O'BRIEN'S LAW

O'BRIEN'S LAW

A ROMANTIC THRILLER

JOHN MCNELLIS

Published by: Hubbard House

Paperback ISBN-13: 978-1-7363525-1-9
Ebook ISBN-13: 978-1-7363525-2-6

For information on distribution and reprint rights, please visit
www.johnmcnellis.com or email john@johnmcnellis.com.

DEDICATION

PROLOGUE

"Tell me again," Inspector Cleary said, glancing up from the scribbles on his notepad, "starting with when you got the call."

"I was asleep at home. The phone rang about 1 a.m.; it was my night guy," replied Davenport, the hotel's general manager. The fiftyish executive was exhausted, his eyes bagged crescent moons. He dug into his suit jacket for his beloved cigarettes, but he was too rattled, his hands too tremulous, to light a match. "He told me Mr. Knox was dead."

"No. Take me through it step by step," the inspector said, lighting the cigarette for him. Holding the spent match, he scanned the presidential suite for a wastebasket. The penthouse overflowed with silk screens and vases, an ornate throne, suits of Samurai armor, a wall of bejeweled swords, carved ivory collections and framed photographs of Malcolm Knox, posing with world leaders from Sir Winston Churchill to the Shah of Iran. As exquisite as Knox's museum-quality possessions were, the inspector was more impressed with the suite's views of Nob Hill and the Golden Gate Bridge. Leaning against a round stone table that sat twelve, he eyed the manager.

"But that's the first thing Gates said." Davenport glanced up, wiping his brow, wondering if the tight-lipped policeman doubted his story. "He said Malcolm Knox was dead, that he had drowned in his bathtub. The tub was jammed with a washcloth and had been overflowing—what a mess—until 1302 called to complain about the water dripping down from their ceiling."

"What time did he say that was?"

"I didn't ask. You should talk to him," Davenport said. He dreaded the prospect of a police investigation dragging his hotel into the papers. The El Cortez's allure lay in its privacy.

"I'm talking to you," the inspector snapped, turning up the heat. He drew himself erect and sidled over to his quarry. He'd had a career's worth of chipping away at stonewalling witnesses. Cleary's trim physique and carriage suggested he was younger than his middle age. Yet after twenty years of investigating mankind at its worst, his face was lined, his hairline in retreat, his fingernails bitten to the quick. "Gates must've gotten the complaint a while before he called you? A half hour, an hour?"

"Probably. He had to find the building engineer first. That must have taken a few minutes. Then the engineer came up, knocked, there was no answer of course. He tried the lock and—"

"That's what Gates told you? The doors were locked?" the inspector asked, pointing across the room to the lacquered ebony double doors.

"We've been through all this—"

"That's the only way in and out?"

"Except for the glass doors leading onto the deck," Davenport said.

"What about those?"

"I told you already: Gates said the deck was locked from the inside. So he called security, our night man came up, knocked and opened the door with the master key. He found Mr. Knox in the tub, shut off the water, called Gates and Gates called the police. It's that simple."

"So the chain wasn't latched?"

"No."

"Old guy like that—how old was he? In his eighties?" the inspector asked.

"82."

"You know that off the top of your head?"

"Yes," said Davenport, grinning at the fading memory. "Seven years ago—in 1970—he threw himself a wild 75th birthday party. Said he had to kick off the new decade in style since it would likely be his last. Probably only invited me to insure we wouldn't call the police."

"A rich geezer with all this valuable stuff—these antiques must be worth a fortune—doesn't latch the chain at night? Hell, this jade table must cost as much as a house." Cleary rubbed the cool stone—the color of money—wondering how the hell the delivery guys ever got it up to the penthouse. "It has to be six inches thick."

"I believe it may be marble, but yes, point taken, Inspector," Davenport said. "But you need to appreciate that the El Cortez is probably the safest hotel in San Francisco. We never have theft issues. Our lobby is small and our guest elevators are directly across from the front desk. We know our guests; most have been coming for years. That's our great advantage. And, as I told you, Mr. Knox has—had—been living in this suite for thirteen years. Without a single incident. It's no surprise he hadn't fastened the security chain. But who knows? Maybe he latched it every night right just before going to bed."

"Anyone else have a key?"

"Housekeeping and security."

"What about his own staff? Looks like he had a secretary," the inspector said, thumbing at the manuscript stacks on the table, the cluttered desk across the vast living room. A sheet of paper in a Smith Corona typewriter. Like a gentlemen's club, the mahogany-paneled suite was redolent of cigar smoke and old scotch.

"Mr. Knox was—how shall I put this?—a difficult man. I don't wish to speak ill of the dead, but I doubt anyone ever trusted him and I'm quite sure he trusted no one. He once told me that gratitude was merely the expectation of future benefits."

"So?"

"So I doubt anyone else had a key. As you've pointed out, even the smallest *objet d'art* in these rooms is priceless."

"What about these? You know anything about this part of his life?"

The inspector tapped a pile of photo albums, files and reel-to-reel film cans. One can was open, several feet of film hanging out. A glance at the film had confirmed the inspector's hunch: amateur pornography. "You could sell these on Market Street."

"I understand he had an active social life. That's all."

"No girlfriend?"

"Ask his associates. Or his nephew."

"We'll get to them. What about this?" the inspector asked, ignoring the manager's pique, crossing the room to a floor safe set inside an open closet. Manufactured by the Victor Safe & Lock Co., the blue-enameled safe stood about three feet high.

"Mr. Knox had it installed when he first moved in."

"Anything in it?"

"I have no idea. I don't know if anyone ever saw it open. As I mentioned, Mr. Knox was not a trusting man. Could be sentimental knickknacks. One man's treasure is another's dross."

"Some kind of dross," Cleary said, bending, examining the old-fashioned safe. "Look: He had it cemented to the floor."

"Please remember, Mr. Knox trusted no one."

"How rich was he?"

"No idea. Wealthy enough to afford this suite."

"That's rich. This penthouse," Cleary said, opening his arms to encompass it, taking in the postcard bridge in the distance, "is crazy rich."

"Inspector Cleary?"

"Yeah?"

"May I ask a simple question?" the manager asked, treading lightly, fearing the answer. He slipped off his glasses and wiped them with his handkerchief. "I know you have to be thorough, ask all your questions and what-not, but isn't it clear that Mr. Knox either had a heart attack—you must have seen his table of medications—or slipped and fell in the shower? And then drowned?"

The inspector shrugged. If the old man had been penniless, he would have agreed; the poor had accidents. Knowing he needed the manager's cooperation, he decided to keep his thoughts to himself. "That could be the case."

"You've no doubt heard that old expression, 'When you hear hoof beats, think horses, not zebras'?"

"That's a good one, got to remember that," the inspector said, grinning without mirth. He jotted a note down on his pad. "Zebras. But I guess I'm in the business of cutting the zebras out of the herd."

"As far as I can tell," the manager pressed, "not a single piece of art or antique is missing. I'll get housekeeping to do an inventory in the morning to confirm that every silver spoon is accounted for."

"Yeah, count the spoons," Cleary said, certain not a dish towel would be missing. It wasn't spoons that had him questioning the bathtub accident, but the dead man's stunning wealth. Someone was about to inherit a fortune.

CHAPTER 1

A NIFTY SOLUTION

In 1979, verdant Jackson Street between Montgomery and Sansome was the loveliest commercial block in San Francisco with its preening two and three-story neoclassical buildings crowded in on either side, its once-moribund warehouses brimming with decorators, antique dealers, and ad agencies. A casual visitor to tree-lined Jackson could browse vendors of silken fabrics, French antiques, and rare books, brushing elbows with buttoned-down iconoclasts who belonged to the best clubs. One could buy an oriental vase that cost more than a car, coffee for fifty cents, or endless hours with fashionable psychiatrists. The Transamerica Pyramid, just five years old, soared a block away, guarding Jackson Square like the Colossus of Rhodes.

Midblock, a small plane tree stood outside a redbrick warehouse that once stabled the fire department's horses. It now served as the law offices of Drummond, Upton and Isherwood. While its façade had changed little in a hundred years, the building was a marvel inside, the height of architectural fashion, with skylights flooding sunshine throughout its exposed timbers, earthquake bracing and open floors. Visitors on the ground floor could glimpse the sky four stories above.

The firm's principal conference room was set in the back right-hand corner of the first floor. The windowless room had two exposed brick walls and a long oak conference table that sat twenty. One early Thursday evening, it hosted a partners' meeting, a dozen men ranging in ages from their early thirties to mid-forties. Their ties were loosened and sleeves rolled up. Between their deep familiarity with one another, the open bar and the platter of chips and guacamole from the Mexican restaurant around the corner, the atmosphere was convivial.

"Guys, let's wrap this up. Anyone object to our making Turner an offer? If he accepts, that'll bring our class of '79 to five. OK? OK then, let's bring him in. Now, what's next on the agenda?" Jack Farwell asked, putting on his reading glasses.

"The Knox overbilling," a smart-ass young partner said, gleeful.

"It isn't a case of overbilling, it's a case of a client underpaying," John Buckley said, his attempt at humor greeted with silence. In his early forties, Buckley had spent his career with the firm and considered himself Drummond's top litigator. Of middling height, he was soft rather than fat, wore gold wire-rim glasses and had lank blond hair combed forward over a broad forehead. He had developed amnesia about his plebeian background on his first day at Yale and had considered himself an aristocrat ever since. He had a sharp wit and a serpent's tongue; few willingly debated with him.

"This isn't a joke," Farwell said. "Everyone's seen Knox's letter: Twenty months have gone by and you're not a step closer to recovering his uncle's estate. You want to give us your side of it, John?" Farwell was the firm's managing partner. Because he was also a certified public accountant, he could actually read a balance sheet. Only forty, he disguised his hands' persistent trembling as best he could.

Wearing his habitual expression—what the simple would call a smile—Buckley tried to explain how he had billed nearly a hundred thousand dollars to the Knox matter while accomplishing nothing. He played to the firm's business lawyers, analogizing his time spent to the countless hours required in obtaining the permits for a high-rise construction project. The groundwork now laid, he insisted his project—the lawsuit—would go up in a flash.

"What a load of crap," Gregg Gordon said. "To pump up your hours, you screwed Knox, billed the hell out of a loser case, knowing *A* he wasn't your client and *B* he was a one-off. That's how you managed to hit your eighteen hundred billable hours despite your sabbatical in Paris."

"If I were your lawyer, Gregg, I'd advise you to never opine on this subject," Buckley replied, his dolphin smile in place. "You spend one hour filling in blanks in loan documents and then bill the poor borrower for eight. That's criminal."

"If you were my lawyer, I'd have an insanity defense just for hiring you. You're leaving Jack holding the bag on this mess. He'll have to write off your time."

"Guys, stop. This isn't getting us anywhere," Farwell said, massaging his forehead. He looked down the table for support from the three partners with power, the lawyers who controlled the firm's biggest accounts; none met his gaze. "Unless we work something out, Knox is going to the State Bar with a complaint. We don't need that aggravation. John and I met with him and we think we might have a plan—"

"Here we go," the smart ass interrupted, laughing. "Why do I even come to these meetings? The deals are all cut in advance."

"Here's the proposal," Farwell said. "Knox will agree that we don't have to write off the hundred thousand now. We can keep it on the books and collect it pending a successful outcome—John still thinks we can win—if, here's the *if*, we give Knox a year's worth of free associate time now."

"So we save John's bacon by screwing some poor associate?"

"Who're you thinking of?" a senior partner asked.

"Wait, wait, don't tell me," the smart-ass said. "You clever bastards. O'Brien."

"Yes, that'll put us two up on Knox," Buckley said, chuckling.

"Goddamn it, John, knock it off," Farwell said. "O'Brien's not that bad, he just lacks focus. He needs some help from you guys. And, as part of the deal, John has promised to supervise him every step of the way."

"Poor kid," Gordon said.

"It's actually a nifty solution," the young partner chimed. "We have to write off half of what O'Brien bills already, he doesn't have enough work, and he needs the experience."

"Let's wrap this up," Farwell said, checking his watch. He just wanted to go home. "All in favor? Thanks, guys. I'll talk to O'Brien first thing Monday morning."

"No rush, he never gets in until ten," Buckley said.

"You just can't help being a dick, can you?" Gordon said, exhaling his fortieth Marlboro of the day toward the rafters. He sighed. Always a half-step from trouble, Francis Michael O'Brien had just been sold into servitude.

CHAPTER 2

FIRST PUNCH

ACROSS TOWN, THE MIDDLE SCHOOL gym in the heart of the Richmond District reeked of sweat the way incense clings to cathedrals. The stucco building was small, with barely enough room to walk around the basketball court. A clutch of secretaries and paralegals stood courtside, talking among themselves but paying little attention to the game, in attendance only to go drinking with the team afterward.

The evening Lawyers' League game was tied at thirty apiece with two minutes left. Tempers were rising as the aging players, those who'd lost a step—and those who never had one—resorted to fouling one another rather than playing defense. The players on the District Attorney's team were angry.

"Come on, guys, suck it up," said Michael O'Brien. He was a ringer on the DA's team, courtesy of Blake Gamble, his law school writing instructor. At twenty-five, O'Brien was the squad's newest member, its leading scorer, and its biggest cheerleader. His mop of curly black hair was tucked beneath his lucky headband, his forearms adorned with decorative wrist bands. Despite his height, he played point guard, staying on the perimeter, searching for open shots.

Inbounding, Gamble passed the ball to O'Brien, who raced down the court, juked his defender, pulled up twelve feet from the basket and shot, clanking the ball off the rim. Four players went for the rebound, two grabbing it in a jump ball. Enraged by an elbow to his ribs, a forward for the Brobeck Phleger law firm head-locked the DA's center and wrestled him to the floor. They scrabbled while the referees stood by, impotently blowing their whistles. O'Brien jumped in, yanking the

Brobeck player from his fallen teammate. Still on his knees, the man wrenched himself free of O'Brien's hold and pushed him back. He rose to his feet and clenched his fists.

"You assholes do nothing but foul," the big forward said, his fists ready. "You're the worst cheaters in the league."

"Who made you the ref, dickwad?" O'Brien said, clenching his fists. "You swing at me, I'm taking you down."

"Michael, back away," Gamble urged. In his mid-thirties, coy about his age, Gamble was a fourth generation patrician who looked like a strip-club bouncer, his broad shoulders and chest heavily muscled from too much time in the gym. He was neither as tall nor as well-read as he claimed, but he did stand by his friends. "Both you guys, back away."

"Go ahead and try, asshole," the belligerent forward said, ignoring Gamble and stepping forward.

"Take your best shot," O'Brien said, grim, dancing lightly on the balls of his feet to his right, eyeing the bigger man.

"Don't do it. No, no, no," Gamble shouted.

The forward cocked his right fist just below his chin, seemingly ready to strike. But before he could, O'Brien punched him hard on the nose. O'Brien's second and third blows struck home as well, and the dazed forward crumpled to the floor. A shaking O'Brien stood over him and glowered at the rest of the Brobeck team, demanding, "Anyone else want to go?"

One referee shouted, "You're out of the game." The young women on the sidelines studied O'Brien as the two teams barked at one another from either side of the downed player. The bolder exchanged expletives and war cries, trusting they'd be held back by their teammates. But lawyers being lawyers, the physical threats and insults soon devolved into technical claims of game forfeiture and aggravated assault.

"Damn it all. What the hell were you thinking, Flipper?" Gamble demanded, using O'Brien's boyhood nickname to soften his words.

Secretly, he was impressed. He'd known O'Brien had a temper—it had erupted in earlier games—but he'd had no idea his protégé was so lethal. He glanced from the big man on the floor, still dazed, back to O'Brien and shook his head.

"I had to protect Romani," O'Brien said, indicating the DA team's center who had by now joined the Drummond staff on the sideline. O'Brien's Boston accent was flaring in his excitement. He flexed his right hand, inspecting it for damage, rubbing his knuckles.

"Romani's half again your size, he can protect himself."

"I'm suing your ass, number 16," the forward said, sitting up, working his jaw with both hands. "I'm going to sue you for assault and battery, take every penny you've got."

"Every penny I've got is in my fucking wallet. Good luck collecting a dime," O'Brien said.

"Apologize," Gamble urged under his breath. The two men had become friends after O'Brien had taken Gamble's Legal Research & Writing class in law school. But Gamble was ten years O'Brien's senior and often treated him like a wayward charge, hectoring him to little effect. "Do it right now. There's a small chance you can make this better. I'm quite sure his legal threat isn't a bluff."

"No way. You saw what he did to Romani. It was self-defense."

"Romani might have claimed self-defense. You can't."

"Don't go professor on me. That prick was fouling us all game. I should have gotten a couple more shots in. Besides, he was going to hit me first, I just beat him to it."

Gamble sighed, questioning whether he had any obligation to report this incident, whether a couple of punches thrown in a middle school gym amounted to anything at all.

The referees restored order by ejecting both the forward and O'Brien and declaring that the game would be decided by free throws. As it happened, both sides missed their shots, each declared itself the winner by default, and the game fizzled out, muttered curses trailing the teams into the evening fog.

"Where'd you learn to punch like that, Flip? That was quite a combination," Jerry Romani said, handing O'Brien the pitcher of beer, his neck still chafed from the headlock. They sat with half the team and several secretaries at a long, boat-varnished table at the Plough and the Stars, a new Irish pub on Clement Street in the Inner Richmond district. Like the Sunset District—its poorer step-sister across Golden Gate Park—the Richmond was a working-class neighborhood slowly squeezing out its longtime residents. The lively pub had a pool table, a couple dart boards, mirrors overlaid with the word *Guinness*, sentimental pictures of the Emerald Isle and a low riser for live music.

"I went to Catholic school. You either learned how to fight at Sacred Heart or got stomped every day at lunch," O'Brien said.

"You punch way better than that." Romani knew street brawling. He'd been an investigator for the DA's office for twenty years before taking an early retirement and a new job as a detective in Sausalito, a tony tourist-ridden enclave just across the Golden Gate Bridge.

"Boxed a little Golden Gloves," O'Brien said. "My mother signed me up to keep me out of trouble. Did OK."

"Now, you simply must learn to control that temper of yours," Gamble said, sipping the house chardonnay. He had an exaggerated posh accent, sounding English to less-traveled ears. It amused his friends and gave his detractors a foothold for complaining about him. "Adults do not get into fist fights, period. Besides, if you hadn't stunned him with that first punch, that chap might have taken your head off. He's as big as Jerry."

"That's why I threw it. The first punch always wins."

"He's right. On the street, that's bible," Romani said, gulping his beer. "That never-throw-the-first-punch advice is a load of crap. Turn the other cheek and get your ass kicked. Anyway, I owe you, kid. Thanks for pulling him off me."

"You'll owe me, too, Flipper, as soon as I figure out how to bury this," said Gamble, drumming his thick fingers on the table, pursing his lips. An hour after the event, he'd had time to consider whether the contretemps might have any effect on him.

"Bury what?"

"Last time I read the Penal Code, assault and battery was still a misdemeanor, and aggravated A&B's a felony."

"Jesus H, it was no big deal," O'Brien said, studying his throbbing knuckles, rolling his fingers. "It'll be forgotten in a week. But I really did pop him pretty good, didn't I?" He laughed, flashing a grin at the brunette who'd made a determined effort to sit near him. Encouraged, she drew her chair closer. But then O'Brien remembered he had a date. He stood, pulled a twenty from his wallet and tossed it on the table, playfully squeezing Gamble's broad shoulders. "I've got to go," he said, addressing the table. "This'll cover my share and Jiminy Cricket here's too. I want to be there the day Blake finally picks up a tab. The church will call it a miracle."

"Can't you stay?" Gamble pleaded.

"Nah, I got a commitment. See you at next week's game."

"If I can get you a pardon from the governor," Gamble grumbled.

CHAPTER 3

APRIL FOOL

THE LATE AFTERNOON AIR WAS clear, almost golden in its translucence, the few clouds highlighting the deep blue sky. A breeze off the bay swirled North Beach's scents, wafting hints of garlic, wine, coffee and spring itself to the Sunday crowds. O'Brien and his girlfriend Roxanne La Rue left Café Trieste with their steaming cappuccinos and walked up Grant Avenue toward Washington Square. Roxanne had said she 'wanted to talk,' and O'Brien had suggested they do so in the park.

"You know time is Irish, don't you?" a grinning O'Brien asked, stalling her. So often misguided, he did know that a woman's desire to *talk* seldom ended well. Scratching his unimpressive bicep, he flexed it, hoping Roxanne would notice. He had to distract her.

"What?"

"Sure. It's o'clock, not clocketti or clockinski or clockberg."

"You're a goof, Michael." Roxanne's laugh was full and musical. With her milky freckled skin, Renaissance lips and figure, Roxanne looked like she'd just stepped from a dairy barn. But it was her hair that one never forgot: wild, curly wheat-brown hair that flew—curled—in all directions. Her hair and her laugh. An opera singer and actress, Roxanne ignored—or was somehow ignorant of—society's mores; she ate salad with her fingers and told others what she really thought of their artistic efforts. Possessed of vast talent and greater determination, the twenty-two-year-old Roxanne knew working as a dental office receptionist was a waystation. Once, in a tender moment with O'Brien, she'd shyly announced her certainty that she would one day be a star. He'd agreed with her.

"Let's sit here," he said as they strolled into Washington Square, pointing at a chipped bench that faced the twin spires of Saints Peter and Paul Church. The small park was buzzing with spring: lovers on picnic blankets, kids playing Frisbee, teenagers eating ice cream, a juggler tossing bowling pins before a small crowd, and ancient Italians perched like sparrows on their benches, watching the world go by. "This, by the way, is Irish time. Sitting with the prettiest girl in the park on a Sunday afternoon, soaking up the sunshine."

"It's nice."

"Nice? Look at this pageantry. Where do you get pigeons like this outside of Manhattan? In fifty years, you'll look back on afternoons like this as the best days of your life."

"What?"

"I don't mean me. I mean the ambience, the day, the coffee, and you."

"You're probably right," she replied, sighing. "Looks like the sunset will be lovely, but we do need to talk. I have to tell you," Roxanne paused to gather her thoughts, letting a trim middle-aged couple pass by. The tourists had walked about ten feet beyond the pair when the woman stopped and turned around.

"Pardon me," she said. "May I take your picture?" She waved a Leica. Not waiting for a reply, she pulled her camera from its case. "You," she pointed at Roxanne, "you're very pretty, but *you*," indicating O'Brien, "you're gorgeous. Like Rudolph Nureyev. I'd really like to take your picture."

The young couple laughed. As the woman readied her camera, O'Brien put his arm around Roxanne's shoulder, squeezing her close. "Come on, Rox, pretend like you like me."

And she did. Always on stage, the gifted actress kissed him full on the lips, holding it perhaps five seconds, then drew back, fanning her face as if overcome with passion. She laughed and the photographer, laughing along with her, thanked them.

Emboldened by the brief reprieve, O'Brien turned to Roxanne. "Can whatever it is you want to talk about wait until morning?"

"Well," Roxanne said, weakening, enjoying the touch of his hand on her thigh. She uncrossed her legs.

"I mean, I know this was only supposed to be a coffee, but why don't we go to the Far East for dinner—"

"So you can maul me in one of those booths?"

"Only reason to go there. The food sucks. But please spend the night with me. It's been a whole week since you came over. I can't sit next to this magnificent body for hours without going crazy. Please. Hey, who's this Nureyev? Some European soccer star?"

Roxanne checked to see if he were joking, then giggled. "Yes, that's it. Now I remember: Nureyev played quarterback for the Moscow Mules."

"Get out of here, you're teasing me. You don't know either, do you? So there, Miss Culture Queen." He laughed and kissed her. She kissed back hard and dug her fingers into his long, sinewy back. Coffee became wine at the Washington Square Bar and Grill, the gilded afternoon slipping into evening. They strolled arm-in-arm to Chinatown. Threading their way down Grant Avenue, past the bustling residents and gawking tourists, O'Brien imagined that he'd been somehow teleported to Hong Kong. The clever waiter at the Far East Café knew the best way to a big tip: ignore the young couple in the back corner booth with its curtain drawn. When they emerged an hour later—O'Brien wearing more of her lipstick than Roxanne—the waiter bowed. Swooping up the check platter, he smiled, benevolent, happy for the three of them.

Roxanne spent the night with the enthusiastic O'Brien, a night in which she hit some of the higher notes in her impressive vocal range and fell asleep exhausted. She awoke a couple hours after sunrise to his pawing.

"Oh my god, Michael. It's eight-thirty, we don't have time. Even if I could fly, I'd still be fifteen minutes late to work," Roxanne said, ignoring his caress. She frowned at the thought that O'Brien might be even more irresponsible than she was. "Don't they care when you show up at your office?"

"We don't punch in or anything, not like a union job. I get there when I want, the receptionist doesn't take roll. It's great. Besides, I'm doing great. They're giving me a big new case this morning, about getting back millions some crooked lawyer stole from some estate." He stroked her freckled cheek with his hand. Then, changing his tone, he whispered, "Please don't go, I can make coffee."

"No, no, no, a thousand times no. I've got to go." Yawning, stretching, Roxanne sat up in bed, drawing the sheet to cover her breasts. "You know, I'm surprised you're not more ashamed of this place," she added, glancing about the cramped studio. She combed her wild hair with her fingers, tossing her head, then groped about on the floor for her bra.

Judging by his apartment, O'Brien was a Parisian, living a café life, returning home only to sleep. His studio was on the ground floor of a three-story North Beach apartment building on Mason Street. The back half of a former garage, the illegal unit held a waterbed, a butcher-block table, a couple of unmatched chairs and a gimpy-legged couch. A new Sony color television balanced on a milk crate. His décor suggested a naïve egotism and a passion for the Boston Red Sox. The kitchenette would have made a chef weep, but one could—by refraining from broad gestures—boil pasta. His postage stamp backyard seldom saw direct sunlight.

And yet a ray caught a disheveled Roxanne zipping up her sheath skirt, backlighting her extravagant hair. Glancing at O'Brien, she wondered how best to let him down. It was too late for him to fall in love. "You still seeing your old girlfriend? What was her name? Shelley something?"

"Kramer. Nah, Rox, honest. I told you we're done."

"Done done?"

"Yeah. We drove each other crazy. All of her games. Then I played my games. Who could be cooler, you know? Couldn't take it anymore."

"You seeing anyone else?" she asked.

"No. Just you, Rox. Running around makes me feel bad the next day—hell, sometimes the next minute. You're the only one I want."

"What a line."

"It's true. I feel like crap. Sex's like a drug that strings me out."

"Maybe, but then you're an addict."

"What's with the interrogation?" O'Brien asked. "You're my girl."

"Nothing, just wondering." She changed her tack. "You said you're starting a new case today, right? Who did the crooked lawyer steal the money from?"

"What? Oh, some dead guy's nephews, I'm not really sure on the details, I've got to read the file before the meeting this morning."

The phone rang. Roxanne hoped it was another woman.

"Hello," O'Brien said. "Hey, B, what's going on?" He turned to Roxanne. "It's Blake Gamble, be just a sec."

She rolled her eyes, laughed, wondering if Michael had a clue about his friend, and then shimmied into the bathroom, little more than a closet with hot water.

"I suppose you're with Roxanne," Gamble said on the phone, hearing her big laugh in the background. "How's your hand?"

"It's OK. That doosh folded like a lawn chair, didn't he?" O'Brien said, laughing.

"You promise never to do it again? I need to know before I decide to bury this. If I don't report it and he files a police report—"

"Come on, he's not going to the cops. Listen, I have to—"

"You won't do it again?" Gamble had already decided to forget the incident, but liked the idea of O'Brien owing him a favor.

"Got to go. Don't want to be late for work."

"You should have been there an hour ago."

With his dress shirt half-buttoned and his tie looped over his

Pierre Cardin suit jacket, O'Brien trotted after Roxanne as she strode up Mason Street.

"I'm so late, I've got to catch a bus. Watch for me please," Roxanne said, turning onto Columbus Avenue, O'Brien a pace behind.

"I'll get you a cab. You know what the biggest lie about lawyers is?" he asked.

"They're good lovers?"

"Hey, I'm serious."

"So am I," she said, teasing him yet keeping a straight face, thinking the occasional self-doubt might do O'Brien a world of good.

"What? I'm a great lover," he loudly proclaimed. An elderly Italian shuffling toward the pair cocked his head, considered O'Brien for a second and shuffled on.

"You're a great lover?" With a jabbing forefinger, Roxanne imitated a sewing machine needle hammering across fabric, finishing within seconds. He tried to smile. They walked a block in silence. Glancing over her shoulder for the bus, Roxanne wondered if she'd at last hurt his feelings. But the morning was too glorious, the air cool on their cheeks, merchants sweeping their sidewalks in timeless ritual, restaurants teasing their noses, steam rising from manholes, bawdy pigeons strutting before them. O'Brien stroked the small of her back.

"OK, tell me the biggest lie about lawyers, you goddamn Greek," she said, kissing his cheek. She would miss him.

"Greek god is what the lady said." He bent to kiss her.

"Tell me before my bus comes."

"Remember that dumb movie we saw last week? Where the lawyer has his crisis of conscience halfway through the movie, suddenly figuring out his client was lying and he had to defend a guilty man?"

"Yeah. Terrible script. And the acting? I could have played the Sandra part so much better."

"Well, anyway it's a load of crap. Criminal lawyers get over their crisis of conscience with their very first defendant or they switch to doing divorces. Day one they're defending someone stone-cold guilty. That's why I'd never represent a criminal."

"That's cynical."

"No, it's reality. I told you about that coked-up defense lawyer I clerked for when I was in school? I sat there in the jail cell with him when his client—this total psychopath—told us how he'd killed three teenagers with a tire iron while they slept in their sleeping bags. Crushed their skulls."

"The guy actually confessed to the murders?"

"Like he was telling us what he had for dinner."

"That's horrifying. A tire iron?" Roxanne asked, feeling queasy. Despite her vocation, she knew little of real drama. "What'd you do?"

"My boss went into a pretrial hearing the next day and started bull-shitting, telling the court his theory was that the Hell's Angels had done it, that his client was innocent. Nothing but lies. My boss could tell I was freaked out and he fired me before I could quit. No, I quit first. At least they convicted the psycho."

Roxanne heard the bus a half-block from its stop. "Let's hurry."

"When can I see you again? Tonight? Tomorrow? I just made five hundred bucks, we need to celebrate."

"How did you do that?"

"Visa raised my limit. Tonight? OK?"

"You and your crazy spending. Sorry, but I've got rehearsals," she said, her gaze fixed on the bus. "Michael, I have to tell you something. Stephen's arriving this weekend. He says he's coming to take me back to New York, this time for good. That I'm the one. I need some time to get my head together. Please don't call me or stop by the office. All right? I'll call you in a couple weeks." The bus opened its doors and she climbed in, only then turning back to look at him. "You want to ride with me?"

"A COUPLE WEEKS?" O'BRIEN WHINED to the bus's lingering exhaust. His holy water Catholicism having long since puddled into Celtic superstition, he stood on one foot to avoid a sidewalk crack and then crossed his fingers, praying Roxanne would glance back at him through the bus's back window.

At twelve, he'd been more Catholic than fish on Friday, serving mass weekly as an altar boy—daily during Lent—certain he had the calling, imagining himself astride the carved wooden pulpit, loved by his parishioners. Then, at a sleep-over, Billy Murphy showed him how to whack off. The next night O'Brien tried it himself. Knowing it was a mortal sin, hellfire the price he'd pay, he'd cried himself to sleep, begging his Lord for forgiveness, swearing he'd never even touch it again. That sacred oath lasted a week. Then he was pounding it three times a day. Hell-bound but unrepentant, his religion faded like a Polaroid in the sun. Rather than confession on Saturday afternoons, he now appeased his gods by knocking on wood and avoiding sidewalk cracks.

Roxanne didn't look back. O'Brien wilted, his chin drooping to his silk tie. He stared down the broad avenue, the great pyramid at its base lost to his turmoil; he scuffed his Ferragamo loafers, cursing his fate.

But a block later an old woman smiled at him, and he smiled back. He reminded himself that a lover who ate rice with her fingers, bathed erratically, shaved nothing, loved staying up all night and was as rootless as a Bedouin was a poor match for a shanty Irishman. It helped a bit. The sky was still blue, the smells as tantalizing, the air as sweet, and a downcast O'Brien, so wrong about so much, was right in knowing this was a morning to cherish.

CHAPTER 4

SERENDIPITY

Marybeth Elliot was annoyed, her fixed shopkeeper smile fooling no one. She had offered the old woman a free cookie instead of her recipe, claiming Serendipity's recipes were a family secret. Pish poshing, the crone pointed out that the cafeteria had just opened. Marybeth bristled at the word cafeteria, but remained silent, wondering why it was that her customers were so seldom right.

Her new shop was tucked into a two-story redbrick building on Montgomery Street in Jackson Square. In preparation for her grand opening, Marybeth had greenhoused the store with hanging ferns, one of the few seventies' fashions she'd embraced with enthusiasm. She'd set a pair of faux Tiffany lamps at either end of the glass counter where the muffins, cookies and rolls were on display. To make it homey, she had each employee bring a picture of a loved one for the countertop. The little shop seated about fifteen, with customers typically buying their coffee and pastries to go. She'd assembled her crew from self-starters at her other two restaurants and, five days into it, she was pleased with her opening. Her sales were better than she'd hoped and far better than she'd projected to the failed restaurateur whose ovens, mixing bowls and baking sheets were now hers.

"Here, please take three cookies, ma'am. On the house."

"Why, thank you, missy," the crone said, pleased with her ruse. "You should tell the owner to hire more girls as pretty as you. It's good for business."

"Thank you," Marybeth said, tucking a loose strand of her short sandy hair behind her ear. After six years as a fashion model, she seldom accepted compliments at face value. People always wanted something.

"I wish my niece's posture were half as good as yours."

"Please excuse me, but I have a situation that requires my attention," Marybeth said, her smile fading. She whipped out from behind the register, halting at the doorway to watch her temporary employee interact with a pair of young women. The sultry, raven-haired Gina Altieri was mumbling her offer of free samples while staring at the sidewalk. The young women walked on. Gina suffered from the same shortcoming as the models Marybeth had hired for her previous grand openings: Despite their beauty, they'd hidden their insecurities behind an icy hauteur, and frosted the shop's best customers—the secretaries, receptionists, and paralegals from the neighborhood.

Smoothing her blue apron, Marybeth strode outside. In her flats, she was still taller than the spiked-heeled Gina and, but for the huge aluminum cookie tray that shielded her sidewalk ambassador, would have stood toe-to-toe with her.

"Having you stand out here is an exercise in futility," Marybeth said, tucking her errant strands once more. Her schooling had ended when her own modeling career proved far too successful to even consider college. Now her lack of education was like freeway noise—it bothered her when she considered it. Over time, this irritant had pearled into a worship of higher education. That she had no use for it and an income that would stagger a university professor made no difference. To compensate, she'd worked hard on her vocabulary, developing a fondness for ornate words. *Serendipity* was a particular favorite.

"I'm sorry."

"Those girls might have come in if you treated them better. You promised you would be nice."

Gina's lower lip puffed. "Well, they were mean to me first, like, they were laughing at me because I'm like a dumb stewardess with no plane out here. I tried to be nice, I really did."

"Stop. You, you can't go around intimidating the public, you either learn to treat—wait, oh, oh gosh. Set the tray down. Look at you. Look what you've done to your apron. It's too low."

Gina glanced down. The *Serendipity* stitched on her apron rode across her mini-skirted upper thighs. "So? If it was higher, no one could see my blouse. What's the big deal?"

Marybeth shook her head, deciding not to explain. "Turn around. I'll straighten it for you."

Gina swiveled on one heel and, looking up Montgomery Street, spied a moody-looking young man, his hands jammed in his pockets, approaching them. She stared at him, wondering whether the young man's broad shoulders were merely the clever tailoring of his suit jacket. She caught his gaze as he approached and said, "Welcome to Serendipity."

"You guys just open?" he asked, taking in the black-haired beauty and the other young woman, a tall, regal blonde, fussing behind her.

"Yes. Here, let me get you a free sample," Gina said, twisting away from Marybeth, the loose apron falling from her shoulders. She bent from the waist to lift the tray from the sidewalk.

"No thanks, I'm not really hungry." He glanced into the shop, trying to remember what was there before.

"Try the muffins, they're the best," Gina said, holding his gaze.

"I lost my appetite a little while ago," the man said, glancing between them.

"Come on, try one. I'm Gina," she said, leaning over the tray, displaying her own wares. "Are you a doctor?"

The man's black curly mane, too long for a professional, confused Marybeth. File clerks did not favor tweed suits. Maybe he was in advertising.

"I'm a lawyer. Hey, this muffin's OK. Remind me what used to be here?"

"Try a cookie," Marybeth said. Her chocolate chip cookies were troubling her. They didn't sell nearly as well as the muffins. That the muffin recipe came with the first shop she bought and the cookies her own recipe only heightened her annoyance.

"You're a lawyer?" Gina asked, giggling. "You don't look like one. You must be pretty good if they let you have your hair that long. Is something wrong?"

"What? Oh, I don't want to talk about it," O'Brien said.

"I'm sorry, maybe I could help?" Gina asked, ducking her chin in a manner she'd been told was fetching since she was ten.

"How's the cookie?" Marybeth asked, ignoring Gina's flirting. She told herself she wanted an honest opinion. And she did, as long it was unadulterated praise. With an upward flick of her hand, she urged the tall lawyer to take a bite.

"Well," O'Brien said, "it's kind of dry, you know, brittle, it could be a little softer."

"Oh."

"Look, it's probably just me. Like I said, I lost my appetite this morning."

"Anything else?" Marybeth asked, giving him a second chance.

"Maybe you could make them a little bigger, give your customers more bang for the buck. Yeah, bigger and softer. More chocolate chips. Does that help?"

"Thank you." Marybeth nodded, drawing herself even straighter, tugging the cuffs of her white blouse which, along with her khaki pants and blue apron, constituted her work uniform. Folding Gina's apron, she gave herself a moment to appraise him. That Gina found the lawyer attractive was enough to damn him. At a convention of Nobel laureates, Gina would find the drummer. The lawyer wore a dove-gray suit, fawn-colored vest and blue pin-striped shirt. His tie was as wide as his lapels, and she thought his pink pocket square silly. She decided the peacock was wearing his salary. "Gina, we need to replenish your tray and continue our private conference. Let's go." Marybeth clasped Gina by the arm, steering her into the shop.

"Jesus H, doesn't anyone want the truth?" O'Brien asked, rewrapping himself in his black mood as he turned toward the offices of Drummond, Upton and Isherwood.

CHAPTER 5

I.N.R.I.

MALCOLM KNOX SAUNTERED INTO THE brick-and-timber Drummond offices and announced his appointment to Michelle, the perky receptionist with the Peter Pan haircut whose cheerfulness endeared her to lawyers and clients alike. Thirty minutes early for his meeting with Jack Farwell, Knox sprawled on a Danish modern leather couch in the open reception area, crabbing his thick weathered hands together in anticipation. Sunshine flooded down upon him from skylights soaring four floors above. Looking up, he admired the Chinese paper moon chandeliers and the exposed, brightly-painted HVAC ducting. The old stable was as airy as a hangar; its windows opened, its ferns flourished, and the firm loved it.

Across from Knox sat a pair of excited German architects, young men armed with cameras and sketchpads, waiting for the assistant office manager to conduct them on a tour of what they considered a wondrous mélange of form and function, modern utility with traditional materials. One gently patted a timber post as if it breathed.

Decades earlier, Moses Isherwood had decided that "The Law Offices of Moses H. Isherwood" sounded threadbare and set about finding a near-extinct firm whose name he could inherit. Messrs. Drummond and Upton had fulfilled Moses's unspoken expectations by retiring soon after their merger. Nobly named, Moses's firm had grown in fits and flukes, averaging a new lawyer for each of his forty years of practice; now a dozen partners tended lush accounts ranging from national banks to international pharmaceutical companies.

Upstairs, Moses's newest lawyer groaned, his forehead on his desk.

"Are you sure Harvey said I had to get that memorandum done today? I could have sworn he got the extension. You're positive?" O'Brien asked, missing his secretary's mischievous nod. "I'm screwed. Who am I going to get to help me? Dillon swore he wouldn't do it again. I haven't even started the research. What am I going to do?"

"You could start by going to the library and doing the research—or maybe you could remember what day this is," Ann Wall said.

"It's Monday. My least favorite day of the year."

"It's also April 1st." She paused, grinned. "April Fools."

"Jesus H. Don't scare me like that, Annie, I'm not a young man anymore. My heart, whew." O'Brien sighed, laughed at his own gullibility, and feather-punched her on the shoulder. "Good one. You really got me." She turned toward the door, heading for Lederhosen, the partner with actual work for her, and he slipped back into his romantic despair and the sports page. That O'Brien had fallen into a position requiring research and writing would have amused the teachers of his youth. As a child, he had read comic books, every word written about the Red Sox, the occasional biography of Babe Ruth, and nothing else. One spring morning when he was thirteen, a Jesuit priest had called on him in class. After O'Brien announced that Kenya lay between Venezuela and Brazil, the priest deftly led him into admitting he had "nearly" read the geography assignment. "I nearly read it," thundered the priest. With a hand on the boy's collar, the Jesuit hustled him to the blackboard and chalked "I. N. R. I." above his head, sentencing him to stand until the bell, commanding his fellow travelers to write two hundred words on the meaning of the Savior's epitaph and thank O'Brien for it.

"I see you've finished examining the files." John Buckley said, standing in O'Brien's open doorway, clutching a brand-new No. 2 pencil and yellow legal pad. Despite his mild sarcasm, he seemed pleased, his dolphin smile in place. "Shall we go? Knox is waiting in Jack's office."

"Tomorrow's opening day. This could be Boston's year," O'Brien said, tossing the Sporting Green, the *Chronicle's* sports section, into his wastebasket. New to the business world, O'Brien still believed that if he was fair, honest and pleasant with everyone, he would be treated in kind. Despite warnings, despite knowing that few associates worked with him for long, O'Brien thought Buckley meant well. He wondered who received the crisp new pencils and legal pads Buckley discarded after a single use. O'Brien trailed him down the hall to Jack Farwell's office. Knox stood outside the door.

"Michael," Buckley said, "this is John Malcolm Knox. You two have a lot in common. You both part your name on the side."

"I have an excuse," O'Brien said, laughing, offering Knox a card that read 'F. Michael O'Brien, Attorney at Law.' "My first name is Francis. After my four older brothers, my mother wanted a girl so bad she was using the name no matter what."

"Everyone calls me Mal," Knox said, shaking hands. He wore a blue blazer embroidered with a Saint Francis Yacht Club burgee. He sported a gold Rolex President that he habitually flaunted by crossing his arms. His powerful hands, weather-scoured face and the tiny boats dotting his tie confirmed his passion for sailing. His pale eyes were bagged and his jaw wattled, but his shoulders were muscled and his chest deep.

"Malcolm is the trustee for his two sons, who were supposed to inherit his uncle's estate, but—"

"They did," Knox said, patting his thinning hair into place. He combed it over from just above his left ear. "I mean they will, but there's nothing left for them. Fitzgerald looted the whole goddamn estate. Fifty million in bearer bonds and stock certificates, all in street name, gone. You know all that, you've read the pleadings."

"But there's nothing like hearing it aloud," O'Brien said, beaming. He wondered how he'd let the time get away from him, wishing he'd read the damn file.

After shaking hands with Farwell, they stood in his office, waiting while his secretary brought in another chair. The second-floor office looked onto leafy Jackson Street. A few years younger than Buckley, Farwell had—as managing partner—less power than the junior associates imagined and more than the rest knew. In a firm plagued with coalitions and fringes, he commanded near-universal respect. He listened to everyone and could still say no, on occasion, to the mighty. And, as the firm's sole accountant, he was the one partner who could have a meaningful conversation with its bankers. Once pudgy, Farwell had lost weight. He was grim this morning, distant, his responses monosyllabic.

Buckley's secretary appeared in the open doorway and, eyes on the carpet, announced that her boss had a call. "Excuse me, fellows," he said, "This is really important. I'll be back as soon as I can. Meanwhile, you two can bring Michael up to speed."

Knox related the story of his namesake, the late Malcolm Knox, sketching his uncle as a Scottish missionary's son whose calling was to a finer cloth, a rogue, a pirate who made his first fortune in China after World War I, selling grain to the Russians, making another during the Second World War by running guns to the Chinese, only to lose it all in the revolution. A sailor who loved the sea almost as much as he loved women, he'd fled bare-pocketed to San Francisco. At the age of fifty, Malcolm had started over, amassing yet another fortune importing Asian trinkets, everything from Chinese folding fans to traditional tea sets, selling for dollars what he'd bought for pennies. Knox portrayed his uncle as a tyrannical mandarin, feared, yet loving and generous to his family, and—despite his countless affairs—loyal in his philandering way to his frail, barren wife Helen until the day she passed.

So how did such an astute man come under the sway of the defendant, Teddy Fitzgerald? Knox said his uncle was too domineering and mercurial to have real friends outside his family. Those near to him kowtowed or fled. That no one could be more obsequious than Teddy

Fitzgerald served him well, but blood served him better: Teddy's father had fought shoulder to shoulder with Malcolm in the Great War.

"But how did Fitzgerald steal fifty million dollars?" asked O'Brien. "Stocks and bonds are registered, aren't they? Didn't he have them in a bank?"

Knox frowned, shooting a quizzical look at Farwell. "This is all in the pleadings. Anyway, that's why Fitzgerald's crime was so perfect. Only Fitzgerald and I knew how much my uncle had. Malcolm lost millions—everything—when Mao marched in. He had no faith in governments, and you have to remember he was a Scot, he hated paying taxes. He didn't trust the Swiss, said they were Nazis with manners. Said he left only a token amount—mad money—in his old account in Basel. No, he kept all his money in bearer bonds, stocks in street name, and gold bars, all in a big safe inside his hotel suite. Malcolm did as much business as he could on a handshake—pity those fools—and paid his bills in cash. And he insisted upon payment in cash whenever he could get away with it. As far as the IRS knew, my uncle was a small-time importer with a modest income."

Farwell was tired. He'd heard Knox's story before, after an old friend had referred the nephew to him. A business lawyer who never went to court himself, he'd brought Buckley in to handle the case; but then Buckley began ducking Knox's calls. He should have just given the case to Buckley outright, let him have the billing credit, but power depended on clients—on billings—and Farwell was a quiet man who appealed more to friends than business acquaintances. He should have known better. Farwell should have known Buckley would overbill the case, producing nothing for Knox and a staggering account receivable for himself. Farwell stole a sad look at O'Brien, knowing he was in for a rough ride.

"You see how simple it was for Fitzgerald. He sneaks into the suite before the official opening of the safe and cleans it out," Knox said.

"And because Malcolm had spun the IRS and even his bankers like tops, no one knew the better. My uncle didn't have a scrap of paper—other than the stocks and bonds themselves—to prove what he was really worth. So this damn Fitzgerald waltzes into court, probating an estate he values at five million, basically just the art and antiques he couldn't squeeze down the goddamn hotel elevator. And the gold bars. They were too heavy for the bastard to steal more than a couple."

"What do they weigh?" O'Brien asked.

"Around twenty-six pounds," said Knox. "Just one is worth more than sixty thousand."

"Wow, that's what I'd make in four years here. Did the hotel let him in? When he rifled the safe?"

"No," Knox replied, his irritation rising at O'Brien's lack of preparation. "He must have had a key. He let himself in. This is all in these pleadings." He tapped the file on Farwell's desk.

"Did anyone else have a key?" O'Brien asked.

"What the hell's that got to do with our lawsuit?" Knox snapped, fixing O'Brien with a piercing stare. "No. No one else had a key. My uncle was extremely security conscious. That's why he lived in the El Cortez."

"But Fitzgerald had one?"

"He must have pocketed one while he was visiting my uncle, ducked out, had it copied and replaced it before Malcolm knew it was missing."

"But Fitzgerald had the safe's combination?"

"Yes, of course. He was the executor."

"If you don't mind my asking, Mal, why weren't you the executor? You were his nearest relative." O'Brien glanced up from his desultory note-taking. "Isn't that the usual way?"

"Why wasn't I the executor?" Knox repeated, swelling with annoyance. "Because my uncle thought the estate needed a lawyer. Because I was too close to him. He put me through Thatcher, then the university. He loved me like a son. And remember: Even though I stood to gain absolutely nothing by his death, nothing mind you—the art and antiques went to museums and the cash to my two boys—Malcolm may have thought it was a conflict of interest."

"Oh."

His head bent, Farwell grinned at his desk, amused over O'Brien's distaste, reminding himself to speak to his associate about learning a poker face. He glanced at his watch, now loose on his wrist. He would give the meeting another five minutes, then wrap it up: O'Brien would devote himself to the case with Buckley personally supervising his every step.

O'Brien walked Knox outside when the meeting ended.

"Whoa. Nice car. You just paint it?" O'Brien asked, lazing a fingertip along the silver 1968 Mercedes cabriolet. He walked around the convertible with its top down, admiring its soft, curving lines and gleaming chrome. Even though he could barely drive and had no interest in owning a car, he caressed the gray leather driver's seat.

"The insurance company did," Knox said, chuckling. "The Union Square garage nicked the front fender and so they painted it for me."

"They painted the whole car because of a dented fender?"

"Well, you have to prime their pump a little. You claim more damage. You just take a key and run it along the side and—voila—your insurance company buys you a new paint job."

"But that's—"

"Good business. It needed a paint job anyway, had lots of dings and dents the insurance company should have taken care of. They just didn't happen all at once."

"OK," O'Brien said, looking away, bending down to inspect the tire's narrow white wall. He noticed its treads were badly worn.

"Anyway, Michael, the first thing we have to do is get those interrogatories answered. You need to make a motion to compel. Get that motion done right and I'll take you sailing on my Sun Tsu."

"Sun Sue?"

"No, Sun Tsu, the great Chinese general. He wrote *The Art of War*. Very famous book. You should read it. What's wrong? That doesn't sound good?"

"I've never been sailing," O'Brien replied, shuddering at the thought of the open sea. "Not a water guy."

"What? Why not?"

"Long story," said O'Brien. "But I don't go for anything bigger than a hot tub."

"My friend, you'll love it, nothing better," Knox said, clapping the young lawyer on the shoulder, knowing O'Brien would work harder if he liked him. "But first, you and I are going to put that bastard behind bars and get my sons' money back. I need you to get right on those pleadings."

"I will," said O'Brien.

"I mean, right now, maybe get a draft done for me to review by tomorrow. And then read Sun Tsu."

"I'm on it. Nonstop."

CHAPTER 6

SAM'S

O'BRIEN REGRETTED SEEING KNOX OUT. He'd tried to like him in Farwell's office; he liked the dashing dead uncle anyway, wished he had him for a client instead. Knox said he was a consultant, but O'Brien had glimpsed his day calendar. There was only one entry for the week. Perhaps Knox was so rich—that Rolex must have cost a fortune—that he did nothing, his claim of insurance-scamming an effort to impress his lawyer. O'Brien trudged the stairs to the second floor, shaking off Knox, allowing his black dog mood to nip at him. He hung his head. How could Roxanne not love him?

"Hey, Mike," Gregg Gordon called from his desk as O'Brien passed his smoke-filled office, two doors down from Farwell's. It, too, looked down upon Jackson Street, but Gordon's blinds were always drawn. "Got a minute?"

"Sure. What's up?" O'Brien was surprised at the invitation, half-surprised that Gordon even knew his name. Had they ever exchanged more than a hello? He'd tell Ann to find him the moment Roxanne called. If she ever did. He wilted onto Gordon's worn green couch.

"Buckley dumped that Knox case on you," Gordon said. A small man, he was shaped like an under-stuffed teddy bear, his face creased, his eyes yellowed, sad. His manner was abrupt, a bumper to ward off sympathy. Gordon had embarked on a slow suicide some twenty years before, forever drinking himself stuporous, never without a cigarette, coffee with cream two meals in three. No one knew what pain prodded him toward the abyss, but even Michelle the receptionist had known about the Jim Beam he hid in his desk drawer and the quips about needing to catch him before lunch. So public was his alcoholism that when he quit drinking—too late for his marriage—every lawyer in the firm congratulated him, the bold begging him to give up smoking as well. Apple-cheeked summer clerks would be astounded to learn he was just thirty-eight: with his sagging face and jaundiced eyes, he looked sixty.

"Yeah, it's great. We just met with Malcolm Knox. Did you see him walk by? I'm going to get to do some depositions and—"

"Jack say anything about the case so far, what Buckley's done?" Gordon asked, lighting a cigarette, exhaling with panache. His hand-carved green marble lighter and matching ashtray were the two objects of beauty in his plain office. The partners had decorating allowances from the firm for their individual offices; Gordon had yet to draw on his.

"Not really. You know, just the preliminary pleadings filed, complaint, demurrer, answer and—"

"I know what the hell pleadings are," Gordon snapped. "Did Jack tell you not to bill your time?" A business lawyer who drafted loan documents, Gordon had few clients and fewer ambitions, yet little escaped him.

O'Brien stared at the small man, remembering the round of drinks he'd won betting with a couple clerks over Gordon's age. Now he felt guilty. He picked at a thread in the arm of the frayed upholstered couch. "No, he didn't say anything about billing. Is something up?"

"But he told Knox you'd be working full time on the case, right?"

"Well, yeah, I guess. As much time as it needs."

Gordon nodded, exhaling away from O'Brien. He took off his glasses, massaged the bridge of his nose. "Mike, listen to me. Don't spend all your time on that case. Do whatever it takes to get some work from other partners. Knock on doors, ask for work. You need to get better known around here. Put in some extra hours between now and year end."

"Sure."

"Don't *sure* me. I'm serious and you need to be, too. Get in early, stay late, put in the hours to impress the guys."

"I will, Gregg. I'm going to get started on a motion to compel right now. And stay on it until it's done."

"Buckley has a way of forgetting. When he tells you to do something, put it back to him in a memo. Put everything he tells you in writing. See this?" Gordon asked, clasping a pen.

"Yeah?"

"Use it."

"Thanks, yeah, Gregg, OK. Appreciate the advice."

O'Brien strode back to his office, sat down, yanked his tie loose and deliberated, trying to shake Roxanne from his thoughts. What was so special about Roxanne's damn director? O'Brien had heard her mention this Stephen before, but he'd thought that relationship over. Now did he even have a chance with her? He shook his head. Why was Farwell so distant, and why was Gordon giving him advice? He ran his fingers through his black curly hair, remembered the sports section and fished it from the trash.

O'Brien had never thought to reconcile his poor math grades with his ability to calculate batting averages, how a two-for-three afternoon would affect a slugger's average. Or how he always knew his meager net worth to the dime without balancing his checkbook. O'Brien could recite nearly every number ever assigned to him: driver's license, social security card, draft card, library cards, even the phone number of a girl he wished he'd had the nerve to call when he was fourteen.

The phone rang in the midst of his fretting over Boston's starting lineup. "Yes," he said, answering.

"Hi, Flip," said Michelle. "Your dreamy friend John Reid is down here. He looks so much like you. I swear he could be your brother."

"Yeah, we get that a lot. I'm the handsome one."

"That's too funny, that's just what he said. Anyway, I sent him up. Is he always so much fun?"

"Michelle, you bad girl, you're married."

"I've got to make you jealous somehow."

"You're killing me. He's coming up right now?"

Reid opened O'Brien's door without knocking. "Vootie," he said, his hipster term for hello. "Check this African thumb harp I just scored for ten bucks. Dig it." He plucked at the metal keys of a hand-sized, hollow wooden box. It sounded nothing like music. "Is this a babe magnet or what? Wicked conversation starter. Let's go get high."

"What the hell, JR?" O'Brien said, chuckling. "It's eleven thirty and I've got a pile of work. Why aren't you at the plant?"

"My boss is on a flight back to Cincinnati. He can't even check on me until four. Let's hit Sam's, get lunch, get high and then get lucky." Possessed of soap opera good looks, easy charm, and an animal charisma, Reid was far luckier than most. That his internal compass was stuck on indulgence meant he always had world enough and time to chase the next high.

"I can't. I really can't," said O'Brien. "I've got to get a motion done on this big new case."

"Dude, come on. The sun's shining, the weather's great in Tiburon. Today's our day. These guns need sun," Reid said, flexing his biceps. Inspired, he yanked open O'Brien's narrow window onto Balance Street, the short alley below. "See these bars? They're not keeping thieves out, they're keeping you locked in. You're a prisoner, you need to break out of here. Yo, try my harp."

"No way am I going."

"We're twenty-five today, we'll be sixty-five tomorrow," Reid said. "The babes are waiting for us. We'll eat outside, get some rays, you'll come back with a tan. You're whiter than an Eskimo's ass."

"I just can't. I've got to be responsible for once."

"Check this bomber." Chuckling, Reid retrieved a joint tucked behind his ear, beneath a wave of thick brown hair. His brown-sugar eyes were almost feminine, his eyelashes the envy of every woman he'd ever hit on. "It's got your name on it."

"That's one thing I'm definitely not doing. I'm not getting high; that'd shoot the whole day."

"No worries, bro. I'll smoke it later. We can just have a couple beers with lunch, take the edge off. Then we get the oysters and the calamari and score. You know how easy Marin chicks are. Tell you what: I'll have you back by one thirty."

"One thirty for sure? No, no, no. What am I thinking?" O'Brien knew his onetime roommate would say anything—to O'Brien, to his boss, to the women he seduced. That Reid would swear true love just to get laid had always bothered him. It was like defrauding an old lady out of her social security check.

"One thirty, I promise," Reid said. "Come on, Blue's right out front."

"Nah, I'm not in the mood. I just got dumped by Roxanne—she's going back to that bigshot director. I'm not up for it."

"So? What do cowboys do when they get thrown? They get back in the saddle. Come on, Flip, you know you want to," Reid said. "Hey, what about calling Alice Kaplan? She's totally hot. Talk about a brick shithouse. If you don't call her, I will. Give me her number."

"There's a marriage made in heaven—a French Lit genius and a guy who plagiarized his way to the bottom of the class." O'Brien shook his head, remembering his brief time with a girl whose brilliance first dazzled, then defeated him. Knowing he wasn't a Rhodes Scholar was one thing, being constantly reminded of it another. "She was way too smart for me, bro. For you…?"

"Dude, the smart babes love me. Remember Gail? She's at Harvard now in some German Ph.D. thing. She adored me."

"Yeah, that was weird. She must have viewed you like some personal anthropology project, like she was studying Neanderthal mating habits."

"Then let's go meet some dumb ones at Sam's," Reid urged. "We'll get there, eat fast and score a couple numbers for later."

"You swear to God we'll back by one thirty?"

"On my mother's grave." Reid laughed.

"She's alive, you dick."

"She won't be by the time you make up your mind. Let's go."

O'Brien sighed, stood, and straightened his tie as if he were going to court. He pardoned himself for his irresponsibility yet again; he would work all night to finish the motion.

"Hey, Michelle," he said as they approached the reception desk, his voice low. "We're going out for a quick lunch. I'll be back by one fifteen. Would you let Ann know, please?"

"Sure, Flip, I'll tell her you'll be back by…three? Bye," she said, admiring the backs of the two lithe young men—one several inches taller, the other broader—as they escaped into the sunshine. They really could be brothers.

CHAPTER 7

HOME COOKING

"No, Michael, I swear she hasn't," said Ann Wall, buttoning the collar of her cardigan sweater. With her spotless desk directly below an air conditioning register, she was often chilled, even on the City's rare hot days. "I promise I'll let you know the second Roxanne calls. But you want to know what I think?"

"As long as it's not 'forget about her'," O'Brien said, squeezing a souvenir baseball in his hand. He was leaning over the screen wall separating Ann's orderly carrel from the hallway, quizzing her in person about his absent love.

"Well, it is," Ann said, enjoying herself, looking past him, watching the nearby secretaries steal glances at O'Brien. The chance to lecture her wayward boss was irresistible. She gazed at him. "It's been almost a week—"

"Barely four days, not even. OK, OK, five days."

"You should find someone who really appreciates you."

"She does, she just appreciates her damn director more."

"I appreciate you. A lot." A twenty-three year old Minnesota girl too sweet for San Francisco, Ann appreciated nearly everything about Michael O'Brien, especially when comparing him to the dullard high school boyfriend she'd married three years ago. O'Brien may never have had any work for her, but he could be so much fun. The other secretaries were envious.

"You're the best, Annie dear. Hey, did I tell you I scored another continuance on the Hart matter? Do me a big fav please and prepare the stipulation for what's-his-name, my opposing counsel. OK?"

Content with his reprieve from actual lawyering, O'Brien decided to reward himself with a coffee. Bounding the stairs two at a time to the firm's fourth-floor kitchen, he remembered the girl with the cookie tray. Maybe Roxanne would appreciate him more if she heard he was dating, or better yet, saw him with the black-haired beauty. Maybe he should visit that new café.

He sprang up Jackson to Montgomery. The sidewalk was empty, the free samples gone, and peering inside, O'Brien could see she wasn't behind the counter. Hoping that a girl who looked like she'd never boiled an egg might be found within a commercial kitchen, he strolled inside. He asked the young, Asian cashier for a coffee. She beamed at him. He flashed a smile, blessed her for the steaming drink, dropped a dollar into a glass coffee mug littered with dimes and asked, "The girl on the street a couple days ago with the samples...?"

"Nice tip, thanks. You mean Gina," the young woman said, grinning as if repeating a punch line.

"Is she, is she…?"

"No, she's not here." Turning toward the kitchen, she called, "Hey, Marybeth. Some guy's looking for Gina. Is she coming back on Monday?"

O'Brien winced, guessing Marybeth was the officious boss. He glanced down, saw he was standing on a floor tile seam, and shimmied off the crack for better luck.

Marybeth emerged from the kitchen, drying her hands on a towel. She slowly reassessed O'Brien, confirming her initial appraisal. Today the peacock was wearing a pink dress shirt and matching paisley tie beneath a blue pinstriped suit, topped off with a green silk pocket square. "We concluded our grand opening festivities and Gina's services were no longer required. I suppose you want that tram—you want her phone number?"

Was she about to say tramp? The word clung to the roof of his mouth like hot pizza. Oh, yes, please give me that beautiful tramp's number, O'Brien wanted to beg. But the short-haired blonde stared him into submission. "Well, ah, I guess—that's OK. Nah, no big deal."

She spun on her flats, withdrew to the kitchen.

Defeated, O'Brien sat with his coffee and *Sporting Green*, thinking he could ask the cashier for Gina's number on the manager's day off. Then he consoled himself, remembering how misleading one woman's description of another could be. Years before, his mother had retailed a friend's niece, urging him to date her, describing her as a "little hippie." Until the moment he'd met the niece at Brennan's for their blind date, O'Brien had envisioned incense, marijuana and hand-shake sex. As it happened, she was wider than a convent door and less interested in free love than the pope himself. Fortunately, he'd spied her first, recovered from his surprise and did his best to make her feel lovely on their one date together. His mother had accepted no blame.

"Is this big enough?" Marybeth asked O'Brien, setting a colossal chocolate-chip cookie on a paper plate before him. She was keen on improving her recipe, annoyed that the damn muffins always outsold her cookies. The peacock's remarks last week had stung.

"Hey, that's my line," he said, laughing at his own cleverness.

"Really?" Marybeth rolled her eyes. "Oh, never mind."

"No, please, wait, I'm sorry, I was just joking. Please sit. And sure, this is plenty big. Perfect."

"You're serious now?"

"Yes, totally," he said, reverently holding the cookie between his thumbs and forefingers in the manner of a priest venerating the host. "A perfect size."

"How does it taste?" She stood over him, tapping an impatient foot.

He turned his wrists outward until it snapped. "I'm sure it's great, but if you could make it softer, gooier. So you can bend it. Texture is important."

"Taste it...please." Frowning, Marybeth sat down opposite O'Brien, her arms crossed, wondering why she was listening to the silly clotheshorse, then reminding herself he was a highly educated lawyer.

O'Brien took a bite and chewed slowly. "It's good."

"Tell me the truth," Marybeth insisted.

"It is good. The problem's with me, not your cookie."

"That's a break-up line."

"No, I'm serious," O'Brien said. "Let me ask you something: Have you ever eaten at an Irish restaurant? Not a pub, a real Irish restaurant?"

"I guess not."

"Neither has anyone else. There aren't any. Why? Because there isn't a single Irish woman who could cook her way off death row. It wasn't the famine that caused the great emigration, it was home-cooking."

"You're joking."

"My saintly mother—Mrs. Patrick O'Brien—she's the worst."

She giggled, then laughed, eyes crinkling. She tossed her head, evaluating the peacock in a different light. He was funny. "I don't believe you."

"Why do you think Guinness is richer than the Queen? The micks had to wash those boiled-to-death potatoes down with something that tasted even worse. Just so they could face their next dinner."

"That's not true," she cried, amused, her voice now relaxed, pleasant. O'Brien saw the beauty in her serious face when she laughed. Her blue eyes were large, set wide apart, and her Slavic cheeks were high, shining. Her smile was art itself: rounded full lips and cover girl white teeth. Her complexion was smooth, her skin tanned from running and her straight hair—no longer than O'Brien's—was parted on the side, falling just below her jaw.

"Tis true. Me lovely mother couldn't bake sand in the Sahara," O'Brien said, adopting a cartoonish brogue. "Now, I'll be telling you about the cookies. So when me oldest brother was a bairn, she bought a hundred-pound sack of ginger snaps dryer than dust and for the next twenty years, whenever one of her lads wanted a cookie, she'd chisel one out—harder than a banker's heart they were—and say, 'wash it down with a little milk'. So a big brother would have a go, gag, then make me eat one just to watch me die. True story. May Jesus roll over in his grave if I'm lying."

"What?" His casual blasphemy surprised her. "Hey, I'm Catholic."

"Remember? I'm Irish. Catholic as the bishop's girlfriend. Thought I had the calling until I was twelve. See," he said, fumbling between his shirt's upper buttons, freeing his crucifix. "I'm Michael O'Brien. Here's my card."

"I'm Marybeth Elliot," she said, examining the crisp card. She had a talent for putting others to work. Maybe the peacock could be useful. "Do you know anything about signs?"

"Sure, let me guess, you're a *Deer Crossing*."

"I'm not talking about astrology. I mean advertising signs, business signs. I want to put up a big Serendipity sign outside and the building department's not cooperating. They say I can't have neon. They gave me this indecipherable pamphlet with all these regulations." She handed it to him. "Could you possibly peruse it for me?"

"You own this place?" O'Brien asked, scanning the shop for the first time. "Whoa."

"Yes. This is my third breakfast-and-lunch dining establishment," Marybeth said, pleased by his incredulity. She ticked off her locations on her fingers, a preening mother with her children.

O'Brien felt a pang when he noticed the tiny diamond on her ring finger. "Does Mr. Elliot work with you, too?"

"Oh, this? This is an engagement ring. I'm not married. Yet. That's my fiancée, the big picture over there on the counter. Scott's a captain—almost a major—in the Army. He's a helicopter pilot, flew combat missions all over Viet Nam. What'd you do during the war?" Marybeth's father, Black Jack Elliot, a decorated sergeant major, had three daughters who thought his every word carved atop Mount Sinai. Marybeth, the one he called his son, shared Black Jack's opinions, among them the certainty that real men volunteered for combat.

"I was stationed in Canada," O'Brien deadpanned.

"Oh." She pursed her lips.

"Boy, I have to stop kidding you. Sorry. I was going to enlist in the Navy after I graduated from college—just to get farther away from my mother's cooking—but the draft ended, the war was winding down and my brother Sean," he faltered, glancing out the window into the distance.

"Yes?"

"He'd already been killed over there."

"I'm sorry, that must have been terrible for your parents."

"My dad's been dead a long time, but yeah, it was really tough on my mother. She adored him. You still can't mention him in her presence. She just starts wailing," he said, shrugging away the memory. "Anyway, how can I help?"

"Well, if you wanted to earn some free cookies, you could figure out a way to circumvent this sign ordinance for me."

O'Brien pondered the pamphlet with its tiny print; having to analyze its minutiae would be a death sentence. He slapped it against his open palm. "Here's what I'd do. I'd ignore this for now," he said, handing it back to her. "I'd go ahead and put up a huge Serendipity banner over your front doors. It could be weeks, months—hell, maybe never—before a building inspector ever shows up. When he does, offer him coffee and muffins, promise to take it down, but do nothing until his next visit, then beg his pardon for the inexcusable delay."

"But that'd be against the law," she said, titillated by the thought.

"So is jaywalking. And I'd do one of those sandwich board signs. You know, the kind you put on the sidewalk in the morning and take in at closing time. Hell, do two. And have one of your busboys hit every car in the neighborhood with a flyer advertising a two-for-one sale."

"I don't do two-for-one sales," Marybeth said. "But maybe a ten percent discount good for a week would work."

"One more suggestion? OK? Don't get mad."

"Tell me."

"Before you buy the sign? Nobody knows what 'serendipity' means and it sounds kind of new-wavy. Know what I mean? Like that weird retreat-place in Big Sur where everybody goes to quote, 'find themselves.' What a crock. What's that place called?"

"Esalen?"

"Yeah, that's it. Bunch of rich stoners. They could find themselves all day long if they got a job," O'Brien said.

"You're funny," Marybeth said, smiling. Her father would approve of that sentiment, if little else about the peacock. "But what are you saying?"

"I'm saying you need a new name."

"Oh."

Missing her tone, O'Brien plowed ahead. "Besides, you have to pay by the letter for those expensive signs. Go for something short and homey, like," he paused to consider. "Like *Beth's Buns.* No, oops, that wouldn't work. But something like that; name it after yourself on the big outdoor sign and paint 'Cookies and Coffee' in the windows. Maybe a cute little drawing of a honeybee."

"Maybe you should be in business for yourself," she replied, her tone curt. What did he know? She glanced about the shop, wished for more customers, and then stared out onto Montgomery. The day was sunny, the haze almost visible in the narrow street. It had been far too long since the last rains. She saw a meter maid writing tickets and reminded herself to feed her meter. "You seem to know everything about running mine."

"Business? I'd be terrible at it, I'm a trial lawyer." Halfway back to his office, he realized he hadn't given Gina another thought after Marybeth had joined him.

CHAPTER 8

THE WESTIE

MALCOLM KNOX SCOOPED HIS DOG'S leavings into a plastic bag and tied it off with a neat half-hitch, frowning at the spot left on the sidewalk. He glanced about for trash—a bit of newspaper—to wipe it away, saw nothing, and made a mental note to examine it again upon their return.

The small dog pranced, pulling at his leash, tugging Knox across the Sausalito waterfront, along Bridge Street, toward the waterfront restaurants, toward San Francisco rose-colored in sunset. With the sun behind Sausalito's hills, the bay glittered black and blue, the rooftops pink across the inlet in Belvedere. The sea air smelled of brine, salt and seaweed. The sidewalk jostled with dogs and their owners, walkers, joggers, lovers and tourists. The smug houses were winking on their evening lights while dawdling cars rolled along Bridge against a backdrop of postcard views. Pelicans ghosted past in formation, a wing's breadth above the bay.

Knox was happy. His dog was over a worrisome rash, and his lawsuit against Teddy Fitzgerald was at last out of the doldrums. His new deal with Drummond—a free associate for a year—had him content with his litigation for the first time in months. It had occurred to him, however, that the firm might have stolen his wind by giving him a boy who, a few months into his career, knew nothing about legal proceedings. Knox had a solution for that: He'd ride O'Brien hard. Oversee the youth himself. Contemplating his charge, he rolled his sea-muscled shoulders back and then his head side-to-side, pleased with its faint cracking. Yes, he'd get his money's worth out of O'Brien, even if he had to threaten to deck him. Maybe he should challenge him to arm wrestle and then slam his fist down on Drummond's conference table. Scare the cocky kid into getting the job done.

Dressed in a jersey and deck shoes, a Saint Francis Yacht Club windbreaker—a club from which he'd been expelled—Knox was ready to fish. His ensemble often led to a bar acquaintance asking about boats and tonight, with his victory over the Drummond partners, he felt lucky for the first time in months. He'd tell her of blue-water sailing, the famous people and places he knew. And between his boat and his adorable dog, he'd succeed. It was the first of the month, and he had money in his pocket. He could stand her three rounds without blinking.

With his prodding, the young man should do all right—after all, he would only be preparing motions; Buckley would still do the sparring with Fitzgerald and his drunken lawyer. And the case was simple: Teddy Fitzgerald stole the money and should be forced to return it. What was not so simple was Teddy Fitzgerald himself.

"Oh, what a little darling. May I pet him?" a big-boned, honest-faced woman asked, bending with delight toward his dog. They stood on the sidewalk in front of Scoma's in the failing light, Knox having strolled past the Trident, thinking it too early to hit the bar. Not the least self-conscious, the tourist squatted like a catcher to make eye contact with the dog.

"Yes. Of course, he loves people," Knox replied, smiling, smoothing the top of his sunburned head. About his age, the woman in her mid-forties was far too old for him, but she and her companion, another truthful Midwestern face in a summer-print dress, were cooing over the dog. So special did he think his dog that Knox felt almost an obligation to allow others to admire him. "Please do."

"He's a terrier?"

"Yes, a Westie."

"That's a West Highland White Terrier, Pam," said her friend. "Like the little dogs on the scotch bottle. What's his name?"

"Skipper."

JOHN MCNELLIS

CHAPTER 9

DAY-OLD

THE PHONE RANG. O'BRIEN FLINCHED. It had to be Knox. A month earlier, he'd have snatched it first ring, bolting from the plodding research that so frustrated him. On good days, he might find an appellate decision proclaiming the right law but with facts distinguishable from his case. On bad, the legal precedent would approach his facts, but decide against him. On most days, however, he found neither, for rather than legal precedent he searched for fellow associates willing to take over his assignments.

Now he stood, backing away from the ringing phone as if it were venomous, inching toward his door, scouting the hall. He clicked the door shut behind him to muffle the phone, slinked past the mailroom, dove down the back stairs, dashed past the reference books no one ever referred to and out the front door.

O'Brien breathed in the morning air and strode toward Serendipity. He nodded at the garish banner only the Department of Building Inspection had yet to notice, and grinned at the hand-painted sidewalk signs that proclaimed chowder the soup of the day. Chowder was one thing Boston had all over the City. Chowder and the Red Sox. And the Bruins. He missed hockey. And real weather. And his mother, his brothers and his friends. He'd run away to California at eighteen to attend the University of California at Berkeley and eight years later he still missed it all. But not enough to move back and face that real weather, his father's past and his forlorn mother.

O'Brien pulled out his silk handkerchief, folded it into three snappy peaks, and reset it in his jacket pocket. He bounced inside the café and asked Nancy, the Chinese cashier, for the usual. Tossing a dollar in the tip mug, he saluted the self-satisfied captain on the countertop, and wondered aloud if Marybeth was in the kitchen. He knew she allotted half her time to Serendipity and the balance to her older shops, but was never sure when he might find her in.

"Will you go out with me?" he asked when she opened the kitchen door. "Please, it's my unbirthday."

"Must I remind you that I'm not unengaged every day," Marybeth said. Carrying a clipboard, she was dressed in a starched white blouse, blue apron and beige slacks, the uniform she wore when they first met, an official conducting a field inspection.

"Come on. Nancy told me your fiancé hasn't been here in, like, forever. What kind of engagement is that? Oh, sorry. I didn't mean it like that," he said, ducking hurt looks from both women. "It's just that if I were engaged to someone like you, I wouldn't let you out of my sight. I'd be your busboy if I had to."

"You and your lines," she said, hiding a smile by dropping behind the countertop to review the shelves of pastries, recalling her helicopter pilot with a detachment remarkable in a fiancée. It had been more than a year since she'd last seen Scott Land, and nearly five since she'd first met him on his way to Viet Nam. Marybeth had seen her father in the swaggering pilot and fallen hard. But by their last night together, she knew Land's pretty words were floating dandelions. She knew his vow of eternal commitment might carry him past one beckoning opportunity, possibly two. When their last hour had arrived, Land presented her with a tiny engagement ring, an enlisted man's special. She'd stifled a laugh, told him an engagement would be unfair to him and handed it back. He'd insisted the ring was hers in friendship and their last hour became as pleasant and innocent as their first. The next day she wore it, announcing her engagement to the photographer and the other models on the Macy's shoot. Before the joke wore off, she discovered the ring was a talisman, protecting her from some—if not the worst—would-be suitors. Although Land and her own family would never hear of it, their "engagement" flourished. That Scott Land was more of an unreliable pen pal than fiancée troubled her not at all. Using him as a shield, she'd dated sporadically, but without effect. Despite her long-suffering mother's admonitions against being too fussy—"Honey, everything's chicken but the gravy if he comes home six nights out of seven"—Marybeth had no intention of settling cheap. Her hometown outside Nashville may have looked askance at women still single at twenty-five, but San Francisco was another story. Besides, she was too busy with her flourishing empire.

"It's not a line, it's true," O'Brien said, crouching to talk to her through the pastry display. "Please, just for a drink, one drink, dinner? Anything? Anything but coffee? Las Mañanitas at five?"

"Please, get up," Marybeth said, shaking her head at the persistent peacock, flicking her hair back. Long since ready to go out with him herself, Nancy stole a look at her employer, wondering if this were the day.

"Will you?" O'Brien pleaded.

Before she could answer, O'Brien's receptionist Michelle popped into the shop, calling, "Flipper. I thought I'd find you here. Mr. Knox is at the office waiting for you. He says it's really important."

Marybeth stiffened at the shapely receptionist's smile and the familiarity in her chirpy voice.

"Knox, oh shit, shit," he said quickly, his Boston accent flaring. "Thanks, Michelle. I'll be right back. Tell him I'll be right back. You want a coffee or a roll?" he asked, fishing in his pocket for a bill.

"No, I'm running to the bank, bye." Michelle pronounced bye with two syllables and skipped out the door, her tight mini-skirt drawing Marybeth's scrutiny.

"A good friend?" she asked, unconsciously tightening her jaw.

"Drummond's receptionist. Nice girl, but it's not that tough a job, she just has to remember not to call the firm 'DUI' when she answers the phone." He laughed, then caught her tone. "Oh. Nothing like that. She's married."

O'Brien looked sincere, but because of her ruse de guerre, Marybeth was well-acquainted with men unfettered by matrimonial vows. "If you'll excuse me, I need to place some calls about a position I'm trying to fill."

"No, no, no. Come on, Marybeth, don't give me that tone. I'm not seeing Michelle, never have. I don't have a girlfriend," O'Brien said. "The only one I used to see moved in with her real boyfriend, and that's the truth. The other truth is, being engaged to some guy in South Carolina you never see is crazy."

"She called you Flipper," Marybeth said, squaring the photographs on the countertop and glaring at Nancy, the source of O'Brien's inside information about South Carolina.

"Remember, I told you my first name is Francis. My big brothers stuck me with Flipper when I was a little kid. I hate it."

"It's kind of cute."

"Use it," he pleaded. "Call me Lassie, I don't care, just go out with me. Someone as beautiful as you should not be waiting for some guy to—"

"There you are, Michael," Malcolm Knox boomed in a gale-force voice. Dressed in a white cable-knit sweater and his yachting blazer, the big man filled the small shop's doorway. Skipper wagged his tail, sniffing the delicious baking smells. "We've got work to do. Shall I buy you a cup of coffee and we'll do it here? Lovely place," he said, ogling Marybeth. "Do you mind if Skipper sits in here with us? He's no trouble at all."

"I do," Marybeth said, girding herself against his leer.

"What? He's no trouble, everyone lets him come in. He can sit on my lap."

"Let's go back to my office," O'Brien said.

"No. We'll stay here. Surely you can let him stay with me?" Malcolm wheedled. "He's such a sweet little doggy."

"Regardless of my personal feelings, the health department will close us if we allow animals inside. The dog will have to stay outside." But for O'Brien's patent discomfort, Marybeth would have left it at that. Instead, she added, "If you sit at number two, that table by the window, and put his leash around the parking meter, it'll be easy to watch him."

Knox grumbled acquiescence, asked O'Brien whether he wanted a coffee or a sandwich. He checked a worn wallet bulging with credit cards. He fingered a single bill. "Oh, hell, sorry, all I have is a hundred. Maybe they can break it?"

"Nah, I'll get it. Order what you want," O'Brien said, grinning at Marybeth. She smiled back as Knox ordered a couple tuna sandwiches, a bowl of chowder and a slice of apple pie. Maybe she could go out with this Flipper once, bring him home to meet Uncle Eloy. He was rather handsome, she conceded, and she recognized his persistence—how many bouquets of lilies had he had sent to the shop over the past month?—as a useful character trait. She'd caught herself daydreaming about improving him, instructing him not to be such an employee, to keep working after the partners left at night, to adopt the muted grays of his profession, to forego pocket squares and breeding-plumage shirts. But she'd stumbled over his hair. Her imagined O'Brien still wore his hair too long for anyone with a day-job. No, Uncle Eloy could wait.

"How about something for man's best friend?" Knox asked, jolly at the free meal assembling on the plastic tray, peering down at the pastries. "You must have some day-old, broken pastry for my dog."

"No, we don't," Marybeth said, her tone clipped, glancing toward O'Brien.

"Oh for Christ's sake," Knox said, his face purpling. "Every goddamn bakery has day-old bread. What is it you don't like about me, bitch?"

The ugly words hung in the air; the other customers in the shop turned toward the big man. They heard the young man growl, "Stop," as he grabbed his client. They strained to hear his muttered words: "She doesn't have any day-old stuff. I'll buy your dog a fucking T-bone steak, but first you're apologizing."

Startled, then enraged, Knox clamped on to O'Brien's outstretched arm and fisted his free hand. He'd once punched a man just for cutting him off on Highway 1, threatening to kill the driver if his road rage were reported to the Highway Patrol. On the verge of striking, of crushing O'Brien, he saw himself in the eyes of the horrified onlookers—witnesses who would testify against him—caught his fury, and lashed it down.

Recovering his equanimity, Knox waved away the incident as a misunderstanding. He rolled his shoulders, smoothed O'Brien's lapels like a tailor fitting a suit, and said, "Bravo. That's the kind of lawyer I need, a fighter." He bowed toward Marybeth. "Please accept my sincere apology. I misunderstood. Here, let me buy that bear-claw for Skipper." He brought forth the veteran hundred-dollar bill.

He knew O'Brien's anger was rooted in their tense relationship, that he should have better concealed his frustrations with the young man's lack of experience and any real progress. Knox nodded inwardly. He needed him now, but the day O'Brien was expendable, he'd pay for this outrage. "Put your money away, Michael. Yes. I'll buy it all—get him another coffee, will you please—and please accept my apology to you as well, Michael. You're a fine young lawyer and I'm sorry if I've been working you too hard. You're doing a good job. All square?" he asked, extending a hand.

"Sure," O'Brien said, shaking.

Marybeth shivered at her fifteen-year-old memory of her father knocking out a fellow sergeant in front of the PX. The hapless man had been openly flirting with her mother. Yet she'd long since decided that using Black Jack as a yardstick for measuring men would see her straight through into spinsterhood.

"Good day, gentlemen," she said, "I must attend to my other establishments."

O'Brien followed Knox to the small table, recalling the day he'd fallen for Marybeth. Weeks earlier, Nancy had mentioned that Marybeth delivered all her unsold pastries each afternoon to Saint Anthony's, a mission that fed San Francisco's poor. She'd said no when O'Brien asked if Marybeth ever mentioned this, and he'd whistled low, remembering his steely-eyed nuns' praise for anonymous generosity. When the cashier added that her boss could have given her workers a tidy raise by selling the day-olds, O'Brien recalled that annoying parable about the vineyard laborers who were paid the same for showing up at sunset as those who'd toiled all day. As a boy, he'd thought Jesus wrong. Now, he supposed it had been His way of telling Catholics to unionize. He cleared his thoughts of charity and glanced at the papers in Knox's hand. "What's that?"

"It's all the lawsuits filed against Teddy Fitzgerald in Marin, Alameda, San Mateo, and of course, San Francisco counties," Knox said. "See, I summarized each complaint and the amount involved. Look at this." He pointed at a list that ran three sheets. He'd looked up 'Fitzgerald' under each county's alphabetized register of lawsuits. "Here, look. He ordered a refrigerator and never paid for it, claiming it was defective. He stiffed a carpenter who fixed a broken window—cheated him over nothing. He agreed to buy a used car, gave the owner a hundred-dollar deposit, drove off with the car and the registration saying he needed it for the loan, and never came back. These are for bad checks. These, the ones I've marked in red, are the lawsuits by former clients, some for malpractice, some for theft, you lawyers call it improper commingling of assets. Forty-seven different suits altogether and that's just here in the Bay Area."

"Jesus H," O'Brien muttered, shocked someone could be sued so often, that a man could be so bad, wishing he'd done this research himself. He ran down the list of Fitzgerald's crimes, marveling at the many ways the lawyer had contrived to steal, from walking on hotel bills to reneging on fee-splits with former partners. Young enough to think evil was as obvious as a street sign, he asked, "But your uncle? Didn't he know Fitzgerald was a crook? How could he trust him with the combination to his safe?"

Chewing slowly, Knox gestured for patience and stepped outside to toss Skipper another bit of pastry, bending to scratch the terrier's ears. "It's time I was blunter with you about my uncle. I've told you he was a pirate. But that's just a romantic expression for a thief, isn't it? You can't get rich otherwise, believe me, I know. I loved him dearly—he was a father to me—but the man had limitations. My uncle wasn't a petty thief like Fitzgerald, he paid his bills, but he was utterly ruthless; he screwed everyone he ever did business with."

"But Fitzgerald?"

"Don't you see? They were spiritual shipmates. Uncle Malcolm suspected he was no good—he had no idea about any of this, of course, but Fitzgerald was his only real friend's son, in a way, his own prodigal son. And Uncle Mal thought Fitz loved him—you've never met a better ass-kisser than Teddy Fitzgerald. My uncle thought they were so alike, so close, that he could trust him, you see? Honor among thieves. Besides, Malcolm had no need to trust anyone, he was going to live to be a hundred and slowly dole out his fortune himself to my boys."

"Didn't he know about his bad heart?"

"Yes and no. The irony—the hell of it—is that Malcolm was a hypochondriac, absolute hypochondriac, always dying of something, this Asian fever, that liver complaint or this blood disease. Well, after fifty years of dying and staying healthy as an ox, he must have decided his weak heart was just one more false alarm."

"Mal," O'Brien said, "What if Fitzgerald isn't lying? Hypochondriacs can get sick, and sometimes liars tell the truth. Maybe the safe really only had the gold bars? Your uncle gave the other money to charity?"

"That flinty Scot never gave away a penny. It was there when he died. Not that I cared—remember, nothing was coming to me—but I saw the stocks and bonds every time I visited. He kept his safe open so he could revel in his wealth. It wasn't going to charity. Besides, if he suddenly started giving away a fortune the IRS didn't know he had, they'd have been all over him. That's why the will was so cagey, leaving the 'residual estate' to my boys without any inventory."

"Guess you'd have had a full-time job investing all that money for the boys."

"Not really. The fee schedule for trustees is barely adequate," Knox said, peering closely at O'Brien. "I shouldn't have gone out of town."

"Hard to believe," O'Brien mused, puzzling over how someone so cunning could entrust an untraceable fortune to Teddy Fitzgerald.

"What?" Knox cried. "What's not to believe? The weather was so damned rotten, we just wanted to get away. We went up to Lake Tahoe, a little motel in King's Beach that allows dogs. Shouldn't have left town, in retrospect, but I'd visited him not two days before the heart attack—come to think of it, he looked a bit peaked. His safe was open then and still full of his damn treasure. It had to be there when he died."

"OK, OK, I got it," O'Brien said. "That makes sense, but I still don't get this Fitzgerald stuff. You and your uncle were really close, right?"

"Like this." Knox crossed two fingers.

"Couldn't you warn him about Fitzgerald, about all—"

"I did," Knox snapped. "Of course, I did, I pleaded with him half a doz—we've done enough here. You need to get back and finish those interrogatories."

O'Brien departed. Alone, Knox wondered why O'Brien doubted his story about being out of town. Uncle Malcolm and he were close; their last conversation had been an aberration. Knox had almost finished his loving biography of his uncle, he'd done the hard work, the research, the first two drafts, when the old man had suddenly turned on him, seizing the work, telling him it would read better in the first person, refusing to advance him another dollar. He'd insisted that Johnny—he refused to call his nephew anything else—hand him the will from the open safe. Malcolm had read him its hurtful details, forcing him to hear first-hand how Malcolm was taking care of Johnny's ex-wife, the woman who'd obtained a restraining order against him but remained an intimate friend of his uncle. Yet still, despite all that, Knox had loved his uncle; the old man was like a father to him. It all could have—should have—worked out so differently. But now he had O'Brien and his damn suspicions.

CHAPTER 10

THE DEPOSITION

The fog huddled against the waterfront, muffling the morning sky, chilling lightly-clad tourists as they awaited cable cars. It pressed against the glass doors of Drummond, Upton and Isherwood, teasing through the dime-wide gap. Ben, the assistant office manager, had swept Drummond's patio clean, removing the previous evening's cigarette butts and beer cans from the boxwood planters that bordered the patio. Then he hosed the entryway down, glistening the bricks.

A late-arriving secretary kissed her unemployed boyfriend goodbye and, stepping from his '56 Chevy, clattered across the patio on spike heels.

Inside the law offices, Teddy Fitzgerald lolled against the receptionist's counter as if the building were his. A heavy man who was light on his feet, he could strut while standing still. His pink face was smooth, his mouth thin and his small nose straight; his clear blue eyes suggested that drink was not among his many vices. He wore a blue suit, a white shirt with gold cufflinks, and a silk tie. He'd chatted up Michelle the moment he sauntered into the building, staring into the depths of her blouse, rhapsodizing about how seldom it was he encountered a woman of her beauty. Spellbound by his swaggering patter, Michelle knew better, but couldn't look away.

A mama's boy whose barbed wit had been his best defense against tougher boys, Fitzgerald had stolen since he was four, starting with his mother's purse, moving on to candy at the five-and-dime and rummaging through the cloak room to ransack his classmates' lunch boxes. He'd used his stolen money to buy friends, treating his hangers-on to ice creams, M&M's and sodas. When caught on occasion, he'd brazenly deny everything, falling back on cunning and his predatory charm. He'd cheated his way through the University of San Francisco, paid his dorm's resident advisor—a math Ph.D. candidate—to take the Law School Admission Test for him and, with a perfect score, was welcomed into Boalt Hall's prestigious law school. Fitzgerald took almost as much delight in duping acquaintances out of their money as he did in seducing their wives.

Fitzgerald's lawyer, Patrick Coyle, sat on the leather couch, ignoring the vignette between his client and the receptionist. The disheveled man was bent over, head in his hands, hoping Drummond's coffee would do for him what no coffee ever had. After yet another night drinking, Coyle, once his family's pride, could barely remember his appointments or how to knot his tie. His career—his life—was drowning a few fingers of scotch at a time, and a practice that once thrived from City Hall to the foot of Market Street now depended on court appointments and charity from old friends. His red curls were thinning, graying. His puffy face was a street map of blood vessels, his cheek bruised as if from a fall.

The blue-doored elevator opened, and O'Brien stepped out.

"Do I know you or are you just Irish?" Fitzgerald asked before O'Brien could say a word. His voice carried past the switchboard and its operator hidden from view, past the decorative reference books. "Coyle, can you believe this? Three micks in a deposition. This could go on for weeks. He looks tough, Patrick, me boy, you'll have to be on your toes with this one." Grinning, Fitzgerald pantomimed a bit of shadow boxing.

Coyle rose with effort, growled hello, shook O'Brien's hand. A big, shambling man in a tweed suit, Coyle was nearly O'Brien's height. He managed a smile, tinged with curiosity, perhaps sympathy. When Buckley's assistant called to inform him that O'Brien would be taking this deposition, Coyle had double-checked Drummond's letterhead: O'Brien's name was now bottom right, the firm's junior-most lawyer.

"Is your waiter coming?" Fitzgerald asked as the trio stepped from the elevator toward the fourth-floor conference room, three doors down from Buckley's office. Buckley had suggested it when he dropped the lawsuit's most important deposition on O'Brien, telling him he'd be steps away should any difficulties arise. He'd assured O'Brien that depositions were simple: The young lawyer had merely to write out his questions in advance and then stick to his script. If he insisted on a complete answer to each question, he'd do fine.

"Waiter?" O'Brien asked, wondering why neither man had brought a briefcase. Fitzgerald was smaller than he'd imagined. As the evidence of Fitzgerald's character had mounted—myriad lawsuits, official reprimands, the tales it seemed every partner had about him—O'Brien had come to view him as larger than life. A lesser Lucifer, not the dumpy little man standing before him.

"Your client, J. Malcolm the sponge," Fitzgerald cackled, glancing at Coyle for approval. "That's what his uncle—may he rest in peace—always called him: the world's largest living sponge."

"He's a consultant."

"Consultant, my lily-white ass. The only thing he consults is his dick when he wakes up in the morning. He's a waiter. He waited for his uncle to die and now he's waiting to get his hands on money that's long gone, that he doesn't deserve."

"And you, you're… you're a thief," O'Brien snapped, flushing.

"Oh, a smart-mouth," Fitzgerald said. "They still teach the elements of slander at law school? You take that class yet, kid?"

"They also teach that truth is a defense." If O'Brien hadn't exactly followed Buckley's instructions, if his script had more doodles—variations on Marybeth's initials—than interrogatories, he'd still given the deposition serious thought. He knew he had to focus on the missing money. He knew fighting with Fitzgerald was a mistake.

"Hey, hey," Coyle said, stepping between the two men. "Save it for the deposition." They withdrew into a room furnished with an oak table, chairs for six and an interior window that looked out onto the third-floor landing below. Like the other offices, the small conference room was painted white and trimmed with unpainted baseboard. The court reporter was waiting, her steno machine ready. A veteran, she knew enough about Teddy Fitzgerald that she'd brought along her stomach pills.

O'Brien managed to get his own name, the date and the time on the record before Coyle's first rambling objection: O'Brien's questions were without foundation, irrelevant, argumentative and calling for speculation.

"Can we get going now?" O'Brien asked when Coyle paused for breath, surprised at the old drunk's eloquence.

"No. I'm not finished. I have every right to state each and every one of my concerns fully on the record and I intend to do so." With a wink at his client, Coyle repeated his ritual objections and, taking advantage of the young lawyer's inexperience, he created a few new objections based on a freewheeling interpretation of invasion of privacy. The court reporter, a Drummond favorite, sneaked a look over her reading glasses at O'Brien.

"This is my deposition and I'm asking the questions here," O'Brien said. He knew he had to take control. "We're not here to listen to you lecture us about the law of evidence."

"You may ask any proper question you wish, Counselor. But my client will not be bullied into answering irrelevant questions. He will not be insulted or forced to reveal anything about his private life or business that is not strictly relevant to this action."

"Would you state your name for the record please?" asked O'Brien.

"William Edward Fitzgerald."

"Your address?"

"Home or office?"

"Both please," said O'Brien.

"I object," Coyle said. "Don't answer that question, Teddy."

"You can't object to that, I'm entitled to know the defendant's address."

"His business address, yes. But his home address is a private matter. Don't answer that."

"You can object, you can put your objection on record, but Mr. Fitzgerald still has to answer," O'Brien said.

"No, he doesn't. And he's not going to. Stop wasting our time, Counselor."

"Your business address?"

"785 Market Street, Suite 1003, San Francisco 94103"

"Your home address," said O'Brien.

"Don't answer that, Teddy. Counselor, you want to end this deposition here and now? You keep asking irrelevant questions and we will have no alternative but to call a halt to this charade."

After an hour that felt like four, O'Brien had established certain crucial facts: Besides his name and business address, Fitzgerald admitted that the only prescription medication he was taking was for his aching hip and that his memory, while fair, could be spotty. During a break in which he'd sought Buckley's advice, O'Brien learned that the senior partner had rushed out of town to meet with a new client. Picking at her words like a vegetarian at a barbecue, Shelly Greene, Buckley's assistant, said he'd promised to call in hourly to check on the deposition's progress.

Five hours later, O'Brien was beaten, as savagely as any schoolboy boxer would have been in the ring with a professional. Yet he was still fighting long after the ten-count. "This is not a court of law, Mr. Coyle. I'll say it again. Mr. Fitzgerald has to answer the questions, even if you think they're irrelevant. You may state your objection for the record, but Mr. Fitzgerald must answer my questions." O'Brien recited the magic incantation, his words were correct, but they carried no conviction. His voice had risen. The young man kept his trembling hands flat on the conference table, his jacket buttoned to hide his sweat.

For hours Fitzgerald had lectured as if paid by the word when asked harmless questions—he burned twenty minutes in describing his first case as a trustee. About everything else, he professed ignorance or lack of memory. The few facts he could recall about the late Malcolm Knox were antiques, his boyhood memories of the man fresher than anything that had happened since the Korean War. Fitzgerald had insisted upon his legal right to educate himself while O'Brien asked his questions: he'd first studied the local newspapers and then turned his attention to his wallet. Grinning at Coyle while O'Brien pored over his notes, Fitzgerald retrieved money, business cards, credit cards, receipts, photographs, a waitress's phone number and a half-crushed white pill. He arranged the debris into piles: cards to toss, numbers to save, currency to arrange.

"May we go off the record?" Coyle said.

"No, let's stay on the record," O'Brien replied.

"Turn it off, Sheila," Coyle said to the court reporter. With a silent plea toward O'Brien, then resignation, she lifted her hands from her machine and sat up straight, stretching her back. "Now, Counselor," Coyle said, "we've been going at this all day. How many times do we have to hear the same questions? When can we knock off?"

"When I get some real answers. If your client doesn't know anything about Knox's fortune, he's going to say so on the record. I don't care how many times you object, I'm asking the questions until he answers." While his adversaries had made the deposition as painful as it was useless, O'Brien couldn't quit. He knew Knox would demand a play-by-play in the morning. "If your client fails to answer today, we're going to continue this deposition and keep at it until he does."

"Oh no, we won't," Fitzgerald hissed. "We're finishing this today. And if you ask one more goddamn question that you've already asked, I'm going to shove that steno machine right up your fag ass and—"

"Teddy, Teddy. Calm down. Let's finish this up," Coyle said, clasping a meaty hand on his client's arm.

"What? Fag…" O'Brien said, recovering from his shock at Fitzgerald's words, bolting from his chair with fists clenched. "If you weren't such a worthless old bastard, I'd take you outside and kick your ass."

"Sit down, Teddy. Sit. You sit, too. Back on the record," Coyle ordered the reporter. "Let the record reflect that Mr. O'Brien threatened to, quote, take Mr. Fitzgerald outside and kick his ass, end quote. That while doing so, he stood and made a threatening gesture with his fists. This constitutes an actionable verbal assault and we are not only going to move for sanctions against the Drummond firm, we're filing a police report against Mr. O'Brien. This is your last warning, sir. Conduct yourself as befits an officer of the court or we are walking out of here. Let's finish this up."

"He called me—" O'Brien stopped, thinking for once before he spoke, realizing they would twist his outrage at Fitzgerald's obscenity into unwarranted homophobia. He took a breath and nodded at the reporter. "No, Mr. Coyle, you're wrong. I said your client's age prevented any such action on my part." He grinned at the reporter. "Now, let's continue. Mr. Fitzgerald, how many lawsuits have been filed against you alleging theft in the last ten years?"

"You skinny little—" Fitzgerald caught himself, his eyes narrowed. "How many phony lawsuits has your client filed against every insurance company from here to Chicago? How many whiplash suits? Knox wears the collar more often than my parish priest."

"Ask him at his deposition." O'Brien said. "How many lawsuits have been filed against you alleging theft in the last ten years?"

"Don't answer that, Teddy. I'm instructing my client not to answer. Irrelevant."

"What did you do with the missing fifty million in stocks and bonds, Mr. Fitzgerald?"

"That's it," Coyle said. "We're out of here. Let's go, Teddy."

"Did you sneak in before the official opening of Mr. Knox's safe and steal all the bonds? Where did you hide them, Mr. Fitzgerald?"

"Off the record," Coyle ordered, lumbering to his feet.

"No, goddamn it. Stay on the record, Sheila," O'Brien ordered. Speaking quickly, he said, "Let the record reflect that Mr. Fitzgerald has refused to answer my questions, let the record reflect that Mr. Coyle doesn't think any question dealing with the money missing from Mr. Knox's safe is relevant to a lawsuit questioning Mr. Fitzgerald's handling of the estate, let the record—"

"Let the record reflect you didn't ask one properly established or relevant question all day, Counselor. No rush on the transcript, Sheila, he didn't touch us." Coyle put a finger to his lips as a gesture to his client and held the door open. The two men walked out, leaving a crumple of old newspapers on the table.

***

THE OLYMPIC CLUB'S BLACK WALNUT paneled bar was scattered with young men and a couple of older guys, smoking, drinking, some watching the Giants game on television, some playing bull dice at the bar, others eating the appetizers—carrots, celery, cheese cubes, stale peanuts and pretzels—that became their dinner. The City's most storied athletic club, the Olympic Club's winged insignia was found on everything from the cocktail napkins to a giant carved medallion hung above the bottles of Macallan and Stolichnaya. The men wore jackets and ties.

"They killed me, absolutely killed me," O'Brien said, staring into his Bushmills. Haggard, he was dressed in the wrinkled suit he'd worn that day, his tie loose, his collar unbuttoned. His heavy curls glistened, damp from his shower ten minutes earlier.

"You didn't do so badly, fourteen points and a clutch of rebounds when the ball fell in your hands," Gamble said, sipping his house chardonnay. "Of course, the chap guarding you was a septuagenarian."

"That's not—cut the crap—you know I'm not talking about the dumb game. My deposition, my big deposition. Hey, Charlie, another round here, please." He waved the empty glass above his head. "All morning and half the afternoon and I got nothing. Jesus H, they kicked my ass. Maybe I'm no good at this crap."

"Remember what I taught your class? Remember?" Gamble asked, leaning across the inlaid brown leather table. At thirty-five, Blake Gamble was a senior deputy on the District Attorney's staff who indulged his weakness for pedantry by teaching Legal Research & Writing at Hastings College of the Law. Between two lost years at Oxford pursuing a doctorate and a lineage so distinguished his unemployed father put on a tie for dinner in his own home, Gamble had cultivated a mid-Atlantic accent. It impressed juries, and was sometimes cited as evidence of his many affectations. Single, Gamble was seldom without a girlfriend, but invariably she would never do. Over the years, he'd shocked his Mayflower mother with white tattoo artists, Hispanic hair dressers, black radicals and Asian cocktail waitresses.

"Nah, nobody listened to you."

"I'm serious. Cross-examination is the most difficult art a trial lawyer has to learn, it takes years. Years. Frankly, I'm shocked a firm of Drummond's stature would allow a new associate to take such an important deposition." Often kind, Gamble decided against mentioning malpractice per se, fearing his downcast friend might at last take a criticism to heart. Instead, he described an unusual procedure for dealing with hostile witnesses.

O'Brien perked up as he considered Gamble's suggestion. "You mean all I have to do is make a motion to conduct the deposition in front of a judge?" he asked. "In court? Just like in a trial? Whoa, he wouldn't be able to pull that crap again—he'd have to answer."

"Yes, yes," Gamble said, "but it's very rare: rarely requested and even more rarely granted. But if the deposition transcript reads as you say, you'd have a decent chance. Every judge in town knows about Fitzgerald. Our office knows about Fitzgerald. Half those chaps who filed lawsuits against him sought to have him arrested first."

"You should arrest him. Arrest him for looting this estate."

"Well, perhaps," Gamble said. Then he chuckled. "But the jails would burst if we went after every lawyer who cheated his clients. Do you mind terribly if I smoke?" Gamble asked politely. His manners were impeccable.

"What about the State Bar?" O'Brien asked.

"It's worthless." Frowning, Gamble considered the small fortune in dues the Bar had already extracted from him. "Make your motion, Flip, ten bucks says you'll win it."

"Done," O'Brien said. He liked betting against his favorite teams: If they lost, he made a few bucks to ease the disappointment; if they won, he didn't care about the money.

CHAPTER 11

CIOPPINO

O'Brien hiked up Russian Hill—up Filbert Street, almost to Hyde, a climb steeper than he'd anticipated. Too winded to appreciate the posh neighborhood and its sparkling bay views, he knocked on the door. On the north side of the street, the duplex was brown-shingled, its trim painted white and its flower boxes pink with impatiens.

"Who are you? Marybeth didn't say anything about a boy. She said she was having dinner with some pest lawyer, not the paperboy," Eloy Duran said. "Marybeth, the paperboy is here," he called, laughing at his own words. He appraised O'Brien. "In, in, in. You can't win her heart standing outside."

O'Brien followed Eloy down a dusty, book-strewn hallway into a living room with bay windows that framed Alcatraz. Rather than decorated, the room was an archaeological dig: books overwhelming shelves, books haphazardly piled across the parquet floor, thumbed magazines stacked two feet high, posters of art exhibits, jazz concerts and a beautiful one of the bullfighter Manolete, painted canvases propped against walls, an easel with an unfinished charcoal drawing, a hand-carved chess set on a steamer trunk that passed for a coffee table, a couch draped with fraying Navajo blankets.

"I know all about you, pendejo." Eloy Duran was so obese that potential seatmates mouthed silent prayers when he swayed down an airplane aisle, so heavy his weight was his life's preoccupation. He wore a laundered T-shirt that sloped snow-white over his mountainous girth, wrinkled khaki trousers and rubber sandals. Despite his size, he was almost handsome, with curly black hair, good teeth and flashing brown eyes that radiated intelligence. Close to fifty, Eloy thought he looked younger and never admitted his age. He claimed his volubility was his defense against being taken for a dumb Mexican. A verbal jackhammer, he speed-talked without pause. To be heard, one had to interrupt him. "Tell me, boy. Do you read? What do you read? Melville? Faulkner? Tolstoy? Surely you read Tolstoy?"

"Well, not—"

"What? You haven't read Tolstoy? You call yourself educated and you haven't read Tolstoy? Marybeth, stay with the pilot, this one knows nothing," he called toward the kitchen, laughing his belly into a shaking mass. He laughed at every third remark of his own and, often as not, at whatever he heard in reply. "But maybe I read too much. Do you know what I always say? The problem with reading is that sooner or later you have to come back to reality. Are you a good boy, Michael? Do you call your mother? How often? Do you send her flowers? Do you send her money from your rich lawyer's salary?"

"I call her pretty much every week, on Sundays after I—"

"Don't tell me you go to Mass. No, lawyers only believe in retainers. Marybeth, she's a believer. Pobrecita. Maybe you can make her understand the Church is dead and God is hiding. No, her god—a jolly old white man with a white beard—never existed. Tell her to stop giving her money away to the scheming priests. Maybe she'll listen to you." Eloy stopped to catch his breath and inspect the laughing young man. "You're a pretty boy. That means you're no good. What's this?" he demanded, jabbing at the small crucifix around O'Brien's neck. "I'll tell you what this is. Nothing. The sign of the playboy, not a token of slavish devotion to some lesser prophet. Every Mexican pimp wears two."

"Eloy, you promised to be good," Marybeth exclaimed, a hint of Tennessee slipping into her pique. She'd marched in with Eloy's homemade tortilla chips and guacamole dip. "No more of that. Flipper, please sit down—not there, that's Eloy's chair, here on the couch. Don't let him bother you. He teases everyone he likes. Well, hi."

"Whoa, you look so great, Marybeth," O'Brien said, stunned. She was wearing a string of pearls, a silk blouse and a black skirt that flattered her long, tanned legs. Her blonde hair was bigger somehow, curlier. "What did you do with your hair? It looks really good."

"Come on, pendejo, you can do better than that," Eloy said, laughing as if he'd told the funniest joke.

"Just a little hair spray and a couple curlers, nothing much." She smiled.

"You look like you're going to Cinderella's ball," O'Brien said, hoping Eloy would relent. "Is this your apartment?"

"I have the little studio downstairs, the garden unit. I can't afford an apartment like this," Marybeth said, glancing at Eloy, her eyes pleading with him to go along with her story. "This is Eloy's."

"Hey, I've got a garden apartment, too," O'Brien said.

"Yes, pendejo, but you don't own the building," Eloy said, ignoring Marybeth's unspoken request. "Do you save your money, Mr. Lawyer? Or do you spend it all on clothes and girls? Are you saving for a down payment on a house? She already has—"

"Eloy, you promised you'd make us margaritas." With a hand at his elbow, Marybeth guided him into the kitchen, returning alone. In a quiet voice, she explained that her parents and youngest sister were overseas while her father finished his Army career in Germany. She had no other family on the West Coast, and within a week of Eloy's renting the apartment above hers, they'd informally adopted one another. For fun, she called him "Uncle Eloy". He was a genius who knew more languages than a UN translator; before retiring to San Francisco, he'd owned a Mexican restaurant in some misbegotten desert town.

"He's usually very perceptive with people. But somehow he doesn't understand Scott."

"Who?" O'Brien asked. "Oh yeah, your army guy. How come?"

"They're oil and water. Scott's conservative and he didn't like Eloy teasing him about the military-industrial complex. He took it personally. Called Eloy a communist."

"Is that even an insult in San Francisco?"

"Is what an insult?" Eloy asked, rejoining the pair, handing them margaritas. "Tell me, pendejo. Is anyone at your blue-blooded law firm offended by your South Boston accent?"

"What? What accent? Oh, you're kidding me. Marybeth must have told you where I'm from."

"Another self-deluded pretty boy, Pobrecita? Where do you find these men? Is there some halfway house for the criminally insensitive in North Beach? Do you find them on the way home? Are the self-deluded the only ones with the nerve to ask out the fashion model?"

"You're a model?" O'Brien asked, surprised.

"I was. Mostly print, just here on the West Coast."

"Whoa, that's great. You have pictures?"

"Where do you think the money came from to buy these flats, Pendejo? Not from her cooking." Eloy belly-laughed.

"I'm an excellent cook, Eloy, and you know it. I wish you wouldn't say that."

"Hey, great margarita," O'Brien said.

"There are two "r's" in margarita, Mr. I have-no-accent," Eloy said. "What makes you think you're good enough for Marybeth? We've already established that you don't read, you have no faith, no self-awareness, and you spend every dollar you earn. What are your hobbies besides chasing women? Gambling, drugs, sniffing glue?"

O'Brien laughed, holding up his hands in mock resignation. "No más."

"So now you patronize me with two words of badly pronounced

Spanish. Stick with the pilot, Marybeth. All this one wants is to get in your pants and brag about it to his friends at the gym."

"You're killing me, Eloy," O'Brien chuckled. "But hell, if she'd even kiss me, I'd take a front page ad out in the *Chronicle* to brag about it. Just look at her. She's the best-looking woman on the planet."

"Hah. Maybe the pretty boy is cleverer than he looks. Be careful with this one."

"I think he likes you," Marybeth said, as they ordered piña coladas an hour later at Scoma's, a Fisherman's Wharf restaurant built athwart a tired pier. The traditional seafood place looked onto the colorful moored fishing boats and was jammed with tourists and locals who liked the bartenders and their generous pours.

"He's quite a character, funny. Is he always like that? Is he really a lawyer, too?"

"Yes, always. He's quite something, isn't he? He may have gone to law school, but he's not a lawyer. I asked him to help me with a lease once and he said he couldn't. I think he failed the bar test. Twice."

"Did he really run for Congress?"

"I don't know. Most of what he says is true or mostly true, but he does tell stories, bless his heart. Besides the restaurant, a lot of his efforts have been futile." Flushed with Eloy's margarita and the piña colada, she smiled at O'Brien, oddly pleased with her adopted uncle's tacit approval of the peacock. She still had reservations.

"Futile?"

"Yes, one failure after another. A friend of his from the desert said Eloy was the world's most successful failure."

"Oh."

They decided to split a Crab Louie and a bowl of cioppino. O'Brien suggested washing it down with a Sauvignon Blanc. Not interested in another drink herself, Marybeth consented, curious to learn how much the peacock drank. As they picked through their dinner, she told him more about Eloy, the stories she'd heard from the stream of friends that visited him—former students, ex-busboys and waiters, activists from his days in this movement or that, the weak and the wounded who viewed him as the Buddha—stories which starred both his acid tongue and generous spirit.

"Enough about him, Flipper," she said finally, glancing into his eyes and then away. "I want to know more about you. How is your job going?"

"It's going great, really great," O'Brien began, "I've got all this responsibility on this new case and, and…oh." He seized his glass and drained it.

"And?" she asked in a soft voice.

"And I. . . Oh, what the hell am I saying? I need another." He poured himself a full glass and slugged back half of it.

"Please tell me."

"It's going terribly. I'm—this is hard to say—I'm sucking at my job." He stared out the window at the gently bobbing boats, biting his lower lip.

"What?" Marybeth was so shocked at his lost braggadocio that she studied him—his angular profile—as if for the first time.

"I did my first deposition this week—you know, a cross-examination outside of court—and I was slaughtered by these two old guys, the witness and his lawyer," he said to the boats. "They tore me apart. I didn't know what the hell I was doing or how to handle them. It was so bad that during every break I ran into the bathroom to wipe off my underarms."

"Really?"

"Then the witness, Fitzgerald—he's the worst—baited me into threatening to kick his ass and they put that on the record and then after the deposition was over, he filed a complaint with the police. I've been lying awake at night wondering how I'm going to explain it if he files a lawsuit against the firm. I don't know if..."

"If what?" she asked. Shorn of his trying cockiness, O'Brien had her interest at last. She studied his pained face, and caught the faint circles of his contact lenses. Her peacock wasn't perfect.

"I shouldn't be telling you this stuff. Probably just all these drinks—Eloy's margaritas were really strong. You know about the maudlin Irish. It's not me. I'm really—"

"No, no, no. Don't recount what you think of yourself. I've heard that enough. Tell me what you were going to say about your case. Please." She pressed the back of his hand, touching him for the first time.

"I don't know what I'm doing. In so far over my head I'm drowning. Maybe I'll never be any good at it."

"Don't say that," she said, slipping into her advisor's role, a task she'd assumed with her younger sisters since the first grade. "It must take years to become a good lawyer, and you just started."

"What's worse is that the senior partner may be doing this to me on purpose." After an awkward pause washed away with more wine, he continued, "I don't know why, why he'd hate me so much. I haven't even been there a year and never worked with him before. I've always been nice to him, why wouldn't he like me?"

"Maybe because he doesn't know you. Maybe he has the wrong conception of you." She hesitated, sipped her wine. "You look and act one way, Flipper, but—"

"What do you mean?"

"I mean, maybe you're nicer than you act—you were sweet with Eloy, playing along with his stories." She'd been struck by the schoolyard glances her uncle stole at the young man, the same look Nancy the cashier gave him at the bakery. "You're nice when you're not trying to impress everybody. Why don't you just tell the senior partner the truth, that you need his help?"

"Good idea. Maybe that would clear the air. I'll talk to him on Monday," he said, taking her hand in his. "Marybeth, I want to tell you something. OK? Well, I've had so much to drink I'm telling you anyway. I like you a lot."

"No, please don't say that. You don't know me." She freed her hand, straightened, inched back from the table. Blushing, she held up a finger.

"Yes, I do. I see you almost every day, I see how you are with your employees, how you treat them, what they think of you, how pretty you look with the kitchen steam flushing your cheeks or when you get jams or powdered sugar on your apron—"

"I don't get jam on my apron."

"Why do you think I'm drinking so much coffee? I've become addicted to caffeine just to see you. Honest. I'm not there for the cookies." His blue eyes had widened, staring into hers.

"Everyone loves my cookies, you know that." She laid her hand on the table, allowing him to take it, touched by his unexpected confession of inadequacy. She stared into her glass. "What about all your girls?"

"What girls? What girls," he repeated. "You asked me that before and I told you. I don't have a wife and kids back in Boston and I don't have a girlfriend. The only girl I was dating dumped me the morning I first met you. It's crazy but it's true, she prefers her New York director to me. Can you believe—"

"There you go again. That's how you annoy everyone."

"Sorry, I'll start over. OK?" he asked, waiting for her nod. "I'm not even thinking about anyone else, I just want to be with you." He was enchanted with Marybeth's voice, her honeyed Southern accent emerging with the drinks. That she'd transformed herself into Cinderella for the evening must mean she cared a little. He gazed at her elegant fingers around the stem of the wine glass, comparing her kitchen-scarred hands with his own unblemished skin, soft hands possessed of so little dexterity that shaving was an adventure. The image of her fingers around the stem stirred him.

"Maybe we could have dinner again next week," she allowed. "You have been nicer."

"And I do like your cookies." He was aware she'd been tinkering with her recipe since his sidewalk critique; a more cautious man might have stopped with the compliment. "I'd like them even better if you put more chocolate in them, you know, real chunks."

"Do you have any idea what ingredients cost? I'm practically losing money on every cookie we sell."

"Raise your prices, double them, your customers won't care. What's an extra twenty-five cents compared with guilt-free sin? Me, I'd rather kiss you than anything else, but half our lawyers and staff have sweets every afternoon. Kiss me."

"No."

"Then I'll have to kiss you."

CHAPTER 12

THE MEMO

BUCKLEY'S MEMORANDUM LAY ON O'BRIEN'S chair when he arrived the next morning in a great mood, whistling *Tomorrow* and thinking of Marybeth biting her lip as she'd said goodnight. He slipped off his suit jacket and picked it up. His face reddened as he scanned it; the jacket fell to the floor. He swore at the cc list at the bottom of the page; crushed the memo into a ball and threw it against the wall; stomped it; tossed it in the trash; and then yanked it out and hurled it outside onto the alley below. A moment later he had to read it again. Anger-blinded, he stormed past Michelle and retrieved the memo from the dry gutter.

O'Brien reread Buckley's opening paragraph: 'Having examined the Fitzgerald transcript, a fundamental lack of preparation, both as to subject matter and the basic art of cross-examination, is apparent. While the former might be overcome with strenuous application in future depositions, the latter may prove elusive crippling if this work is truly indicative of your innate level of skill.' Seething, O'Brien wondered if the murder of a lawyer were a lesser crime, like shooting a rabid dog. Probably in Texas. Furious, he'd walked a mile before concluding the wisest course was to say nothing to Buckley, to go about his business as if the memorandum were inoffensive, merely instructional.

He stayed this wise course for ten minutes. Then he ran back to the office, raced upstairs to the fourth floor and burst into Buckley's stylish office. Buckley was chuckling into the telephone. He inclined his head toward a chair for O'Brien and suggested with a wave of his pudgy hand that his associate close the door. Then he swiveled away.

O'Brien remained standing, shifting his weight, resisting the temptation to jump over the desk and throttle the bastard. Buckley's sunny office faced east. Its two tall windows looked past the Alcoa Building, toward the Bay Bridge and the rising sun. The shelves and bookcases were blond oak, the room was painted white and its exposed fir rafters were high above, crossed by a blue air duct. The office had a glossy feeling, as if a society decorator had chosen the English desk, beige couch, table lamps and chairs with an eye toward a magazine spread.

"Sit, sit," Buckley said finally, hanging up the phone, his dolphin smile in place. "What can I do for you?"

Trembling, O'Brien dropped the memorandum on the polished, empty desk. "This," he said.

"Let's take a look at this, shall we?" Buckley widened his smile and examined the memo as if for the first time. "Been through the wars, has it?" He snickered. "The trouble with writing, even truly good writing, is that nuances are subject to misinterpretation; inflection is everything. Rereading this—I dashed it off after a late night's work—I can see where a sensitive soul might infer a harsher judgment than I intended. In the final analysis, I may have made a mistake in not going over this with you in person."

"What? What are you saying?" Ready for a confrontation, this distant relative to an apology caught O'Brien flat-footed.

"Michael, sit down. Relax. Everyone knows you've only just begun here and that cross-examination is a fine craft that takes years to perfect."

"What?"

"Take it easy. Sit, sit. My partners know I belong to the old school, where young attorneys aren't coddled—they're tested early." Buckley then delivered a closing argument, taking time to elaborate on his theme, claiming one had to coal-walk to learn trial work—to carry a great litigator's bags every day during a six-month trial, to prepare until

2:00 a.m. each night for the next day's witnesses, to research motions until the pages blurred.

A crumpled O'Brien sat staring at his shoes until Shelly Green knocked on the door, announcing a conference call. She had standing orders to create one every time an associate was in Buckley's office more than ten minutes. "We're finished here, aren't we, Michael? Good. Before you go, let me tell you the one about the lawyer, the judge, and the nun who get washed up on the desert island."

Slouching downstairs, O'Brien suddenly recalled Gordon's advice—the caution he'd urged in dealing with Buckley—and detoured to his door. "Got a minute, Gregg?"

With a red pen, Gordon was making corrections in the margin of a contract, fitting his form deed of trust to his client's latest deal. His windows were open to the summer morning—a concession to non-smokers—and the air in his office was cool. It still smelled like a bus station. Gordon flicked out a fresh cigarette, lighting it with his sad flair, his jaundiced eyes surveying O'Brien. "Buckley?"

"Yeah."

"Asshole," he said simply, as if telling a tourist a street name. Gordon dug out his copy of the memorandum from a desk drawer. "You see this?"

"Of course I saw it. It's to me. Wait a second—are you telling me he'd send the partners a copy of a memo addressed to me and not give me one?"

"It's easier to make your getaway before the victim knows he's dead." Gordon's words were flat. "Why are you here?"

"Well, I wanted to check something, ask you what you thought—"

"Why should I?" Gordon asked. "I told you what to do the last time you bothered to stop in. You didn't do it. I don't like people wasting my time."

"Sorry, I'll go. You're right, I didn't listen to your warning about

Buckley. I guess I thought he liked me, I just couldn't believe he was out to get me for no reason. At least he promised to tell you guys the memo was too harsh, that I wasn't that bad."

"Sit down," Gordon growled, "and listen this time. Buckley's already talked to us. He said he had to go easy on you in writing—"

"That motherfucker."

"You going to listen to me this time?"

O'Brien nodded.

Gordon repeated his sermon: Demand work from other partners, put in a sustained effort, work crazy hours—bill 200 hours a month for six months running— attend the Bar's evening courses on pretrial preparation, ask key partners for advice on cases. He had to convince the firm that he really wanted to be a lawyer, that the craft was important to him, that Drummond was his life's ambition. To counteract the nearly indelible impression he'd already given the partnership, O'Brien needed an influential partner to stand up for him, to insist Buckley had him wrong, that he was doing serious work, that he was serious himself. Without a champion, O'Brien was doomed.

"Should I talk to Farwell? Get some work from him?"

"Jack?" Gordon replied, glancing away. "Jack can't help anyone. Don't bother him. Talk to Cain, he's a good guy, get some work from him. Or Richmond, he's a little goofy, but he's all right. And don't screw up that Knox case anymore."

Watching him depart, Gordon wondered why Buckley had it in for O'Brien. Was he offended by O'Brien's blue-collar roots? Or the lesser schools he'd attended? He pursed his lips, puffed on his cigarette. Maybe Buckley was doing the kid a favor. Maybe he should be rooting for O'Brien to escape. If only an asshole like Buckley had chased him from the law fifteen years ago, where would he be today? He blew a smoke ring toward the ceiling, and gazed out the bright window.

CHAPTER 13

RUFFIAN

It was early, the City sleeping off another Saturday night, sun low above the Oakland hills. The streets were dry—the great drought gripped California by the throat—but the cable car tracks were damp from the fog. A young couple was running on the empty streets, the woman's long-legged canter so splendid it seemed gravity had given her a pass. Ten yards behind her, cursing himself for agreeing to run a damn marathon, O'Brien was wondering why running was even considered a sport. Boring and painful, it was the kind of hard work he'd shirked all his life. Dribbling a ball, O'Brien could fly across the court for hours, his vigor on unconscious display. But jogging? It was more tedious than legal research. Could he fake a sprained ankle? He had to come up with something.

When he'd suggested a dinner date two days earlier, Marybeth had countered with a Sunday morning run. They could get to know one another better that way. O'Brien had hesitated, then accepted her challenge, figuring he could talk her into a leisurely jaunt, perhaps to Fisherman's Wharf and then back to North Beach for cappuccinos.

He'd sauntered over to the Tower Records on Columbus. As he approached the parking lot, he grimaced. Marybeth was stretching with intention—like an Olympic athlete—her expression stern. Doubled over in a pike, she'd straightened her legs, her palms pressed flat on the asphalt. She'd brushed aside his suggestion of hanging out until the Buena Vista opened, insisting they do a real run: the Golden Gate Bridge and back.

And now they were a mile into it.

"Marybeth, wait, wait please," he called to her. Improvising, he dropped his hands to his knees, wiping his face with his Red Sox sweatshirt, hoping to impress her with his muscled stomach. "I don't know what's wrong. Must be the altitude."

"We're at sea level, Flipper, very funny." From the rub-some-dirt-on-it school, she pursed her lips. That her peacock was all show and no go was hardly a surprise. Why was he wearing those silly wrist bands? "Come on. You'll loosen up after another mile."

"Think I've got a side stitch," he said, warming to his excuse. "Yeah. Big pain right here just below my ribs. Want to feel it?"

"Will you be recuperated in a couple minutes?" she asked. "We've just started."

"Wish I could promise you that, but Jesus H this really smarts. Look, there's the Safeway," he said, pointing out a market notorious among singles as the place to shop for dates. "Why don't we get a couple bagels and orange juice and relax on the Green? The sun's coming out."

"I don't care for orange juice." She slipped off her headband, tucked her hair behind her ear, and snapped it back into place. "Wait here, over there on the grass. I'll sprint a little and be back in half an hour. All right?"

O'Brien started to object, caught himself and straightened. Letting her run while he dozed wasn't such a bad deal. "OK, all right, I'll see you over there."

Marybeth spun and ran.

"Holy cow," O'Brien murmured as he watched her tear up Marina Boulevard. Free of O'Brien, she'd lengthened her stride and accelerated to a gallop. He stood stock-still, mesmerized. A fair athlete himself, he was in awe of physical gifts—as a boy, he'd worshipped the ill-fated Tony Conigliaro—and he was seeing one now. He stared until she rounded the bend.

He bought a bottle of Martinelli's apple juice and a couple sesame seed bagels at the Safeway and crossed to the Marina Green. He rolled his sweatshirt into a pillow and sprawled on the grass. Despite his considerable ego, O'Brien asked himself what she was doing with him. She had three restaurants and her own home; she was beautiful and ran like a gazelle. No, a thoroughbred. And he was circling the drain. He shut his eyes, telling himself not to think about it.

"Miss me?" Marybeth woke him thirty minutes later. She stood over him, glistening with sweat. "I stopped on Chestnut and got you this." She handed him a tube of Ben-Gay. "For your stitch."

"Whoa, that was thoughtful, thanks," he said, sitting up. He stuck the tube in his pocket, thought better of it, and lathered his side with the cream. "Speaking of whoa, you know what you remind me of? The way you run?"

"What?"

"One of the greatest racehorses of all time."

"You're comparing me to a horse?" She laughed. She'd heard a lifetime of compliments, but this was unique.

"Not just any horse. *Ruffian*. The most beautiful horse ever, the best mare ever. She was a mare, but she still beat all the stallions every time. She won ten races in a row—"

"I remember her," Marybeth said, delighted. "The tragic horse they had to put down a couple years ago?"

"Yes, after the Kentucky Derby. The poor thing ran her heart out, then broke down. They had to euthanize her. She was the greatest horse ever. Better than Secretariat. It was so sad." He glanced away. "Sit, please. You can use my sweatshirt."

Marybeth noticed a tear welling in his eye. "Are you a horseracing fan?"

"Not really. Been to the races a couple times and lost my ass. I just followed her in the papers—she was the best. Sorry, hey, I got you apple juice. And here's a bagel."

"You listened," she said, gazing at the juice, impressed. "Thanks." She sat down beside him and broke a piece from the soft bagel.

"Hey, so you must have run in high school—what were your events? The hundred? Quarter mile?"

"No, I've never competed."

"What? Are you fuc—are you kidding me? You run like Steve Prefontaine and you never competed? I don't believe it." O'Brien fell silent. He plucked a blade of dry grass and chewed on it.

"I couldn't, I was always working," Marybeth said, deciding she had to say something. "Remember? I was a model. I had to take jobs whenever they came up, I couldn't commit to practices."

"Even in high school?"

"Before that. When I was eight, my mother started dragging me to pre-teen beauty contests all over Tennessee and then at every base we were stationed at—Little Miss This, Little Miss That—and the next thing I knew she had me modeling in newspaper ads."

"The weird kind where they make little girls look like strippers?"

"Yes, that kind." Marybeth looked away, wondering again whether she would ever forgive her mother for turning her into a Barbie doll, for making her childhood a never-ending series of charm schools, lessons and classes: music, singing, speaking, dancing, makeup, even runway walking classes. And of course, the bizarre beauty pageants. Marybeth's plain mother had been envious of her since she was a toddler, even jealous of her husband's innocent fawning over her, wishing she'd received a tenth as much of his attention as his precious Marybeth. Her mother who was at once proud and resentful of her oldest daughter. Her mother who'd insisted Marybeth pay rent to help out the family. Marybeth had known the cost of beauty long before it ever occurred to her that she might be beautiful.

"Is that why you don't wear any makeup now?"

She gave O'Brien a sidelong glance. Perhaps he was more perceptive than she thought. "Tell me something: How did you end up in San Francisco?"

Tapping the sweatshirt, he said, "I came to Berkeley in '69 as an undergraduate and just stayed."

"But Boston is full of colleges. Why did you come here?"

O'Brien was used to this question, and had a pat answer. "You know that song, California Girls, by the Beach Boys?"

"Sure."

"Well, they weren't writing any songs about Boston girls, so I—"

"There you go again with that smart aleck stuff, Flipper."

"I'm sorry," he said, raising his hands. "Sorry. OK." He paused, flicked away the blade of grass, and stared at Alcatraz. "The truth is, my home life was bad, my father was dead, my mother was—is—in perpetual mourning and my brothers had scattered." If it worked out with her, he might tell her the rest one day, why he'd been forced to defend his dead father's honor on every playground he'd trod since he was twelve, why he'd developed a hair-trigger temper and a talent for boxing. "I was clueless about college, had no idea what I wanted to do or be. I didn't even think about being a lawyer until my senior year at Berkeley. California just sounded cool. You know? Summer of Love. How about you?"

"Me?"

"Yes, why aren't you back with your family in Tennessee?"

"I told you my dad is career Army—he's stationed in Germany right now—there's nothing for me in Knoxville except relatives I hardly remember. We were always stationed somewhere else. When I was a teenager we were living here at the Presidio, then he was transferred to Fort Bragg and now he's in Wiesbaden."

"So you stayed here alone when he was transferred? Wasn't that hard?"

"Not really, I had my modeling career. I was peaking just as they were about to leave. Peaking at eighteen," she said ruefully. "If I'd only known how short my career was going to be. Anyway, I couldn't stand the dieting, the cattiness, the vacuousness of everyone involved."

"But leaving your parents behind?"

"That wasn't so bad. It was like I was in a sorority with the other models. A sorority of extra-dumb girls." It was her turn to decide the truth could await another day. Her mother had insisted she remain behind to pursue her career, that Fort Bragg was no place for a star like her. Marybeth had cried herself to sleep the first two weeks after her family left.

"Well, except for the beauty part, you couldn't have fit in with them," he said. "You're really smart."

"We can take a cab back, Michael, if your side's still bothering you."

"Let's just walk. We can play a game: You ask a question about me, then I'll ask one about you. Whoever answers the most, wins."

She agreed, took his hand, and they strolled toward North Beach. "That was sweet, what you said about Ruffian," she admitted.

They chatted amiably, O'Brien making his small jokes, Marybeth enjoying the moment away from her demanding business, each feeling a surprising comfort and companionship now that they'd settled into the date, each unaware of how far they'd soon be driven apart.

CHAPTER 14

THE MOTION

THREE PINK PHONE MESSAGES FROM Malcolm Knox cluttered O'Brien's chair, the last one with a note: I won't go to lunch until I hear from you. Just great, O'Brien thought, now it's my fault if the prick starves to death. He stared at the papers on his desk, the motion that refused to write itself. Sighing, he set aside his outline and the favorable appellate decisions. He thumbed through the deposition transcript, double-checking the passages where Fitzgerald and Coyle had been most recalcitrant. Their caustic words played worse on paper, an ugly defiance of the judicial system. He picked up the outline. He read it. He read it again. It was almost there on the page: how he could marry the facts to the law, where he could insert his highlighted appellate passages, and where he might quote the ugliest of his opponents' remarks.

The phone rang. "Hello."

"You're supposed to let me know where you are, Flipper. You weren't at that darn coffee shop again, were you?" Ann Wall asked. Because her desk was outside Lederhosen's office on the third floor, a floor and half the building's length away, O'Brien had the intolerable freedom to come and go without her leave. She visited him often, delivering his scant mail, dropping off interoffice memoranda and pink phone slips. He produced so little secretarial work that her visits were ceremonial, but the gentle young woman did act as a windbreak for him, shielding him from everyone, especially female callers. "Knox called again, said it's urgent."

"I know, I've got all three of—"

"He just called a fourth time. Said he's on his way here."

"Jesus H, Annie. Call him back and tell him, tell him," O'Brien paused, groaned and said, "Tell him I had to run up to the law library to do some last-minute research, but that our motion will be filed tomorrow. Tomorrow. Got that? Then call Blake and tell him I can't play in tonight's game, I've got to finish this motion."

"But what do I tell Noxious tomorrow when he wants to see the motion?" Ann Wall was an Iowa girl with luminous cheeks, a clear conscience and a twenty-six-year-old husband who'd plotted their retirement to the dime. With his dreams of bass boats and home-dug night crawlers, her Jimmy was out of place in San Francisco and, in sadder moments, she suspected she belonged with him back among the cornfields. Married too young, Ann sometimes wished she had a scandal or two among her memories, but she had no gift for deception.

"Tell him he can pick it up. And if you don't want to work late tonight—real late, Annie—ask Bev to get me a night temp to do a lot of typing."

"You're not teasing me? You're really going to do it?"

"I've got to—it's my ass—can you help me? Would it be OK with Jimmy if you stayed late?"

"He's not my boss, you are. And besides, all Jimmy does is watch that dumb TV. There's leftover hot dish, he won't care."

O'Brien knew what he had to do. The judge's decision might be a coin toss, but the motion itself was straightforward and weeks overdue. He knew writing wasn't so hard, he simply had to shut his door, sharpen his pencils, and with scissors and tape at hand, write the damn thing. Instead, he flung his door open to run one errand, then another, photocopying this page and that, fetching the Shepard's Citations, searching once more for the perfect precedent. At length, he ran out of excuses; he had to write. Five minutes after Ann's third call asking for something to start on, O'Brien scissored his first appellate decision and pasted it onto a long yellow sheet of paper. With little originality—he'd steal the summary of one decision from a subsequent case that quoted it—he set out the law on defiant deponents, fattening his motion with quotations. But the words ran away from him; he tossed his scribbling into the trash, and started over with Fitzgerald's testimony.

The hours passed, the firm grew silent and the summer sky darkened as O'Brien shuttled pages and inserts to Ann. He ordered a pizza when they were too hungry to concentrate. She had to retype one finished page when they found it flecked with tomato paste. Much later, hours after Jimmy Wall was asleep and dreaming of trophy fish, Ann told O'Brien the motion was indistinguishable from those she pounded out for Lederhosen. He was pleased.

He put her in a cab he refused to share, claiming he needed to get his head together. He walked up Montgomery and turned onto Broadway, skipping over the sidewalk cracks. He felt the night's depth—the madrugada, as Eloy would describe it—and glanced about: the tourists, barkers and strippers had vanished. Shorn of its vulgar ornaments, the avenue was more sad than tawdry. With nothing to ogle, the cars trickling off the freeway roared past him, racing toward the yellow-tiled Broadway tunnel. O'Brien took a right on Columbus, heading for Washington Square, toward his apartment. The fog rolled east. He should have been delighted; he'd finished his best legal work ever, but his fleeting sense of accomplishment was marred by thoughts of Buckley. He could find nothing—no misunderstandings or slights—to provoke the partner's antipathy. He'd laughed at Buckley's jokes, thought him sophisticated and clever, even admired him. O'Brien wondered whether he truly had no aptitude for trial work or Buckley was simply out to get him. It would never occur to him that Buckley might have disliked him on sight.

By the time he reached his studio—after 2 a.m.—he craved sleep, dropping so hard onto his waterbed it rippled for a minute. As he drifted off, his thoughts unmoored, wandering from Marybeth, to some detective work he wanted to do for Knox, to Gordon's advice, and back to Marybeth.

***

ANN BUSTLED DOWN TO THE lobby, bringing the impatient Malcolm Knox the motion and a cup of coffee and leading him to the small first-floor conference room to await O'Brien. Narrow, with a curving back wall and flooded with natural light, the pleasant room looked past Drummond's patio onto Jackson Street.

"I'm sure Mr. O'Brien will be here any minute, Mr. Knox. It was a long night for him finishing this for you."

"That's quite all right. I'll read it while I wait." Dressed for town in his nautical blazer and tie, Knox sat and read, nodding his head, occasionally jabbing his finger on the motion. Twenty minutes later, he exulted to the empty room, "The son of a bitch nailed it." He was halfway through his second reading when O'Brien walked in with a Serendipity coffee.

"Goddamn it, Michael. You did it. You pinned that bastard. We're going to win this."

"Do you really like it?" O'Brien grinned big. "That's great, but you know judges will hardly listen to trials, let alone some guy's deposition. We're going to need a lot of luck. And a little Sherlock Holmes."

"What?"

"Well, I've been thinking about how we win this. Assuming you're OK with spending the money, we should hire a private investigator to interview the bellboys, maids and the front desk clerks at the hotel. Maybe somebody saw Fitzgerald. Stealing all that loot must have taken several trips."

"But that would cost a lot," Knox said, reaching for his coffee.

"It'd be worth it. If a maid says she saw him at the hotel two days before the official opening of the safe, we rest our case and he goes to San Quentin. Hell, if it's the money you're worried about, you could do it yourself. Even I could do it, but my hourly rate is too high to do really useful work." O'Brien laughed.

"Me?" Knox removed his reading glasses, cleared his throat and said, "Out, out of the question, I'm too busy with my consulting business. Couldn't possibly, couldn't possibly."

"But—"

"No. Not happening on my watch. Period." Knox was caught off-guard. Why was this idiot lawyer staring at him? He knew his words sounded strange, forced. O'Brien must know how little consulting he did, how false his excuse rang. He had to think. Knox gripped the table to steady his hands. "Didn't mean to sound abrupt. Do you have other ideas?"

"We could interview the cleaning service at Fitzgerald's office building. The night janitor may have seen him returning with heavy bags—maybe he stole one or two of the gold bars. Maybe the janitor saw some odd wrapping paper in his trash."

"Yes, now you're on to something. Not such a wild goose chase, talking to one man instead of a dozen. I could call the building manager and find out who does the cleaning. Good idea, Mike. I'll follow up on that. You've really been thinking about this, I'm impressed. Anything else?"

"Two things: Here's the best one. Switzerland," O'Brien said. "Fitzgerald's really smart. Hell, he went to Boalt. He had to know you'd sue to recover the money—so he must have a contingency plan if things go wrong. Let's say we somehow present the court with proof your uncle had the fifty million when he died. Fitzgerald either coughs up the money or goes to jail forever, right? He knows that. He also knows he can't commingle it. You said your uncle had a Swiss account. Well, if it's as hard to close a Swiss account as an American one, that account may still be open—"

"Goddamn it. Why didn't I think of that?" Knox clapped his weathered forehead. "Of course, Fitz takes the money to Switzerland and stashes it in my uncle's account. That way he can swear he never stole it. And when the coast is clear, he's home free. Or, if he becomes a fugitive, the money's already abroad. That's what he must have done. That's goddamn brilliant, Mike."

"Problem is, there's no way to check my theory. The Swiss bank would never confirm he made a deposit—even if we had a court order, they'd ignore it."

"First we need to prove he went to Switzerland after my uncle died." Knox lapsed into thought, drumming his fingers, then smiling at the solution. He'd spent several years as a stockbroker, and learned a few tricks before getting fired for churning his clients' accounts. He could call Fitzgerald's office, posing as a travel agent soliciting new clients; after accepting a rejection with grace, he'd ask the name of the agent who inspired such loyalty. He could then call that agent and say he wished to duplicate the trip to Switzerland that his old pal Fitzgerald had touted. "I can handle that. But you mentioned two things—Switzerland and what else?"

"I'd like to submit a supplemental declaration from you. It'd be simple—you just say you saw all the loot in your uncle's safe just before he died."

Knox swallowed. "It wasn't just before, it was at least the week before. No, more like two weeks. Not sure of the exact date." He glanced toward the ceiling. "Funny, I know where I was when I got the call about Uncle's death—at the Lake—never forget it, like when Kennedy was shot. But the last time I saw him? Can we say several weeks before? What's wrong? That not good enough? I could check my calendar."

"But you told me you'd seen him two days before he died," O'Brien said, his doubt writ large. He'd learned the hard way that poker wasn't his game; his face was easier to read than a stop sign.

"No, I couldn't have."

"It's in my notes from our first conversation."

"You must be mistaken. I've noticed note-taking isn't your strong suit. I must have said two weeks before."

"OK. Two weeks is better than nothing. You good with that?"

"Let's say within a month just to be safe. Don't want to lie."

"If that's all you got."

"What are you thinking, counselor?" Knox searched his attorney's face, remembering his interrogation in the damn coffee shop, how he'd doubted his relationship with Uncle Mal, questioning the executorship.

"Nothing, I'm good. OK, I'll get back upstairs and get on this. I'll call the bank as soon as you confirm Fitz took the trip. We have this conference room for another half hour if you want to make your calls from here. Talk to you soon." O'Brien stood, jabbed a hidden middle finger at his client and retreated.

Watching his young lawyer depart, Knox imagined himself decking the arrogant punk. He smiled.

CHAPTER 15

A DAY IN COURT

"We know you, Mr. Fitzgerald," Judge Arnold Black said, peering over the rim of his bifocals. "Every judge in The City and County of San Francisco has heard of your antics. I have read your deposition transcript. You—and you, Mr. Coyle—ought to be ashamed. You, sir, will answer every question truthfully and you, Mr. Coyle, will keep your mouth shut. I will judge the relevancy of Mr. O'Brien's questions. If you fail to comply with these simple instructions, I will cite you with contempt and then, after forty-eight hours in the company of your peers at County Jail, we will resume this deposition. Do you understand me, gentlemen?"

The two men nodded. The only spectators in the City Hall courtroom were the clerk and court reporter; neither displayed interest in the middle-aged men. The bailiff had gone for coffee. The courtroom belonged to a bygone era, a time when all wore coat, tie and hat. With its high ceilings and somber wood paneling, the hushed chamber seemed a secular church, the judge's bench its raised altar, the jury box its choir, the rows of seating its pews. Dressed in his court suit, O'Brien sat alone at the counsel table nearer the high windows. He nodded along with Fitzgerald and Coyle as if the judge had been talking to him.

"Mr. O'Brien, you may proceed," the judge said after Fitzgerald had been sworn in. A small, wizened man past seventy, Judge Black had retired, but remained on the bench part-time to help with the case backlog. A brilliant superior court judge, the old man had a habit of cradling his bald, splotchy head in his fingers while listening to cases, appearing half-asleep until he attacked.

"Mr. O'Brien, I suggest you eliminate the unnecessary. If he answered the question to your satisfaction here," he said, jabbing the deposition transcript with his thumb, "don't ask it again, go right to the heart of the matter. Interests of judicial economy."

"Yes, your honor, I'll go straight to the heart of it," O'Brien said. He retrieved three sets of papers from a folder. "I have copies for the court and the deponent of two sworn declarations. One, we obtained from a bellman who happened to be smoking on a stairway landing when he encountered Mr. Fitzgerald carrying what he thought were heavy suitcases downstairs. He distinctly recalls the event because he had never seen a hotel guest with luggage in a stairwell before. And he remembers Mr. Fitzgerald's joking reply to his offer of help—Mr. Fitzgerald told him he was training for a marathon St. Patrick's Day pub crawl. The other is my declaration about a phone conversation I had with Eva Muller of the Suisse Bank of Basel, Switzerland. She remembered Mr. Fitzgerald's visit ten days after the late Mr. Knox's passing. Suisse Bank was where the late Mr. Knox kept his secret account, your honor."

"Your honor, I object, we haven't seen—"

"Silence, Mr. Coyle. Sit down. Mr. O'Brien, wait one moment, hold those papers. Sit." The judge paused. He understood the grave error the young lawyer was about to commit and wondered if he could do anything to prevent it. Too often, Judge Black had seen justice lost through inexperience or ineptitude. Too often, he'd felt himself gagged by his role, a witness frozen before a car wreck. Moments ticked by as the judge considered, knowing how delighted Fitzgerald would be to seek his recusal. "Mr. Coyle, I'm willing to hear your objection to the introduction of these documents."

Patrick Coyle exchanged glances with his client and lumbered to his feet. Shifting from one foot to another, Coyle appeared to be in pain, favoring his right leg, leaning hard against the counsel table. "Your honor, my sole objective in this proceeding is to clear Mr. Fitzgerald's good name as soon as—"

"Do you object, sir, yes or no?" the judge asked. "I'm not going to grant any continuance. I'm sure your client would be most delighted to clear his good name." The judge knew his heavy sarcasm would evaporate on the written page, how innocent his words would read in a transcript of the proceeding.

A pale, frantic-eyed Fitzgerald tugged at Coyle's trouser leg beneath the counsel table to get his attention.

"Your honor, I have never viewed the judicial process as a poker game where one side hides its hand," Coyle said. "It is only fair that we be allowed to review these baseless allegations before this deposition continues—"

"You don't object, thank you." In a tone more exasperated than snide, the judge continued, "Mr. O'Brien?"

"Yes, your honor?"

"Sir, you're aware you have no obligation to produce these documents before you take this deposition?" the judge asked, checking the moving papers for the name of the plaintiff's lead attorney. "Have you discussed this with Mr. Buck—"

"Judge," Coyle started, but checked himself, ducking from the old man's withering glare.

"Yes, I'm aware, but the sooner the truth comes out, the better," O'Brien said.

"Noble sentiment, noble indeed," the judge muttered, cradling his head. "In that case, give the papers to Mrs. Valiente to mark for identification."

"Your honor," Coyle said, "would a short recess—no more than ten minutes—be in order to permit us to review these papers?"

"I have no problem granting Mr. Coyle a recess, your honor," said O'Brien, confident justice would prevail.

"No, Mr. O'Brien, it's apparent you wouldn't," the judge said. He perched the glasses on his nose, gaveled a recess and asked his clerk to bring the briefs for the next day's hearing.

Ten minutes later, Fitzgerald resumed the stand. The judge read an unrelated motion during O'Brien's initial questioning but set it aside when the young lawyer, tapping on the counsel table, asked Fitzgerald the value of the safe's contents at the time of Knox's death. Fitzgerald shrugged his shoulders, smiled—obsequious as a courtier—at the judge and explained that he wasn't an accountant. O'Brien pressed him. Fitzgerald daggered a look at the young lawyer.

"Approximate to the nearest million dollars, Mr. Fitzgerald," the judge ordered. "One million should be leeway enough even for you."

"Roughly twenty million dollars, your honor," Fitzgerald said, looking the judge in the eyes.

"Twenty," the judge barked. "It was much more, wasn't it? Before you answer, let me remind you, sir, that Swiss banks are notorious for freezing disputed assets. One cabled order from this bench will prevent you from ever getting your hands on that account. And another order will keep you incarcerated until you turn over your passport. Could it have been as much as fifty million dollars?"

Fitzgerald narrowed his small eyes. "It could have been as much as fifty million, I didn't count it," Fitzgerald said after a long pause, his voice weak, lacking its usual bluster, his eyes darting at Coyle as if the truth were his fault. Fitzgerald wanted to admit nothing, to attack. A heated deposition would shred the bellman's testimony to mush, and he knew the plaintiffs would get nothing from the Swiss bank. That O'Brien had only his own declaration as evidence was proof of that. The young Swiss woman likely gave him no more than the time of day; even if she'd confirmed Fitzgerald's visit, she would recant if pressed. Had it not been for Coyle's threat during the frantic recess to withdraw as counsel of record, insisting he would be gone if the charade didn't end, Fitzgerald would have brazened it out.

"We will take another five-minute recess, Mr. Coyle, to allow your client to arrange to deliver his passport to this court before he leaves this morning. Mr. Ghormley," he said to the bailiff, "you will escort Mr. Fitzgerald to the public phones and then escort him back here. He will not leave your sight. Mr. O'Brien, you will furnish me with the bank's telex address and phone number. We will advise them that no funds may be withdrawn without a certified court order."

When Fitzgerald returned to the witness stand, dogged by the happy bailiff, he shot O'Brien a vicious look.

O'Brien resumed his deposition. "Mr. Fitzgerald, did you remove bonds and stock certificates with a value of approximately fifty million from the safe of your client, Malcolm Knox, and deposit them in Mr. Knox's account at the Suisse Bank of Basel, Switzerland?"

"Objection, your honor, the question assumes facts not in evidence, is compound—"

"And artless as well, but Mr. Fitzgerald will answer it now," said the judge.

"Yes," Fitzgerald said, staring at the floor.

"Did you fail to include the value of these assets, the fifty million dollars, in your final, sworn accounting of the Knox estate?" O'Brien asked.

"Answer the question, Mr. Fitzgerald. Now," said the judge. The bailiff looked up from his newspaper and glanced from Fitzgerald to Coyle.

"Yes."

The enormity of Fitzgerald's admissions stilled the courtroom, all eyes upon him. The bailiff sat straight, fingering the grip of his holstered revolver, hoping the master thief would make a run for it. The court reporter straightened and rolled her neck about her shoulders.

"Your honor," Coyle said, clearing his throat to break the silence. "I would like to give Mr. Fitzgerald a chance to explain how he happened to overlook these assets. How his pressing caseload—"

"*Overlook,*" the judge snapped. "Overlook fifty million dollars? Mr. Coyle, my best advice to you, sir, is to sit down and keep your mouth shut. Anything you say will only get you in this deeper. Sit. Pray tell us, Mr. Fitzgerald, how you came to overlook such the trifling sum of fifty million dollars."

Fitzgerald tumbled through a tale about a hectic trial schedule, the death of an aunt, his wife's shingles, his failure to supervise his office staff. Inspired, he recalled that a paralegal in his office—he couldn't remember who—had prepared the Knox inventory and presented it to him for signature on a chaotic afternoon.

"Are you quite finished, Mr. Fitzgerald?" the judge asked. "Do you have any other excuses for failing to include fifty million dollars in the estate's final accounting? No? Mr. O'Brien, the court is assuming you intend for Mr. Fitzgerald to confirm the companies which issued the stocks and bonds held by the late Mr. Knox, the exact number of shares of stock, who aided him in removing the estate's assets, who prepared the fraudulent inventory and so on." The canny old judge scratched his head, satisfied he'd given the inexperienced young lawyer a roadmap home.

O'Brien grinned. "Yes, your honor."

WHEN THE DEPOSITION ENDED, THE judge—with a grim nod toward O'Brien—and his clerk withdrew through the private door into his chambers. The reporter raised her arms toward the ceiling, stretched, rolling her neck again, and then marked her tape of the morning's proceedings with a felt pen and twisted a rubber band around it. Fitzgerald rushed out, trailed by Coyle. O'Brien stood and gathered his notes.

Only one of the three elevators was in service; a queue awaited its arrival. O'Brien and his opponents saw one another as he rounded the corner.

"I'm going to get you, queerbait," Fitzgerald murmured, puffing himself large. His standing swagger returned, his belligerence as palpable as a prison fight. "Next time I see you, I'm taking a shit in your pretty pocket handkerchief."

"No, Fitz, don't," Coyle said, shaking his head, stepping back from Fitzgerald. He smiled at the onlookers in apology.

"No, you've got it backwards," O'Brien said, unfazed. He stepped toward Fitzgerald. "I'm getting you. I'll have a motion on file tomorrow seeking to remove you as executor of the old man's estate, demanding a full accounting for the estate and sanctions against you both. You're going to jail and my client's sons will get their money."

"Your client's sons. What a fucking laugh," Fitzgerald said. "You don't know shit, you swish-dicked moron. Those boys are the old man's sons. That's why they were inheriting everything. Tell Sponge-Boy everyone knows his pretty little wife loved taking it up the ass from the old man. She divorced your dickless wonder to become Mal's full-time mistress. That's why they hated each other." Fitzgerald cackled, thin and harsh. "Let's get some lunch, Patrick, the Knox estate feels like treating."

"What a pack of lies," O'Brien said.

"Wait, wait," Fitzgerald said to Coyle, snapping his fingers, beaming like the grand marshal of the Saint Patrick's Day parade. "That's it. There's our defense. The old man and Sponge-Boy hated each other. That's why I stashed the money in Switzerland. I hid it because I was afraid Knox'd killed his uncle and would stop at nothing—even murdering the poor boys—to get at their money. I was acting in their best interest, waiting for the cops to nab him before I released the estate. Sacrificing my own good name for their sake."

"That bullshit's going to get you nowhere," O'Brien said.

"Come on, Fitz, save it," Coyle growled, grabbing his client by the arm.

"No, listen. First, we demand the boys get paternity tests and then depose the ex-wife—she'll crack like Mexican concrete. She'll admit she spent more time sucking the old man's cock than brushing her teeth."

"Let's get a drink. You coming down?" Coyle asked O'Brien, holding the elevator door.

"No." O'Brien would walk the two flights of stairs before spending another minute in Fitzgerald's hateful company.

"Watch your ass, queerbait."

As the elevator doors slid together, O'Brien heard Fitzgerald chortling to Coyle. "I had to do it for the boys' sake. They're going to canonize me one day, Patrick, me boy."

O'Brien's euphoria plummeted with each step downstairs. He'd never felt so dirty, Fitzgerald's obscenities blackening him like chimney dust. He was silent in the taxi back to the office, awash in unaccustomed reflection, wondering if the judge had been trying to tell him something. Should he have gotten Fitzgerald's testimony on the record first? Before he revealed his declaration? What should he tell Buckley? Just that he'd found the missing fifty million?

CHAPTER 16

SECOND CHAIR

THE MORNING AFTER THE DEPOSITION, Buckley asked Shelly Greene to summon the firm's junior-most lawyer. O'Brien slouched on the couch and set aside his yellow pad. This was not to be a working session. Buckley reiterated his congratulations of the day before, this time with neither surprise nor pique. He told the young lawyer he'd done a fair piece of work and that he would relish reading the transcript.

"Did you put an overnight rush on the transcript?" he asked.

"Yes."

"Good." Buckley ratcheted up his dolphin smile a notch and said, "Michael, I've given this matter due consideration and decided that our client's interests would be best served if I personally handled the next hearing."

"What? The hearing to dismiss Fitzgerald will be a total piece of cake. Judge Black practically arrested him yesterday. That should be mine."

"I'm afraid some hearings are simply too important for any but the most experienced litigators to assume first chair. But your presence, as second chair, will be critical. Essential," Buckley said. "Knox can't complain about double representation while we're recovering fifty million dollars." O'Brien was silent. Wrinkling his brow, Buckley extemporized, "Tell you what. I'll even do the first draft of the motion this time."

O'Brien studied the gray carpet, glanced at the wooden rafters, at a small bust of an obscure French composer, everywhere but at the grinning first chair. Although he wasn't surprised—his fellow associates had predicted this hijacking over congratulatory drinks the previous evening—he was hurt, the injustice tearing at him. The partnership would hear only how Buckley had saved the fifty million. Clenching his jaw, O'Brien decided that Buckley could learn about Fitzgerald's scorched-earth defense in due time. The first chair could then inform Knox that his wife's infidelity was part of the public record and that Fitzgerald suspected him of murder.

BUCKLEY DOVE IN WHEN THE transcript arrived the next day. After instructing Shelly to hold his calls, he arranged his scissors, tape, fresh yellow pads and no. 2 pencils before him, sprayed his glasses with a cleaning solution he'd bought in Paris—American products left a residue—and began to read. He bit his lip over his associate's appalling mistake; if the worthless O'Brien had only managed to get Fitzgerald's blatant lies about the estate's value on the record first, and *then* produced evidence to the contrary, they would have a perjury charge. Concerned, he sped ahead to where Fitzgerald admitted the Swiss trip and the missing fifty million dollars. Sighing, Buckley picked up the earlier transcript, the one of Fitzgerald's deposition at the Drummond offices and, dashing through it, sighed again. The record was too muddy for a perjury charge to stick based on Fitzgerald's testimony then. Buckley sipped his coffee, reminding himself how essential he was to the case. If not perjury, if not outright theft, Fitzgerald was guilty of gross misfeasance. Buckley would nail him to the wall.

He read through the transcripts at an hourly rate pace, comparing Fitzgerald's courtroom answers to those he gave in the Drummond deposition. After scissoring out the choicest quotes, placing them side by side with the probate court accounting, Buckley wrote swiftly, with one-draft confidence. He prided himself on his crisp style of writing, dismissing legal phrases as crutches for the illiterate. He avoided Latin and often resorted to Bartlett's for flair. He worked for some hours.

When his first draft was finished, he thought it needed only the slightest polishing. It pleased him.

Buckley's draft demoralized O'Brien when he read it the next morning. Sticking it in his back pocket, he left his jacket behind and went out for coffee. He huddled over a table in the corner and reread the brief slowly, parsing each paragraph, following Buckley's taut logic like an engineer reading blueprints, oblivious to the cashier's occasional glances. He knew he could never write like that, fine words singing off the page, leading the reader to an inescapable conclusion. Rather than accuse Fitzgerald of theft or lying under oath, Buckley convicted him of the foulest negligence. With his trademark humor, Buckley wrote that only B-movie amnesia might excuse Fitzgerald's "Fifty Million Dollar Lapse." He demanded Fitzgerald's removal as executor and sanctions against him. In reading the motion a third time, O'Brien pondered the district attorney's office. Maybe he should swap his soft carpeted halls and Colombian coffee for the cracked linoleum and vending machines at the Hall of Justice. Gamble had assured him that their motions came out of a can, that deputy DAs were too busy putting away bad guys to have time for research and writing. O'Brien loved the idea of putting away bad guys, but knew from his boyhood that real criminals often went uncharged, let alone convicted. Yet it was pleasant to think he could put killers behind bars. If only the DA didn't prosecute recreational drug users, he'd have called Gamble that moment, but he thought marijuana harmless—inhaled an acre's worth at Berkeley—and though he seldom smoked now, he couldn't stomach the hypocrisy of convicting small-time dealers.

Instead he called Marybeth Elliot.

CHAPTER 17

SECOND CHOICE

"WHERE HAVE YOU BEEN?" MARYBETH asked, her voice strained. She stood parade ground straight behind the glass counter at Morning Stop, her first bakery on California Street, a five-minute walk from the Drummond offices.

"I was crazy busy on my Knox case after our dinner and then every time I came to find you, they said you were at one of the other shops," O'Brien said. "I kept missing you. I left messages. Can we talk? Maybe have dinner tonight?"

"Let's talk now, it would be preferable. I want to try my competitor across the street." She pulled her apron over her head, reset her hair behind her ears and came around the counter. Outside, she glanced up and down California, waited for a half-empty cable car to rumble by, and then jogged across the busy street, O'Brien in her wake. She studied the Daily Grind's storefront, deciding its black and gray geometric fretwork looked like a warehouse in Richmond. The owner must be male, she concluded.

"I'm thinking of leaving the firm," O'Brien said when they sat with their coffee at a window table, Marybeth with a direct sight line to her own shop's front door. "Maybe going to the District Attorney's office, maybe working with a small personal injury firm. What do you think? You look beautiful, by the way."

She smiled away the compliment, then considered the Grind's smudged, neglected windows; the manager must be male as well. "You mean the District Attorney's office here?" She studied the shop's hand-chalked wall menu, comparing prices with her own. Perhaps she should raise hers.

"Yes. Blake Gamble—I told you about him—thinks he can get me an appointment with the DA. Don't worry, I wouldn't leave San Francisco."

"That's nice."

"That's nice? What the…?" O'Brien said. "Why don't we have dinner tonight?"

"I can't."

"Tomorrow night?"

"No, I—"

"Friday night, Saturday night? Breakfast, lunch or dinner? Snacks at midnight, name it." O'Brien laughed, but fear nipped his readable face. Then it settled in over Marybeth's silence. He touched her hand. "Whatever I did, I'm really sorry for it and I'll never do it again."

"It's not you." She couldn't look him in the face, returned to examining the wall menu instead. She'd made her decision—it had to be right. In the two weeks since she'd last seen O'Brien, Scott Land had been calling her night and day from South Carolina, wooing her non-stop.

"Please don't say that. Everyone knows what comes after 'It's not 'you'."

"I can't see you anymore." A swift glance toward him was all she could muster; she looked out the window. "I have something I have to tell you. My fiancé's coming back. He's so sure he wants to marry me and help me with the business and be my partner that he's willing to take an early retirement from the Army. He thinks we could grow the business to maybe even ten shops. Maybe more. It'd be so much work, but it'd pay off in the—Flip, are you OK?" Shocked, her prepared speech ran aground. "Michael, please don't do that. Please don't cry."

"I'm not…no way I'm crying here. It's just allergies." He glanced away, swearing at himself, rubbing his eyes with his sleeve.

"Are you sure? I'm truly sorry. It's just, Scott and I have known each other for years, we've been talking about this," she said, trailing off. She reached out to touch him, but knew it would make it worse. She studied the crease in her trousers, pinching it together with her thumb and forefinger. "He and I are so similar, military backgrounds, he wants to help with the business."

"You said that. Is he flying his helicopter here? To Chrissy Field?" O'Brien forced himself away from her words—from their import—forced himself to think of anything else, anything to keep from crying. She couldn't see him this way.

"I don't think so. Why?"

"I'd like him to crash-land on a couple guys, if I can just get the bastards together in a field." O'Brien tried to laugh. He'd rolled the paper menu into a tube and held it beneath the table, worrying it in his hands. He crossed his fingers, tapped the table's underside and asked in a breaking voice, "Are you going to marry him?"

"I don't know, maybe, I think so, my parents like him, well, my mom anyway. I don't know. Probably."

O'Brien pushed himself up from the table, his lower lip quivering.

"Wait," she said, "where are you going? Come back. Please."

He stopped a few paces from their table and wiped his face with a napkin before turning to face her, his eyes brimming.

"Please, don't go." His pain hit her hard. "I don't want to end it like this. Regardless of Scott, we should be friends." She knew her words were wrong. "That's not what I meant. I'm not absolutely certain what's going to happen—I do like you."

"I can't, I can't listen to this. Goodbye." He bolted, his shoes scudding across the tiled floor, echoing in the empty shop.

Marybeth felt gut-punched, empty, as if she'd just learned of a close friend's death. She realized she was crying when a tear dropped onto the check. Nowhere near as certain of her charms as the world supposed, she'd interpreted O'Brien's absence after their last dinner as a rejection. He'd found her boring or uneducated—she'd seen his stifled smile at her big words—or maybe he had another girl, maybe the old girlfriend had changed her mind. Something was different. Instead of seeing him several times a day at Serendipity, she'd had sporadic phone calls apologizing for his absence. And she was busy with her other shops—her best manager had quit—and then Scott Land had begun his siege. His long absence and handsome picture were his best weapons.

"Oh, damn," Marybeth cried, plucking a thumbnail from between her teeth, a habit she thought she'd conquered at twelve. O'Brien's flattery and flowers had been easy to dismiss, but not his pain. Was she making a mistake? Yet if he cared so much, why had he left her alone? She reached for the check, calculating fifteen percent on the three dollars before tax. Then she noticed the ten dollar bill O'Brien had left on the table and her tears flowed anew. He was so terrible with money, she told herself. How could they ever be compatible?

CHAPTER 18

KRISTEN

THE PARTY BEHIND HIM, MALCOLM Knox readied himself for the City. He avoided looking at himself in his bathroom mirror, focusing instead on his finicky hair, but his puffiness was inescapable in daylight. His drunken celebration had kicked off a week earlier when he'd read the motion to remove Fitzgerald as executor. He'd seen the fortune for himself in Buckley's glorious words, his stewardship of fifty million dollars. The fees and expenses he could charge. The first-class trips he could take with his boys around the world: the Galapagos on a private yacht, the Great Pyramids on camelback, a Big Five safari to South Africa.

He'd begun the festivities at home, drinking highballs by himself in the Sausalito duplex he'd purchased with the proceeds from his father's modest estate. A pair of flats over a carport, the utilitarian box was painted a cadaver gray. Knox had bought it for the top unit's views—Richardson Bay, Belvedere and Angel Island—and its ten-minute walk from downtown. The duplex was just minutes from the Trident, the town's most popular restaurant. In better times, he went there to troll the laughing young women; in worse, he tossed back Johnny Walker alone, hunched over the bar. The bartenders knew him, they knew his claims of sailing greatness and of a fortune at the horizon's edge and though they sometimes pitied him, they'd cut off his credit. With his fifty million dollar motion in hand, however, last night his drinking friends, if not management, had stood him to as many rounds as he could handle.

The party had been his best week since Kristen left him a dozen years before. Now, on the eve of gaining his fortune, Knox's waking dream was to win his wife back. He'd married Kristen Orlopp, an assistant buyer for Macy's, at the single moment in his life when he'd appeared prosperous. After years of idleness punctuated by fleeting jobs, Knox was enjoying a brief success as a stockbroker and rounding out his image with a membership at the Saint Francis Yacht Club. He worked hard to impress the beauty, whisking her away to winery weekends in Napa, golfing at Pebble Beach, dining at the Blue Fox, and introducing her to his dazzling Uncle Malcolm. He succeeded for a time, but each day after their quick marriage another bill arrived, another acquaintance made a slighting remark, and another ugly truth surfaced. Knox's résumé unraveled, his bank account emptied, and Kristen learned her international yachtsman was from Sebastopol, a quaint apple-farming town an hour north of San Francisco. His alcoholic mother had walked into the Mendocino surf five years before, leaving neither a note nor anyone to mourn her. A cousin explained that Knox blamed his father, a decent hard-working farmer, for her death and his own failures. She'd walked out after the birth of their second son, leaving Knox alone, still in love, near broke, and embittered.

He walked downstairs to find his mailman at the box. As the mailman squatted to pet Skipper, Knox tore open a manila envelope, saying, "This ought to be good, Eric. The response from that crooked lawyer I told you about." Odd, he thought, no note from Buckley.

He began to read.

The mailman nodded and walked away. Skipper was wagging his stumpy white tail as his master crumpled onto the stairs' lowest step. The dog curled himself small.

Knox could only scan Fitzgerald's personal declaration, the lies so scurrilous he couldn't read them word-for-word. He cursed, swearing the boys were his, swearing he would get those goddamn lawyers. "Oh, God," he cried, clutching his pounding chest. Moaning, massaging his chest, he inhaled deep to slow his breathing. Skipper whined at his feet.

"No. Don't think, don't think about that—take it easy—forget his lies, no, they're my boys. My boys. That's it, calm, calm, calm down, no heart disease, calm, calm," he murmured, cataloguing family deaths. He lay there fifteen minutes, his head propped against a step, scratching Skipper. Unsteady, he rose, reached for his keys and leash and stumbled toward his Mercedes.

Knox knew the lies about his sons could have only arisen within Fitzgerald's scabrous imagination—Kristen would never have intimated such a monstrosity—but the murder charge? If Fitzgerald had suspected murder at the time, he would have rushed to the police. What better way to steal the estate than by directing attention elsewhere? No, this was new, someone was talking to Fitzgerald. O'Brien. It had to be O'Brien. Seething, he recalled O'Brien's doubts about his relationship with his uncle and his questioning of the Tahoe alibi. He remembered how he'd mishandled O'Brien's idea of interviewing the hotel staff and his attempt to trick him, trying to place Knox in his uncle's suite too close to the event. Goddamn lawyers were blood-brothers, thieving, lying bastards enriching each other at the expense of their clients. O'Brien must have bragged to Fitzgerald about what he suspected. O'Brien had done it. And now O'Brien would pay.

CHAPTER 19

MUSICAL CHAIRS

BUCKLEY'S HALF-SMILE WAS GONE. HE'D lost it on the first page of Fitzgerald's opposition papers. Never before had he read such vicious personal attacks in a court filing. He winced, slipped his glasses off and pressed down on his eyebrows with his thumb and forefinger. He dropped the vitriolic brief on the floor and, deciding to work on something else, buzzed Shelly, directing her to place a few calls for him. The first lawyer she put on hold questioned whether her boss had lost the use of his hands. On the call, Buckley defended his practice as sound time-management, further antagonizing his opponent.

After a few desultory calls he returned to the awful brief. Although it read like a crime novella, Fitzgerald had crafted his allegations with care, avoiding outright declarations of fact. Rather than claim Knox had killed his uncle, he stated that a confidential police source had disclosed an ongoing investigation into Malcolm Knox's death, that unnamed detectives considered it a homicide and his nephew a person of interest. Using legalese, Fitzgerald said he was informed and believed that Knox had been outraged over his ex-wife's longtime affair with his uncle and the sticky gossip about his sons' paternity, but that he'd swallowed his fury as long as his uncle's financial support continued. Fitzgerald declared outright that he was personally present when the old man cut off his nephew's support just weeks before his death. Given these facts, Fitzgerald claimed it was reasonable to sequester the estate's assets until the police concluded their investigation, lest he risk turning over the boys' fortune to the murderer of their natural father.

The story was so fantastical that Buckley checked whether Fitzgerald had signed the sworn oath page. Judge Black would have stricken such unsubstantiated declarations from the record and likely jailed both Coyle and Fitzgerald for contempt, but Judge Black was no longer hearing the case. The defense had done far more than libel Knox. They'd sought Judge Black's removal for bias, quoting his severe reprimands during the deposition hearing. The proud judge had recused himself upon receipt of the motion, and the hearing had already been reassigned to Judge Herbert Hedgepath. And, in a stroke of genius, the defense had hired William Mott as co-counsel. A self-styled iconoclast, Mott was the sole independent—likely a closet Republican—on San Francisco's Board of Supervisors. In a city where Republicans failed to beat write-in candidates, Mott was as close to a conservative as the business community could elect. And, as big money's darling, he was among the most powerful men in the City.

Buckley worked out the algebra. He calculated a great case against a weak judge and an influence-peddling civic leader. The equation had its charms; the case was so strong he would doubtless prevail on appeal, but Fitzgerald's gutter tactics weighed on him. Knowing Fitzgerald's personal attacks would now be directed against him, he wondered what despicable lies the defendant would tell.

Buckley was no coward. He was unafraid of a bigtime juice lawyer, or of having his name smeared across the public record. No, he was a fighter. Nodding, he told himself he would tough this one out all the way to the Supreme Court. Steadfast, he went home that evening and, over a young Bordeaux and an old movie, he began questioning if he were neglecting his other cases.

The next morning he announced a spring cleaning to Shelly. He told her to call the opposing counsel in all his major cases to schedule their next hearing dates. Buckley would juggle his appointments if necessary to accommodate their requests. Later, tugging at a bloated earlobe, he compared her list with his desk calendar. He thanked her—he always thanked staff—and requested the phone number of Abraham Lasky, the one true star among his opposing counsel. He would place that call himself. Ten minutes later, he directed Shelly to summon O'Brien.

Slumped against a broken piling, O'Brien loitered among the Asian and Mexican fishermen at the foot of Broadway on Pier 7. It'd been a week since he'd last seen Marybeth, each day worse as his hopes faded and his aches intensified. He'd tried oblivion drinking, but that caused more pain than it relieved. He had no gift for hangovers. He'd also considered sharing his grief with Gamble, but thought the better of it. No one could help him. After a morning wasted, he drew himself straight and trudged back to Drummond.

"Flipper, where have you been?" asked Michelle. "Shelly's been looking for you everywhere. You look terrible. Are you all right?"

"Having kind of a tough time. I'll be OK."

"She said to tell you that Mr. Buckley wants to see you right away."

"Tell me something, M. You think he's a total dick? I really do," O'Brien said in a voice loud enough to suggest indifference. "I won't quote you."

Pleased by the confidence, Michelle tittered, but shook her head. "He's always really nice to us here. He remembers our names and everything. He even brought us donuts once. No, twice. That was nice."

"The guy's good with staff, have to hand him that. See you." He stepped into the elevator and jabbed the fourth floor button.

"Michael. I have good news and bad news," Buckley said when O'Brien appeared in his doorway. "Sit, sit. The really bad news is that the bad news is for me. I can't make the Knox hearing. Abraham Lasky—yes, the Abraham Lasky—is insisting he depose Rittenaur in the U.S. Plastics case the same morning as our hearing. He can't make it any other day. So the good news is you get to handle the Knox hearing…" Buckley paused, startled by O'Brien's disheartened, faraway expression. "Michael? Are you all right? Talk to me. I'm offering you a wonderful opportunity. You're doing the Knox hearing."

"Yeah?" O'Brien asked, his tone sharp, snapping back into focus.

"Yeah?" Buckley fluffed himself like a brooding pigeon, measured his words, and fought his rising guilt with anger. He might have justified—to himself at least—tossing O'Brien to the hyenas when the Knox case was a worthless nuisance, but now it was a major lawsuit: delegating it to the firm's most junior lawyer was malpractice, plain and simple. "When a senior partner offers you the first chair in a key hearing, I'm confident the correct response is not a smirking 'yeah'."

"Why you really giving it to me?" O'Brien glowered at him.

"Why? I told you why—I have a conflict on a far more important case. I'm sensing something else here. Are you—let me put this delicately—uncomfortable facing Fitzgerald again?"

"John, depositions are scheduled weeks in advance, but this Lasky bullshit pops up overnight? Let *me* put this delicately, why the fuck are you bailing out? You worried Fitzgerald's going to slam you?"

"That's it. This conference is over." Buckley stood, his voice pitched higher. "You're handling the hearing—you botched the deposition, you will clean up your own mess. Every first-year law student knows you get a witness's story on record before impeaching him. We're done here."

O'Brien rose, walked to the door and pivoted. "Hey, John, put this quote in your next back-stabbing memo: Fuck you, you chickenshit bastard. You're nothing but a goddamn coward." As his words reverberated throughout the fourth floor, he slammed Buckley's door and stomped to Shelly's carrel. "Hey."

"That went well," she said, a conciliatory smile flickering across her face. She knew too much about Buckley and not enough about the intriguing O'Brien.

"I had to do it, that guy's been fucking me every chance he gets." He ran his fingers through his Byronic curls, trembling with rage, trying to shake it off. He breathed deep. "I'll get over it. Hey, heard you're leaving us for law school, right? Congrats. I would have gone to Stanford, too, but the admissions office checked my grades—just no trust in the world." He laughed, but it sounded forced. "One question: Did Lasky call Buckley or vice versa?" O'Brien tapped his knuckles against the wall. "Have to know if I guessed wrong when I blew my career. Don't say a word, just point in his direction if pencil-dick set the depo."

With a shy smile—she thought O'Brien's self-immolation gallant—Shelly pointed at her boss's door.

"The fucking weasel." He slipped downstairs, cheerful for the first time in a week. At least the cards were face up now. Certain Buckley's next elegant memorandum would rank his insubordination among his lesser crimes, O'Brien pondered his next step for no more than a moment before deciding to throw the first punch. He wandered the halls, regaling the partners with his tale of Buckley's perfidy and cowardice. He found eager listeners. With each retelling, O'Brien climaxed his astounding success—nailing down the missing fifty million—with Buckley's theft of his glory. To a man, they nodded knowingly when they heard Buckley had bailed out; it surprised no one that he would retreat when the cannon rolled into view.

By day's end, O'Brien had spoken with everyone. Rather than fire him over his handling of the Knox matter, the partners were applauding his efforts, telling him not to worry about the hearing's outcome, reminding him that 'final' was an elusive concept in litigation. Win or lose, the hearing would be appealed, and Fitzgerald would be libeling half the City for years to come before any money was recovered. Despite their private support, O'Brien knew Buckley could force his departure. He was done. To walk away on top, he had to win the hearing. He liked his chances.

He might have been a trifle less sanguine had he been aware of Judge Hedgepath's well-earned nickname, or the extent of Bill Mott's power.

CHAPTER 20

BAR SERVICE

Like a side chapel in a forgotten cathedral, the Olympic Club's bar was dark and empty, sepulchral: the televisions blank, the pewter bowls of carrots, celery and peanuts untouched. It smelled of cigarettes and Lysol. Two men—one a gnome-like belligerent suspected of secretly living at the club, the other a drunk who couldn't live up to his father's fame—drank beer and argued football at a leather-topped table in the far corner. The elderly, red-jacketed bartender was wiping down the immaculate bar top with a cleaning spray. He grinned when two younger men, fresh from the showers downstairs, sauntered in, laughing over some small joke.

"Hi, Charlie, how's it going? A beer for me and a white wine for my whining white friend here," O'Brien called out. "Kicked his ass in one-on-one. Whoa, it's dead in here. Where is everybody?" He looked around, saw the glaring gnome and stared back at him—he didn't care if the little prick was big with the unions.

"A chardonnay, Charles, if you please," Gamble said, and turned back to O'Brien. He caught his reflection in the long bar mirror and flicked an errant curl behind his ear. "It's August, everyone's off to Pebble or the Lake."

Charlie poured the drinks, muttering about the club's dress code requiring more than a loose tie hung like a goddamn cowbell. O'Brien automatically signed the drink chit, ignoring Gamble's feeble effort to grab it.

"Hey, toast me, B. I've got great news. Buckley punted the big hearing back to me."

"The removal hearing? That's extraordinary." Gamble sipped his wine—contented—pleased with his surroundings. He so loved the Olympic Club: the idiosyncratic hundred-foot swimming pool with its stained glass cupolas four stories overhead, the weight room where the gym rats gossiped, the nap room where the City's power players slept off their bacchanalian excesses, and the tiled steam room. Especially the steam room. He missed that feeling of utter relaxation every time he traveled. Even the club's four-year waiting list appealed to Gamble; he loved being on the inside, the rush of entrée into VIP rooms.

"He's an extraordinary chickenshit. As soon he saw that Fitzgerald is accusing Knox of murder in the reply brief, he weaseled out, dumped it right back on me."

"Fitzgerald accused your client of murder?"

"Basically. You should read his brief, total fiction. And he accuses me of being gay." O'Brien laughed. "Hell, maybe I should be, every other guy in town wants me."

"You really should work on your insecurity, Flip."

"I'm kidding. But hey, it would double my chances."

"Droll. Do let me know how that works out for you," Gamble said. "Meanwhile, this is serious. Murder? Really?"

"Not exactly. Fitz says he stashed the fortune because he suspected Knox of whacking the old guy. Oh, and he forced Black to recuse himself, got the case assigned to Hedgepath and brought in William Mott as co-counsel."

"He what?"

"You heard me," O'Brien said.

"Bill Mott is defending your removal motion in front of Judge Hedgepath?"

"Yeah."

"I need a moment." Gamble fumbled for a cigarette, found a crumpled empty pack. "Charles, is the cigarette machine still broken? I'll be right back, going to run across the street."

O'Brien caught the bartender's tie-tugging gesture, grinned, buttoned his shirt and tightened his knot. It occurred to him his father would be about the same age as Charlie. His mother was crazy. His old man was dead, O'Brien told himself for the thousandth time. His father had vanished when he was twelve, Mrs. O'Brien insisting he was off to Lourdes for a drinking cure, the south half of Boston knowing the goddamn Italians, weary of their front man's skimming, had dumped Patrick Sean O'Brien's body off Thompson Island. Patrick's pub friends knew the mob was his undoing and that he never should have left Southie. His youngest son knew other things. He knew his father was a drunk with a temper so fearsome that he'd often wished him dead; that he had failed as an accountant (despite a gift for numbers) and that, in a surprising turn of luck, he'd become the owner of a superette in Chestnut Hill, a Cypress Street deli financed by shadowy partners for whom his old man collected thin envelopes of cash from the neighborhood. He knew the mob had executed him. Tortured by the nightmares of his father's black-water drowning, O'Brien also knew he would never swim again.

"Flip," Gamble said, patting O'Brien's shoulder as he retook his seat. "You need to know a few things. Judge Hedgepath has been known as the 'Hedger' since before you were born. He's never made a difficult decision in his—"

"This is an easy decision. Fitzgerald stole the money and we found it. Simple. End of argument; we shoot the bastard. Bang."

"Your conviction is persuasive. It persuades me you slept through law school. Nothing is ever simple in litigation, and who do you think used his influence to have the case switched to the Hedger? Bill Mott. He could be the biggest hitter in the City, and he didn't get there by being a bad lawyer. Your senior partner was right the first time: This hearing is too important for you to handle. Even I would be outgunned. You must insist that one of the firm's partners handle this. There. I've said what I have to. Another beer?"

O'Brien shook his head, memories of his drunken father's screaming matches with his mother quenching his thirst. O'Brien had always sided with his mother. "You don't understand. I have to do the hearing myself."

"Pray enlighten me."

"Promise not to lecture me and I'll tell you what happened today. Promise?" Taking his nod as assent, O'Brien recounted his interview with Buckley. "And then as I was walking out, I said, 'Put this in your next back-stabbing memo: Fuck you, you rotten chickenshit motherfucking bastard.'"

"No." Gamble shook his head, questioning, disbelieving and believing in the same moment, thrilled and appalled by O'Brien's rage. "Really?"

"Yes. That's why I have to do the hearing. He's firing me one way or another—I have to win this one to go out with my head up."

"They should fire you. Reptile or not—and frankly, I can't believe he's as bad as you maintain—he's your employer. How many times have I told you about your temper and how—"

"No lectures. Just tell me how to win the hearing."

"I don't know if I can," Gamble said, "but I do know that your record for the appeal must be impeccable. Even if you insist on going it alone, you damn well better get the firm's best wordsmith to reply to Fitzgerald's libels."

"I can do that."

Looking at himself in the bar mirror, Gamble considered his protégé. No advice he could give would prevent his slaughter. "Enough of that. You should see this new deputy we've hired. She's in misdemeanor arraignments and hotter than the hookers there. I'll introduce you, if you—oh. Why the look? Sorry, old boy, I thought it was over with that bakery owner."

"It is, way over. She's marrying the other guy." O'Brien drained his beer. "Anyway, I get dumped by the woman of my dreams, I'm about to get whacked in court and then, win or lose, I'm getting fired. You know what the really good news is?"

"What?" Gamble laughed along with the chuckling O'Brien.

"Things can't get any worse."

"He's right over there," Charlie said to a ferrety middle-aged man carrying a manila envelope. The ferret approached and said, "Francis Michael O'Brien?"

"Yeah? That's me."

"Here." He tossed the envelope at O'Brien as if feeding a tiger and was a step away before it hit the bar.

"What the hell?"

"I think," Gamble said, laughing louder, "you've just been served."

"Jesus H." O'Brien slammed his fist on the bar, drawing another glare from the gnome. "It's that asshole who jumped Romani in the game five months ago. Remember? He's suing me for fifty thousand dollars. I barely touch the guy and he says I fractured his jaw? That's it, I quit. I'm never playing in the lawyers' league again, it's like playing with twelve refs anyway." O'Brien pressed his forehead to the bar. Then he sat up, stretched his arms wide, and tilted his face toward the ceiling. "Lord, why hast thou forsaken me?"

"You did deck him. Remember how proud you were? And what did I tell you then—"

"Blake. Fifty thousand dollars. I don't have fifty dollars, my credit card bills are killing—no, stop." He shook his head. "You've got to be my witness, tell the judge I was acting in Romani's self-defense. Romani will testify, too. We're tight. Did I tell you he wants me to join his Parks-and-Rec team?"

"Only twice."

"I'm going to Sausalito next week to play with his guys, see how we fit. Anyway, with you and Romani on my side, we can beat this bullshit."

"Perhaps." Gamble recalled Flipper's rescue of the headlocked Romani. Sighing, he slipped into his professorial mien as easily as an old sweatshirt. "But you really did sleep through law school: Only Romani can claim self-defense—you weren't threatened. You have no real defense at all; you punched a man who never touched you. But don't worry, these lawsuits always appear much worse at first blush."

"That's so reassuring," O'Brien said, huddling forward, running fingers through his damp hair.

"If you like, I'll call this rat-chaser for you and attempt to explain your inexplicable poverty. That should bring about a quick settlement."

"Ha. I'm glad you're so lighthearted about this because he's suing your office, too. Says here the District Attorney's office had a duty and obligation to prevent violent types like me from playing on their—"

"Let me see that." Gamble snatched the complaint. It named his office as a codefendant. "Oh, Christ. Oh, no. I'll be blamed for having you on our team." He flicked out another cigarette and lit it.

"You might want to finish that one first," O'Brien said, pointing at the still-smoldering cigarette in the ashtray.

"You don't understand. I'm this close to moving up to murders and now this. Flip, I'm screwed. Screwed," he cried, his equanimity and cultivated accent lost. Gamble could see the horror movie: He would stand in front of the District Attorney as if before a firing squad, the chief deputy sneering on the couch, the old man's administrative assistant with her notepad. The D.A. would look out the window, sigh, and quietly tell Gamble how disappointed he was, how let down he felt by Gamble's inexcusable failure, somehow pulling off the same WASP guilt trip the aristocratic Mrs. Gamble had used to control her son for thirty-five years.

"Don't worry, B," O'Brien laughed, cheered by Gamble's misery, "these lawsuits always appear worse at first blush."

"Very funny. This is my career we're talking about. And I'm an innocent bystander." He gulped the last of his wine and glanced at his watch. He had a dinner with a beautiful café-au-lait massage therapist he'd yet to spring on his mother. "I have to be off. I told Colleen I'd pick her up at 7:30."

"Why are you always late for your dates? You'd better call her." He glanced about the lifeless room and sighed. "I should get a date, too, but I can't yet. Marybeth said she wasn't absolutely certain. I'm stuck in purgatory."

"Flip, it's over. You're in hell."

CHAPTER 21

A LITTLE KISS

"That was one fine dinner," Scott Land drawled, leaning back in the red leather booth, patting Marybeth's thigh, luxuriating in the restaurant's studied refinement. Ernie's white tablecloths were ironed flat, its golden candles aglow, and its black-jacketed waiters reverent. Its subdued lighting flattered its diners almost as much as its effusive maître' d'. The graying male patrons were dressed in blue and their honeyed women in silk. Set in an old brick building across Montgomery Street from Serendipity, Ernie's was a gathering spot for the rich Pacific Heights crowd; they came after the ballet or the opera or to celebrate a birthday or simply to be seen. The scents swirling about the dining room—hollandaise, horseradish, rare beef, old wines and warhorse perfumes—whispered quiet, confident money. Land had insisted they share the Chateaubriand for two with creamed spinach on the side. Weaving tales of their separate pasts with thoughts for their future, they had eaten at a leisurely pace, Marybeth surprised at the way Land picked at his food, reminding her of a model before a big shoot. He stroked her leg. "I swear I could eat like this every night."

"Have you given any more thought to securing a position?" Marybeth wore a simple red cocktail dress, a strand of faux pearls and a splash of makeup. She sat straight, her hands clasped in her lap. She brought her wine glass to her lips, pretended to drink, and set it down.

"Oh, yeah, yeah, of course, but once I'm done with Uncle Sam, I might take a little time off. Get my game back. I'm not putting worth a damn." He was a three handicap. "You sure look pretty tonight. Give me a big smile, Marbeth." He tossed back his wine, kissed her cheek.

"Thank you."

"I could get used to this. I do feel like I belong here." With his good looks and easy manner, Scott Land could belong anywhere he wished. He had tousled auburn hair, chiseled cheeks and a razored jaw. His eyes were blue and his smile dimpled. With his Yves Saint Laurent blazer and insouciant air, he might have been the restaurant's landlord. After high school, Land had spent two years trying to sell vacuum cleaners, quit in frustration, and joined the Army to fly. "'Sides, Marbeth, I'm serious about working with you. If I had another job, it'd be harder for us to have kids. See, you got yourself three of these coffee shops now, but once I get to speed, why, we could have six or seven in no time. And then, soon as you're feeling comfortable with me running things, you could start having babies. Don't that sound good?"

Marybeth studied the table candle: steady throughout the long meal, it was sputtering. Land had arrived in San Francisco a week late—tanned and relaxed, carrying a golf bag and a whiff of cigar. Sounding rehearsed, he'd declared his love at the baggage claim, hugging her, announcing his eagerness to settle down. He'd had better luck in the garage elevator, kissing her, fondling her, pressing against her, reminding her of his animal exuberance, of her own inactivity. Inside her car, he'd unzipped his pants, pressed her hand on his crotch, and reached into her blouse. She'd pleaded with him to wait. He'd nuzzled her ear, laughing.

He settled down and they were talking like old friends before they reached the City's outskirts, Land telling her of Army life, stroking her cheek and kissing her ear as she drove. Marybeth asked if he minded stopping by Serendipity. She needed to sign checks. He walked about the restaurant with its hanging ferns and Mucha posters, lavishing praise on everything from the neon sign to the napkin dispenser. Marybeth rarely spoke about money, but despite her misgivings about Land, she was flushed with anticipation. She whispered Serendipity's monthly income, pleading with him not to repeat it. Concentrating, Land multiplied that number by twelve and then recalled that Serendipity was just one of three shops. He broke into his biggest smile, greed radiating from him like heat from a sauna. She'd stepped back.

A day later, Marybeth was wilting again beneath that dry blast. She carefully rotated the sputtering table candle, trying to free its wick. "It feels like we're rushing things, Scott. You just arrived yesterday—"

"Rushing? Hell, I proposed to you four years ago. I've been waiting for you ever since." Running his hand down the banquette, he squeezed her backside. "The only rush I'm in is to get you back to that apartment of yours. The South shall rise again."

She took his hands and gazed into his eyes. Inexperienced the first time they'd been together, she'd supposed sex was always that quick, questioning all the bother. Berkeley's Sexual Freedom League had mystified her. But that was years ago. "Would you care for the rest of my wine?"

He fished a cigar from his blazer, cut the end with a small pearl-handled pocketknife and flicked open his Dunhill lighter.

"Scott, I don't know about South Carolina, but restaurants here prefer you not smoke cigars."

"I'm sure this fine dining establishment won't mind this little bitty cigar." He exhaled a plume of smoke. "See? No fire alarms ringing. Now, I do believe we were talking about our future. To us." He finished her wine and blew a smoke ring that lingered above their table.

"Sir, if you would be so kind to join us in the bar, we would like to buy you and your lovely friend a drink," the suave maître d' said. Adroit at making directions sound like requests, he pulled out Marybeth's chair.

Rising, Marybeth admired the free drink offer's ingenuity, and considered how she might adapt it for conflicts with her own patrons.

"Works every time," Land said once they'd settled in the bar. "You want a free drink in a fine dining establishment, you light up a cigar. Drink up, Sugar, it's free." He raised a cut crystal glass of Courvoisier.

"You planned this?" she asked, embarrassed.

"Marbeth, as beautiful as you are, as good-looking a couple as we are, they should be paying us to sit here. We're their best advertisement. Somebody walks in, sees us, well, they know they've come to Jesus. Now, speaking of coming to Jesus, should we visit a little about my starting salary?"

"It might be preferable to work out your role first."

"Why, of course." Lacing his fingers behind his head and closing his eyes, Land replayed the mercantile daydream that had coalesced since his arrival. He spoke of directing a chain of shops from The City to San Diego, assembling a crack team to handle day-to-day management—real CEOs didn't get their hands dirty—leaving him plenty of time for Marybeth and the kids and working on his game. How they'd have second homes at Pebble Beach for the summer and Palm Springs for the winter. As he waxed on, Marybeth crossed her legs, shifted away from him, and gazed at the industrious bartender. He, she observed, was a hard worker.

Rather than passion, disenchantment had sparked almost from the first moment she'd embraced him at the United gate. She'd made the mistake of wearing heels. Like a childhood home, Land was smaller and less impressive than she'd remembered. But it was neither his size nor his cigars nor his love of golf. Before, he'd spoken of heroes and aces, of wars and glory, of dodging anti-aircraft fire to save the lives of pinned-down riflemen. Her heart had soared with his heroics. Now, his talk drifted to money whenever their conversation luffed. He wanted to understand restaurant economics, whether she'd thought about opening shops outside San Francisco, whether she might bring in investors to finance an expansion. Marybeth compared him with O'Brien, weighing her captain's greed against the peacock's maddening indifference to money.

The bill came and Land snatched it. He read the total on the bill's second page and sucked in his breath. He set the bill on the table and, with a forefinger, went through it line by line. He'd insisted upon taking her to Ernie's, crowing that everyone knew it was the finest restaurant in town. He'd dismissed her objections about the cost, telling her a man only proposes marriage once in life and it had to be done right.

"Is something wrong?" she asked, reaching beneath the table for her purse. "Let me pay, please. How much is it?"

"No. I took you to dinner. This is mine," he declared. "I do think they slipped this cognac in here somewhere. Yawl don't tip on taxes out here?"

"I can deduct it as a business expense, we did engage in a conference about my shops; I like your idea about expanding outside the City. Please. I've been most fortunate, I can afford it."

"Nope, this one's all mine. There," he said, slowly piling bills on the table.

"Well, I'll make it up to you."

"Let's get out of here before they start charging rent. You going to finish that?" he said, grabbing her untouched cognac before she could answer. He emptied the glass, stood, swayed, and held her chair. They walked out into the cool evening.

"Are you OK, Scott? You look a little tepid. Oh, I'll be right back," she said, "I left my compact inside." She rushed back to the table and, smiling at the black-jacketed bartender, added a couple twenties to the meager pile, thinking her peacock would approve.

"Why don't we take a taxi instead of walking," he suggested, his words thick. "I do believe I'm sloshing too much for a romantic stroll home." He gave a waiting cabbie her address. He opened the door for Marybeth, stumbled around to the other side and dropped in. Nodding, the cabbie lurched his yellow Dodge down Montgomery Street.

"What are you doing?" Marybeth asked as Land fumbled with his zipper, her whisper failing as the driver grinned, visible in his rearview mirror.

"Just walking the dog after dinner. Little fresh air's best thing for him. You said something about making it up to me."

"Zip that up right now," she said.

"Marbeth, all I want is a little kiss. Come here." Land leaned over and drew her face to his, kissing her hard on the mouth. He seized her hand and tugged it toward his groin. She jerked her arm back.

"I don't like this, Scott. You're hurting me," she cried. "Please stop now."

"Soon as you give me a little kiss," he said, pressing against her neck, pushing her head toward his lap. Drunk enough to despise—if not himself, then the fact that he'd come to San Francisco for the money—humiliated by her wealth and success, he needed to dominate her.

Grabbing his hand from the back of her head, Marybeth broomsticked his ribs. He groaned and she straightened. Composing herself, she addressed the cabbie. "It's quicker if you turn here and go back up Columbus and then left on Filbert."

"Yes, ma'am," the driver said. "Are you all right?" He saw her curt nod in the rear view mirror and then looked to the road ahead.

Land hung his head and slurred, "Sorry, Marbeth. Just wanted a little love. Sorry, sorry, sorry. I'll make it up to you. I swear I will. Nice dinner, huh?" Abandoning conversation, forgetting his open fly, he slumped back against the seat and closed his eyes. Marybeth was silent the dozen blocks to her apartment, pasting herself against the passenger door, staring straight ahead.

"Keep the meter running," she whispered to the driver when they arrived. "And don't let him out of the car."

The driver floored the emergency brake, hoping it would hold against the steep slope.

"Wha—we're home?" Scott asked, stirring.

"Close your eyes, Scott, relax. Relax, I'll be right back." Marybeth dashed inside her apartment, threw together Land's overnight bag, grabbed his golf clubs and his half-drunk bottle of Jack Daniel's—a housewarming present for her—and ran back to the cab.

The driver looked up when he heard her door slam and was standing by the open trunk before she reached the curb, reaching for the bags. She haggled with him for a half-moment on the price of an airport trip and then made him promise to see his passenger inside the terminal.

Hiding her tears from Land, she stood a step behind his door. "Here's your bottle and money for tonight's dinner. Scott, it's over. Please don't call or write me. Don't say anything. No, hush. Don't make it any harder. Hush now."

Land realized his peril—his pending loss—and shook his head, trying to clear it. He fumbled for the handle, then pushed open the door and, leaning heavily on it, climbed out.

"Get back in the car," Marybeth demanded.

"No, Marbeth," he said, straightening to his full height, "I don't believe I will. I'm your fiancé and I'm—"

She slapped him hard across the face. He stumbled back against the cab. She said, "If you're not on the next flight to South Carolina, I'm calling the police and reporting you for attempted rape. The cabbie will be my witness, right?"

"Yes, ma'am," the driver said. "Absolutely."

"Now, get out of here," she said, pushing the tottering Land toward the open door.

Whether it was the legal threat or his rising stupor, but this time Land didn't resist. He slumped back into the seat, his head cradled in his hands. "Go, just go," she said to the cabbie.

Marybeth watched the cab disappear. She stared at the crest of Russian Hill until another car forced her onto the sidewalk. Tears slipped down her cheeks as she wondered what had happened, whether he had always been so horrible and she so blind, or if he'd somehow changed. What was wrong with her? That Land might want her only for her money was such a blow she cried out as if struck, then sank down upon the curb and bowed her head to her knees, sobbing.

"Pobrecita," Eloy sighed, coming out of the apartment behind her and placing his hands on her heaving shoulders. For once he was silent, content with stroking her. "Pobrecita," he murmured. "Come, Cosita Linda, come inside before I embarrass you in front of the neighbors you think you've fooled."

"Oh, Eloy, look at you. Look at you," she said, giggling between her sniffles, wiping her eyes.

Draped like a house painter's drop cloth, his splattered T-shirt stopped at his stomach's widest circumference, exposing a vast speckled underbelly. He was barefoot and a bath towel clung precariously beneath his waist, giving a Polynesian twist to his slovenliness.

"The trailer trash bullying the poor dumb Mexican," Eloy said, laughing, his brown eyes flashing with the pleasure of diverting her. "So it's been since the Alamo. Nothing changes. Come, Cosita, I will make you a cup of jasmine tea."

She rose, wiped her eyes again, swatted at the back of her dress and followed him into his apartment. Within minutes, she was cheered by Eloy's cackling tale about a disciple impregnating his scheming girlfriend, a story she'd heard before. He was half-shouting from the kitchen as he bustled about, making chile relleno, for he was less likely to serve a beverage alone than to keep his opinions to himself. She was nearly composed, she would think about it all later, she would pass the evening in Eloy's company. Just as her churned-up emotions were settling on the seabed, she remembered how her peacock had run away from her.

"Are you starting that again?" Eloy asked. "How much tissue do you think I have? Is your pilot already married? How many children does he have?"

CHAPTER 22

FLIPPAH

STILL BREATHING HARD, ROXANNE LA Rue ran a hand through her preposterously thick hair, fanning it out across a pillow on O'Brien's bed. She wiped sweat from the pool on her stomach, his mingled with hers, and finger-painted a heart on his thigh. She loved his taut-muscled body. "It has been a while for you, hasn't it?"

"A while? No way. Why it's only been…" O'Brien paused, knowing he had to mask his melancholy. "Can I count back in junior high when I got lucky? My girlfriend accidentally gave me a little tongue when she kissed me good-bye. Total score." He forced a chuckle, rolling on his side to face her. A wave surged across the waterbed, and he wondered if they eventually evaporated. Like his spirit, his seemed a few quarts low. He'd been unable to keep thoughts of Marybeth at bay, even in his most intense moments with Roxanne. With the sexiest body he'd ever had beneath him, his thoughts still kept drifting back to his Ruffian. That athletic girls were seldom worth a damn in bed provided no solace. He just wanted Marybeth.

"Junior high reminds me, Mr. Never-Keeps-a-Promise. How many times have you sworn you'd explain your nickname?" Roxanne lifted his glasses from the flea-market nightstand, tried them on and grimaced. Michael really was blind. He'd recounted the childhood taunting he'd endured and his mother's steadfast refusal to purchase contact lenses. Now, he only wore glasses when alone.

"Never. It's my darkest secret."

"Tonight, you're talking. Our last night together, darling, before I go off forever with my other darling to New—"

"Your *real* darling," O'Brien said, finding a way to share his despondency in a light more flattering to Roxanne. "OK, tell you what. Sing me that sad song about leaving on a jet plane and I'll tell you. Deal?"

Always ready to perform, Roxanne sat up, flung her hair back and sang. Her throaty mezzosoprano carried far beyond his studio's open windows, filling the night like a ballpark national anthem. O'Brien beamed at his diva singing naked in bed, but his joy soon faded. He knew Roxanne had never been more than passing fond of him. And while he adored her body, thrilled to hear her sing and loved kidding around with her—she was flat-out fun—he understood they were hopelessly mismatched: she a pagan and he Catholic to his soles.

A tear slid down his cheek as Roxanne crescendoed the last verse:

Don't know when I'll be back again

Oh, babe, I hate to go

She giggled and bowed, knowing she'd nailed the simple ballad. She ducked her chin and clucked when she saw his tear. She wiped his cheek and marveled at her damp finger. "I'll take this as high praise."

"The highest. Sorry, I get a little sentimental. You know, the maudlin Irish."

"You and that Irish stuff. Even your grandparents were born here. Flip, you're American. Do you hear me going on and on about my French ancestry? Admit it, that tear was for me."

"It was, it really was. I'll miss you so much, Rox."

"Really?" She studied O'Brien.

"Really and truly." He crossed his heart. He would.

A sadness flickered in her eyes. "You could have had me, you know. All you had to do was stop running—oh, never mind. It's too late. This is our farewell party. Just tell me about your nickname."

"What?" O'Brien exclaimed. "You always had your director. You told me that from the beginning."

"Stephen was my defense against you. Against you and your happy wanderer," Roxanne said, tapping his crotch. "And now—finally—he's serious and you never will be."

"Oh, God. Jesus H," he said, hanging his head. "No, no, no." That couldn't be true. She'd proclaimed her prior commitment—her love for Stephen—on their first date. She'd never expected O'Brien to be faithful to her. "I'll be right back," he said, pulling the bathroom door tight behind him. He ran the faucet cold and splashed his face half a dozen times. Had the director just been O'Brien's excuse for his philandering? But Roxanne and he were totally incompatible, she'd said so herself many times. Or was that another of her defenses? Did he know a thing about women? "I'm such a fucking idiot," he whispered to the unforgiving mirror.

"I'm so sorry," he said as he emerged. "I don't know what to say. I never thought you were serious."

Roxanne stroked his cheek. "It's all right, Flip. We're OK. We were never meant to be. Besides, you've already moved on to that coffee shop lady."

"No, I told you she dumped me. I don't have anyone."

"Her loss, she doesn't know what she's missing," Roxanne said, stroking his cheek. "Now, tell me about your nickname."

"You really want to hear it?"

"I'll cherish your dark secret forever," she said, laughing, lightening the mood.

"OK. When I was about four I saw this little rubber seal at the market, about this big, and it was brown on top with a white tummy, really cute big eyes—like Bambi, only cuter—and a little black nose and it squeaked when you squeezed it. I begged and begged until my mother finally got it for me and it was my favorite toy, every time I had to take a bath, this little seal, Flipper, was with me. I slept with it. Get the picture? Little boy, favorite toy."

"Flippah," she repeated, mimicking his Boston accent.

"No, 'Flipper'."

Roxanne nodded; she'd long since given up trying to convince O'Brien of his accent.

"So two of my brothers, Sean and Patrick, decided to autopsy Flipper to find out what made him squeak." O'Brien blessed himself.

"Sean was the brother who, who—"

"Yeah, the one who got killed in Viet Nam, but let's not," he paused, shaking his head. "Anyway, my oldest brother, Michael—"

"But you're Michael," she said, giggling. "Oh, no, that's right. You're Francis Michael. Too poor to have your own name, how sad."

"Yeah. The micks save their imagination for poetry and excuses. I can only be Michael on the West Coast. But my oldest brother—remember he's the anesthesiologist, the married one my mother beats me over the head with—he used to look after me, he tells Sean and Pat he'll kick their asses if anything happens to my Flipper. So they don't do anything."

"That's the story?"

"Nah. They didn't do it, but it was still their fault, they got me thinking about it. I'd lay awake wondering about Flipper's magical squeaker. One day I had to know, so I stuck the little guy behind a tire on the neighbor's car—remember I'm only four—and when he backed up, boom, my poor seal was pizza and my idiot brothers thought it was so hilarious they never stopped calling me Flipper. Even my mother was laughing behind my back."

"Poor baby, don't be blue," she said, leaning over him, brushing across his chest, kissing him. Then she laughed. "How tragic, a boy starting life with a broken flipper."

"Funny. Now I remember why I never tell anyone the story. Go ahead, kick me while I'm down," he said, toying with her breasts. "Everybody else is—Jesus H, but these are lovely."

"Poor Flipper," she said, running her fingers through his black curls, enjoying the touch of his lips. "But, as my mother used to say, if you have your health, you have everything."

"I didn't tell you about my touch of the clap?"

"That's not funny. You're kidding, right?"

"Yeah, of course. It's my financial health that's clapped up. A guy's a little late with a couple payments, the bank acts like it's a federal crime. I'm good for it."

"I know what you're good for. Come here. Put your teeth on it." A long pause. "Yes, like that. Harder, yes, yes, yes." Her eyes glazed over. It was a long while before they spoke again.

CHAPTER 23

FAREWELL

MARYBETH HAD DRUNK HER TEA with Eloy, nibbled at his flan, listened to his stories and, as they both knew she would, told him what had happened. Eloy quizzed her, firing five questions to her every answer.

"So he wants your money? I'm the only man who doesn't. Why do you think the rich marry each other? Why do you think lawyers get rich writing prenuptial agreements? Everyone wants your money."

"Is this your idea of comforting me?"

"Pobrecita, you are the luckiest girl in San Francisco. You have a successful business, no debt and you own this wonderful building—look at this view. Instead of sipping tea like abuelas, we should be drinking champagne to celebrate getting rid of that duck assassin. Did you really want to go back to your cracker roots? Didn't you swear you'd left the bayous behind? That you were done shopping at the PX?"

"Scott was an officer. And I'm proud of my background and my family, especially my dad. Real men are fighters, they join the military and protect us."

"That doesn't mean you should marry a drunken redneck. Or that you can't rise above your background. Look at you, always trying to better yourself, always reading, always working, and you wanted to throw it all away on Captain Bass Boat?"

"You know nothing about bass boats."

"I've had a lifetime of being called a fat Spic by their owners. Enough about the rapist. What about the other one? The one who doesn't read? The pretty boy who thinks his charm lets him get away with everything? Don't tell me you're going back to him?"

"No."

"Good. He was too clever by half. What happened with him? Did he leave you? Now what? Why are you crying now?"

"I think I broke his heart and—"

"What heart? He's a playboy."

"I'm serious. When I told him I was going to marry Scott, he started to cry. Really cry. He ran away from me—*ran*—in a public restaurant. I broke his heart."

"So you got rid of two terrible suitors in one stroke. Penelope would be proud."

"Who?"

"The wife of, oh, never mind. Don't tell me you care for the worthless lawyer?"

"It doesn't matter. He'll never talk to me again."

"Tonta. Whoever lost a man by telling him she loved another? I'll tell you. No one. Must I teach you everything? Do you think he found another girl overnight?"

SHE COULDN'T SLEEP. SHE DECIDED stretching her legs, a little exercise, might help. A walk took her down Filbert into North Beach and then onto Mason Street. Marybeth thought she remembered where O'Brien lived. He'd pointed out his building once during a cab ride to dinner. She wouldn't dream of ringing his bell, but the thought of seeing his name on the door pleased her. She read the names beside the buzzer: a Mondello, a Dal Porto and an Occupant. It was Busalacchi next door and Aghilarre on the other side; she circled back to the first building. She tucked her hair behind her ear, glanced at her watch. He had to be asleep and, if she were wrong, she'd be waking some poor old Italian.

Standing on the porch, she saw a figure approaching through the inner door's curtained window. Early by her standards, Roxanne La Rue had pressed one last wet kiss on O'Brien and slipped away, buttoning her blouse as she tiptoed down the hall, carrying her bra. She saw the tall blonde with the puzzled look as she opened the grated metal security door.

"Excuse me," Marybeth said, "Pardon me?"

"Yes?"

"Is this Michael O'Brien's building?" Marybeth's gaze flickered to the Saturday-night bra.

Roxanne laughed, but rather than music, her voice carried an edge. Flipper had just sworn he was heartbroken and alone, his one girlfriend about to be married. Yet here was a beautiful, imposing blonde on his doorstep. Roxanne saw a quintessential California girl, the type who preferred orange juice to wine, would rather jog than read, and thought Bellini only a drink. The type who invariably looked down her elegant nose at Roxanne and her bohemian theatricality. Damn O'Brien. At least in the beginning, he'd freely admitted his social life.

"Sure, Flipper's inside. But he's a little tired, if you know what I mean," Roxanne said, jiggling her bra.

"Oh, oh, I—I. Oh, I'm sorry." Marybeth blanched, bending over as if punched. When she rose, tears were streaming down her cheeks. With an anguished look, she strode away.

Roxanne frowned as she walked to her brother's crumpled Citroen, a heap so worthless one would only lock it sarcastically. She hadn't meant to hurt the California girl, only to put her in her place. Although she prided herself on living large—free of society's strictures—she felt small, the blonde's tears over her words calling forth her horrible days at junior high, a time of constant torment. Could she make amends by telling Flipper about his late-night visitor? But that would require an explanation and worse, an apology. And she was late, and packing for New York was such a chore. Besides, it was his fault: If he owned a car, he'd have driven her home and run into the skinny blonde himself. She dithered. Squeezing the battered emergency brake, Roxanne promised herself she'd call him in the morning.

CHAPTER 24

THE HEARING

O'BRIEN WAS EARLY. NERVOUS, FEARING a cab breakdown, he'd allowed himself time to walk to City Hall and arrived forty-five minutes before the hearing. Judge Herbert Hedgepath's courtroom was in the basement of an annex a block from City Hall. With its low ceiling and linoleum floor, its judicial trappings looked out of place, as if they had been set up inside a government cafeteria. Overhead, strip fluorescent lights buzzed. O'Brien wondered whether judges were sentenced there as punishment.

He sat alone in the first row of public seating, behind the bar, shy about taking his place at the plaintiff's table. He wore a gray suit, a white shirt and a solid blue tie: a working lawyer at last. He'd labored hours over his speech, writing out his arguments; he'd had Ann type them on three-by-five cards. He rewrote as he practiced, memorizing, scratching out one phrase, inserting another, dumping one argument for its repetition, a second for its weakness. He had to win. He had to beat Fitzgerald so convincingly that the Hedger would have no choice but to rule in his favor. With his unprecedented preparation, he liked his chances, the optimist in him thinking he'd shock everyone from Fitzgerald to the strangely quiet Knox.

The judge's clerk, a blur of a woman with a dowager's hump, entered from the private door and sat at her desk. Without glancing in O'Brien's direction, she stirred her papers and then dialed a hushed phone call. The portly bailiff arrived a few minutes later, racing sheet in hand, and surveyed his domain.

O'Brien was poring over his frayed cards, hunched, his lips moving, when Blake Gamble clapped him on the shoulder.

"Good luck, old man," Gamble said.

"Whoa, B, what are you doing here?"

"I'm across the street at the Mayor's community outreach meeting. Wish I could stay, but I'll be missed in a few minutes. This start at ten sharp?"

"Should; it's just us on the calendar. I really think I'm going to win."

Gamble smiled, patting O'Brien's shoulder again. "Yes, I'm sure you do. But do keep the appeal in mind. Whatever happens, insist the old hack hear your whole argument. We want the record as clear as possible. Understood?"

"We?"

Before Gamble could reply, Edward Fitzgerald sailed through the courtroom's doors, his raucous cawing suggesting he'd just heard an obscene joke. Coyle limped after him. Fitzgerald tapped Coyle, pointed toward O'Brien and Gamble, and murmured, "What'd I tell you? Look at those two. Teddy boy can smell them a mile off. Let's go fuck with them."

"Leave him alone, Fitz," Coyle said, checking his watch. "Let's wait outside for Mott, make sure he really knows what this hearing's about." Coyle wore the same wrinkled suit from the Judge Black deposition. Whatever had pained him then appeared to be worse now. "I need to sit down."

Giving the finger to O'Brien's back, Fitzgerald pivoted, popped his shirt cuffs and stalked out.

"So that's the famous Edward Fitzgerald. I thought he'd be taller," Gamble said. "Anyway, listen, Flip. Remember: a clean, clear record. Good luck."

Fitzgerald pushed back through the doors minutes later, followed by Coyle and a tall man who greeted one and all as if he were running for mayor. William Mott directed Fitzgerald to sit in the first row, hailed the pleased bailiff by name, asked the blushing clerk about her daughter's wedding and then turned his attention to O'Brien. "I know you. I've seen you play basketball at the club. Bill Mott," he said, shaking O'Brien's hand. "I'll get your vote after the hearing."

O'Brien remembered Mott. He'd seen him in the occasional half-court game, firing nothing but bricks and fouling like he was swinging at a piñata.

In his mid-forties, Mott had reached his pinnacle: He was a financial conservative who ignored the mayor and his fellow supervisors, appealing instead directly to the voters, ceaselessly arguing for fiscal responsibility. Political cartoonists satirized him as a balding beanpole, all forehead, nose and glasses. Mott held the swinging gate open and followed Coyle to their table.

"All rise," the bailiff said as Judge Hedgepath entered. Herbert Hedgepath was a kind, decent man who lacked both the experience and imagination to believe in true evil. A lackluster lawyer, he'd been a partner at the City's finest law firm, but only because his father's name was on the door. His influential partners, unable to fire him, had conspired to have him elevated to the bench.

"Good morning, Bill," the judge said, smiling at Mott.

"Good morning, Herb. Excuse me, your honor," Mott said. "Before we get started, I think we need to do something for you down here. I'm going to have my AA look into getting this place painted and replacing those old lights. Brighten it up. See if we can do something about the rumbling in that duct."

"That would be so wonderful, Bill," the judge replied.

O'Brien stared at the floor tile, unable to watch the second-most powerful politician in San Francisco turn the old judge into a fawning supplicant. He knocked on wood, crossed his fingers and tapped his crucifix.

Mesmerized by Mott's power-play, the other participants failed to notice the courtroom's late arrivals. Malcolm Knox, nautical as always in his club blazer, slipped into the last row. He looked exhausted, hung over, gray bags beneath his watery eyes, jowls hanging loose, grazing his collar. Blake Gamble and an older man lingered just inside the doors. Gamble whispered something to the dapper, silver-haired man, pointed out Fitzgerald and then excused himself. The gentleman then sat in the second row and drew forth a gold pen and a small notebook from his pocket.

"Your Honor," Mott began, "if Mr. O'Brien has no objection, I believe we can cut through a great deal of this. What we have is a simple misunderstanding that's been—"

"I do have an objection, Mr. Mott. This is my motion and I'm entitled to present it before you mischaracterize it," O'Brien said, his words tumbling out hot.

"All right then," Mott said.

"Shall I begin, your honor?" O'Brien asked, gripping his three-by-five cards, standing straight. "This is a simple case, a case about the theft of fifty million dollars. Edward Fitzgerald was appointed the executor for the estate of an old family friend, the late Malcolm Knox, and before his client's body was cold, Fitzgerald looted his safe, stealing millions upon—"

"Your honor," Mott said, not bothering to stand. "The only truth—"

"Unless you're objecting, Mr. Mott, I will continue with my remarks."

"I'm sure everyone is objecting to your remarks, counselor. If you thought about them carefully, you'd object yourself." Mott rose and changed gears, adopting the tone he used to conciliate warring neighbors. "Your honor. May I save us a little time here? Mr. O'Brien is obviously a fine orator, but I can see he's out for blood and too much of that has already been spilled. May I have just a moment?"

True to his nickname, the Hedger nodded. "Yes, Mr. Mott. Mr. O'Brien, you will have your opportunity."

"Your honor, you've studied the moving papers," Mott said. "You know the ugly accusations they contain—vicious allegations by both sides. When I met with Mr. Fitzgerald and my old friend, Patrick Coyle, I asked them how we could set those aside, how we could right this ship. Rather than steal the estate's money, Mr. Fitzgerald had safeguarded it out of an overabundance of zeal. Now, he realizes his suspicions against Mr. Knox are groundless and—" Mott paused to play to the audience. He spied the elegant gentleman taking notes in the second row and came up short.

"You were saying, Mr. Mott," Judge Hedgepath said.

"Yes, your honor. Let's focus on the fact that no damage has been done to the estate. All of the money is present and will be accounted for shortly. My suggestion is that we table this hearing until Mr. Fitzgerald's team can prepare an amended final return. I'm sure my client will stipulate to a court order compelling the accounting to be filed within—say—two weeks?" Mott glanced at Fitzgerald, as if this suggestion were extemporaneous. Fitzgerald nodded at the judge, his upraised face mild, almost meek. He appeared calm, but his right foot hammered beneath the table.

"But Mr. Mott," the judge said, "What about the plaintiff's demand to remove your client as executor? How does a delay address that?"

"If you permit Mr. O'Brien to blacken your record with further accusations of theft and malfeasance, my co-counsel will have no choice but to explain why Mr. Fitzgerald felt he needed to safeguard the money. Mr. Coyle will explain how his client came to believe—wrongly, I might add—that the plaintiff was involved in Mr. Knox's death." Mott looked away from Fitzgerald and Coyle.

"Your honor," O'Brien said, noticing the odd interplay among his opponents, the distance Mott kept from his team. "I can see why

Mr. Mott is the president of the Board of Supervisors; the man could sell rain to the Irish. But the facts are simple: Fitzgerald filed a final accounting for the Knox estate that was fifty million dollars short, fifty million that Fitzgerald stashed in a Swiss bank. That is a fact. That is the only fact we have before us. To combat that one fact, Fitzgerald concocted—before my very eyes—this terrible, terrible lie against Mr. Knox. No one other than Fitzgerald himself has ever dreamed that a murder was involved—"

"You told me yourself he did it," Fitzgerald barked, leaning forward in his seat, grinning wildly at his own lawyers' horror. "You said Knox killed his uncle because the old man was screwing the hell out of Knox's wife."

"Your honor, I *never* said that," O'Brien cried.

Mott stared at a buzzing light fixture. Coyle hung his head. Standing in the back of the courtroom, a furious Malcolm Knox eyed the bailiff, then stormed out.

Judge Hedgepath flinched as if slapped. He drew himself erect, caught the eye of the dapper gentleman in the second row, and said, "Mr. Fitzgerald, you, sir, you have gone too far. You are behaving contemptuously, living up—or down, if you wish—to your, your *reputation*. I came into chambers this morning prepared to give you the benefit of the doubt, but you, sir, are in contempt of court. I am fining you one thousand dollars, no, three thousand dollars, and if you utter another word, I will double that. Mr. O'Brien, I apologize to you for Mr. Fitzgerald's outburst. You may continue."

"This horrible man, your honor, should not only be removed today, he should be behind bars," O'Brien said.

"Your honor, if I may," Mott said, conciliatory, glancing back again at the gentleman in the second row. "Mr. Fitzgerald is fighting for his professional life, he is under incalculable stress. While not forgivable, I would submit that his reaction just now was in some measure understandable. You were right to fine him, and if his amended return is not perfect, you should remove him as executor. But an order removing him now would only delay closing the estate. Let's do the right thing for the Knox boys."

"Your honor, that's as far from the right thing as I am from the NBA," O'Brien said. "Letting a fox count the chickens he ate makes no sense. Besides, as long as he's executor, he's not only charging the estate his own outrageous fees, it's paying for this whole defense—his big-shot lawyers must be charging five times my hourly rate."

"Mr. Fitzgerald will waive his executor fees for the past..." Mott paused. He looked to Fitzgerald, who held up two fingers. "He will waive his fees for the past six months."

"Judge," O'Brien said, "that's insulting. Have Fitzgerald personally reimburse the estate for all of his fees, all of his defense costs and all of my client's legal fees. If not for Malcolm Knox pursuing this, Fitzgerald would have gotten away with his fifty-million-dollar theft."

"You're asking a great deal, Mr. O'Brien," the judge said. "I'll take that under advisement."

His three-by-five cards forgotten, O'Brien knocked on the table, smiled at the judge and then his opponents. His glance lingered for a moment on Fitzgerald. The defendant was slumped against the bar, his obscene belly hanging low. "Your honor, I'm only a first-year associate. But my firm has lots of experienced trial lawyers who could have handled this case. They sent me because this case is open and shut—you don't need a million-dollar lawyer to convict a man when his own testimony condemns him."

"Ingenious argument," the judge murmured, scratching his chin wattle. He focused on O'Brien, realizing he was hardly more than a boy.

"Mr. Mott said he wants to do the right thing. I will be happy to stipulate to a two-week continuance if they will agree to one condition." O'Brien waited, hoping Mott would blindly agree to his condition.

Mott stared at his yellow writing pad, leaning away from Coyle.

"Please continue," the judge said, gesturing for him to get on with it. The young lawyer had his interest.

"You'll note in the file that Judge Black was so worried about the fifty million dollars that he sent a telex to the Swiss bank ordering it not to release any funds to Mr. Fitzgerald."

"Yes, I remarked upon that."

"I've done some research. In short, putting money in a Swiss bank is a lot easier than getting it out. The Swiss would love us to fight for years while they keep all the money. The right thing to do would be to wire the estate's holdings back to a San Francisco bank today, into an account under the court's control."

"Mr. Mott? This sounds like we're making progress. Do you need a moment to confer with your client? Mr. Fitzgerald?"

"That would be helpful, your honor. Thank you," Fitzgerald said, the portrait of humility as he buttoned his suit jacket.

"In fairness to you, sir, you should know that if you refuse Mr. O'Brien's suggestion, I will grant his proposed order exactly as written, removing you as executor as of this moment and imposing the sanctions Mr. O'Brien just requested."

"Your honor," O'Brien said. "At the defendant's deposition, Judge Black ordered that he remain in his bailiff's custody until Fitzgerald's passport was delivered to the court. If you ordered him to remain in your custody until the Swiss confirm they're wiring the money and couriering the stocks and bonds, I think we would all sleep much better."

"Your honor, Mr. Fitzgerald is not a flight risk, he is a long-standing member—"

"Another excellent suggestion, Mr. O'Brien. Gentlemen, we will recommence this hearing in fifteen minutes." Judge Hedgepath's gaze moved beyond Fitzgerald to the man in the second row. The judge nodded to him, rose, and left the courtroom with his small retinue.

Mott, Coyle, and Fitzgerald huddled over the bar, gripping the wooden railing. Mott scanned the emptying courtroom over the others' heads. He knew they had nothing to discuss; they had no choice. O'Brien was gathering his cards and note pads into his borrowed briefcase.

"You lost, fag-boy. I'm still executor," Fitzgerald hissed at O'Brien. "But you're still on my shit-list. I'm going to nail you."

"Ed, knock it off," Mott said.

"You're executor of nothing, you pathetic old bastard," O'Brien said. "It's not even worth kicking your ass."

"When you least expect it."

"Stop it, Fitz, stop it right now," Mott said. "Why do you keep digging your own grave? We had it going our way until your crazy outburst. Let's get out in the hall; we need to talk. Now." He pushed Fitzgerald past O'Brien. Coyle trailed them, limping, nodding to the young lawyer.

"Nice job," the second-row gentleman said to O'Brien, dropping his small notebook into his pocket. He extended a hand. "Shame it had to go this far."

"Thank you, sir, but it's not over yet and I don't want to jinx it. We still need to get all that money back and get him removed as executor. Excuse me, please. I need to find my client."

"I believe the judge will rule in your favor," the gentleman called after him. "And, by the way, you're right: Fitzgerald should be behind bars for a long time."

O'Brien stopped, turned back to consider the man for a moment, wondered who he was, then grinned and flashed him the thumbs-up.

CHAPTER 25

MY BOYS

Judge Hedgepath's ruling thirty minutes later delighted O'Brien: Fitzgerald would remain in the bailiff's custody until the court recovered the estate's assets from the Swiss. The defendant had fourteen days to show cause why he should not be immediately removed as executor, and independent auditors would oversee the final accounting.

O'Brien thanked the judge, ignored his opponents, and fairly skipped into the basement hallway, for once oblivious of a floor's luck-busting cracks. Knox was nowhere to be found. He dashed up the stairs to the ground floor entrance and out into the misted morning, onto McAllister Street, peering about for his client, ready to shout his joy. No Knox. He walked to the corner of Polk Street, casting about, unable to believe his client had left. At a loss, he hesitated, then decided to catch a cab in front of City Hall.

"Michael," Knox shouted from across Polk. He'd been pacing back and forth along the sidewalk edging Civic Center Plaza, knowing he'd see his lawyer on his way to the cab stand. He was trembling, as if flu-wracked, his ruddy sea face plum with fury. He stood with his fists clenched to his hips.

"Hey, great news, huh?" O'Brien called, picking his way across the busy four-lane street to join his client. A patrol cop honked at him for jaywalking.

"How could you?" Knox snarled.

"How could I what? Jesus H, Mal, didn't you see what I just—hey, are you OK? You need to sit down? There's benches over there." He indicated the Plaza, a joyless park of rectangular lawns, pavement and overly pruned London Plane trees.

"You told him. You're all spreading goddamn lies about me, my Kristen and my boys."

"Are you crazy, Mal? How can you possibly be upset?" Intending to shake hands, O'Brien had stopped ten feet from Knox. "You saw what just happened—"

"You told him."

"The only thing I told Fitzgerald was to shove it. You've spent the last six months telling me what a pathological liar he is, but the moment he says something about me, you believe him? I find your boys' money and—"

"My boys, *my* boys," Knox shouted. It was too early for the government bureaucrats' midmorning coffee in the Plaza, but the few passersby stared at the furious man.

"That's what I said, your boys. I get your boys' money and you don't even say thanks. You should be kissing my ass from here to Broadway."

"Did the judge remove Fitzgerald?"

"What are you asking me for? You were there."

"I stepped out. Did he?"

"Not yet, but we—"

"*But* nothing. Goddamn it." Knox straightened and stretched the fingers in his right hand, ready to fist it, but then he spied the squad car on City Hall duty. His mind raced and, planning ahead, he intuited the need to appear on good terms with his traitorous lawyer. He lowered his voice, deepening its menace. "You lost. And you told Fitzgerald I killed my uncle."

"Everybody knows Fitzgerald's lying like crazy, even his own lawyers. Especially his own lawyers. You were there—you saw how Mott handled it, he didn't repeat that crap about you."

"You betrayed me."

"You're talking crazy, Mal. You should see a doctor, you're overwrought. Seriously, you might give yourself a heart attack."

"I'm crazy? No, what's crazy is some punk junior lawyer betraying me. That's beyond crazy. That's suicidal." He glared at O'Brien and lumbered away, toward the public parking garage beneath the Plaza, muttering obscenities.

O'Brien watched him for a moment, then pivoted and jaywalked back across Polk to the cabs waiting in front of City Hall. The driver said the Broadway Tunnel would be quicker—downtown traffic was bad. O'Brien nodded. He shrugged away thoughts of Knox, knowing it was over, he was finished with him. Buckley would relieve him when the Swiss complied, as soon as he could cadge another associate into being Fitzgerald's punching bag. Then he'd have O'Brien fired. How much notice would they give him? He needed help, but Farwell's door was always shut. Maybe Gordon could swing him a few extra weeks with pay; the old grouch liked him. Maybe it was time to move back to Boston.

"Forget Jackson Street. Take me to the pier instead, that one straight ahead, at the bottom of Broadway, Pier 7." He doubled the fare for the cabbie's tip and wandered onto the decaying wharf, threading his way across its failing deck. The breeze blew wet on his face, riffling his hair, chopping the bay a white-capped green. He felt silly in his court suit walking past the hard-scrabble fishermen. Some were fishing as an excuse to drink, while others looked as though dinner depended on their catch. Most were smoking, cupping cigarettes against the wind. O'Brien peered into their buckets as he passed, wishing them silent luck, questioning whether bay-caught fish were safe to eat. He leaned against a piling and stared at the soaring financial district and then back at the fishermen. He shook his head. He saw little romance in drunks praying for tainted rock fish, less in the callous commercial center.

Should he quit before they fired him? He could think of no occupation more soul-gutting than what passed for litigation in the big city:

a ritualized paper war with trifling difference between its victors and victims. Quit and get away from Buckley and Knox on his own terms. O'Brien understood Buckley: the prick was a garden-variety backstabbing coward. But Knox? Knox was off-the-charts crazy. How could he be so devastated by Fitzgerald's ridiculous lies? If Mal thought the boys were his, they were his. Even if they weren't, the old man was dead and the boys had to be at least his—what?—cousins. Close enough.

CHAPTER 26

THE RECEPTIONIST

Amazing Grace, How sweet the sound

That saved a wretch like me

O'Brien's singing was off-key, but he was giggly drunk and elicited only smiles and shaking heads as he tottered from curb to storefront up Columbus Avenue. "Good evening, madam. Quite a lovely dog," he said to an ancient woman bundled against a chill only she felt. She was walking a lively Havanese. "New leash, eh? You've given him a new leash on life?" He laughed. The woman nodded, then dealt a tight smile, knowing the young drunk would not be laughing in the morning.

Nor had he been laughing earlier that afternoon at the Hall of Justice. O'Brien had cabbed it to 850 Bryant and found Gamble in the dingy third-floor office he shared with another deputy, their rubber-topped metal desks facing opposite walls. For many—not just the accused—the Hall was the halfway marker to hell, their lives changing forever upon entering the gray stone-clad building. Yet, despite its broken-tile floors, peeling paint and grimy neglect, Gamble loved it. Every inch of it, every minute he was there. He loved being a City insider, being privy to political scandals too juicy even for the *Chronicle's* gossip columnist; he loved wielding his fleeting power over criminals and more so their attorneys, nodding beneficently as he strolled the Hall's corridors, going from one hearing to the next, laughing with fellow deputies, praising judges for their insights, dispensing advice and wisdom, a suzerain of a minute kingdom.

"So what do you think?" O'Brien asked.

"Your client may be crazy, but you definitely would be if you leave

Drummond before you secure another position. That just isn't done," Gamble said, regarding his fingernails with a critical eye. It had been three weeks since his last manicure.

"Jesus H, Blake, what's the big deal? I just tell the next employer I couldn't stand the bullshit, the endless paper bullshit, the interrogatories and all the motions that lead nowhere. Anybody I'd really want to work with would get it."

"Yes, he would get it. He would get that you're a spoiled dilettante who could quit on him just as easily. Flip, no one *voluntarily* leaves a job without first securing a new one. Anyone who says he did is lying. We get resumes like that all the time. Where do they go? Round file," Gamble said, finger-shooting his waste basket.

"Speaking of that," O'Brien began, hopeful. Perching on the desk opposite Gamble's, he picked up a five-inch bronze key—an antique that looked like it unlocked a castle door—and twirled it.

"Flip, I can't—don't touch that. Leave his desk alone. Kling's a nut about right angles, everything has to be squared. Put it back just the way it was."

"Satisfied?"

"Yes," said Gamble. "Now is simply not the time to bring you in for an interview. Remember? We're being sued because of you."

"Shows I'm a fighter. The DA's got to like that."

With a Kleenex, Gamble nudged O'Brien's shoes off Kling's immaculate desk. "He might... once I determine how to get the office dismissed from your lawsuit. It's not as if we had foreknowledge that you were a menace to society."

"Cute."

"Anyway, didn't you notice who I brought to your hearing?"

"You came alone and then bolted," said O'Brien.

"I came back. I brought—" the telephone rang. "Gamble. Yes? Oh, yes, your honor. I'll be right down." He hung up the phone. "I'm needed in chambers. Would you be so kind as to hand me my jacket?" Gamble stood, buttoned his suit and brushed his teeth with a forefinger. It dawned on him that Flipper had no idea what the District Attorney looked like. He laughed. "Never mind. I'll tell you later."

"Hi, Flipper, where have you been all day?" Michelle asked.

"Fighting crime in the streets. Miss me?"

"You know I did. I always do." She leaned against the desk, rolling her shoulders forward, working her cleavage.

O'Brien swallowed dry. He dropped his bag, one of the firm's battered trial briefcases, and steepled his fingers on the wooden countertop. He glanced up through the skylights, shook his head and returned her gaze, struggling to keep his eyes above her throat.

"You look beat," she said, angling her face, her chestnut bangs falling across her lovely brow. "A bunch of us are going to Las Mañanitas after work. You should come; a couple margaritas can't hurt you."

By a quarter after five, a boisterous group of secretaries, paralegals and young lawyers were trooping out Drummond's misaligned front doors, the lawyers heckling one another about the fraudulence of their hours billed, the others swapping gossip. They walked up Jackson Street toward the mildly garish Mexican restaurant around the corner. No one noticed the burly man across the street, intent on the antique shop's display window.

The man spied O'Brien in the group and strolled behind, watching the revelers turn the corner at Montgomery. He guessed their destination. He walked the several blocks to his Ford and then sought a parking spot with a discreet view of the restaurant.

Two drinks couldn't hurt him but six could, and O'Brien was sailing large, a few blocks from home. He could still feel Michelle's thigh pressed against his, her breath in his ear when she feigned a need to be heard, her breasts brushing against him when she reached for the guacamole. Maybe he should have invited her back to his place for drinks—she swore she had a very modern marriage—but no, he'd met her sweet, starving artist husband at a firm picnic. He shook away his libidinous regrets, telling himself he could always call her another time, and sang out:

I once was lost, but now am found
Was blind, but now I see
'Twas Grace that taught my heart to fear
And Grace, my fears relieved

The driver had waited until O'Brien stepped out from the restaurant's front door. In the waning twilight, he saw O'Brien hug a young woman before the others joined them on the sidewalk. The driver held his breath. If O'Brien went with her, he'd have to return another day. "Good," he said aloud when his prey walked up Montgomery alone, waving good-bye to those lingering beneath the bar's blue awning. The driver opened his trunk, pulled out a worn jib and, folding the sail into a compact rectangle, lashed it across the car's hood and front bumper. He eased out of his parking spot and headed toward North Beach, knowing O'Brien's route would take him up Columbus Avenue. He'd double-park next to the North Beach Playground on Greenwich and wait until the young lawyer stepped into the intersection. He circled past O'Brien just before Washington Square and parked opposite the playground, his motor idling.

O'Brien stepped into the intersection, stumbled, spied a pizza-sized sinkhole halfway across the street and laughed at its silent challenge. He drew himself up—a drunk Olympic long jumper—rocked back, sprinted and leapt, clearing it by a yard. Turning to admire what he considered his medal-worthy accomplishment, O'Brien froze at the sight of a car roaring toward him, then leapt again, this time so far the onrushing Ford only clipped him. Yet the glancing blow sent him flying into the night, screaming. The car barreled into a hard right and gunned up Columbus.

An elderly couple who'd been scuffling down Mason heard the racing car, but only glanced up at O'Brien's shouts. The sedan—its lights off—sped past them so quickly they could only later guess about its model to the cop, maybe a Plymouth.

"You're lucky you only broke your arm," opined the chuckling ER doctor at San Francisco General. "Maybe all that hair cushioned the blow to your head. This," he tapped O'Brien's forehead, "should be a lot tenderer than it appears. And I guarantee your butt is going to ache tomorrow."

"Lucky I was drunk—hell, I still am," O'Brien said, feeling his taped back. "I think you should prescribe another round of margaritas. If it's doctor's orders, who can object?"

"My nurse. Your fumes nearly killed her. I'll be shocked if she doesn't go on disability." The doctor, a worldly man in his mid-fifties, was enjoying his few minutes with O'Brien. A bantering, well-dressed hit-and-run victim was a welcome respite from his daily rounds of stomach aches, overdoses, and knife wounds.

"Who is it that God looks after? Widows, orphans and drunks? Thank you, Jesus. Doc, how long do I have to wear this thing?" His right forearm was in a white cast from elbow to wrist. He wiggled his scraped, bandaged fingers.

"Here's my number," the doctor said, jotting it on a slip of paper. "Call me tomorrow when you're sober."

"I might not be sober tomorrow. Not every day someone tries to kill me. Seems like that calls for a celebration. I know. How about some Quaaludes? Just enough to see me through the pain. Say, two years' worth?"

The doctor laughed along with O'Brien. "You wouldn't believe how many hit-and-run accidents we see."

"It was no accident, doc. The guy tried to run me down. Hell, the witnesses said the car's lights were off."

"The driver was probably drunker than you. You said you were goofing around, doing some kind of running jump across the street, right? Maybe you confused him, maybe he thought he could get around you."

"The dick could have passed me all day long on the left."

"The driver had to be high—it's going around," the amused doctor said, smiling, testing the flexibility of O'Brien's fingers. "He could have been on acid or PCP, or maybe he was one of those crazies Sacramento dumped on our streets."

"What?"

"The liberals think the crazies are the only truly sane among us—that French fantasy—and the conservatives don't want to spend the money on state mental hospitals, right? So Sacramento shut down all the hospitals and now those patients are living on our streets. Next time you see a homeless guy, ask yourself how sane he looks. Anyway, maybe one of them stole a car. Good luck, Francis," he said, reading from the chart.

"You're free to go now, Mr. O'Brien," the nurse said. "You want me to call a cab for you? You need any help getting to the front door?"

"No, that's all right—no, oh hell, yes, it's really starting to hurt. Thanks." His head ached as he picked at the gauze and bandage wrapped around his forehead. The bored cop had thought it was an accident. "Kid," he'd said, "If he wanted to kill you, he'd have backed up and done it again."

The old dog walker had been right: O'Brien was not laughing in the morning. His head pounded, his arm throbbed, his back spasms so painful that standing was anguish. Keeping the cast dry in a plastic garbage bag while he showered was more than he could manage.

"Oh my God. What happened to you? What happened to your

arm?" cried Michelle when O'Brien limped in, his suit jacket caped over his shoulders, his tie unknotted. Her eyes were red and puffy, her mascara a blur. "Is your head OK? Were you in a fight?"

"Sort of," he said, shuffling toward the elevator like an old man with bad news. "Went a round with a Sherman tank, it—ah, hell, I got hit by a car, hit-and-run."

"Poor baby. Come here, let me look at you."

With a guilty glance, he shuffled toward her, mumbling, "I don't know, I'm already stiff enough." She stood, leaned over the counter and touched his face. He brightened, weighing his wounds' upside. "Could you go for the rugged, outdoorsy—hey, what's the matter? You've been crying."

"Jack's dead," she blurted, no better at the announcement the tenth time than the first.

"Jack? Jack Farwell? You're kid—you're not kidding. You're serious. Oh God." O'Brien tried to cross himself, but the pain stabbed him. "With all those kids, oh, no. Wait, wait, wait. Jesus H. What happened?"

She shook her head, snatched a Kleenex from the counter box and blew her nose to Vaudevillian effect. "You know, his cancer, well, it—"

"He had cancer?" Images rained down on him: Farwell's belt loose at the last notch, his fingernails too long, his secretary's evasions, Gordon's odd comments from months before.

"Doesn't it blow your mind? Stomach cancer, I just heard about it last week, it was a big secret, but I thought you knew. Anyway, he had like just started the radiation and chemo stuff a couple months ago and decided that was a total bummer, so," Michelle paused to honk again. "So poor Jack stopped his treatments. He let the cancer take its course."

"I understand. I even kind of get it. I mean this," he said, flourishing his cast-bound arm, "This hurts like hell and it's nothing compared to cancer. Living with that pain? Whoa." He winced at Michelle and turned away. "Bye."

"Where you going, Flip?"

"Home. It was a mistake coming in, I have to lie down. The pain pills just aren't doing it for me. If you call me a cab, I can hobble out to the street by the time he gets here. Tell Ann I'll call her later."

Picking up the phone, Michelle realized someone would have to bring O'Brien lunch if he wasn't to starve. Dinner, too.

CHAPTER 27

THE FUNERAL

THE MORNING WAS GRAY AND fog damp, a chill cloaking the small Sunset District church. Jack Farwell's funeral had filled the chapel with mourners. Its pews were jammed, its choir loft creaking under unaccustomed weight, grievers everywhere leaning against its unadorned walls and columns. The stucco church was neither imposing nor ornate; its cross-topped steeple had no bell and its interior held neither statues nor icons. It was so plain that O'Brien thought the protestant interior more akin to a New England town hall than a church.

The widow and her five small, fidgeting children sat in the front pew. The children glanced about at the crying adults, wondering if they were in trouble. Eulogy followed eulogy, few speakers controlling their emotions, and an affecting portrait of a kind and generous man emerged, Farwell's devotion to his family and his congregation a surprise to those who only knew him at Drummond.

Three days after his mishap, O'Brien still staggered with pain, each step a struggle. He stood with effort, propped against the nave's back wall. His broken arm was slung in a silk square, his forehead bandaged. Unshaven, he wore a black blazer draped over his shoulders like a matador. Despite the perfumed sling, little of the dandified boy remained about him. His blue eyes were brooding and angry.

O'Brien hardly knew Farwell, but had thought him fair and evenhanded. He knew Farwell was good with numbers, preferred scotch to bourbon, and enjoyed the view of a passing skirt. Now he questioned whether Protestants felt guilt, too. Had Farwell suffered over dumping Knox on him? Was that why he'd been so inaccessible? Listening to the tributes, O'Brien wondered whether half so many would attend his own funeral. His eyes teared. The minister asked the assembly to join together in song, the organist played, and O'Brien sniffed quietly for the fatherless children, empathy springing from his own childhood.

He wiped his eyes, shivered away thoughts of suffering waifs, and glanced about the gathering. The Drummond lawyers were all present, partners and their wives scattered throughout the chapel, the younger lawyers alone, mostly standing. Buckley and his melodramatic wife were two rows behind the widow. Gregg Gordon slouched against the back wall a half-dozen mourners away, openly crying. O'Brien rubbed his cheeks with his sleeve and limped outside to the church patio as the song ended, skipping the benediction.

"Hello, Michael," Knox said, rising from a concrete bench.

"What are you doing here?"

"Paying my respects, same as you. Jack was a friend. We weren't close, but he'd be pleased to see me here. What happened to you?"

"I was in a hit-and-run," O'Brien said. Studying his client, he straightened despite the pain it caused, clenched his jaw. "You didn't hear about it?"

"No, I didn't, I've been out of town. Skipper wanted to run up to the Lake so we left right after the hearing. Sorry about that morning, I was so upset. I didn't understand we'd actually won, that the money is coming back from Switzerland. Congratulations on a marvelous job."

"You were at Tahoe?"

"Yes."

"Wait, that was..." O'Brien stopped himself. Knox had said he was at the Lake the night his uncle died.

"That was?" Knox smiled, straightening his club tie. "Anyway, I apologize, Michael. I was just telling a friend that I'd pushed you too hard. But this was so critical for my boys—you understand—Fitzgerald is such a goddamn devil and you're so inexperienced. I thought I could help."

"Yeah, I bet."

"But maybe it is time for us to move on. Is there someone else who could help Buckley finish the case? One of them, perhaps," he said, ducking his chin toward a knot of somber young men and women emerging from the church.

"Go ask them."

"Let's shake," Knox said, extending his weathered hand.

"No. You threatened me the last time I saw you. We're done."

Knox flushed. He'd decided the best way to learn whether O'Brien had told anyone was to go to the funeral, chat up the Drummond lawyers, and let their attitude inform him. Knox knew Buckley had no idea and, judging by his reception thus far, neither did anyone else. "Ah, there's John. Shall we at least tell him about our parting?"

"You tell him. Tell him how I saved both your asses." O'Brien shuffled across the flagstones to join a clutch of associates. Trembling, he steadied himself by clinging to his cast with his good arm.

The other lawyers attributed O'Brien's silence to his injuries rather than any overwhelming sorrow for Farwell while they, in the bloom of youth, struggled to avoid joking in front of the truly bereaved. His head bowed, his eyes closed, O'Brien heard their words as if from a distance, cursing himself for his stupidity. Why couldn't he at least fake civility with Knox? Why'd he have to antagonize the bastard? He rapped himself on the head.

"Careful there, Flip. One more knock on the head and you'll start doing your own research," one associate said.

"No chance of that," said Lederhosen.

Debbie Taylor, one of a handful of female associates, touched O'Brien's sling. "Hey, I've seen this shawl somewhere before. Where'd you get it?"

To the group's surprise, O'Brien shook his head, mumbled something about paying his respects, and hobbled away.

The offices of Drummond, Upton and Isherwood might as well have been closed. The morning funeral over, its lawyers were busy distracting themselves from disturbing thoughts, perhaps among them the wisdom of devoting a lifetime to formalized quarreling. Those who'd craved a glorious drunk had gathered at the Royal Exchange, Farwell's favorite bar. Others had straggled back to the office, nodding to their subdued secretaries who were reading or chatting quietly among themselves, waiting while the legal engine idled. Some had gone home with their wives. A few just walked.

Buckley had left his wife with the widow and circled back to the office, masking his cheer with downcast eyes and a funereal mien. He comforted the red-eyed Michelle with a few words and rode the small elevator to the fourth floor. He nodded at Shelly, murmuring about the ceremony's gentle grace. He shut his door, straightened the bust of his French composer—he would write another memo about the maddening janitors—and contemplated the Bay Bridge. The fog had dissipated, but an ugly haze hung about the bay, smirching the view, forcing him to consider the great drought. He'd liked Farwell, their wives were close, and he regretted his passing. As managing partner, Farwell had been more than fair to him, a few said partial. Buckley saw himself making an impassioned plea to the partnership on the widow's behalf. But that still left Farwell's profit points in the partnership. And his clients.

Buckley rocked back and forth, his hands clasped behind his back, staring out the window. With his lank hair combed onto a broad forehead, he resembled a petty Napoleon. His thoughts turned to Knox, the half-smile on his lips. Knox was now his alone. He'd write off O'Brien's wretched billings on Farwell's watch and then collect the fifty million dollars. He could bill a thousand hours now and hear nothing but praise from Knox. Teddy Fitzgerald was at last irrelevant; his power was gone; even if he wasn't removed as executor, he could only distribute assets under court supervision to the rightful heirs. Buckley reached for a No. 2 pencil in the brass cylinder and wrote "Paris" on a yellow legal pad. "Shelly, it's a quarter to five," he said into the intercom. "Why don't you take off? But before you go, please ask O'Brien to come up."

If only he would quit. Buckley's memorandum detailing O'Brien's vulgar defiance had backfired. At the ensuing partnership meeting, someone said it was unfair—wrong—for a partner to air disputes through one-sided memos. Another had questioned whether he'd supervised O'Brien at all. That toad Gordon even suggested O'Brien had saved the firm from a malpractice suit by finding the fortune that Buckley had once insisted was fictional. Then Gordon sent the memo trumpeting O'Brien's victory over Supervisor Mott, underscoring the word *unassisted*. If Gordon knew anything about litigation, he would have known that the judge had decided the matter before the hearing began. Judge Hedgepath had made up his mind based on Buckley's superb brief. And now this damn accident. Buckley could augur votes better than a ward boss: no one would fire a hit-and-run victim who'd just won a major hearing. Even if he couldn't draft a thank-you note. His gutless partners weren't booting O'Brien any time soon; Buckley had to force him out.

"We meet again," he said to O'Brien, his tone jovial. "Sit down, please sit."

"I'll stand. Ann is bringing Shelly the files. Knox is all yours. Is there anything else?"

"Yes, there is, Michael." He stepped around O'Brien and closed the door. "Isn't standing uncomfortable? No?" He tried a few pleasantries, asking if the arm were painful, if the police had any leads, how he was coping, whether he needed anything from the firm.

O'Brien's silence lengthened with each question, his eyes cold, glowering at Buckley.

"Perhaps it is best we just come to the point," Buckley conceded. "It's time for you to leave Drummond. You've been here nearly a year and it simply hasn't worked out. Despite my misgivings about your—let's be frank—lackluster grades at a second tier law school, I thought you were bright and personable. I was for you initially. You are personable, Michael, but perhaps we can agree that your skill sets fail to match our needs. I'm willing to recommend a generous severance package if your departure can be accomplished swiftly."

"You speaking for the partnership?" O'Brien was controlled, his legs apart, shoulders back, good arm at his side.

"Of course."

"There are fifteen partners? And a couple of the old guys never vote, right?"

"Your point?"

"I just left six of them drinking at the Exchange—everyone's telling cool stories about Jack. They all thanked me for my great work on Knox, a couple even said they were sorry for the raw deal I got from the firm. Gordon—he was sober—said I was doing a great job."

"That's all very lovely. Gordon is an addled alcoholic we keep around out of a misguided sense of obligation and the others, as you say, were drunk. You probably also heard them tell our female associates they were good-looking." Buckley appeared unruffled, but he picked up his French letter-opener—a silver blade—and tapped it across his palm. O'Brien was different. If anything, he was even more uncouth, with his unshaven sneer and broken arm. Something else bothered Buckley: O'Brien seemed distant, uncaring. Where was his boyish desire to please?

"Anything else?"

"Didn't you hear what I just told you? Do you think I don't know my own partners?" Buckley's voice had thinned into annoyance. "This offer and my goodwill evaporate if you walk out that door."

"Your goodwill," O'Brien said. "Where would I be without your goodwill? Tell you what, John. Fuck your goodwill. And, just for your next fucking memo, fuck you."

"You really do have a way with words. If you can string thoughts together better than words, ask yourself about that 'raw deal'. Did my partners explain it to you? No? Let me fill you in: Your client threatened to take the firm to the State Bar on groundless charges. Rather than honorably defend ourselves, your good buddies voted to buy off Knox by giving him seventeen hundred hours of free time. Yes, the firm wrote off a whole year's billing just to appease that stuttering idiot. Once they reached that decision—after hours of rancorous debate—how long do you suppose it took before your pals selected the least valuable associate to sacrifice? Guess."

O'Brien lowered his gaze to the ornate Persian rug. He knew it had to be true: Farwell's awkwardness in his presence, Knox's off-hand remarks and Gordon's advice, all tiles in a dark mosaic.

"Guess who joked that selecting you would put us two up on Knox," Buckley pressed.

O'Brien reached for the door.

"If you want to see something truly funny, ask Lederhosen to do his imitation of you worming out of a research project."

"Is that all you got?"

"You're a pathetic joke here."

"Does anyone like you, John? Did anyone in your whole life ever really like you?" O'Brien limped to the elevator, nodding at Shelly in her carrel, congratulating himself for holding his temper, then condemning his own cowardice. He should have said nothing at all. No, he should have crushed that smug face with his good fist.

He locked his office door and lowered himself onto the carpet, using his guest chair as a handrail. Did the associates know about the humiliating Knox bargain? If they didn't, they soon would; Buckley would see to that. O'Brien picked a fleck of dried blood from his cuff, sighed, realizing he had nowhere to go and no one to see.

He unbuttoned his collar, gripped the crucifix as if to free himself of his superstition, but stayed his hand. He couldn't blame Jesus for his luck.

CHAPTER 28

RATTLED

"THANKS FOR THE RIDE, DAVE. And the killer weed," O'Brien said to the first-year associate whose office adjoined his own, bending to climb out of the rumpled Volkswagen. The world spun the wrong way as he stood. He gripped the car's paint-faded roof. "Whoa, didn't realize I was so stoned until I got up. How do you smoke that shit every day?"

"Training, Flip, training. Hey, you ought to get one of these. It's called a car."

"Not me, I'm a driven man." O'Brien could manage a straight country lane if the car had an automatic transmission, but he'd ruined his brother Patrick's clutch in Boston traffic as a teenager and been skittish about driving ever since. He leaned into the window, resting his cast on the door. "And thanks for, you know, listening."

"S'cool. Everyone knows Buckley's a dick. You want the rest of this for later? No? Take care, man." Dave waved goodbye and putted off toward Marin.

O'Brien stood in the street, his head whirling. He saw a parked car half a block away start up with no lights on. He jumped onto the sidewalk, shivered and then laughed when a Corvair rolled by, the driver flicking on her lights and doing her lipstick as she passed. He sat on the stoop, rubbed his forehead and wondered how long the high would last. His vision moved a single frame at a time, a silent movie cranking on a rusty sprocket. An Asian couple walked out of the corner laundry. Did they have guns hidden in their laundry bags? "Just can't smoke his shit," he told himself, "it weirds me out." After a time, he remembered the vanilla ice cream in his freezer. He unlocked his mailbox, fingers crossed against creditors. As he opened the aluminum panel—his silent movie advancing a couple frames—he heard a dry rattling. He peered into his mail slot: A tightly-coiled snake exploded out. The diamond-back caught his arm, sinking its fangs into his soggy cast, hanging from his wrist like a remora. O'Brien screamed and leapt, flinging his arms about his head, hurling the hapless snake against the porch.

And then he ran.

"I SWEAR TO GOD, IT was this long," O'Brien said, holding his arms out wide. He stood in the middle of Gamble's gracious parlor, his pain quelled for the moment more from his adrenaline rush than Dave's potent marijuana.

"You're quite positive it was a rattlesnake?"

"It sounded like a marimba band, must have had a dozen rattles. Jesus H, look at these fang holes in my cast. You'd be talking to a dead man if it wasn't for this. My lucky cast. Can I get a refill? Top it off this time?"

"Maybe you should catch your breath." Watching Flipper chug his rare Bordeaux like deli beer broke Gamble's heart. Just his luck he'd been holding the Chateau Petrus when his protégé burst in with his high theater. He'd have to liberate another bottle from his parents' cellar.

"Thick as my forearm. Well, this thick anyway," O'Brien said, putting his thumb and middle finger together. He plopped down on the polished cotton floral couch, slugging back the wine. "If it weren't for the rattles, I would've guessed cobra. King cobra."

"Careful with the claret on that settee." Gamble's silky apartment would have been less remarkable had it been in stately Pacific Heights rather than perched above Alamo Square, a genteel outpost in the wild Western Addition. Filled with his family's pictures and antiques—his grandmother's 19th-century French armoire dominated the parlor—the high-ceilinged apartment with its rounded bay windows and sweeping views seemed better suited for cotillion committees than a swinging bachelor. Having once been mercilessly teased about his decorating by his rugby teammates, Gamble was chary of guests and invited few to his home. O'Brien was an exception; oblivious to his surroundings, he couldn't tell a duvet from a horse blanket.

"I'm lucky to be alive."

"Flip, a snake a fifth that size would never fit in your mail slot. They barely hold a couple letters and a magazine."

"Jesus H, Blake. Lazarus comes back from the dead and you're quibbling. Look at these fang marks; see how far apart they are. That snake was huge." He scratched at the cast, deepening the minute punctures. Before he retold his tale, the fang holes would be more impressive.

"Undoubtedly."

"Don't be a smart-ass. Someone's trying to kill me and you're joking around. First, I thought maybe Fitzgerald, but in the cab over here, I figured it out: Fitzgerald is the worst—an absolute criminal—and I may annoy the hell out of him, but he's got no motive. He'd rather have *me* suing him then someone who actually knows what he's doing."

Gamble arched an eyebrow at O'Brien's uncharacteristic admission of a shortcoming, deciding against remarking upon it.

"It has to be Knox." O'Brien drained his wine, set the glass down on the federalist end table, the coaster unnoticed. Following Gamble's pointed stare, he shifted his glass. "Knox told me once that betraying him was suicidal. How ironic would it be if he really did whack his uncle? Fitzgerald's biggest lie ever turns out to be true? He wasn't lying when he said Knox was broke and that his uncle had cut him off. Bang: motive in a barrel." He tried to conjure the circumstances of the old man's death. A heart attack? A slip-and-fall in the shower? "Knox said he was at Tahoe the night his uncle died."

"So?"

"You can get back from Tahoe in 3 ½ hours without traffic. Maybe three if you crank it. So Knox drives up, checks into his motel, goes to an early dinner, chats up a few people to establish his whereabouts, then roars back to the City, pops his uncle and is back at the Lake by 2 in the morning. Works, right?"

"In a cheap murder mystery, yes. In real life, probably not. A hundred things could go wrong with a facile plan like that."

"That doosh is nothing but facile plans. Trying to kill me with a car and then a king cobra? Maybe he's just not that smart."

"But wasn't Malcolm Knox ruled an accidental death? Nothing suspicious?" Gamble sipped his wine, inhaling deeply, taking care to savor its bouquet, grimacing at O'Brien's empty glass. If it weren't for the undeniable hit-and-run and now the snake—Flipper couldn't have made those up—Gamble would have dismissed his young friend's ramblings as further justification for the laws against marijuana.

"The cops probably weren't thinking murder with a geezer that old. Maybe Knox was clever enough to stage it right. So now he thinks I'm trying to rat him out and he has to whack me, too. Make sense?"

"No, but murderers' actions seldom do," Gamble pontificated. "The mistake smart people invariably make when contemplating a crime is in thinking that the criminal is clever. They never are. Their stupidity is often stunning, their motives appalling or simply ridiculous. That's why all those elaborate murder mysteries are just silly fictions."

"That mean you're with me, Professor?"

"Well, it's more logical than a snake volunteering to nest in your mailbox. Now, as soon as you're feeling better," Gamble said, wistful over his wine, "we should get down to the Northern Precinct and file a report. Attempted murder is serious."

"Nope, no way, never. Knox will say he doesn't know jack about a snake and, an hour after denying everything to the cops, he'll be home planning his next attempt, polishing his shotgun. I'm out of here," O'Brien said, reaching for the bottle. "Vino's not bad."

"So glad you like it." Gamble held the empty bottle at arm's length, contemplating its glorious provenance. He drummed his fingers on the coffee table—what to do? How could he help his friend? He began his standard reluctant witness speech about testifying, about doing the right thing for society, about the police providing protection, but he faltered midway through. He had pushed this dreary homily so many times he knew it by heart, but Flipper was a dear friend.

"You know the cops can't protect me. And no way is anybody locking up Knox because of my busted ass or this cast. Jesus H, I keep getting the sonofabitch wet," he said, scratching at the cast, "it's flaking like crazy. Anyway, maybe I'll quit, declare bankruptcy, wipe the slate clean, go back to Boston, start all over. They love me back there."

"All right, you don't have to go to the police, but you simply cannot throw away your life and your career. Boston? Really? If you truly need to get away, you could," Gamble hesitated, affection overcoming his better judgment. "You could use my family's cabin at the Lake."

"Tahoe? What would I do there? Remember? I don't swim."

"You could read and relax and commune with nature… except you never read and you couldn't find nature with the Boy Scout Handbook."

"Yo."

"But the cabin is only ten minutes from Stateline, just outside Zephyr Cove. You could throw away more money you don't have at Harvey's or Harrah's, or chase girls."

"But isn't your family using it?"

"They're at Pebble for the next couple weeks, for the Concours. You would have to promise, promise, promise to be so careful. No guests. Mother would die—after killing me—if anything were stained or broken."

"I don't know. Speaking of mothers, I'm still thinking of going back to Boston. I really do miss the old girl's cooking." He couldn't keep a straight face and Gamble laughed with him.

When a bottle of more modest vintage was gone, O'Brien gave in, agreeing to take his three weeks' vacation and decide nothing until his return. Gamble told him about the District Attorney's favorable impression of the Hedgepath hearing, promising he would arrange an interview.

"I still think you should file a police report. If only we had the snake as evidence."

"The snake," O'Brien cried, remembering the rattler was still at large. "Oh, Jesus H. We need to do something about that."

"Well, we could search for it ourselves... or, we could anonymously tip off the cops about your killer."

***

THE POOR KILLER WAS CURLED beneath a faded advertising flyer on O'Brien's porch, recovering from the bit of amphetamine its handler had forced down its throat. The snake froze when it sensed footsteps on the sidewalk six feet away.

Marybeth Elliot stood outside the building, more out of loneliness than Eloy's chiding. She wore a sweat suit, running shoes and a headband. She might have been jogging and just happened past. Or, she might have been patrolling his block for an hour, hoping to catch a glimpse of Flipper alone, ready to sprint at the sight of another woman on his arm. Marybeth wanted to ring his doorbell, but her memory of the smug, wild-haired beauty dangling her bra stopped her.

Still, she couldn't stand there forever like a fool. She began to stretch, one long leg, then the other, as if loosening up for another bridge run. As she pressed her palms against the pavement, another image surfaced: Eloy taunting her anew, this time for weakness. Marybeth recalled the hurtful conversation they'd had after her last visit to Mason Street. She'd sobbed her tale of Flipper's perfidy to her impassive uncle.

"So tell me, Tonta," he had said, his mottled arms folded across a salsa-stained T-shirt, "Is he a Franciscan? Did he take vows after you dumped him for your cracker? Why should he keep his shorts on while you dropped yours? You broke his heart, not his cock."

"I told him about Scott from the beginning. I was honest with him. I wasn't sneaking around. Eloy, you don't—"

"A fake engagement is honest?"

She'd gone to bed that night dismissing his irritating words; all too often Eloy twisted his opinions to amuse or shock. But why was he so blind? O'Brien had sworn he had no one, while Land's picture was on her counter for the world to see. How could Eloy equate the two? He was just wrong.

"Hey, Miss. Yeah, you," a stocky young patrolman barked from his cruiser. He had double-parked across from Marybeth, his patrol car's light bar flashing red and blue. "You the one who reported the snake?"

"Snake? You mean a real snake?"

"Yeah, oh," the cop said, his tough-guy air evaporating when she rose, turned and faced him. Smiling big, he jumped out of his squad car, locked it and joined her on the sidewalk. He crossed his arms, pushed the backs of his hands against his biceps and flexed, trying to impress her. "Someone called in a report about a ten-foot rattlesnake at this address. You haven't seen anything suspicious, have you?"

"Rattlesnakes don't get that big. Maybe someone's pet boa constrictor escaped. They're not jeopardous," Marybeth said, frowning, envisioning her peacock sprawled in the hallway inside, slowly dying from venom. "Maybe you should alert the residents? I can ring the bells for you."

"Nah. I don't want no panic here. It's probably just a joke—the stuff we hear—but I've got to check. Maybe this planter box? You live here?" he asked, smiling, withdrawing his baton. "I'm single."

"I'm married."

"Oh." He stood back from the hedge, poking at the boxwood with his long nightstick, teasing one clump of leaves aside, then another.

"I doubt you'll find anything in the upper foliage, officer. Rattlesnakes are ground-dwellers. You might want to inspect the soil underneath those dead leaves. Shall I hold the light for you?"

"No, miss, you need to stay back." He squatted and prodded at the groundcover with his baton. Despite wanting to impress her, the patrolman was well inside of cautious: If he could reach a viper with his nightstick, it could return the favor. "Doesn't look like anything in there."

"Maybe under that newspaper there? Snakes like to hide."

"OK. Stand back." The cop approached the porch steps as if he were leading the bomb squad. He flicked at the advertising flyer with his baton, knocking it away. The snake rattled, the cop shrieked, leaping back and dropping his baton. The coiled snake, its rattles a blur, cocked its head in striking position.

"Why, it's only a little diamondback," Marybeth said. She picked up the nightstick. "He can't be more than eighteen inches long. He must be a baby."

"Sta—stand back," the cop cried. "He could attack."

"It's all right, officer. Snakes can only strike about half their body length. This little guy's good for less than a foot. Besides, he won't bother us if we don't bother him." Marybeth liked snakes. For a sixth-grade science project, she'd caught a garter snake: To the disgust and delight of her classmates, she'd let it slither all over her as she extemporized on its habits and habitat.

She noticed the cop's hand shaking on his holstered gun. "What are you going to do?"

"I, I'll radio Animal Control to pick it up—it's their problem."

"What will they do? Will they kill it?"

"We don't do catch-and-release with deadly snakes," he said, his voiced tinged with cop sarcasm.

She decided to take charge; that way she could call Flipper in the morning, explain how she'd happened to see the squad car as she was jogging by, heard about the rattler and how she saved the day. Flipper would be delighted; men so loved self-reliant women. "There's no reason to call them. I'll do it for you."

Before he could object, Marybeth darted forward and pinned the dazed snake's head down with the baton. It thrashed violently from side to side. "You're sure the little guy has to die?"

"Yeah, I'm sure," the cop said. "But you need to back away."

"If I let go now, he'll escape." She kept the baton pressed hard against the snake's head as she mounted the first step, then the second, carefully angling the baton from near horizontal to vertical. With a sad nod toward the cop, she drove the nightstick down, crunching the rattler's skull like a stinkbug.

"Hey, good job."

She handed him his baton. "May I keep it?"

"Nah, you know, it's evidence, has to go back to the station, Animal Control, proper disposal, all that b.s."

Marybeth had been hearing men's lies since she was fourteen; she heard one here, guessing the cop wanted the snakeskin as a trophy. "Be careful. Rattlers can still bite after death, a reflex mechanism. Back in Tennessee, my dad used to cut the heads off and bury them deep, wouldn't let us touch them." She hid her grin when he bent from the waist to gingerly poke at it with his nightstick.

"Can you open the trunk for me? I don't want to drop him and set him off."

"Sure."

He let the body slide down the baton and shut the trunk. "That about does it. Here's my number in case you need anything."

She sighed, sat on the stoop, and regretted her part in the snake's demise. The poor thing was harmless. She turned away from the blood on the step. She rose to leave, but the doorbell caught her eye. "Ring the bell, Marybeth. He wants you to," she said aloud, remembering Eloy's advice. She took a deep breath and pressed the buzzer. She pressed again, this time longer. A third, then a fourth time. Then she knew he had to be in bed with that slut. Marybeth ran—hard down Mason, hard up Filbert—all the way to her flat. She was out of breath, panting, but country silent for fear of encountering Eloy. She slipped inside her empty studio. Suddenly, switching on the light was more than she could manage. She sat in the dark and cried.

CHAPTER 29

COOKIES

Little Johnny Knox had always been a dreamer, roaming the seven seas with his pirate Uncle Malcolm, sailing away from his pathetic parents and his Old Testament grandfather. He fantasized himself popular instead of mocked, his mother holding a fresh apple pie rather than a highball, his dirt-farmer father sophisticated, his grandfather—a man who could not be fooled—dead.

As the decades passed, Knox grew more adroit at rearranging reality, ignoring the inconvenient, reworking the malleable, polishing the lovely: Rather than unemployed, he was a consultant; instead of an insurance cheat, he had bad luck with car accidents; his alcoholic mother's suicide was a tragic accident; instead of heartsick over his dissolute son, his father was a simpleton.

And Uncle Malcolm had died of a heart attack.

Knox had risen early, pacing his living room, staring down Fourth Street, fuming over his tardy newspaper. He ran downstairs and snatched it before the delivery truck rumbled away, scouring its pages for mishaps involving lawyers, finding nothing. He checked it again, reading each article to the last paragraph, reminding himself of the *Chronicle's* notorious typesetting, so inaccurate the piece could have been inserted anywhere. He dialed O'Brien's home phone number, nodding at the ringing. The day before had begun well. The back-up receptionist said O'Brien had not come to work. But when Knox called later, the tarty receptionist sounded strained—was he imagining this?—when she claimed no one had heard from him. And O'Brien's secretary hadn't called back, ignoring three messages. Did they all know? Surely, someone would have gone to O'Brien's apartment if he went missing without a word.

"Skippy," Knox called. The white terrier sprang from his window perch and clattered across the hardwood floors. Knox scooped Alpo into a beige ceramic bowl and set it next to the water dish. He scratched the happy dog behind the ears and, falling into baby-talk, encouraged him to eat. He opened a can of discount tuna for himself, drained the oil, tapped it into a mixing bowl and threw in mayonnaise, salt and pepper. Searching the afternoon newspaper, he ate from the bowl, wiping it clean with a thick forefinger.

"All done, Skip? Good boy. Let's go to the City, shall we?"

"I NEED TO TALK TO my lawyer. That *gone* bullshit is not satisfactory. What about this simple message don't you understand?" A secretary on the second floor peered over the railing to check on the shouting. "Where is he?"

"You may not talk to me like that, Mr. Knox," Michelle said, recoiling, sitting straight. "You must lower your voice and not use any vulgarities. Sit. Sit over there. I will call Mr. O'Brien's secretary for you. Sit."

Knox stood his ground—two feet from the receptionist's counter—rocking back and forth, a seaman braced for a gale. He scowled at Michelle. She gave as good as she got, glaring back at him.

"Do I need to call Ben? Or 9-1-1?"

Swearing under his breath, Knox dropped onto the leather couch. The damn receptionist had told him nothing, but she'd shown no concern over O'Brien's welfare, and her bristling suggested she'd been ready for their encounter. She knew he was the enemy. He watched her murmur into the telephone, covering her mouth, her large eyes darting toward him.

"Pick up that white phone when it rings. Ann is calling you."

"But I want to see her," he said. "Phones are no good." It rang. "Hello, Ann. How are you?" he asked, his voice wheedling.

"Mr. Knox," Ann Wall said, reading from the notes O'Brien had dictated to her. "Mr. O'Brien is no longer working on your case and has instructed us to refer your calls to Mr. Buckley. Shall I transfer you?"

"No. I mean, not now. Ann, we're friends, aren't we? I need to talk to Michael. Where is he?"

"He's out of state. I'm not at liberty to say more."

"But I must talk to him."

"I'll let him know you called if I hear from him. He did say to tell you he would 'repay your recent kindnesses' just as soon as he could."

"What?" Knox slammed the phone into its base, cracking it. He rose, shook a finger at Michelle and walked out. That O'Brien might disappear had not occurred to him. No doubt a private investigator could find him, but that cost money and, worse, dealt another hand into the game. He had to find O'Brien himself. He swatted at the patio's flies, told himself to go back inside, apologize to Michelle and offer to pay for the phone.

At that moment, Marybeth Elliot marched into the patio from Jackson Street, striding past Knox without a glance, her eyes fixed on Drummond's glass doors. Knox recognized the insolent bitch at once; every time he passed Serendipity, he remembered how she'd treated Skipper. He stared at her panty line, pondering revenge.

"Hi, I'm Marybeth—"

"I know you, Marybeth, I only like buy coffee in your shop every day," Michelle said, bubbling. "I have to tell you; your shop is so cute. I just love it. And the cookies—the chocolate chips are fabulous."

"You really like them?" Everyone adored Marybeth's cookies now. Her shops were selling more cookies than all her other baked goods combined and, despite Flipper's expensive ingredients, profiting wildly. She still credited him—to herself at least—with the idea of making them bigger, softer and gooier, but somehow she remembered Flipper's idea about doubling the prices as hers alone. She'd had to impose a four-cookie-per-customer limit at her California Street shop, and she now had employees who did nothing but make cookie dough. With her eye on two more locations, she was considering a central bakery. "Thank you so much, but speaking of Serendipity, I just overheard a couple of your secretaries there talking about Flip—Michael O'Brien. Was he in a bad accident? Is he all right?"

"Oh my gosh, let me tell you." Michelle catalogued his injuries, his broken arm, banged head and certain concussion. She claimed Flipper had shoved a pedestrian out of a runaway truck's path, sacrificing himself for a stranger.

"Really?" Marybeth asked, her eyes widening. "That's so brave. Wait. Did *he* tell you that?"

"Oh, no," Michelle swore. "He didn't say a word about it. Ann, that's his secretary, heard it from a friend of hers whose brother knows one of the paramedics from the accident scene."

"Is he here? I haven't seen him at all lately."

"No, he's out of town." She glanced past Marybeth toward the doors: Knox was pacing outside. "He had some trouble and left suddenly yesterday."

"Did he go back to Boston?" Marybeth asked. Then she recalled Flipper's Manhattan girlfriend. "Or to New York?"

"We don't know where he is. He said it'd be better if we didn't know. I'll tell him you came by when he calls in. I'll tell Annie to tell him, too. OK?"

Marybeth jotted her home number on her business card and handed it to Michelle. "Oh, and would you please inform him I didn't get married? That's correct, I'm still single." She thanked Michelle, strode out and found herself staring into Knox's bloodhound eyes.

"You're Michael's girlfriend, aren't you? With the coffee shop around the corner, right? I'm Mal Knox, how are you?" He stood too close.

Marybeth remembered him vividly, the embarrassing scene and his hundred-dollar bill trick. He had called her a bitch. "You're blocking my way," she said, trying to step past, but he'd planted himself where the patio narrowed, a few feet from the front doors. "Please let me by."

"I'm trying to get ahold of Michael. Could you tell me where he is?" Knox retreated a half step.

"No."

And then she was gone, Knox muttering after her. The goddamn bitch had snubbed him again. Swearing, he swatted at the flies and followed her to the sidewalk, watching her march up Jackson Street. Then it occurred to him: rather than find O'Brien, make the traitorous bastard find him. No more halfway measures or gimcrack ideas; this time, Knox needed a meticulously thought-out plan, one plotted to the last detail. Just as he had before.

***

Knox could recall every detail of his last encounter with Malcolm, the wind-lashed rain scouring his rental car, streams flooding Geary Boulevard's gutters, the potted ficus trees bending away from the wind. He'd been alone in the street, prowling past the El Cortez's entrance again and again, hidden beneath his slicker, bucket rain hat and oversized umbrella. He'd halted beneath the lobby's awning, peered inside and, breathing deep, lumbered through the revolving doors, furling his umbrella about his head as he crossed the lobby, shaking it out, keeping it between himself and the registration desk as he stepped into an open elevator. Knox had ridden to the third floor, stepped out gingerly as if anticipating a security guard, and then, head down, plodded up the back stairs, stopping at the tenth floor to regain his breath. He'd reached the penthouse level and glanced down the ornate, mirrored hall, crept past the demi-lune table with its fresh orchids toward the presidential suite, where the old man had lived for years. The storm flickered the hall lights and he twitched. He eased an oiled key into the lock, nudged the door open a hand's width. He heard strains of an opera—Puccini—and waited, listening. Hearing neither conversation nor stirring, he slipped inside, and shimmied out of the yellow slicker. He opened a small shoulder bag, and pulled out a buckshot-filled knee sock, a homemade sap that he'd encased in three socks, the outermost silk.

His uncle sat at a marble table in the living room, staring at the ceiling for inspiration, feeling the Puccini. Across the wide room, a blue-enameled steel safe stood open; if he wished, the old man could drink in his wealth. He was working on a manuscript—the last draft of his autobiography—and he had two squared stacks of typing paper, one fresh, on either side of a worn Smith Corona typewriter. In the midst of Cho-Cho's climactic death song, the old man paused, sipped his scotch, closed his eyes and pressed his fingertips together, disappearing into his past. Then he saw Knox. "You goddamn weasel," he shouted, anger urging him to his feet. "I told you I was done with your wretched sniveling. Get out before I call security, you goddamn sponge."

"Good bye, Uncle." Knox swung the weighted sock, smashing Malcolm's left temple. The old man's expression passed from rage to disbelief as he staggered back, swayed and fell toward the Oriental carpet. Knox caught him as he crumpled and held him close, searching the blank face that had terrorized him since time out of hand. The light had gone out in Malcolm's eyes within moments. Knox laid the old man atop his yellow slicker and felt for a pulse. He waited a minute and felt again. He examined the crushed temple, blood trickling from it, its deep purpling halted by the old man's death. He stripped off his uncle's clothes, inspecting each item, hanging the jacket and trousers in the palatial cedar-paneled closet, tossing the shirt, socks and underwear in the antique Chinese woven basket the old man used as a hamper.

In the master bathroom, Knox set out slippers and placed a bathrobe and pajamas on the brass hook next to the shower tub. Then he retrieved the body, leaving it wrapped in his slicker. Grunting, he shouldered it into the tub, set the corpse face up and turned on the shower, adjusting it to the right temperature. He threw in a wash cloth and a bar of soap for verisimilitude, and then wiped away his presence.

Back in the living room, Knox inspected the carpet on his knees, combing it for telltales. He rose and saw the Laphroaig on the table. He considered the forbidden twenty-five year old scotch for a moment, then gulped the old man's drink, grimacing at its burn. He grabbed the bottle from the bar, poured himself an ambitious glass and raised it in his gloved hand, a tribute to his fallen host. He stopped. Hamstrung by a lifetime of obeisance to the old man, he swore as he poured the shot back into the hated bottle. Taking his leave, he lingered before the open safe as if it were a private chapel, worshipping the bearer bonds, the stock certificates tied with dime-store twine, the velvet-lined cases with their gold coins and bars. He considered the Cohibas—Cuba's finest cigars—in the walnut humidor, certain only the dead knew how many were left, certain no harm would come from taking a few, but the old man's ghost spat at him and Knox shut the safe empty-handed and spun its dial.

The sock felt heavier going down the fourteen flights of stairs.

CHAPTER 30

FREE PARKING

Knox knew what he had to do: Kill the girlfriend and O'Brien would be on the next plane home. The bastard would attend the funeral, and Knox could track him until the right moment presented itself. Then he'd snap his neck. He concocted a plan: he would leave a compelling letter on Elliot's windshield—pretending to be an enraged girlfriend of O'Brien's—a note so gripping she'd read it on the spot. He'd run her down as she stood by her car. He'd gotten away clean with O'Brien's hit-and-run; he could do it again. This time he wouldn't miss. Twilight would be perfect: dim to foil onlookers, but light enough for Elliot to read the jealous girl's mesmerizing threats. He'd need another rental from that rent-a-heap agency in Hayward that took cash, held a credit card to insure the car's return, but didn't ask questions.

Posing as a city building inspector, Knox called Serendipity, and learned that Marybeth closed the shop on Tuesday evenings. Late the next afternoon, he tucked his glove-typed note under her windshield wiper—the envelope read simply, "Bitch"—and waited six cars away in a shabby Chevy Nova with his jib sail fastened to its hood.

The shop had closed at five. The dishwasher who doubled as the night janitor was mopping up. Marybeth sat at the high round stool in the kitchen corner that passed for her office, tabbing troublesome sections in the lease for a new Sansome Street location. She would never pay a lawyer to review a whole lease for her—she could do that herself—but she'd found a young associate at Lerner, Randolph and Desmond, a firm around the corner on Pacific Avenue, who was willing to interpret the tricky parts while she waited. She'd jot down the exact start and end of their time together to compare against his later bill, unaware the moonstruck lawyer would have happily worked for free. She tucked her hair behind her ear, noting a section on condemnation with two question marks.

She was tired. Shoulders slumped, she leaned against the counter. When she'd been working fourteen-hour days in her first shop, Marybeth had sustained herself with a vision: One day she would have efficient managers running many shops. She would jog, pursue her college degree, lunch with friends, and her only worry would be where to invest her excess cash flow. Now, with store revenues exceeding her fondest hopes, Marybeth was working sixteen-hour days with less pocket money than she'd had as a teenage model. Managers called in sick at a sniffle, took drugs, stole, overslept, slept with employees, refused to sleep with employees, and slept in the kitchen while their disgruntled staff boiled coffee or burned cookies. Anybody good quit and Marybeth had learned that nothing was as expensive as success. She was appalled at her contractor's estimates for the Pine Street kitchen work.

The floors were done. The dishwasher was wringing the grizzled mop out in the steel sink. Marybeth had finished reading the lease, memorizing a few new legal words to impress Eloy and her staff. She sipped her last coffee of the day, sighed, and decided she'd have to renegotiate the construction allowance from the landlord. "You'll drop those trays by Saint Anthony's, Marty?" she asked, indicating the day's unsold cookies and pastries.

"Yes, Ms. Elliot. You know I'm the most popular guy in the Tenderloin? You should see the homeless line up when I pull these out. Good night."

As the late summer day faded into dusk, the City's lights flicked on. Marybeth locked Serendipity's front door, preoccupied by money. She thought it hard-won and hard-kept; her parents had aged themselves raising four daughters on a sergeant's pay. As much as it hurt, she'd understood her mother's relief when a seventeen-year-old Marybeth tearfully agreed—upon her father's transfer to Fort Hood—to stay behind in San Francisco, pursue her modeling and support herself.

She was generous, her donations to food charities amounting to thousands of dollars in baked goods each year. And because that was too easy, she threw a fat check in Saint Dominic's collection box each week. Yet she hated paying for parking and would search blocks to avoid a garage. She fought the meter maids daily, constantly dashing out to stick quarters in her parking meter. Most days she won.

Marybeth wondered at the envelope stuck in her Saab's windshield, then frowned when she glimpsed its cover. Opening the letter as she unlocked her car door, she stopped, reading, frozen by its first line: "You're stealing my boyfriend, you fucking bitch." At that moment, she heard a car blasting up Montgomery. It was racing in her direction, suddenly veering toward her. She threw herself against her car, screaming as the Chevy just missed her, clipping the outer edge of the Saab's open door with its covered bumper. Faster than sight, the door flung forward, ripped into the side panel and then snapped back, crushing her right leg against the door frame, cracking her shin like a wishbone. She glimpsed a little white dog inside the speeding car as she lost consciousness.

Knox hadn't counted on her opening the damn car door. Standing in front of it, she was protected; he couldn't risk tearing the door off and damaging his rental. Had she only read the note before she opened the door, his plan would have worked. With Skipper barking against the passenger window, Knox focused on the rear view mirror and sped up Montgomery. The Saab's door was shuddering forward, its force spent, Elliot collapsed on the pavement. Had he actually killed her? Had she recognized him? He had to know. He turned left onto Pacific, pulling into the corner lot. If the attendant had seen anything, he would know how to react. But the Asian kid was busy, cramming a Jaguar into a tight space. "I'll be back in a few minutes," Knox called, his voice trembling. "The keys are in it." Skipper jumped out. Hesitating, Knox decided the dog would be good cover.

A shopkeeper—a seller of architectural books—had run back inside to call for an ambulance. A couple who'd been having drinks at the swanky bar down Gold Street was hovering over the unconscious woman. Her leg was bad. The jagged shin bone had knifed through her flesh. Blood everywhere. The young woman who stroked her wrist was as pallid as Marybeth.

"My God," Knox cried, cradling Skipper in his arms. "What can I do to help?"

"Some guy ran inside that bookshop to call an ambulance. Go tell him to call the police, too. Do you think we should move her?" Marybeth's head lay against the door frame, her body twisted onto the asphalt, slacks blood-soaked below the knee. Her right leg had another joint, two shards of broken shin.

"No, don't try to move her. We need to wait for the paramedics. Did anyone see what happened?" Knox asked, glancing about for the note. He sidled toward it.

"No, we were around the corner when we heard a scream and a metal crunching sound. She's not going to die, is she?" The young woman's hysteria was rising.

"She's going to be fine," the paramedic said a few minutes later, the silent revolving lights from his ambulance flashing red, orange and white onto the gathering crowd. "Now, please stand back." They strapped Marybeth on the stretcher, loaded her into the ambulance and sped away.

With the balled note in his pocket, Knox remained on the sidelines until the cop had quizzed the crowd about the accident. No one had seen anything, but the mild bookseller was incensed: how could an accident on Montgomery Street possibly go unobserved?

The weary cop pushed back his hat, scratched his forehead and looked skyward for a better answer than the only one he had. "It happens all the time."

CHAPTER 31

THE UNDERSTUDY

ROXANNE LA RUE WAS WORRYING a thick strand of her wheaten hair, twisting it into honey-colored twine. Determined to do the right thing, she still couldn't knock on the damn door. She balanced on one foot, then the other. Hesitating, she looked back at the Citroen, hoping the emergency brake would hold against Filbert Street's slope. She'd regretted her remarks for weeks, wondering if she'd ruined Flipper's relationship with the athletic blonde. And now she was back in San Francisco, hoping her acceptance of a last-minute understudy role would lead to stage time. In her hours of memorizing lines unlikely to ever be heard, Flipper and his California girl had nibbled at her conscience. Maybe she had come to tell him her wedding was off. What if she were his great love? Roxanne remembered his girlfriend owned a cafe called Serendipity. She'd scanned the Yellow Pages, called the shop, and had the manager confirm her description of Marybeth. Yes, she was single.

Roxanne called again the next day.

"Serendipity, how may I help you?"

"Yes, this is Ursula Le Guin from Western Onion. I'm trying to deliver roses and a singing telegram to a Miss Elliot. But the address we have on file must be out of date."

"Could you deliver them here? No, wait, that won't work. She won't be in for a while. Let me get that home address for you."

Standing on the porch, hesitating, Roxanne rehearsed her lines: It was all a misunderstanding, they were simply old friends, surely Marybeth had platonic friends as well. A young woman of infinite pluck, Roxanne still wished she were anywhere else. She tapped lightly on the door.

"Who the hell are you?" Eloy Duran barked, throwing open the door. He was newly shaved, his wet hair combed and curling, his T-shirt fresh from the laundry. His laces were untied on his good brown shoes; he could no longer reach them. Thus clad, his friends would have known he had an appointment. A lover of youth and beauty, Eloy was delighted to have this beautiful young woman at his doorstep. He launched his usual barrage. "And what do you want? Which are you? Jehovah or Mormon? I'm not buying magazines from any crazy cult."

"No, wait, please, don't shut the door." Roxanne flinched at the braying bulk filling the doorway. "I'm looking for Marybeth Elliot. I'm a friend—"

"Then, Miss-friend-I've-never-seen-before, why are you ringing my bell? Why don't you know she lives downstairs? Why are you dressed like a hippie? Are you going to a costume party? Who are you really? Do you have a car?"

"Yes," Roxanne said, answering the last of his questions, looking back, fearing the car had rolled all the way down to North Beach. She laughed to mask her anxiety.

He smiled at the music in her voice. "You really want to see her?"

"Yes, I have to give her a message."

"Then let's go."

With Eloy in the sprung passenger seat, the Citroen listed sadly to the right. Roxanne pressed herself against her door, leaning away from the man who'd expanded like baking bread in the small car. She drove to the hospital, soon realizing the strange man was harmless, even amusing. She laughed at his questions, answering some. She squeezed in that she was a singer and an actress and that she happened to be an old friend—just a platonic friend—of Michael O'Brien's and that she feared Marybeth might have misinterpreted a chance encounter outside his apartment.

"You say you're an actress?"

"Yes, I've been in—"

"Get a real job. That's the worst performance I've ever heard. You were screwing that boy every chance you got." He waited a moment for her stunned indignation to register and then laughed, his head thrown back in delight.

"But it's true," she cried, righteous in her momentary belief.

"There's no such thing as a platonic relationship—Plato didn't have platonic relationships. He was Greek, remember." Eloy laughed again and gazed upon the lovely young woman inches away from him. "And neither do you. Look at yourself in that cracked mirror—you were built for sex. You've been putting out since you were fourteen—"

"No, no, no." But his laughter cut through her denials. "Well, only if you count second base…and only outside my sweater." She giggled, her pique slipping away as she recalled a teenage tryst with a singularly inept boy. Roxanne checked herself in the rear view mirror. He was right; she was built for sex. That she was serially monogamous with men who failed to realize she was a sexual Ferrari—and with whom she was forever stuck in first gear—was their loss. And hers.

"Hah. Do you know what Baptists call actresses? Prostitutes, Jezebels, putas."

"Don't forget strumpets and harlots." She laughed. "And floozies—that one's still popular back in Chicago."

"All right, Miss Too-Clever Shameless, you're going to sell Plato to Marybeth, she'll believe it. But first we need a plausible story." Eloy was so enjoying himself—lovely girls who could banter were a rare commodity—that he'd forgotten the chronic pain in his lower back and the new one that prevented him from turning his neck to the right. He would soon remember them both.

The hospital perched on Nob Hill's western slope. Marybeth's double room had a view to the south: city bustle, the bay and soft hills in the distance. Her elderly roommate was recovering from, as she put it, an operation on her plumbing. The old woman watched the wall-mounted television at full volume and, when not dozing, whiled away her time haranguing the nursing staff. She was not unkind, however, and insisted they check on the girlie each time they attended to her demands.

Marybeth's bed was closer to the window. Her view would have been better were the room not brimming over with well-wishers' flowers and chocolates, the windowsill awash with bouquets of roses and potted azaleas. She lay with her right leg in a cast suspended at a twenty-degree angle. Her leg, shoulder and head ached, but Marybeth had refused half the pain pills, claiming they made her woozy. When present, Eloy demanded she take them, claiming she was supposed to be woozy, rest her only doctor.

The old woman feigned sleep when the fat man and a hippie girl walked into the room. She might have complained about the Mexican devil and his blasphemies, but in the quiet moments between her television and her own snoring, the old woman had heard Marybeth's whimpers of pain, and knew he comforted her. Now, she heard the devil introduce his hippie to her roommate. She heard Marybeth's surprise. She couldn't hear what the hippie was selling, but whatever it was, it left Marybeth delighted.

The hippie gushed, "Hope to see you again soon" and bolted out the door.

"Wow I didn't think I was that innocent, Eloy. I never would have guessed Roxanne was a lesbian," Marybeth said, joy radiating from her like bonfire heat. "Her girlfriend, lover—what do they call it?—is really waiting in the car downstairs?" She beamed at Eloy's nod and laughed aloud, then caught herself, the effort painful. "Funny. Flipper never mentioned a gay cousin."

"He will, Linda, he will. Next time he sees you. Have you heard from the pendejo yet? But why would he call, he thinks you're married to Captain Dummy. Why don't we call him?"

"I told you, I can't call him. It wouldn't be right."

"Tell him your snake story, tell him about your cookie success."

"But no one knows where he is, I think he must be back east somewhere." Marybeth glanced about her flower-dappled room, sighing. "It's so lackluster lying here in bed all day."

"Lackluster," he repeated, pouncing, rolling the word like a first sip of wine. But he caught himself, remembering that his campaign to rein in her *Reader's Digest* vocabulary was on hold until she recovered. "Who do you think he is? A secret agent? A spy? You think he's drinking champagne on Broadway? The boy went home to his mother's. Call his mother."

"Eloy, I don't even know his mother's first name and there are 162 O'Briens in the Boston phone book. Oh." She blushed at his raised eyebrow. "All right, I called a few. What am I supposed to do here all day? Funny that his cousin didn't know where he was. And it's strange, too, the way she teased me that night, making it sound like she was his girlfriend. Darn, I should have asked her Mrs. O'Brien's first name. Do you have her number?"

"So now I'm your receptionist?"

"Oh, speaking of that, the cute receptionist at his law firm promised she'd give him a message for me."

"Why should she do you any favors? She's probably screwing him, too."

"What? Who's screw—what are you talking about?" Marybeth lifted her head, moist, dirty hair clinging to the pillow. But she was accustomed to his salacious teasing and, after a moment's reflection—Eloy had never glimpsed the receptionist and only spoken to Flipper in her presence—she dropped back onto her pillow. She picked up a clipboard with a page-and-a-half of calls and tasks. The sweet lawyer from the Lerner firm had brought her a potted cactus, offering to finish her lease at no charge.

"Nothing. Nada, Cosita Linda, just an old man talking nonsense." Eloy looked away. "I meant the girl would be jealous of you, of your beauty and success. But someone must know where he is."

"He's mentioned an old roommate, John Reid."

"That's worse than O'Brien. How many ways are there to spell *Reid*?"

"Wait." She recalled his mentor. "There's a Blake Gamble who—"

"*Blake Gamble*? What's his middle name? Wellborne? Yet another over-pampered rich boy. The revolution can't come too soon."

"Flipper said he's a district attorney here. They play basketball together. He should be easy to find. Oh…" Marybeth turned away from Eloy, toward the window, recalling why she'd stopped her Boston search. Flipper's tears. The scuffing of his shoes as he ran away in the grimy coffee shop. She could still hear his soles against the linoleum. Why would he ever want her back? "No, let's not call him. If he's forgiven me, he'll call. Did I tell you how heroic he was? How he saved a school girl from a runaway truck? They give medals to civilians for bravery, don't they?"

"I'll call this aristocrat for you." He shook his head. "I want to complain about the dogs shitting all over our sidewalks, the owners should be jailed—and then I'll call the pendejo. I'll tell him all about your accident, Pobrecita, and we'll find out how much he really cares. I'm sure he'll be delighted to hear about the lesbian's visit."

CHAPTER 32

TAHOE

"YOU GOING TO GET THAT?" Reid asked, wiping foam his mouth, his Budweiser tallboy cradled in his lap. He leaned back on a canvas beach chair, alongside O'Brien, baking in the late morning sun. Sweat and Hawaiian Tropic suntan lotion smeared across Reid's softening, creased stomach. The alpine lake sparkled before them.

"I told you: Blake said not to answer the phone. Jesus H, my head's killing me. Can't believe they don't have any damn aspirin in this house."

"That was the fourth call in the last hour." Reid drained the beer, opened another, tilted back to adjust to his best sunning angle. Eyes closed, he tossed O'Brien a beer. "Can't let this one get warm."

"No, I'm still wasted from last night. I don't know how you do it, JR."

"Seriously, you should get the phone, bro. Maybe Gamble's mother's on her way up."

"He'd send the Coast Guard if she were coming. I'll call him later. Collect." Massaging his temples, O'Brien managed a small laugh at the chances of Gamble ever accepting a collect call. Groggy, he frowned at his blotching pink skin—the Irish were a sunless race—and scratched at his cast's ragged edge.

The young men were recovering from the night before, sunning on the deck of what Gamble called the cabin. Except for its size, the rambling green clapboard residence did resemble a cabin; but at six thousand square feet, it was designed to accommodate a whole clan. Inside, the river rock fireplace, knotty pine walls, and furniture more ancient than valuable suggested old, restrained wealth. In counterpoint, two mounted bucks and one moose head, a handful of animal-hides posing as rugs—Reid longed to steal the snarling grizzly—and a Remington statuette on a log coffee table conjured up a baronial hunting lodge. The home was inconspicuous, even drab, but its setting—a double-wide lot with a private beach and pier on the bejeweled lake—was irreplaceable. Had they been worldlier, the young men would have been more impressed with O'Brien's free accommodations.

"Want to smoke a doob?" asked Reid.

"I don't know. Maybe. My head's so messed up, it might help. We should eat something first. I'm starving."

"Liquid diet, bro. Take a slug."

"Hey, sorry about last night." O'Brien shut his eyes against the fresh memory.

"It's OK, she went for you. What a rack. Jesus would've climbed down off the cross for that body."

"Really sorry, man, I shouldn't have…" O'Brien cringed, raised his hands in defeat. Reid had met a bleached blonde Pan Am stewardess at the bar, bought her a drink and had been well on his way when they joined O'Brien at Harrah's blackjack tables. The casino was crowded on a Friday night, smoky and noisy, slot machine bells ringing, winners' joyful shrieks rising above the cacophony. Suzanne—was it Suzanne?—had slipped into the chair between the two young men and let Reid gamble for her. O'Brien had known his role: make his friend look good. And while Reid trotted out his best material, O'Brien goofed around, joking with the couple, the dealer and the table at large, cheery despite his losing cards. He extolled Reid's virtues and deflected the stewardess's skepticism about his friend's professed monastic lifestyle. But a couple more rounds of drinks, another $100 lost and Suzanne was squeezing O'Brien's thigh beneath the table. Reid figured it out, shrugged and left for the bar. Another round of vodka and Galliano found O'Brien and Suzanne on the beach outside the casino, rolling in the cool sand, using his shirt as a blanket, their lithe bodies blue in the moonlight.

"That was, that was. . ." Suzanne paused, reaching for a kinder word.

"*Quick.* Sorry, it's been awhile. If I don't do it every day, well…"

"No, it was really sexy, Flipper. Passionate. I liked it. You liked it?"

"It was great."

"Really? You don't sound sure. But you really like me?"

"You're great," O'Brien said. He'd known how low he would feel afterwards. "You're really great."

"Why don't you come back to my place? My roommates aren't up this weekend, we'd have it all to ourselves. I make a fabulous omelet," she said, shimmying into tight jeans that showcased her backside. Smiling, she banged the sand from her tennis shoes. "Come on, let's go. It'll be fun. I'll show you what I can do in a real bed."

"I can't," O'Brien mumbled, weak. "Can't leave JR alone, you know, old college roommates' weekend."

"Oh… You sure?"

"Yeah, sorry," O'Brien said, standing, rubbing the sand from his hands, buttoning his fly. He tried to look her in the face, but failed. He clapped his tennies together.

"OK, you're up all week, right? Why don't we get together and hang out tomorrow afternoon? You could come over or I could come to your place. Zephyr Cove?"

"Yeah, right, but no, that wouldn't work. We've got plans."

"Sunday?" she asked, dismayed.

"Sorry, I'm just not… sorry. Hey, give me your number and I'll call you when we're back in the City?"

"Give you my number so you can throw it away? Do you know how many guys would kill to have a piece of this?" She patted her butt. "How many guys I say no to on every flight?"

"You're really pretty—"

"I'm really pretty? Fuck you. I'm gorgeous and you're blowing it with the best piece of ass you'll ever see. Don't touch me. Jerk. Leave me alone. Fuck you." She stalked off, her head and shoes held high. O'Brien wilted onto the sand. He gazed out over the black lake, the bright stars. He let his forehead fall into his hands.

"Flip, Flip, where are you, man?" Reid asked, popping his sunglasses to consider his silent friend. "You're zoning out on me."

"Sorry, just thinking about last night. I really suck at that."

"You're such a fucking Catholic. You're dying to get laid and then you feel guilty for two weeks afterward."

"I guess I've had a lifetime's worth of casual sex."

"Not my lifetime. I'm firing this bad boy up. You need an attitude adjustment." Reid lit the joint, took a monster hit, handed it to O'Brien.

"Couldn't feel worse." O'Brien inhaled, then coughed it out. "That's your Hawaiian shit, right?"

"Only the best."

O'Brien tried another hit. "Want to hear about this dream I had last night?"

"Cool."

"This is strange: I was with Jesus," O'Brien began. "Yeah, man, Jesus. He was like a friend, a regular guy dressed in American clothes. He was lying on a couch and slowly dying. You remember the painting by that French guy where the guy is bleeding out in the bathtub? It's called the death of somebody famous? Kramer had it in her bedroom."

"Figures. What a crazy bitch. Still can't believe she dumped you."

"She didn't dump me. Nobody dumped anybody. We were just too much alike."

"Prettiest couple in town," Reid said.

"Lot of good that did me."

"You moped around for a month after that one…and PS, she dumped you."

"Anyway, as Jesus's life was oozing away, I'm kneeling on the floor, completely helpless, sobbing, burying my head against his body. Then he died. I felt so terrible—no, so terrified—I had to force myself awake."

"Heavy."

"The death of God. Give me that," O'Brien said.

"Smoke the whole thing, bro. You need it."

"No idea what it means."

"It means you shouldn't be drinking those fucking Harvey Wallbangers," Reid said. "That shit's sweeter than cherry cough syrup."

"I'm going cold turkey after today. This whole week."

"Know what else it means?"

"What?"

"You feel guilty over snatching my snatch."

"I should have left you guys when she grabbed me. That's not it, though. I knew you didn't care. What's bothering me is that I keep fucking up. All I really want is a girlfriend and I keep blowing it. First Kramer, then Roxanne—"

"You told me Roxanne always had some New York squeeze, right? So you guys were never going to happen. Not your fault," Reid said.

"I don't know now, maybe I had that wrong. If Rox hadn't been sure I was dating half the town, it might have been different. And then Marybeth walked out on me."

"Maybe they think you're too skinny. Time to bulk up," Reid said, flexing his right arm. "Hey, you getting that phone or what? Or at least call our host?"

"All right, all right. I'll call him."

O'Brien returned a few minutes later, laughing. "What do you know? Blake took my collect call… for about ten seconds. He says I have to call Marybeth's uncle, something important, but I can't use the phone unless it's collect. If he won't accept the charges, can I borrow Blue and run over to the Z? They have a pay phone on the front porch, right?"

"Next to that little market. You could pick up a couple more sixers while you're at it. Might be a thirsty afternoon." Reid sprawled back in his chair, craned his face sunward. O'Brien trotted into the cabin.

CHAPTER 33

THE MESSENGER BOY

"YOUR NAME AGAIN, SIR?" THE long-distance operator asked.

"Michael O'Brien. Eloy, accept the damn call please."

"Am I a millionaire?" asked Eloy. "How many pendejos must I support? Tell him to call the messenger boy on his own dime."

"I can't do that, sir. I'm terminating—"

"No, operator, I'll accept the charges," Eloy said. "I want to hear why Mr. Rich Lawyer can't afford a phone call. I always knew you were a phony, pretty boy."

"I'm sorry, Eloy, I can't use the phone here to call out—"

"So you're in prison? What did they get you for? Commingling funds? Criminal conversation? Practicing law without a license?"

O'Brien laughed. "I've made a criminal mess of practicing law, that's for sure. How are you?"

"You could give a shit how I am." Eloy laughed. "You only want to know about Marybeth."

"Well, is she—"

"No."

"No? No, what?" O'Brien demanded, filling Eloy's dramatic pause. "No, she's not living happily ever after? No, she's not married?" His heart racing, he jumped up from the bar stool and, stretching the phone cord to its limit, banged on the picture window framing the lake. Reid ignored the dull thudding. "Quick, tell me. Tell me please."

"She sent the pilot packing."

"Hang on a sec." He dropped the phone, dashed to the back door and shouted, "She's not married." Without turning, Reid raised a languid thumb.

"Sorry, Eloy, you were saying?"

"She's in the hospital."

"The hospital? What? You're not kidding?" O'Brien tapped his crucifix against his chest. Between the hangover and the marijuana, he was a half-beat behind, snagging on a word here, a word there, struggling with the conversation's flow.

"No. She was hit by a car—nearly killed—in a hit-and-run in front of her shop on—"

"A hit-and-run?"

"Must you repeat everything I say? Yes, a hit-and-run."

"But is she OK?"

"I just said, she was nearly killed. Her leg was smashed, but, gracias a Dios, she'll recover."

"Her leg was smashed," O'Brien said, his mind racing, but awash in too many disparate images. He had to concentrate. "Wait, did anyone see the car?"

"No, Sherlock Holmes. No one saw anything. Marybeth only remembers seeing a white dog on the front seat."

"A white dog? Oh, shit." O'Brien slumped onto the kitchen counter, running his hand through his hair. "Oh, Jesus H. Eloy, I'm, I'm… I need to call you back. I'll go find a pay phone, get quarters and call you in a couple hours." He hung up, stumbled onto the porch and down the short path to the lake. He waded out thigh-deep, shivered, bent over and plunged his head in the sixty-two-degree water. It stung like a slap in the face. He did it again, holding his head under a couple seconds longer.

"What the hell," Reid called from the deck.

"Trying to sober up."

"What's going on, man?"

"Marybeth was hit by a car, a hit-and-run. She's in the hospital. I'm messed up."

"Whoa. First you, then her. That's Twilight Zone shit."

"I've got to think, JR. I'm going for a run, clear my head. Just relax here, I'll be back in a while."

O'Brien was mistaken in thinking he could dance. He thought he couldn't run, but was again mistaken. While slow, he could run an hour and still play the next game of three-on-three. But, unlike his Ruffian, he took no joy in it, running was simply hard work. Yet now he jogged onto Highway 50, figuring he might sober up over the five miles to Stateline. He needed to think, but that proved harder than running. He concentrated on avoiding oncoming cars, the pine cones and fallen branches that littered the shoulder. Thirty minutes in, he spied the Round Hill Safeway and convinced himself he needed aspirin more than another couple miles of roadwork. He bought a coffee, chewed the aspirin to speed its effect, and slouched against a boulder on the grassy berm that edged the highway.

Knox. Knox was out of control. Was he insane? What could he gain by killing Marybeth? Knox'd already tried twice with him, would he try again with Marybeth? Why? Killing her made no sense; Knox could gain nothing from it. Then he remembered Gamble's dictum about the rational substituting logic for a criminal's warped thinking. Were their lives worthless as long as Knox was alive? He knew the law could do nothing for him—his scant evidence couldn't have been more circumstantial; the police would never arrest Knox, nor would the DA ever prosecute. The law would only further enrage a psycho.

What could he do? A restraining order would only prove Knox's guilt after O'Brien was dead and buried. Threatening Knox with mayhem was a dangerous waste of time. He could flee, return to Boston for good, but then Knox would go after Marybeth. Could he kill him? No. But what choice did he have? If he didn't he was as good as dead himself. Knox would keep coming. He'd made three murder attempts already. Still high, O'Brien remembered his father's murder with a shudder. No one had ever been charged with that. Although the Boston detective knew better, although he knew the older O'Brien had been murdered for stealing from the mob—everyone knew—the detective had just interviewed the usual suspects, come up with nothing, and quietly closed the investigation. People got away with murder every day of the week; Knox would get away with O'Brien's. Besides, Marybeth's life was in the balance now too. No, he couldn't do it. He tried to dismiss that damn woodpecker that hammered his skull whenever he thought of killing. Not only did he have to do it, he had to get away it. How? O'Brien argued with himself, dithering back and forth, punching the loamy soil in frustration. He chewed a blade of grass, then another. Two more aspirin.

He fetched another coffee, slogged back toward the cabin—his shins barking at him—chewing on roadside pine needles. He stopped at the woodsy Zephyr Cove Resort, bought two six-packs of Budweiser and a couple bags of Lay's potato chips. With the change he called Eloy.

"It's me. Flip—Michael."

"Are you rushing to the hospital, Mr. I-Love-Her-So-Much?"

"Don't start that crap again. Just tell me what happened to her. Simple, declarative sentences."

Surprised by the determination in O'Brien's voice, Eloy narrated the event with fewer detours than usual.

"So, the car swerved into her mid-block and the cops didn't think it was intentional?" O'Brien asked.

"Do you want to know where all the C students from your high school ended up, Pendejo? They're policemen. They make you look like a brain surgeon. They have no clues: maybe the crash was intentional, maybe a drunk, maybe the car had a steering problem."

"Montgomery Street is straighter than a ruler. It had to be intentional. But the police have nothing?"

"When are you coming to see her?"

"Soon as I can. How long is she in the hospital for?" O'Brien asked. As long as she was hospitalized, Marybeth would be safe. Knox was crazy, but he wasn't stupid; he wouldn't attack her there, surrounded by a hospital full of witnesses.

"The doctors won't say—the pendejos know nothing—at least a few more days."

O'Brien had to hurry. He had to get to Knox before Marybeth was released. But he had to warn her now. "Eloy, don't mess with me on this. Tell Marybeth the hit and run was intentional, I'm sure of it. And that she has to be super careful after she gets out. I mean super careful. Tell her I have to go to Boston to visit my mother. She's… she's ill. I'll come see Marybeth the moment I get back."

Some minutes later, he handed Reid a cold beer.

"What's up, Flip?"

"You're going to Boston."

CHAPTER 34

THE ALIBI

"I'M DOING WHAT?" REID POPPED his sunglasses, chugged the last of his lukewarm Budweiser, and searched O'Brien's face for the joke. Instead of a punch line, he saw uncharacteristic resolve.

"You're going to Boston. All expenses paid. You'll have a great time. Hustle up, we've got to pack and hit the road. I'll put these empties in the neighbor's trash. Remember: we have to strip our beds and put the sheets in the washer. Do you remember where I put Blake's departure checklist?"

"Seriously?" Reid ran his palms up his stomach, over his matted chest, scooping up tanning oil and beer sweat and flicking his hands toward the forgiving lake.

"I'll explain on the way back. Maybe there's space on the red-eye tonight."

Within the hour, they were climbing out of the Tahoe basin, the '56 Chevy wagon struggling with the grade. Once they'd left the town's casinos, fast food and trailer parks behind, the vast blanket of Jeffrey Pine felt clean—primordial—somehow unsullied by the gray highway that snaked through it. The national forest pressed down on both sides of Highway 50, softening the snow-chain pitted freeway. Reid smoked a joint as he idled along with one finger at the bottom of the wheel, O'Brien faking hits to stay clear-headed.

"You ready to explain this yet?" Reid fiddled with the AM radio, catching only static.

"Let's wait until we hit Sac. I've got to figure out the details, what

I can and can't tell you. You remember, the attorney-client privilege stuff."

"Yeah, the attorney gets the privilege of fucking his client."

"Pretty much it." As they wound down through the forested mountains, one station, KNBR, played cat-and-mouse with Blue's push button radio. A moment of clarity, a minute of crackling. The Giants were playing an afternoon game. No way to know the score. They drove in silence, wrapped in their separate worlds, Reid content, stoned, slowly warming to the idea of a free if inexplicable trip to Boston. O'Brien fidgeting, tapping his fingers, picking at his cast, wondering how he could ever pull it off. Spying a runaway truck ramp alongside a steep downgrade, he imagined a brakeless eighteen-wheeler roaring hell bound through that waist-deep gravel. Was the ramp supposed to save ill-fated trucks or merely sidetrack their crashes?

A couple hours later, the last foothill behind them, the road straightened and the earth flattened. Peering down Highway 50's rifle barrel, they beheld Sacramento—a white collar government town—in the plain's hazy distance. They were more than halfway home. They swung through a Taco Bell drive-through off the freeway, Reid ordering enough for three, O'Brien a couple tacos and a coke.

"OK," said O'Brien, slowly unwrapping his taco. "How do I explain this? I really need your help, but for your sake—to keep you in the clear—I can't explain too much." O'Brien knew better, there was no keeping Reid in the clear if his plan failed. But he was desperate.

"Here comes the Vaseline," Reid said, choking down a beef & cheese burrito in a couple wolf bites. Eating was the fastest thing Reid ever did.

"You know how everybody says we look just like brothers?"

"They always say I'm the handsome one."

"The blind ones do." O'Brien sipped his coke and laughed at their running comic quarrel. Despite their protestations to the contrary, each thought the other the better looking. "Anyway, I need to do some stuff in the City that I, I…"

"Need a major alibi for?" Reid filled in the blank.

"Yes."

"This is all about your crazy client, right?"

"I can't say. Anyway, so if you'll do it, I'll buy a round-trip ticket to Boston in my name, give you my ID, credit card, you stay there for three or four days—you can stay at my cousin Mikey's. He's fun. You remember when he stayed with us senior year. You go out to lunch, dinner, use my card, spend what you want." O'Brien bit into a taco, the corn shell cracked and hot sauce dribbled down his black Polo shirt. Sighing, he wiped it, making a worse mess and wondered why he was bothering to eat; he wasn't hungry and couldn't taste a thing. "I'm going bankrupt anyway."

"Really?"

"Sure, spend whatever you like."

"I meant the bankruptcy."

"Maybe, I don't know. I suck with money. Anyway, I'll get a message to you to come home quick as soon as I . . ." O'Brien stopped, took a careful bite and chewed for time. He had to protect Reid as best he could. "As I finish my business. It'll be really important that you rush back the moment I call you. It'd be a huge favor."

"I don't know, Flip. Boston in August?"

"Come on. I'll give you my black book, I'm done with it anyway. Mikey will show you around."

Reid dipped a couple fingers into a plastic cup of refried beans and cheese and licked them clean. Sated, he contemplated his life's central ambition: getting laid. He wiped a dash of beans from the steering wheel and swallowed it. "You could be in luck. I just remembered that Gail's at Harvard."

"Gail Finney?"

"You remember her. I could stay with her. She'd love it. She's totally into me."

"I'll never figure out what these Ph.D.s see in you."

"It's what they see in *them*. My own Ph.D.—my pretty huge dick."

"First time I've heard that bit of brilliance…today." O'Brien managed a laugh at the old joke. "But sure, stay with her. I could call you there. So you'll do it?"

"Yeah, what the fuck. But what about your mother? A Boston alibi only flies if your mom's on the plane."

"You've met her. She's tougher than her own cooking. I told you how she always had to cover for my old man. She'd cut off her thumb before she'd talk to the—to anyone she didn't know about me. I'll call her."

"Cool."

They had merged onto Highway 80, passed the farm town of Dixon and its drought- withered fields, and were driving through Davis when, catching sight of the University, Reid remembered his joint. Steering with his knees, he deftly rolled the back of a match book into a roach clip, fished the nearly spent joint from the ashtray, lit it and drew down hard. Refreshed, he bobbed his head—occasionally in time—to *Take it Easy*, the Eagles song he considered his personal anthem. He lowered his visor against the late afternoon sun and tapped on the air conditioner that had blown nothing but hot air for ten years.

"Oh, and don't hustle any of the stews on the plane, you can't be too memorable." Lost in the details of his plan, O'Brien gazed out the window, seeing nothing. "Maybe you should wear my Sox hat, look down the whole time, maybe even at a book, pretend you can read."

"Long as it has pictures," said Reid.

"Last thing: can I borrow Blue while you're gone?"

"Course. But one small detail you may have overlooked."

"Yeah?"

"How am I going to explain how I got so much better-looking when they check your ID at the airport?"

"Easy. Tell them you lied about your height and got fat," said O'Brien.

"Nah, I'll say it was serious gym time that got me these guns." He flexed his right bicep and kissed it.

"You do have the guns. Anyway, so here's what we do. We go to your place, you pack up for the week, then we head over to mine, hang out, mellow, get some dinner and then call a cab for you about 8:30."

"Wait, you've got my car and you're not giving me a ride to the airport?"

"Bro," O'Brien said, with the patience of a new kindergarten teacher. "I don't own a car. How did I get to the airport? We call a cab, the company has a record of picking up Michael O'Brien at 2154 Mason Street for an airport run. And I have a receipt." He grinned, squeezed the back of Reid's neck and returned to his thoughts of Marybeth, tapping his lucky crucifix, praying for her full recovery. He yearned for her, but knew he couldn't visit. Dare he call her? No. It played so much better if he could convince Knox—and, if necessary, the cops—that they were long since broken up.

"Whoa, Flip, you've really thought this through."

He called his mother. Mrs. O'Brien stifled her tears, caught herself before asking any questions—she knew from alibis—said she'd handle it. A chastened O'Brien promised to visit in the fall. He called the office, left a message with the answering service. He rang Ann, told her he was fine, but needed to visit his mother. She asked if they could have lunch upon his return. Finally, he called Blake, assuring his mentor he would not be looking for a job in Boston, just a quick family visit. He'd be back within a week.

Hours later, a freshly stoned Reid caught American's red-eye.

Carrying his thumb harp and a worn copy of Siddhartha, he'd decided he would impress Gail Finney with his spiritual growth, his questing beyond the bourgeoisie, proving he wasn't—as she'd playfully accused him—just another cog at Procter & Gamble. His cover was simple: He wore his Ray-Bans and tucked away his extravagant brown curls inside O'Brien's Red Sox cap. Reid looked similar enough at a glance.

O'Brien told his landlord Sal that he was going to Boston for a week and asked him to check his mailbox; it had a way of filling up with junk and bills, especially since he now so seldom checked it himself. He threw together underwear and T-shirts for a week and jumped in the Chevy. He eased Blue onto Lombard Street, timed the traffic lights, and was cruising across the Golden Gate Bridge in minutes. He was heading for Corte Madera, a bedroom town of commuting stockbrokers, lawyers and accountants, ten minutes beyond the bridge. No one knew him there and it was close to Sausalito. He checked into the Best Western motel with Reid's credit card. Exhausted, he tried to sleep. But between the traffic noise and picking at his half-baked, boyish plan, he lay awake for hours, reality flooding his thoughts like a king tide. Could he really kill Knox? No way. But he had to. He couldn't. Not in a million years. O'Brien remembered the one time he'd ever killed anything bigger than a spider. How his twelve-year-old self had stalked that beautiful speckled woodpecker through the woods behind his house. His soul-sickness when at last he'd shot it. His heartbreak at seeing its magnificent feathers explode and float like dandelion seeds. He'd buried the bird shallow in the November ground, sneaked his brother Sean's BB gun back into the forbidden closet and hadn't touched a gun since. Yet Knox was a mortal threat to Marybeth. He had to die. O'Brien just couldn't do it.

Frustrated rather than worn from tossing and turning, he rose from the lifeless bed, climbed into his Levi's and a sweat shirt, and slipped down the walk-up motel's back stairs. He wandered aimlessly, pulling on a pint of Jim Beam, away from the rumbling freeway, toward the looming Mt. Tamalpais. If he couldn't kill Knox, could he beat him in a fight? Even if he did, would it stop him? Maybe it would, maybe if he thrashed Knox in public, in front of gaping bystanders who'd call the cops and have them both arrested. A bloody witnessed brawl might do it. He'd explain to the cops why he started the fight, how Knox had tried to kill his girlfriend. His client would be tagged with such a compelling motive for O'Brien's murder he'd have to back off. Or would he? Knox was crazy, already a murderer with nothing to lose. Besides, did O'Brien have a chance of winning a fist fight? Would the bystanders break it up if it got too ugly? O'Brien figured he'd be OK as long as they boxed, fought at arm's length, but that it'd be disastrous if the big man closed on him. He could get the first punch in, probably the second, but unless he knocked Knox out, unless he beat him senseless, he was cooked. His client outweighed him by fifty pounds. If O'Brien had learned anything in his few Golden Gloves bouts, it was that weight mattered.

Did he need an equalizer?

CHAPTER 35

THE FERG

THE OAKLAND COLISEUM'S FLEA MARKET was as much tourist attraction as sprawling outdoor bazaar, the crowds jostling one another on a warm Saturday among the pulsing, colorful aisles. Separated from the Nimitz freeway by a rusted chain-link fence, the market smelled of exhaust, burned rubber, frying meats and patchouli oil. The itinerant vendors—Bedouins in a tent-and-awning city—were eager, hopeful, hawking everything from spider plants to tie-dyed T-shirts to macramé candle holders to merchandise burgled from half the Bay Area. And wind chimes. Every other hippie vendor sold driftwood chimes and amateurish sand candles made from boxes of Crayola. The sellers of corn dogs and sodas were delighted by the lines outside their food trucks.

"You looking for a belt?" a lanky young man asked, popping up from his work bench when O'Brien glanced at his goods: crudely made belts, shoulder bags and floppy hats. Leather that looked better on the cow. "Check these out. These are custom-made. See? No buckle holes. I knock them in once you choose your belt." He held up a small hammer and a pencil-sized steel punch, pantomiming the action. He grabbed a belt. "See, you put it on. We measure the exact spot that fits you. I punch a hole there and a couple more on either side. You get a perfect fit."

An unshaven O'Brien was wearing Reid's *Grateful Dead* sweatshirt, a knit ski hat and aviator sunglasses. "A belt? A belt?" He laughed, patting his legs. "These jeans are tighter than my high school girlfriend. Got nowhere with her."

"I hear you, brother. How about a hair clip for your old lady? These are pretty wild." The peddler nodded toward leather clips hanging on a wire below his awning. "I'll throw her initials in for free."

O'Brien studied the vendor. His shoulder-length hair, moustache, leather bracelets and pirate shirt suggested the right attitude toward law and order. Could he ask him? "Sorry. Not sure I even have a girlfriend right now. But mind if I ask you a question?" Toying with the Puka shell necklace about his throat, the skinny peddler nodded. "OK, I'm looking for a way to protect myself. You know? A little self-defense."

"Yeah?"

"Yeah, this big dude is out to mess me up," said O'Brien.

"What are you looking for?"

O'Brien made a fist, extended his forefinger and pressed his thumb down a couple times.

"Man, that's heavy."

"Yeah."

"I don't know," said the peddler.

"Anyone here into stuff like that?"

"You didn't hear it from me, but go see the Ferg. Two rows down on the left, just past the taco truck, he's got the psychedelic VW van with a big smiling sun painted on the side door. Luck, man."

The Ferg was hustling a couple girls when O'Brien found his stall. A tie-dyed sheet, anchored to the sunburst van and held up by poles, shaded the jumble of wares spread across the length of a cheap Indian cotton bedspread. Eyeing the Ferg goat dance about the teenagers, O'Brien picked up an unboxed car radio with the word *Cadillac* emblazoned above its channel buttons, wires dangling from the rear. He examined another, a *Blaupunkt* and then a *Ford.*

"These new?" O'Brien asked.

"Better than new, man," said the Ferg, pensive, watching the giggling bell-bottomers saunter away.

"Guaranteed?"

"Guaranteed until you get around the corner."

O'Brien laughed despite himself, delighted at the man's honest mendacity. The Ferg laughed harder. "Did you see those chicks?" he asked, indicating the teenagers. "Un-fucking-believable. How does an ass defy gravity like that? I got to try them again later. Fuck, I got to get laid today."

"How's that work for you here?"

"Are you kidding, man? Like a fucking charm. I hit on maybe fifty a day. More if the quality is good. If even *one* says yes, I'm in like Flynn. I'm getting laid a dozen times a week. Beauty of living and working out of my van. My bedroom's always ten feet away." The Ferg laughed, his hands on his hips, a satyr unbridled. "How about you? You look like you get plenty of action."

"Yeah, well. I don't know. A little. But I'm no good at it. Gets in my head."

"Man, it's what we all live for. Pussy, pussy, pussy. It's like my fucking oxygen." His words ran together.

O'Brien considered the short, powerfully-built man. About forty, the Ferg had fading reddish hair and a freckled, smiling face. While not handsome, energy crackled off him like a downed power line.

The Ferg pointed to the radio in O'Brien's hand. "You looking to upgrade your car stereo? I got way better than that piece of crap. I can set you up. Unbelievable price."

"I'm looking for something else, something you wouldn't spread out for the public."

"Hash pipe, man? I got them in the van. Maybe a bullet?"

"Bullet?" O'Brien said, startled. "You mean like for a—"

"No." The Ferg chortled. "For blow. You know." He tapped the side of his nose. "Fucking great for sex, but I had to swear off. Was killing me. Tough on the hard-on. Nothing worse than a blow-softie."

O'Brien took a deep breath. "Actually, I'm really looking for a, a—"

"A what?"

"A gun."

"A gun? A handgun?"

"Yeah," said O'Brien.

"You ever shot one before?" asked the Ferg, turning serious.

"No, but I need one for self-protection. This big fucking bastard wants to kill me."

"Come here. Sit down." He waved a hand toward his office: a pair of frayed folding lawn chairs tucked between the van and his merchandise. "You look like a smart guy. Professional, I bet. Let me ask you something: Do I look like I should be working at a flea market? Do I fit in with these greasy low-lifes?"

O'Brien thought he blended in like a drop of ketchup in a bottle, but said, "No, you really don't."

"That's right, I don't. But after five years in Vacaville on some bullshit charge—swear to fucking God I was totally innocent, didn't defraud anybody—I'm unemployable. You know who I met in the joint?"

"Guys like me?"

"No. The guys who whacked guys like you," said the Ferg. "You know the only thing a handgun's good for? A Jack Ruby. Gut-shooting some poor fuck from two feet away. You know what it sucks for?"

"Self-protection?"

"Good guess, sport. Here," the Ferg said, jumping up, enthusiastic, grabbing the fun in the moment. He snatched a small, silver-plated candleholder from his counter. "Stick this in your jeans, like a gun. Walk over there about fifteen feet, yeah, out in the aisle. That's it. Just stand there. Now when I say go, pull it out, point it at me and say click. Got it?"

"Yeah."

"Go." A whirling Ferg was at O'Brien's throat before he had the candleholder halfway raised. "See?"

"Fuck."

"Unless you're doing two taps to the back of the skull—and even that's likely to get all fucked up—stay away from guns," said the Ferg.

"I have to protect myself. This guy's tried to kill me twice."

"You right-handed?" The Ferg pointed to the tattered cast on O'Brien's forearm.

"Actually, I'm lucky, I'm sort of ambidextrous, my old man bought me a baseball glove for lefties when I was—"

"Can you punch with your left?"

"Got a decent jab."

"What about a hook? Show me," the Ferg said. He assumed a sparring stance, feet wide, bandy legs bent, jailhouse arms raised. "Come on, show me. Do it. No, do it again, like you mean it. Once more—step into it." O'Brien whipped his arm around, stopping his fist at the Ferg's whiskers. "That's OK. Not bad. Wait a second." The Ferg jumped in his van, rummaged and returned. "Stand in front of me—block the view." The Ferg scanned the bustling aisle, reached into his back pocket and dropped a piece of polished metal in O'Brien's hand.

"Whoa, brass knuckles."

"Put them on and make a fist."

O'Brien slipped his fingers through the holes and squeezed. He felt powerful. He shadow boxed with the unaccustomed weight of metal on his hand, a series of quick jabs.

"That's just the way to crush your hand," said the Ferg. "You can't punch straight wearing knucks, destroys your hand. Forget the jabs, go with your hook. And stay away from his bones. Roundhouse into the guy, hit him hard—pow, pow, pow—in a soft spot. The gut, the shoulder, wherever, just stay away from his head, and I guarantee he'll leave you alone. OK, that's enough. Put it down."

"Jesus H."

"You want it?"

"Hell yeah."

"Ten bucks," said the Ferg. "Stick it in your pocket, no one's watching."

O'Brien handed him the cash. "Thanks, man."

"Not sure I'm doing you a favor. Just be fucking careful. Possession's a crime and if they catch you with them after you hit somebody, you're doing real time. Got it?"

"What?"

"You heard me. Knucks are like using a gun."

"Ah, shit," O'Brien said, squeezing the knuckles in his back pocket. He couldn't use them in a public fight. Unless he was about to be killed.

"If you use 'em, lose 'em."

CHAPTER 36

BAR TALK

"Mr. Buckley just left for the day, Mr. Knox," said Shelly Greene into her phone, pursing her lips. She hated that lie. Buckley had left hours earlier, but she had his standing orders. Awash in the late afternoon sunlight, Drummond's fourth floor was deserted, half of its lawyers on August vacation, the others having followed Buckley's lead. Inwardly, she sighed at Knox—law would be lovely if it weren't for the clients—glanced at her monthly calendar, and x'ed out the date with a felt-tip pen. She had only eight days before leaving for school.

"Shelly, this is the fifth call I've made to him since yesterday."

"Yes, sir, I've passed on all of your messages."

"Is he ever going to return my call?" asked Knox.

"I hope he will. I'm sorry."

"I really need to speak with him. In my shoes, what would you do? Please help me."

"Well," she said, sympathy arising from guilt over her role in Buckley's deceptions. "I know he's coming in tomorrow morning. If you were in the lobby by, say, 8:45, you'd see him when he arrives."

Knox was at Drummond's front desk at 8:30 the next morning, announcing his appointment with John Buckley. He apologized to Michelle for his last visit, offered to pay for the phone he'd broken, and then sat with his coffee and the firm's *Wall Street Journal.* He told himself to be pleasant. To smile. "Michelle, may I ask you a question?"

"All right."

"Has anyone heard from Michael O'Brien?" He studied her face. "I must speak with him soon."

"No, not a word." She glanced at the tiny stuffed bear next to her phone, a carnival prize given to her by an admiring partner who'd said it was in friendship. She knew better. "He must still be on vacation," she added, hoping the detail would bolster her lame answer.

"Come on. He has responsibilities, he must have called in."

Michelle hesitated, bit her lower lip. She had nowhere to hide, no one to back her up. A well-loved child from a happy family, she had no gift for lying. "Not that I know of."

Knox nodded, interpreted her hesitation, and decided that O'Brien was aware of Marybeth Elliot's accident. He had to be. Knox's plan might work after all; O'Brien was bound to rush to his girlfriend's side sooner or later. O'Brien was certain to confront him. Knox would be ready. Satisfied, he took up the newspaper.

Buckley strolled in forty-five minutes later, said good morning to Michelle and, following her glance, saw Knox glaring at him. "Why, Malcolm," Buckley said, his dolphin smile in place. He extended a moist hand. "What brings you in? Didn't Shelly tell you I was phoning this morning? Did she explain we've been absolutely snowed under?"

"No," Knox snapped, crushing Buckley's hand in his grip. "She said you were unavailable. So snowed under you didn't take any work home? Where's your briefcase?"

"I was here late last night."

"No, you weren't. I called yesterday at four and Shelly said you'd already gone."

"I'm not debating my calendar with you, Malcolm. Now, if you'll excuse me, I've got a very bus—"

"No. I'm not excusing you." Knox stepped between him and the elevator. "We're going to discuss our litigation strategy. Now. You're not putting me off."

"Litigation strategy? Litigation strategy?" Buckley's smile broadened, a twinkle in his eye. With Farwell dead and O'Brien gone, Knox had no way around him. "You're forgetting this isn't one of your trumped-up slip and falls in which you defraud some backwater insurance company." Buckley stepped toward Michelle as if she were a juror, captured her eyes, and continued, "And I shall retire long before the day I require your litigation advice. But since you're bent on this contretemps, I shall describe our working arrangement from this point forward. When I need a question answered or your appearance in court, Shelly will call you. Shelly—rather, her replacement—will send you monthly status reports and—"

"No," growled Knox. Buckley had intimidated him from the start with his impeccable schooling, his French-larded speech and his lancing remarks. In their first meeting, Knox had been fascinated with the range of Buckley's intellect and his vicious skewerings. But Knox's fascination with the law and its vassals had long since faltered. He rushed Buckley.

"You may call my assistant with any questions—let go of me," the attorney cried. "Michelle, note the time and date and the fact that Malcolm Knox has forcibly grabbed me by the lapel. And that he has refused to let me go. And that his fist is clenched. Barbara," he yelled to the only secretary on the first-floor, his voice stretched thin. "Come here. You're a witness, too. If you touch me, if you don't let me go this instant, I'll—"

"What? Sue me?" Knox laughed, short and ugly. "Sue me for wrinkling your jacket? Here, let me smooth it off." He dropped his hand, leaned into Buckley. "I have a better idea. Tell your story to the State Bar, right after I tell them mine, tell them how you billed me a hundred thousand dollars for barely opening a file. Our deal is off—you got rid of O'Brien. The State Bar is going to hear about what a goddamn thief you are."

Free from the larger man's grasp, Buckley jumped inside the elevator. "No, it's not. We had an agreement and we performed. I found your fifty million. You are not going to the State Bar. Do you hear me? You are not breaching our agreement." Buckley poked away at the elevator's door-close button. "You'll be in breach of contract if you say one word. Breach. You think you like litigation? You utter one word to the State Bar, one word, then burying you will become my career ambition, my raison d'etre." When later recounting the scene, Michelle would describe Buckley's remarks as an unbroken screech.

The elevator door closed. Knox raised his clenched fist as if to strike the solid-steel door, caught himself, snarled and strode out.

On the drive back to Sausalito, Knox coddled Skipper with head-scratching and soft words. He was free to act: With the fifty million in the court's control, with payment only a matter of time, any firm would take his case. Would Buckley really file suit? Would Drummond's management committee allow a public scrutiny of his billing practices? Climbing the stairs to his third-floor flat, Knox paused to contemplate the rich town of Belvedere across Richardson Bay and, for the first time that day, he smiled. His boys would need a nicer home to visit him on his every-other-weekends with them. As trustee, he could buy a posh waterfront home in their name. Any probate judge would approve a solid real estate investment like that in a heartbeat. From a desk drawer Knox pulled out the file he'd prepared early in the year and reread it. He dialed the State Bar.

"Ms. Konecny? May I call you Frances?" Knox asked a few days later. He was sitting in a boxlike office with a pleasant, sad-eyed attorney at the State Bar. The fusty room was cramped, cluttered with stacks of manila folders, all complaints against miscreant attorneys.

"Ms. Konecny, thank you," she said. "Now, please tell me in your own words what happened with your lawsuit against this Mr. Fitzgerald and what your issues are with the Drummond firm."

Knox recounted his tale, trying to be ingratiating, showing the examiner how the papers filed on his behalf in court—the complaint and the answers to Fitzgerald's three demurrers—contained fewer pages than the bills Buckley had sent him during the action's first year. Knox set the two stacks, the legal work and the bills, side by side for her to compare. He explained how he'd nearly gone to the State Bar at the beginning of the year, the settlement he'd reached with the firm and then, reluctantly, O'Brien's results.

The examiner said, "To sum up, the firm overbilled you badly for a year plus, charged you one hundred thousand dollars for accomplishing nothing. Then, to compensate you, they gave you a free associate who managed to recover your fifty million. Then the firm took him away, thereby, in your mind, breaching your settlement agreement, yes? Is that a fair summary?"

"In broad-brush, yes, but it's so much more egregious than that. Look at this bill from Buckley. This is for a trip to Beverly Hills, the ostensible purpose of which was to interview—not depose but *interview*—a former business partner of my uncle. Between travel time, file review and research, Buckley billed twenty hours over two days to conduct this fact-finding mission. Just look at his hotel bill. Winston Churchill on safari would have charged less. Look at his dinner bill. Good lord, the man has no shame."

"That is a surprising sum. But, Mr. Knox, had Buckley accomplished in the first year what the associate did in the second, wouldn't you have been delighted to pay one hundred thousand dollars for the recovery of fifty million? This would no doubt be the firm's defense."

"Not if it should have cost ten thousand," said Knox. "Drummond doesn't work on a contingency basis. If a single phone call got my money back on the very first day, I would expect to be billed for that one phone call, not for an around-the-world cruise."

"All right. I'll review the file in detail and then contact the Drummond firm to get their side of the story."

"Their side?"

"There are always two sides, Mr. Knox. But you have raised legitimate concerns. While Drummond may have rectified your billings through the free time of the associate—a rather nifty solution, by the way—admonishing the firm may nevertheless be appropriate. I promise you I will speak with them."

Knox's elation evaporated before he hit the Golden Gate Bridge. He should have obtained new counsel before he burned Drummond. His next counsel would be in a terrific bargaining position. With fifty million in the balance, a contingency fee lawyer would be exorbitantly expensive; they insisted upon a third—sometimes, half—of the money they recovered. Yet hourly lawyers were as adamant about being paid monthly. And Knox was broke. His challenge would be to find a patient hourly lawyer, tough enough to go mano-a-mano with Fitzgerald. Knox's thoughts drifted from treacherous lawyers to poisonous snakes and on to O'Brien, wondering if the quisling had already returned. Knox had thought O'Brien half-bright and hot-headed, but he'd never supposed him a coward. Was it possible he wouldn't return? No, he must be back; Michelle knew something. He had to stick with his plan: he would lure O'Brien into attacking him and kill him in self-defense.

He needed to stop his mind from racing, to think things through clearly. To breathe. He'd drop the Mercedes at home, change, walk the mile to the yacht harbor and add another coat of varnish to his boat's toe rails. A simple task that—like knitting—allowed one to both concentrate and relax.

"Want to go for a walk, Skippee?"

They strolled to the harbor, Skipper prancing, Knox preoccupied. He fetched a can of Epifanes from the *Sun Tsu's* cabin, put on his tile-layer's knee pads and cleaned the rail. It dried. He began varnishing. But his brushwork was mechanical, distracted, his thoughts hostage to his attorneys. O'Brien had to be dealt with. Knox tapped the small Beretta in his pocket, decided again his plan was solid. He'd stick with it at least another week, chumming himself, hoping for a strike from the cocky school boy. If it didn't happen within a week, then maybe he'd frightened the bastard into leaving California forever. Knox grinned at the image of his lawyer cringing behind his mother's apron in Boston. It didn't matter. No matter where he fled, Knox would hunt him down.

As it happened, O'Brien was less than fifty yards away.

CHAPTER 37

THE BARFLY

UNWILLING TO CALL THE OFFICE—HE was sure calls could be traced—O'Brien had no way of pinning down Knox's address. But he knew his client lived in Sausalito and that he was always puttering with his boat. He remembered Knox had told him the boat was named after some Chinese guy who'd written a war novel. The Corte Madera library was a couple blocks from the Best Western. The assistant librarian had heard of Sun Tsu and *The Art of War*, but didn't recommend it. Too Machiavellian.

O'Brien drove Blue to the Sausalito Yacht Harbor only to discover hundreds of sailboats and motor yachts clinging to its long piers like so many barnacles. Finding the *Sun Tsu* proved harder than learning its name. Misled by Knox's bragging and his own ignorance of sailing, O'Brien had focused on the swankiest boats. He laughed aloud when at last he found the snug, but unremarkable Islander. It was berthed at pier end, across the marina inlet from the Spinnaker restaurant, visible from its parking lot. He had a choice: He could watch the harbor's southerly approach from the public lot between Bridgeway and the entrance, or he could surveil the boat directly from outside the Spinnaker. After fifteen minutes in the restaurant's parking lot, he realized that loitering there looked suspicious and settled for the public lot.

O'BRIEN FIDGETED IN BLUE, TRYING to read baseball news as he scanned the boatyard. Nervous, he picked at his cast—he'd wrapped it three times over with duct tape—and tried to listen to the radio. If only there'd been a Giants game. Every so often he jogged to the Spinnaker to see if Knox had slipped by him. A few hours later, he spied Knox ambling toward the harbor from downtown. O'Brien sank in his seat as he watched his ex-client disappear behind the boardwalk's storage lockers. He waited twenty minutes, slunk to the Spinnaker, and saw Knox on his deck. Odd how harmless—how innocent—the murderer seemed as he varnished, occasionally talking to his dog. How powerful Knox's shoulders looked as he knelt on his deck. O'Brien shivered. He had to do it, call Knox out, start a fight. But not at the marina. It was too private; free money couldn't draw a crowd. O'Brien reasoned that if Knox had walked to the harbor, he must live nearby and that he'd return the way he came. O'Brien could track Knox on foot. He'd park the station wagon south of downtown and await Knox from Viña del Mar, the triangular pocket park a block from the harbor. O'Brien would discover where he lived, and then follow him from there to some crowded public spot.

O'Brien was contemplating Marybeth for the twentieth time, worrying over his chances of winning her affection now that the fiancée was gone, when Knox strolled into view three hours later. Using the park's central fountain as a screen, O'Brien studied the big man as he passed—led by his prancing dog—then disappeared beyond the Hotel Sausalito. O'Brien trotted after him, peered around the corner of the building. Knox was sauntering down the walkway on the bay side, stopping to chat with Skipper's random admirers. O'Brien crossed the street and stayed fifty yards back. Each time Knox paused, O'Brien would bend down to re-tie his sneakers, crouching behind parked cars, garbage cans and fire hydrants. Bridgeway became Richardson, and Knox climbed the hill. O'Brien hurried, afraid he would lose him among the neighborhood's short blocks. He saw Knox turn left on Second Street and right on Main. He rounded Main in time to see Knox turn left onto Fourth.

Knox had disappeared. He had to live close by—within the first block—but which house? O'Brien was stymied until he remembered the Mercedes. Find it, find the house. He dashed back to Blue and returned, cruising up Fourth. He spied a covered car in a carport beneath a three-story gray box that a hard shove might tumble. The shape beneath the canvas looked right. He parked around the corner, walked back, scanning the windows in the ugly duplex for observers, nodding as he saw the signature Mercedes painted hubcaps below the cover. He parked Blue on the north side of Main facing the intersection. Then he walked downtown to get a ham-and cheese-sandwich, the *Examiner* and a *Sports Illustrated.* Having heard Knox brag about his wild excesses and unbelievable luck at Sausalito's waterfront bars, O'Brien hoped he'd visit one this evening. He would confront Knox as he left the restaurant, in front of the knot of diners waiting for a table.

The sun was setting behind Sausalito's hills when Knox stepped from his top-floor flat, gazed toward his imagined Belvedere home across the inlet, glanced at the street below and descended the stairs. At the intersection, he checked his surroundings while appearing nonchalant. He saw nothing, patted his pocket for reassurance and strolled down the hill, destined for the Trident.

The fashionable restaurant was jammed on this warm August evening, indoor diners amidst the forest of hanging ferns and potted palms envious of the patrons on the deck with its dazzling city views. The crowded bar was already boisterous, the regulars—the long-haul afternoon drinkers—were smoking, half-shouting over the din, making small talk, flirting with giddy tourists hoping for a table. Knox leered at the hostess as he strode past the reception desk.

"Yo, Mal, how's it going? The usual?" the bartender asked with a welcoming smile.

"No, Scott, need to keep it in first gear tonight. I'll just have a beer—give me a Heineken."

"Sure. You hungry?" At forty-five, the balding, pudgy bartender was too old for the bar's hip clientele, but he was a boyhood friend of the owner. He wiped the bar in front of Knox with a towel. "I'd get you a menu, but hell, you could recite the whole thing blindfolded."

Knox snorted, pleased. "I could, couldn't I? And yes, I'm famished, nothing like varnishing to work up an appetite. You should see the *Tsu*, her rails are gleaming. I'll take you out sometime. Maybe you get us a couple dates and we'd do an afternoon, sail around Angel, maybe out the Gate."

"You see those two?" said the bartender, ignoring the proposal he'd heard too many times before. They had yet to go sailing together, and Scott was only half-convinced the boat even existed.

Knox waited a beat, then followed his look. "Not bad, old boy, not so bad at all. Any other time, I'd buy them a drink, but I may need to be sharp tonight."

"Got it. Dinner then?"

"I'll get the steak with the double-stuft potato."

Knox slyly appraised the two women in the circular booth. Very not so bad, particularly the redhead. She was the perfect age for a barfly—too old to expect more than a meal, too young for her face to betray her drinking. Maybe he'd buy them a drink. Despite his certainty that O'Brien would return, and soon—Michelle had given it away—the chance of the punk confronting him tonight was slight. Besides, if he were to spy O'Brien, he could feign being a hapless drunk, easy prey. A couple beers would lend his act verisimilitude.

Outside, O'Brien strode back and forth, skipping over sidewalk cracks, tapping his crucifix, picking at his cast, then at his forlorn plan. He felt sick to his stomach. He had to challenge Knox in front of a dozen witnesses, bellow accusations of attempted murder, and, once the fight started, hope the onlookers would not only call the cops, but yank Knox off him if it turned ugly. To insure Knox's arrest, O'Brien had to ignore his ironclad law and goad his ex-client into throwing the first punch. Then he'd dance aside and counter-attack: a jab-cross-hook combination. With more luck than he deserved, his flurry would stun the big man long enough for the crowd to break up the fight, the cops to arrive and arrest them both. The heavily wrapped brass knuckles—his threadbare security blanket—rode useless in his back pocket. The Ferg had been right, using them meant serious time. They had to be his absolute last resort.

Inside, Knox flamed out. Laughing off three rounds of generous drinks, the curvaceous barfly had parried him, suggesting that he give her his number instead. Giggling, she promised to call him. With an élan borne of countless such failures, Knox handed the redhead his number and the two women teetered out, their mission—free drinks—accomplished.

"Have one on the house, Mal," the bartender said, pouring a double Seagram's. "You didn't want that bitch anyway. Seen her before, basic snow queen, harder than lake ice."

"Yeah, not my night. Put the dinner on my tab, Scott?"

"Sorry, you know what Jeff said."

"Tomorrow, I'll be back in tomorrow and pay it all off. Deal? Then we'll go sailing. Deal?"

"Tomorrow for sure?" asked the bartender.

"I swear. And then we'll do the high seas."

"All right, Mal. Deal. Hey, you OK? Want me to call you a cab? I was pouring some fat drinks for you guys, wanted you to tap that bitch. You probably shouldn't be driving."

"No, remember? I'm a ten-minute walk away. I'll be fine. The night air will set me right." Knox lurched out into the night, widening his eyes to the dark, and headed home, thoughts of O'Brien lost in his pique over the barfly. He should have played it differently, offered to accompany them to the next bar. They'd been headed to Wimbledon's, and after a couple more drinks there, who knows what might've happened. If only he'd had the cash.

"Oh shit," O'Brien cried as he emerged from Scoma's, the lively seafood place next to the Trident. He'd dashed inside to relieve himself and, between his rising fear and haste, left two buttons on his Levi's undone. Knox was wobbling away, a hundred yards down Bridgeway. O'Brien watched him stumble, trip, and then right himself, veering as if windblown. He was drunk. O'Brien hesitated, wondering what to do. Should he await Knox's next public appearance? He was already too far away from the bar; a fight now, in the quiet residential neighborhood, would go unwitnessed. There would be no arrests to set Knox's motive in stone, and no Samaritans to help if the bear closed on him. But Knox was drunk. O'Brien's odds of winning a fight against him, of inflicting a real beating, were much improved. Maybe a real beating was enough. He could stir up such a ruckus the neighbors would call the cops. Maybe his own arrest alone for assault and battery would provide Knox with too much public motive for killing him. He thought Knox might be a coward. He dithered, going back and forth. Then he remembered Marybeth's pending hospital release and trotted after Knox. He couldn't risk Knox going after Marybeth the moment she was released.

Knox staggered up the gentle hill, breathing hard. He remembered O'Brien as he crossed Third Street. He whipped his head back, saw someone—or something—freeze, patted his pocket, and trudged on. His mind raced as he rounded Fourth Street, quickening his pace. He was certain O'Brien was tailing him. Steps from his driveway, Knox dug out the Beretta, hefted it, flicked off the safety and set it in his waistband, the grip riding outside.

Behind a laurel hedge twenty yards away, O'Brien shuddered at the sight of the pistol, his mind instinctively replaying the Ferg's rush-the-gun demonstration. He could do it. He could get the gun away from Knox before he had a chance to use it. O'Brien reached for the knuckles, slipping them onto his hand. They would be his last resort.

Knox slowed. He had to draw O'Brien in close. The shooting would play better as self-defense if it occurred on his own property. He glanced about the dark carport. His tenant's car was gone. Knox made a mistake: He switched on the light at the back wall, momentarily blinding himself. Blinking, he saw O'Brien and barked, "There you are, you traitorous bastard."

O'Brien sprinted toward Knox. The big man went for his pistol, but O'Brien was on him even as he jerked it free from his khakis, hitting his neck hard, blocking Knox's right arm with his cast. Knox's shot hit the ceiling, his hand forced high by O'Brien's forearm. Knox caught O'Brien with a left cross, a wicked blow that would have shattered his cheekbone had he not rolled off the punch. Knox lunged for O'Brien, intent on closing on him. Dancing out of the way, a desperate O'Brien whipped his fist back and slugged the big man, throwing his body into the punch, hooking into his Adam's apple, crushing his windpipe.

Knox gasped, his air cut off. He dropped the gun and clutched his throat with both hands. He staggered back, gurgling, retching, imploring O'Brien for help, grabbing at the young man's collar. He flailed, lurched, tumbled, and fell hard, thudding his head against the concrete apron. His gasps stopped.

O'Brien froze, the gunshot still echoing in his ear, the silence now more deafening. He crouched over Knox, then prodded him gently with his tennis shoe. Nothing. He prodded him again. "Oh, Jesus H. Christ, what have I done?" Stunned, he stared at his left hand as if it belonged to someone else. The knuckles slid from his open fingers, falling to the concrete, bouncing. He dropped to the oil-stained floor and sat, his head cradled in his hands. Certain the neighbors would be swarming him in a moment, San Quentin prison roiled his consciousness. But then he opened his eyes, saw nothing across the street, no lights flicked on, no commotion. Perhaps the carport's closed sides had muffled the shot. He toed Knox again, this time harder. Like his water bed, the body gave way to the touch, then fell back. Nothing. "Oh, shit, shit, shit, I killed him. Fuck me, Jesus." He listened for the sounds of opening doors, of rushing feet, of alarmed chatter—of a distant siren—but the night was silent, the neighborhood as still as a midnight park. At length, disbelieving the eerie quiet, he rose, flicked off the carport light, stumbled to the street and scanned the houses on either side, walking halfway down the block. Nothing. Suddenly, his deed's enormity over-swept his fragile relief. He staggered a few paces, braced himself against a small live oak and heaved. And heaved again. Wiping away the strings of saliva, tasting the sour vomit, he retched once more, this time dry.

O'Brien straightened and stepped toward Blue. He should turn himself in, the police would agree it was self-defense: Knox had a gun, he'd shot at O'Brien, he'd tried to kill him twice before. Then he slapped his forehead. "What the fuck am I thinking? The knuckles, the fake Boston trip? Me outside his house. They'll say I was stalking him and charge me with murder one." He retched dry again. "What am I going to do?" Shaking, O'Brien listened hard, squeezing his arms across his chest, but heard only the sparse traffic on Richardson below. He had time. The Boston alibi might work. Grab the knuckles and get the hell out. He trotted back to the carport, snatched up the knuckles, then froze, the rivulet of blood dripping from Knox's skull taking his breath away. He forced himself to look away, but the Rolex caught his eye, the solid-gold Rolex. A robbery. Make it look like a robbery, his self-preservation instinct screamed. He hesitated, then squatted, unclasped the watch, slipped off Knox's golden signet ring and fumbled through his pockets for his wallet. He remembered the gun as he rose. A stolen pistol was worth more than a hot Rolex—no mugger would ever leave it. Unable to look at the corpse again, O'Brien stumbled back toward the station wagon.

He turned right on Alexander and followed it out of Sausalito, climbing to the freeway, thinking he would head north, but, improvising, he thought twice when he beheld the Golden Gate Bridge. Driving under US 101, he pulled into the small lot across the highway from Vista Point. Looking back over his shoulder, he strode onto the bridge—the forlorn Pacific side—stopping beyond the northern pylon, nearly halfway across. He gripped the orange railing in both hands, bent over and laid his forehead on the chilled steel, oblivious to the sharp flaking paint. What had he done? After a time, he told himself to stop thinking, and pitched the Rolex toward the black sea, along with the gun, the wallet and ring. He ripped off his sweatshirt and tossed it over the rusted railing. Then, remembering the Ferg, he threw the knuckles far into the night. Half afraid the evidence would be floating, O'Brien glanced over the railing, seeing only the black water below.

Ten minutes later, he pulled into the Chevron station at the Mill Valley off-ramp and found the pay phone. "Hi, Gail. It's Flipper, sorry to call so late. Did I wake you guys? What? Honestly? I'm pretty fuc—no, no, no. I'm OK. I'm really OK, just a little tired. May I talk to John, please?"

"Vootie."

"JR, I need you to come home right now. Can you catch the early flight tomorrow morning?"

"Dude, it's already tomorrow morning here," said Reid. "It's after 1."

"I need you to come home as soon as you can, man. *Please*."

"You OK, Flip? You sound totally weird. Told you not to drop acid at night. Freaks you out." Reid laughed.

"I'm, I'm really messed up, bro," said O'Brien, regarding his left hand; it had yet to stop shaking. "Will you please come home right away? There's a late morning flight."

"It's cool."

"Remember, wear my Cal sweatshirt and the baseball hat. And, if you can do it without her getting a really good look at you—like just before landing—grab a phone number from a stew. Make sure you tell her your name's Flipper."

"You're dancing with the devil," Reid said.

"Cab it home and get a receipt."

"Some serious shit."

O'Brien hung up, thought about calling his mother. She'd be up, but the silence that would greet his words would be unbearable. He tapped at his crucifix, but it wasn't there. "Oh, no, no, no. Goddamn it." No way could he return to look for it; he was screwed. "Wait, wait, wait." He steadied himself. "Just breathe." He felt for cuts around his throat; there weren't any. It would be free of his blood. And too small for fingerprints. Surely a bloodless crucifix was evidence of nothing.

CHAPTER 38

MURDER IN SAUSALITO

"Yo, Blake, it's me," O'Brien said, cradling the phone against his shoulder as he shifted through a pile of junk mail. To celebrate the return of her prodigal boss, Ann Wall had crowned the stack of worthless correspondence she had organized into categories with a red rose in a chipped coffee mug. Making a game of it, O'Brien was wadding offers of affordable life insurance and continuing legal education into balls and tossing them at the trash basket he'd placed near the door. The sunlight flooding his barred window promised another warm day.

"Flipper?" Gamble said. "What time is it in Boston? It's early here, only 7:30. When are you coming back?"

"I'm back, I got back yester–"

"You're back? Why didn't you call?"

"I'm calling now," said O'Brien.

"You could have called yesterday."

"Jesus H, I thought my mother lived in Boston. You're my first call. I was zonked yesterday. Still on Boston time so I came into the office early to catch up before anyone gets here. Anyway, want to shoot hoops at the club after work? Maybe I'll even buy you dinner for Tahoe."

"That sounds grand… but wait, you're simply not going to believe what I have to tell you, what I'm reading right now. Are you ready for this?" Gamble sat at his kitchen table in his sunny Alamo Square flat, sipping French press coffee from his mother's third-best china, reading the *Chronicle*. "This is simply unbelievable."

"What?"

"Your client, Malcolm Knox?"

"What about him? Miserable prick."

"He's dead, murdered the day before yesterday—"

"Very funny. Today's not Christmas and he's not dead."

"I'm quite serious. I'll read it to you. The headline is 'Murder in Sausalito', the line below reads, 'Executive slain outside home'."

"No way," O'Brien said, holding his breath, knowing this was the first of many hurdles he'd have to leap. "No fucking way. That's crazy."

"Listen to this: 'At 11:30 Monday evening, the brutally beaten body of John M. Knox, 46, a Sausalito financial advisor, was found outside his home at 108 Fourth Street in Sausalito. He was beaten about the neck and head, his larynx crushed.' Wait, there's much more. 'His wristwatch and wallet were missing... A neighbor recalled hearing what she thought was a firecracker around 10:00 pm...Investigating officers and Sausalito Police Chief Colin Ramsdale had no clues to the vicious murder.' Can you believe it?"

"That's incredible. What do you think happened?"

"Maybe a hold-up where the perp got twitchy. Maybe Knox refused to hand over his money."

"A robbery in front of a guy's house in Sausalito? No way. There's no crime in Sausalito." O'Brian rolled his eyes toward heaven, beseeching, crossed his fingers, knocked on wood.

"Stranger things have happened, but you're right, we're not talking about the Tenderloin. Besides, the newspapers seldom get the true story. The cops never tip their hands; they hold back details. Nothing in here about a gun. Or blood. Or gunshot wounds. We'll see. Anyway, you are one lucky son of a bitch." Gamble swore on rare occasions, usually to prove he was one of the guys.

"I wanted him to leave me alone, I didn't want him dead," said O'Brien. "Have to say I'm delighted, though. Wow."

"Delighted? You simply must be ecstatic. Now, aren't you glad we didn't file a police report on your cobra?"

"*We*? You insisted I file a report. But yes, what a break. I don't need some detective going proctologist on me."

"That'd be quite the compelling motive. Good thing you were in Boston." Gamble paused, awaiting his protégé's confirmation. He shook his head, thinking that if he truly suspected O'Brien of murder, he'd been a prosecutor for too long. But he had to ask. "You were, weren't you?"

O'Brien was ready. "The paper said Knox was whacked around ten Monday night? I was on the flight home from Boston nine hours later, American's non-stop at ten a.m. If you like, I'll give you Krissy's number, the stew I met on the flight. She's too old for me."

"Sorry, Flip, I'm a prosecutor. I had to ask."

"It's OK. The cops will have their hands full. There's a conga line of guys who hated Knox. Start with Fitzgerald and Buckley and move on to the guys he screwed in his bullshit fender-benders."

"Surely Fitzgerald's too cagey for that. But one never knows."

"No, *one* never does." O'Brien gently mocked his mentor, exhaled, passing his first test. "I've got to grab a *Chron*. See this good news for myself. See you at the club at 5:30?"

CHAPTER 39

PAY-BACK

THE YOUNGER OF TWO DETECTIVES sat in O'Brien's single guest chair, jotting notes as the older one leaned against the back wall. For all the formality their rumpled Kmart sport jackets and clip-on polyester ties lent them, the disheveled detectives might have been wearing overalls. The younger man asked the questions while the senior detective smoked, looking out the open window, avoiding O'Brien's gaze. "When was the last time you saw Mr. Knox alive?"

"I already told you, about three weeks ago, at Jack Farwell's funeral." Behind his desk, O'Brien sat on his hands. Having swallowed half a red before the interview, he was barbiturate calm, but still feared his trembling hands. He reminded himself to answer every question as if he were innocent, but knew nothing.

"And you had a big blow-up?" The detective, Barry Lenak, was tense, his face florid. A one-time jock whose drinking had the better of him, he was thirty going on early retirement. A high-strung man, he liked nothing better than browbeating witnesses. He drummed his pen against his palm, an excited foxhound running his prey to the ground.

"No," said O'Brien, his patience becoming labored. "Like I told you, we had some words on the church patio. Ask anybody. There were tons of guys around."

"What if I told you Buckley said you two almost duked it out?" The wiry man leaned in toward O'Brien, over the desk, staring hard.

"I'd say Buckley's a liar. Look, I already told you I couldn't stand Knox. Nobody could, that's why these pricks stuck me with him."

Lenak glanced over his shoulder at his silent boss. The older detective shook his head.

"That bruise on your cheek," Lenak pressed, "nasty, must still hurt, is that about a week old?"

"About." O'Brien bit his tongue, recalling the advice lawyers always gave to witnesses facing hostile depositions: Pretend you're in a hurry, that you've got an appointment, answer with as few words as possible. He ran a hand through his black hair and then tucked it underneath his leg.

"And you got it…?"

"I told you, a pick-up game back in Boston. Some jerk elbowed me when I was rebounding."

"You got his name?" Lenak asked.

"You ever play three-on-three in a public park?"

"Anybody's name?"

"Nah," said O'Brien.

"You have a doctor look at it?"

"It's a bruise."

"Why you wearing your jacket?" Rising from his seat, Lenak placed his hands on the oak desk and leaned in close. "It's not cold in here. You worried we're going to see you sweating?"

"What? It's a fucking law office, Sherlock," O'Brien flared, losing control, regretting his words even as they tumbled out hot. He stopped, raised his palms as if slowing a car, and wrestled his tone back to conversational. "It's a little formal here. We always put our jackets on when we have visitors."

"You got a temper, kid. That reminds me," Lenak said, grinning at his boss, sifting through his notes. "Looks like you decked some guy in a basketball game earlier this year. Want to tell us about that?"

"Some guy was beating the crap out of one of our guys, I pulled him off. A scuffle ensued." O'Brien glanced toward the older detective; he was studying something in the alley below. "My teammate's a great guy, I had to help him out."

"A scuffle, my ass," said Lenak. "You flattened that guy. You got a hell of a punch. It got you and your law firm sued."

"What's that have to do with Malcolm Knox?"

"OK, you like bouncing balls. Follow this one: You hated Knox. You got a bad temper. You know how to punch. Somebody with a bad temper punched out Knox with his left hand. You can only punch with your left hand," he said, indicating the fresh cast on O'Brien's forearm. "Knox punched that somebody back with his left hand. Your right cheek is bruised. You connecting the dots here, counselor?"

"I got a dot for you, chief: *Boston*. I'm done here." O'Brien rose.

The silent detective unfolded his arms, cleared his throat, swallowing the bitter cigarette taste. He put a firm hand on Lenak's shoulder, pressing him back into his seat. "I'm sorry, Mr. O'Brien, Barry doesn't mean to be confrontational. It's just that all these coincidences have created some doubt for us."

"What am I missing here?" O'Brien buttoned his jacket and masked his trembling hands by picking up a beanbag paperweight from his desk. Telling himself to stay cool, he squeezed it hard, fighting the temptation to throw it in Lenak's vulpine face. But what about righteous indignation when falsely accused of murder? He should take it up a notch. "Knox gets killed during a robbery while I'm in Boston, he's got a hundred enemies, and you have doubts about *me*? Wait, check this out." O'Brien fished in his pocket, pulled out a crumpled American Airlines cocktail napkin. "Here. I'll make a copy of this for you, and you can call this girl Krissy. She's really hot. Ask her if she was working economy on the 10 am flight from Boston on the 15th. Ask her if she gave her number to *Flipper*. And just in case she's handing out her number all the time, remind her I was the one wearing a Cal sweatshirt and a Red Sox hat."

"Can we have that?"

"I'll xerox it for you."

"Who else can verify your presence in Boston?"

"I told you, my mother. Half the girls at Brennan's. Call the bartender...Nick. Check my Visa card bills. Are we done here?"

"What fucking bullshit," Lenak snapped, pushing himself out of his chair and slapping his palm on the oak desk. He wagged a finger in O'Brien's face. "If you're so fucking innocent, why're you shaking like a fifteen-year old in a whorehouse?"

"Any idea who might want him dead?" the lead detective asked, gripping his volatile partner's shoulder.

"Other than you, kid," Lenak said, his hands fisting. A vein in his forehead throbbed.

The lead detective sighed. "Mr. O'Brien, do me a favor, would you? Go xerox this napkin and your driver's license and give us a moment," he said. He shut the door behind O'Brien, then glared down at the smaller man. "What's with you, Barry? You want to a pop a guy in a law office? Your girlfriend dump you again? What's this kid's motive for killing Knox? Come on, give me one."

"I don't know, he didn't like him, give me some time to sweat him, I'll get it—"

"He didn't like him? Fuck, nobody liked him. Knox was a total shit, a 'goddamn leeching sponge,' and that's a direct quote from his dead uncle, the one guy that supposedly loved him. And remember what his ex-wife said, too. You think this O'Brien kid did it because he's nervous around you? *I'm* nervous around you. You're a fucking psycho." The senior detective rubbed his temples and gentled his tone. "Barry, first, this kid ain't got a motive, second, he's half Knox's size. He took him on? Come on. Third, his alibi looks pretty solid—if he was on that morning flight, no way was he here the night before. Let's finish this up."

"But, Jer, I know he did it."

"Bust his alibi then. Check with the airline, call the stew, check his Visa charges. Call the bar where he said he was hanging out, fax the bartender his I.D. Get him to confirm it. But no way are you going to Boston on some fucking boondoggle. I don't have the budget for that. Now, bring him back in."

"Where was I?" the lead detective asked when O'Brien returned with the photocopies. A big man, he seemed caged by the small office. "Any idea who might want him dead?"

"Sure, Teddy Fitzgerald," O'Brien said.

"You're right, kid, but his alibi's a shitload better than yours," Lenak said. "Who else?"

"I don't know. He sued a lot of people, he faked injuries, car wrecks. Maybe one of those defendants went ballistic. Fitzgerald's lawyer has a list of all Knox's lawsuits. You could get it from Buckley."

"What about Buckley?" the lead detective asked. "Did you know those two had a violent argument here just hours before Knox was killed?"

"No," said O'Brien. "Remember? I was in Boston."

"Let's cut through all the bullshit," Lenak said. "Kid, you willing to take a lie detector test? Clear your good name?"

"Sure, detective."

"Really?" The detective was shocked. No one agreed to lie detectors. "That's great. When? Today? We can probably get an examiner here this afternoon."

"I'll tell you when," said O'Brien, grinning to soften his words. "As soon as I get released from the psych ward."

"What the fuck?"

"As soon as the false-positive rate on polygraphs isn't thirty percent, you can strap me in all day long. Remember? I clerked at the DA's office, I know about polygraphs."

"Jer, what's that tell you? The smartass won't clear his name."

"Tells me he went to law school. Mr. O'Brien, we'll probably get back to you in a few days. You're not planning to leave town? No more Boston?"

"Nah, I'm here. I might move back home in a while, things aren't working out so great here."

"We know where to find you," Lenak glowered, as the detectives left.

"Don't give me that look," the older detective said as they crossed Drummond's patio. "And don't let me find out you spent two weeks interviewing horny stewardesses—talk to this one and tell me what she says."

"Maybe that cocky prick's just high-strung, but I got this feeling about him."

"Check your feelings about Buckley, too. His alibi sucks worse than my ex-wife—and he's got the mo. He had to be pissed about Knox going to the State Bar."

"That wuss's all talk," Barry said. "Ten bucks says the only time he ever made a fist was to whack off. But the kid? He's a fighter."

"Buckley could have hired somebody. Fitzgerald could have hired somebody. Anyway, time to go see the great inspector Cleary. That'd really be something if we solved his murder for him."

"Yeah," Lenak said, brightening at the prospect. "Where's the El Cortez?"

"On Geary. Just past Union Square. Cleary says he's buying lunch at O'Doul's—all we can drink—if this baby fits the penthouse door." The detective fingered the key he'd found in the Knox's desk.

Cleary had called after reading about the Sausalito murder, explaining that he'd always liked Knox for his uncle's death, but with no evidence and Knox possessed of a decent alibi, he'd had to let it go. He'd never bought the heart attack decision and kept the file at the top of his personal cold cases file. According to Cleary, the old man's killer must have had a key; the only other explanation—the killer was expert at picking locks—didn't wash. If the Sausalito key opened the El Cortez penthouse, Cleary could close out the old man's murder, knowing the murderous nephew had kept the key as a souvenir. The two detectives both thought Cleary's theory intriguing, but the key was missing its fob—no way to connect it to the El Cortez other than by sticking it in the lock.

Ten minutes later they were greeting Cleary and Davenport, the hotel's general manager, in the lobby of the El Cortez. While Cleary was eager, impatient, rocking back and forth, delighted to meet the Sausalito detectives, Davenport might have been a pall bearer. Davenport examined the key, acknowledging that yes it could be one of theirs, but that Schlage—he reminded them that it was a San Francisco company—made keys for every business in America. He ushered his guests into the small elevator and pressed the penthouse button. The detectives were high spirited, the manager stoic on the slow, rumbling ride to the top floor. When the elevator opened, Cleary almost ran to the penthouse.

"Sonofabitch, will you look at that?" Cleary said, as he opened the lacquered double doors with Knox's key. The three detectives laughed, gleeful as small boys chasing a puppy. Cleary clapped the Sausalito detectives on the back, telling them how much he looked forward to buying them lunch.

Davenport didn't join in the merriment. "What does this mean?" he asked.

"It means you don't change your locks often enough," Cleary said, laughing.

"That will be rectified as soon as you gentlemen depart."

"Kidding aside, it means your old man Knox was murdered by his nephew," said Cleary. "But don't worry, it won't hit the papers. The nephew got his just desserts—someone whacked him—and there's no way to prove a thing. I'm just closing out the file."

O'BRIEN HAD WAITED THIRTY MINUTES behind his closed door, trembling despite the barbiturate, flapping his suit jacket, airing his wet armpits, wondering how soon before they'd be back to pick apart his story. Refusing the lie detector looked bad, but he'd had no choice. All he had was Boston.

He managed a wink at Michelle as he left the building. He walked down Montgomery Street and turned up Post toward the Olympic Club. He undressed in the basement locker room, hanging his suit jacket and shirt to dry on separate stands, and then sat in the Jacuzzi for half an hour, dazed. He padded to the steam room, hoping to sweat out the red. Then he tried the nap room. When that failed, he showered, dressed, blinked at the sun as he emerged from the club and headed toward the office. With the light against him at California and Grant, O'Brien found himself staring at Old Saint Mary's Cathedral, a small 19th century red-brick church. "A cathedral my ass," he said, but he blanched when he read the stony admonition on its clock tower: "Son, Observe the Time and Fly from Evil." He convinced himself Ecclesiasticus was speaking directly to him as he strode—jittery—across Chinatown. Rounding Jackson Street, he heard someone too close behind him.

"Stop right there and raise your hands slowly above your head."

O'Brien froze in compliance, visions crowding him: should he run, fight, plead? He inched his arms skyward. Big hands frisked his sides and roughly spun him around.

The man burst out laughing as O'Brien's mouth dropped. The senior detective—the very Jerry Romani whom he'd rescued at the basketball game months earlier—said, "Oh, Jesus, if only I'd had a camera."

"Romani, what, what the, what—"

"Had you going, Flip. Really had you going," Romani laughed. Despite Cleary's celebratory drinks, he was sober enough.

"You bastard," O'Brien gasped, his hands on his knees, looking at the pavement. He buttoned his jacket.

"Wish I'd had a camera," Romani repeated, sucking in a deep breath to stop laughing. "Let's keep walking."

"Jesus H. You scared the hell out of me. You just took ten years off my life. I'm dying before I hit sixty."

"You weren't making it to forty anyway, the stupid fights you get in."

"Hey, did I do OK?"

"You didn't sign a confession."

"I'm innocent, Jer, you have to—"

"Save it, Flip," Romani said, his face tightening, humor gone. "I talked to Blake Gamble—he tell you? No? He thinks you're innocent, knows you were in Boston, said you couldn't pull it off if you wanted to, but—"

"I am innocent," O'Brien cried, his sweat running again.

"I *don't* want to hear that again. Never. Understood?" Romani said, scowling. "*Understood*? All right. Tell me something. You think Knox whacked his uncle?"

"I know he did. The old man had cut him off, Knox was desperate for money. The official story—falling in the shower—was bullshit. Knox knocked him on the head and drowned him in the tub."

"It's going around," Romani said.

"That's why he kept trying to kill me. I'd figured it out and he thought I was going to turn him in. That's how I got this," O'Brien said, tapping his cast. "The bastard knocked me halfway across Columbus. Jesus H. I just thought of something. Check out the police report on my hit-and-run, then check to see if Knox rented a car the same day and if his Mercedes was really in the shop. Hundred bucks says they find my ass print on the rental."

"You just gave me your motive, Flip." Romani put his hand on O'Brien's sleeve to quash his protest. "Save it, you were in Boston.

Assume I'm buying that for the moment and tell me the rest, tell me about this snake thing Gamble mentioned."

Over the next several blocks, O'Brien recounted the snake tale while Romani sifted truth from hyperbole. Gamble had explained why the attorney-client privilege had prevented O'Brien from reporting the old man's murder.

"Your girlfriend, what's her name?"

"I don't have one."

"Flip, what'd I tell you about the bullshit? The girl Blake said got hit by a car? Another hit-and-run, right? Knox did it?"

"Marybeth Elliot—I heard that she was in an accident, but I haven't talked to her in weeks. Honest."

Romani sensed the truth, scratched his chin. "I get it. Hypothetically here, counselor, so save the denial crap, you figured if you're not her boyfriend, you don't have a motive for beating the crap out of the guy who popped her." He shook his head. "You dumb shit, you already had a motive. Smart guys always make the same mistake—they think everyone else is stupid. Like we couldn't see through that. Serve you right if she fell in love with her doctor at the hospital while waiting around for your lying ass to visit."

O'Brien flushed. He'd thought himself clever and gallant in not calling her. "Jer, her friend Eloy Duran told me she saw a little white dog in the car that hit her—it had to be Knox."

"OK, Flip, forget about it." It all made sense. Knox had murdered the uncle and twice tried to kill O'Brien. Even tried to kill the girlfriend after that. "You own a gun?"

"No, never. Never even shot a real gun."

"Knox own one? A .38?"

"How the hell would I know that?"

"Maybe you saw it the last time you saw him. We found the slug in the carport's ceiling. Maybe he tried to shoot you with it. Maybe you confronted him, he pulled the gun, you struggled, it went off and you traded punches," Romani said, brushing O'Brien's bruised cheek with the back of his hand. "Maybe just *maybe* your lucky punch was self-defense."

O'Brien looked wretched. "I was in Boston, Jer. Please."

"Save it. Let me ask you one last thing."

"Anything." O'Brien jammed his hands in his pockets, fingers crossed.

"Barry calls that stew. She going to confirm it was you? Or your magical fucking twin brother? Don't give me your innocent crap, just answer my questions. He digs into the flight manifests, your Visa bills, it's all going to check out? The bartender's going to ID you when we fax him your driver's license? He's going to have it today. Pretend the goddamn lie-detector's on, cause if Barry finds something, I guarantee you're having your day in court, got it?"

"I swear, Jerry, it'll all check out. Cabs from my place to the airport and back, me being on that flight, the stew, my mom."

"We look at your phone bill, your gas bill, anything like that going to show us you were home when you were supposed to be in Boston?"

"I swear I was gone that whole time. Ask my landlord, Sal. He lives upstairs. I asked him to toss my mail inside my door for me. My mailbox is too small for all the junk. Your guy won't come up with anything."

Romani nodded, swallowed hard. He knew his duty, but he also knew Knox had been a murderer bent on further killings, and that it had been not only an accident, but self-defense. He knew O'Brien. The kid had a temper, but he was OK, certainly not a cold-blooded murderer. It must have been accidental. He reached in his pocket. "Flip, I got a suggestion for you."

"Sure, I could use one, this has been pretty—"

"Find a church out of town somewhere and go to confession.

You're the worst liar I've ever met." With an odd look, one O'Brien would never forget, Romani held out his hand and then walked away. O'Brien's palm had closed around something as they shook hands.

His lost crucifix.

CHAPTER 40

THE LONG GOOD-BYE

O'BRIEN TRUDGED TOWARD PIER 7, clutching the necklace like rosary beads, pondering its fate. He had to keep it to prove his innocence; he had to toss it. His Lord had betrayed him. Had any detective other than Romani found it at the scene, he'd already be behind bars. He had to be done with his crippling superstition.

He considered Romani, the other ringer Gamble had sneaked onto the DA's basketball team to win a championship no one else cared about. Was Romani repaying a debt or accepting street justice? Would he change his mind? O'Brien knew Italians were as trustworthy as Gypsies, yet Romani had just become an accessory after the fact. Or had he? Maybe it was a subterfuge designed to wrest a confession.

O'Brien crossed the Embarcadero and studied the failing pier, frowning at the sea slapping against its rotted pilings. He side-stepped around its gaping holes, gazed into a fisherman's bucket and asked whether he was having any luck. The smiling Mexican admitted no English. Shuffling down the wharf, he wondered why the hapless fishermen kept at it; surely they'd end up with more fish working any job instead of loafing all day on the pier. He came to the end, glanced down at the broken necklace, hesitated. He kissed the tiny figurine, asked for forgiveness, promising to cherish it always, and stuck it in his pocket.

"YOU'RE REALLY QUITTING?" ANN WALL'S voice cracked, her mascara moist. She'd asked the same question three times in as many minutes as she first watched, then insisted on helping O'Brien sort his personal belongings. With her help, a five-minute task had no end in sight. She had to arrange everything just so in the cardboard banker's box. They had to decide whether certain objects—chiefly, a Webster's dictionary and his coffee mug—had passed from the firm to Flipper through some medieval concept of usage. The sweet farm girl claimed she needed instructions on reviving his maidenhair fern.

"You might as well take the ruler, it's too bent now for anyone else to use—what did you do with it? Does your cheek still hurt? Oh, you don't have to leave, Flipper." Ann fought back tears; she couldn't swallow. She knew she'd never see him again.

"Annie, I suck as a lawyer. I feel like a fraud when I'm giving clients advice and you know I can't, I can't," O'Brien paused, his self-indictment sticking in his throat. He was touched by her pain and, with nothing to do and nowhere to go, delighted she'd converted his packing into more ritual than a high mass. Knowing how much worse this parting could be, he thanked his lucky Jesus for leading him away from at least this one temptation. "I can't even write a shopping list. You know it. And sitting behind this desk in this dinky office faking it is, is…it's not me."

"You could move upstairs, you could take Gutierrez's office."

He laughed aloud. "Annie, Annie, Annie," he shook his head, his fondness for her rising. She was lovely—her apple cheeks begged to be kissed—but no, he shook himself. "Give me a hug."

"Don't give him a hug," Gregg Gordon growled, opening the orange door. "He gets enough damn hugs. Give him some common sense; that's what he needs. What happened to your face?"

A blushing Ann slipped out, asking O'Brien to summon her as soon as he'd finished with Mr. Gordon. As an older man might, Gordon gripped the arms of the guest chair and lowered himself. Flicking the door shut, he said, "Nice girl. Her *husband's* nice, too."

"Gregg," O'Brien said, coating the word with indignation. "I never touched her. That was just going to be a hug—she's sad because—"

"I'm not here to lecture you. Bev just told me you were resigning."

"Yeah, maybe I should have told you guys first."

"You're making a big mistake," Gordon said.

"I'm no lawyer. Hell, I don't listen to my own advice, why should anyone else?"

"Cut the clever crap, Mike. You could be a good lawyer, you just need time—you haven't been here a whole year yet. Everyone's timid at first, everyone makes mistakes. It takes five years to learn any job worth having. You could do it."

"Yeah, maybe, but what would it do to me? You know any old litigators who aren't full-time assholes? You are what you pretend to be."

"Don't give me that Vonnegut shit." Gordon reached into his shirt pocket, swore under his breath, and said, "You could try real estate, do transactions—"

"Nah, how boring is that? Taking notes while business guys bullshit, and then filling in the blanks all day. I'd rather drive a—oh, no offense, Gregg, I mean some guys like it."

"Let me narrow your job search: Forget diplomacy."

"Sorry." He ran his fingers through his curls, massaging his bruised cheek. "I don't know about the job, don't even know where I'll live. Maybe Boston, things just haven't worked out here. Being a sports announcer would be cool."

Gordon cocked an eyebrow, wondering whether O'Brien had a clue what his bricklayer voice sounded like. "If you're bent on giving up the law, what about this computer stuff down in Santa Clara? That could be the future. My brother-in-law just made a bundle working for some little company that makes software for computers or something. And he's no rocket scientist."

"That's a fad—once the government buys their new computers every five years, who's left to buy them? Nobody. Besides, I'm not into business. I don't know, maybe advertising, like becoming a creative director for some cool ad agency—I'm pretty good at spotting which commercials work."

Gordon tugged at his pocket, aching for a cigarette, fearing he couldn't prevent the young man's terrible blunder. He envisioned a joyless O'Brien selling refrigerators in a backwater mall, a string of failures pinching him like bad shoes. "You've got the ticket—don't drop your bar membership, it's a bitch getting back in."

"There's something different about you."

"How about this? Instead of quitting, take a couple months' leave of absence, bum around, have fun, get your head together." Gordon wanted to apologize, to tell O'Brien the firm had made a big mistake. They'd let him drift without direction and then burned him with that damn Knox case.

"They'd never give me a leave. Buckley's been trying to fire me from day one."

"Buckley's out." Gordon grinned, his words triumphant.

"What?"

"He's off the management committee and we're cutting the shit out of his profit share. As far as the firm is concerned, he's toast. Between his bullshit sabbatical and the Knox mess, the partners had enough." Gordon's eyes crinkled in pleasure. Leaning forward, shedding years in his enthusiasm, he spilled the partnership's internal politics. At length, he concluded, saying, "So, that's how he had it over Farwell."

"Their wives were best friends, whoa. But that's got nothing to do with the firm."

"It'd be nice to think so," Gordon said, amused by O'Brien's naiveté. "Anyway, the new managing partner can't be pressured with society crap."

"Jesus H. I completely forgot, we needed a new one. Who is it? Carlson? Mercer?"

"Me."

"You? Get the f—get out of town. Whoa, Gregg, that's great. Hey, wait a second. Now, I get it. You're not smoking, that's what's different. Wait, don't go away." He jumped up, yanked open his door and glanced at Gordon's office across the floor. "You really aren't smoking. No haze in there."

"Sit down, you're making me nervous. No goddamn big deal. You don't miss a thing, kid, maybe you ought to be a private investigator."

"Really?" O'Brien asked, mulling its allure for a moment. "Oh, funny. I'll find something. This advertising idea kind of appeals to me."

"You ever been inside an ad agency or talked to anyone who has? I didn't think so. Talk about snake pits. This is your life we're talking about, Mike. Here it is: I'm sending a memo out that you're not resigning, you're taking an indeterminate leave of absence. Take six months, whatever, then come back and see me before you do anything stupid. OK?" The small man rose and offered his hand. "Hell, we'll even give you a month off with pay—you deserve it after all of Fitzgerald's bullshit. Shake, damn it, my arm's getting tired."

"Thanks." O'Brien clasped his hand with both of his. "That means a lot coming from you, but no, Jesus H. I can't do it. I'm out of here. But I'll come visit, I promise."

Gordon sucked in between clenched teeth. He would still write the memo, extract his partners' consent to re-hire the young man, but he questioned his motivation. Did the firm really owe it to O'Brien, or was it that he'd miss the youth's mirth and bantering, his guileless flattery of every woman he encountered? Where would the sepulchral second floor be without O'Brien's histrionics over the Red Sox?

"Excuse me, Mr. Gordon," Ann said, as she tapped on the door. "Michael, you have a phone call. I told her you were in a meeting, but she says it's very important." A study in disappointment, she pouted, "It's that Marybeth Elliot."

CHAPTER 41

WHAT'S IN A NAME

MARYBETH ELLIOT SAT IN A conference room on the forty-eighth floor of the Bank of America building. The room faced south, gazing down upon a view few tourists ever saw: tangled freeways, blocks of faded industrial buildings, a decaying waterfront and the hazy south bay. With its ornate floral wall coverings, gilded table lamps and antique crystal chandelier, the sumptuous conference room whispered Louis Quatorze. Marybeth sat at the head of the conference table, her cast-bound leg resting on an upside-down wastebasket. She'd spent the morning at I. Magnin, picking a suit that bespoke financial independence.

"I really should have been accompanied by an advisor, Mr. Woudstra. I'm feeling out of my milieu," Marybeth said, smoothing her blue skirt, glancing from one man to the other.

"Please, call me Karst," the suave investment banker replied. He pointed to his partner. "And this of course is the man with all the answers: please call him Donald. And yes, you should have all the advisors you need. This is a big room. We can fit in all of your advisors." He laughed. "But we thought this first meeting might be simpler, just a get-to-know-one-another occasion."

"All right. I'm only here to listen anyway. Where are you from originally?"

"Amsterdam," said Woudstra.

"Oh, so you're Dutch?"

"Yes, nearly German, but thankfully, America arrived in time." He chuckled. "You sure you wouldn't care for a cookie, Miss Elliot? They're really quite special." He waved at the lustrous table's centerpiece: an arrangement of cookies on a silver tray. He'd sent his Harvard MBA assistant to buy the cookies from Marybeth's shop down California Street. Beaded with condensation, a crystal decanter of fresh milk stood next to the tray.

"No, thank you," she said, smiling, tense. The dollars these elegant men threw around like wedding rice were breathtaking. She fussed with her notes, squared her clipboard.

"A cigarette? No, of course not. I keep telling myself I'll quit, but the flesh is weak. You know the Dutch: Our vices are innocent, our virtues questionable."

The trim, fiftyish investment bankers lacked neither animal desire nor compassion. Yet when they focused on the sandy-haired young woman, they looked past her beauty and leg-length cast. They saw money. "Are you quite comfortable, Miss Elliot? I could find a pillow for your leg? Yes?"

"No, thank you, I'm fine," Marybeth said.

"Perhaps you would prefer to stand?"

"No, I'm quite comfortable. Do you own other food companies, Mr. Woudstra?"

"Karst, please. Yes, we own an ice cream company in Belgium. A pretty OK little company, but nothing like the potential of your cookies." In Woudstra's estimation, this unremarkable young woman had somehow hit upon a winning formula. He'd stood in the lines snaking outside her shops, watched harried clerks selling cookies faster than they could be baked. Cookies that cost pennies to make and sold for nearly a dollar. Woudstra envisioned a nationwide chain of shops, kiosks and mail-order cookies. With a glance at the Morbier Comtoise wall clock, he pressed on. "Miss, Ms. Elliot, I don't wish to sound impertinent—there's a business reason to this question—you're a very lovely woman, but do you photograph well?"

"As a matter of fact, I do," she said, straightening her skirt. Flooded with recollections of photo shoots, she smiled. "I was a professional model from the time I was fifteen. Mostly print, some runway work. That's how I acquisitioned my first breakfast and lunch dining establishment, with the savings from my modeling."

"Yes, of course, I should have known the camera would find you enchanting. I asked because we believe that you should be the spokesman for the new company, your picture on the label, you starring in the commercials."

"Really? *Me*? In the commercials?" She asked, delight in every word.

Woudstra grinned. She reacted as he'd anticipated. He had not become wealthy by failing to do his homework. "It's rather a clever play on the old standard—the grandmother selling the candy, the black nanny selling the syrup, the matronly housewife with the, you know," he snapped his fingers enthusiastically. "Help me here."

"The cake mixes," Marybeth said, more delighted still as she envisioned a part-time return to her earlier, simpler career.

"Yes, just so, cake mixes. And now in today's hip marketplace, we have a beautiful young woman selling her own cookies. What do you think, Donald?"

"I can't think of a better way to kick off the company," the junior partner said, nodding eagerly.

"We just need a great name, something comforting, a name that says homemade, that says warm cookies cooling on a window sill." Woudstra clasped his arms behind his head, closed his eyes and leaned back in his chair. Donald copied the pose.

"You don't like Serendipity?" Marybeth asked, frowning. "I really researched it before opening my third shop. I'm planning to name all of my new shops Serendipity."

"Oh, Marybeth. May I call you Marybeth? It's a wonderful name for San Francisco, so clever and meaningful. But I'm afraid it may be too arcane—too obscure—for Middle America. Remember we're talking about going nationwide."

"I like the name."

"I love it," said Woudstra. "I truly do. But may I tell you something? That's why you would have Donald and me. We're here to guide you. Please forgive me for rambling, but when I first started out, I let myself be persuaded by my entrepreneurs, I let them convince me I was wrong, that I should follow their approach. And do you know what happened? As often as not, we lost money. The wonderful skills it takes to start a company—the vision, the drive, the determination, all your fabulous talents—well, taking a small company to the next level, taking it public, requires different skills. That's where we come in."

"I may not wish to go public."

"Of course, that's entirely up to you," said Woudstra. "But please consider this: If you choose to stay small, to remain private, if you don't catch this cookie train, how long do you think it will be before someone copies your formula, creates their own chain of cookie shops and goes public?"

Rather than answering, she glanced out the window, trying to control her breathing. The dreams these men had for her little company dwarfed her own. Going public with hundreds of shops? Could this be real? What if it didn't work out? Would she be left with anything other than her face on a cookie box? Could she trust these slick businessmen? She raised a tempting thumbnail halfway to her mouth before catching herself.

"Marybeth?"

"You're saying I don't have the skills to enhance my own company. But what you're really implying is that you want control. That's it, isn't it?" If only she had an idea of her company's true worth. She needed time.

"Not at all," Woudstra said. "You would still have two seats on the board, you would be the chairman, you would simply have line officers handling the day-to-day—"

"But you would own a majority of the stock and I would be just a figurehead for the company. I don't like that. Suppose you fired me the day after we closed our deal? You could do it, I'm well acquainted with the vagaries of business. You're a nice man, Mr. Woudstra, but let's stop here. Please write down your proposition and then I'll meet with my advisor. Besides, I need to compare your offer with the one from," she paused, pulling her hairdresser's card from her purse. She, too, did her homework. "Yes, here it is, the one from Excelsior Partners. Mr. Manchester was very nice."

"You're talking to Manchester?" Woudstra exclaimed. "I didn't know they did retail."

"Please excuse me, gentlemen. I need to get some circulation back in my leg." Marybeth rose with grace, picked up her crutch. "If you like, I'll come back this afternoon to give you a chance to put your best offer on paper."

"No, no, please, we don't need that much time. Hardly any at all. Shall we reconvene in forty-five minutes? We can put you in an office and let you make calls."

An hour later, Woudstra was offering Marybeth three board seats, veto rights on major decisions and three times what his assistants had told him her concept, her recipes and her shops were worth. But he was caught up in the game; he loved closing deals with promising entrepreneurs and nurturing their businesses. He was positive that gigantic gooey cookies were the next big thing. Woudstra had convinced himself—and apparently Donald—that Marybeth was the concept's x factor: a beautiful young woman who could bake, who could nibble cookies while looking like a movie star, who could subliminally convince millions of women that a mid-afternoon sweet presented no threat to their waistlines. "The financial risk would be all mine—you would have none—while we grow to two hundred stores. And if that goes well, it's on to Wall Street."

She peered out the window, seemingly enchanted by the view of the south bay.

"Marybeth? Marybeth, are you with us? I'm sorry we've taken up so much of your time. Well, what do you think of our proposal? Would you like to consider this or could we perhaps come to terms? Just in principle. Nothing binding," Woudstra said, forcing himself—and with an arched eyebrow, Donald—to nibble yet another cookie.

To conceal her delight over his offer, Marybeth concentrated on one annoying fact: F. Michael O'Brien's failure to call. Eloy had promised he'd explained everything. He swore Flipper knew it was over with Scott Land, that he knew she cared. And yet, Flipper had never once come to see her in the hospital, nor in the weeks after her release. What was wrong?

"Is something troubling you?" Woudstra asked with a becoming gentleness.

"Oh no, no, nothing."

"Would you like to call your advisor? We could leave the room. Yes, Donald, let's give Marybeth all the time she needs. Just let us know when you want us back. Meanwhile, we'll think about a new name, something that keeps you front and center, something homey."

"Yes, please," she said, her face the picture of tranquility, tapping into her years of holding poses for bitchy photographers. When they shut the door behind them, she clapped her hands: She finally had a legitimate reason to call Flipper. The Lerner lawyer was away, and she had to discuss this proposal with someone. That Flipper knew nothing about valuing companies or board seats or down rounds was no deterrent. For the moment, she only needed a sounding board, and Flipper had been surprisingly good with practical business advice. She dialed his number, pleading first with the chirpy receptionist, then the frosty secretary to put her through.

"Michael—Flipper, hi, it's Marybeth."

"Marybeth," O'Brien gushed. "Wait, wait, wait. Please don't go away."

Marybeth thrilled at his wild excitement. Through his muffled phone, she heard indistinct sounds and a door closing.

His words rushing together like startled blackbirds, O'Brien cried, "Marybeth, are you all right? How's your leg? When can I see you? *Now*? Can I see you now? Is it really over with that pilot guy? Please let me see you now."

"I'm in a meeting right—"

"Where? Are you downtown? I'll run right over. I have to see you, I have to see you right now. It's been so long. Please, please, please."

And Marybeth's laughter, the delight of a happy child, floated out into the elegant hallway. Woudstra and Donald raised their foreheads, wondering what it could mean, for the laughter carried no hint of triumph or slaked greed. Rather, it conveyed such a simple, pure joy that for a moment the investment bankers forgot their dreary mercantile art.

CHAPTER 42

OSCAR WILDE

"I'm not gay, Eloy," Blake Gamble snapped, a crack in his cultured voice. He checked his watch. "What could possibly be taking Flipper so long?" he asked, fuming over O'Brien's absence, failing to see the ballyhooed charm in the Mexican sea elephant.

Eloy's living room troubled Gamble as a visit to a cancer ward might a hypochondriac. The natty deputy DA clucked over the tumbling books, the dust mice, the leftist newspapers covering a steamer trunk, the unframed canvases propped against walls, the chess set akimbo on the hardwood floor. Yet he rather liked the avant-garde posters: the warrior Che Guevara, the flower-bedecked Frida Kahlo. And until the conversation's annoying turn, he'd found himself admiring the bullfighter Manolete leaning a hair's breadth away from an onrushing bull.

He stood as far from Eloy as the room permitted, gazing at an Alcatraz pink in the gathering darkness, wishing he could reopen that worthy prison. Earlier, Gamble had thought it great fun listening to Eloy rope and brand the City's sacred cows, but this was beyond suffering. He draped an arm around his amused girlfriend. "Flipper can tell you about all the women I've dated. Look at Cassandra here. Does she look like a man?"

Eloy regarded Cassandra over his smudged half-moon reading glasses with exaggerated sympathy. He wiped his hands on his T-shirt, spotting it with hot sauce. "You've already told me about your women, Pendejo. That's why I know you're gay."

"You people think every man is gay."

Eloy lowered his pendulous chin to consider him. "How do I know you're gay? Putting aside your ironed Levi's, the pointed boots—there's only one kind of cowboy in this town, bucko—and that silver-buckle belt. How? Because I'm sure every woman you've ever dated is as unsuitable as this poor linda."

"Hey, I'm in the room here," Cassandra said. A Wells Fargo Bank vice president, she'd had little experience being teased by strangers. "Talk behind my back, that's all right, that's normal, but not in front of me as if I don't exist."

"That's just it, Pobrecita, you don't exist. You're beautiful, you're smart, you're probably a great lay, but do you think his socialite mother is going to welcome a black girl with open arms? Has he taken you home yet? No? Why? Because unless you're wearing a maid's uniform, she's dialing 911. Will he marry a girl his family doesn't approve of?" Eloy barked his staccato laughter. "According to pendejo numero uno, you've had a Chinese tattoo artist, a French circus performer, a Colombian dancer, a Turkish masseuse—where do you meet all these girls? The UN? You think dating inappropriate girls is just a rebellion against your Mayflower mother? No, it's your way of avoiding marriage."

Gamble looked away, urging himself to exercise a conversational form of noblesse oblige—to take a page from his mother's book of etiquette—and ignore the Mexican's absurd ranting, to grin and bear it. There was nothing wrong with ironing a crease into jeans or wearing a silver belt buckle. Despite his haphazard self-education, the Mexican was clearly unsophisticated, applying his pueblo's mores to San Francisco society. Gamble told himself to find the humor in Eloy's tirade. It wasn't easy.

"Inappropriate," Cassandra repeated, irate. Her background was more patrician than anyone else's—save Gamble's—at the small party.

"Is he appropriate for you? Wouldn't your parents throw this phony white bread out on the street?"

Cassandra pursed her lips, silently acknowledging the truth of Eloy's words. She was indeed afraid to introduce Blake to her parents.

"Just because I find debutantes boring doesn't imply I'm gay," Gamble said.

"You may not even know. After all, Oscar Wilde was the last man in London to learn that Oscar Wilde was gay."

"Oh, stop, Eloy," Marybeth exclaimed, stumping into the room on her cast, carrying a tray of salt-rimmed margaritas. "Would you stop beating Oscar Wilde with a dead horse? You don't know Blake well enough to be so rude. Offend me instead. Besides, if that Earnest Important play is so great, why didn't they make a movie about it?"

"Actually, they have, but thank you, Marybeth," Gamble said, smiling, admiring her as one might a portrait in the National Gallery. He took a margarita. "These look fabulous. All for me?"

"Yes, please drink them all. And you, Eloy, you just hush. I swear." It had been three days since her exhilarating meeting with Woudstra. Three days in which O'Brien had seldom left her side. Her eyes shining, her cheeks aglow with pleasure, she wanted to impress his friends. After greeting Cassandra at the front door and complimenting her lovely cocktail dress, Marybeth had hobbled downstairs, changing into a silk blouse, adding a string of pearls.

"Congratulations," Marybeth said, toasting Gamble, smiling at Cassandra and fixing Eloy with a look. "You must be so proud. It's not every day such a horrible man goes to prison. Flipper said you did a great job putting together all the evidence against Fitzgerald, that prosecuting white-collar crime is really hard. How many years will he get?" She picked up the *Chronicle's* metro section—open to the arrest on the third page—and wagged her finger at the picture of Fitzgerald snarling behind bars.

"That orange jumpsuit is rather becoming on him, isn't it?" Gamble said, his equanimity returning. If the irritating Mexican wanted to think he was gay, why should he care? He knew he wasn't. "He's not quite in prison, he's only in jail. We had Fitzgerald picked up late yesterday so we wouldn't have to arraign him until Monday morning. But he may have already made bail. We'll convict him of grand theft, but without any priors, he won't do serious time. It's a wonder the man's never been convicted before, but the real question is whether he'll be disbarred."

"Of course he will. The man has stolen more money than Bonnie and Clyde," Cassandra said. Gamble had already recounted the litany of Fitzgerald's crimes to her.

"It would be pleasant to think so," said Gamble. "I personally reviewed the State Bar's file on him. It's two inches thick, yet he's never received anything worse than a reprimand."

While Eloy pouted—his feelings hurt by Marybeth's chiding—Gamble ticked off examples of convicted lawyers who hadn't been disbarred. He laid out the sentencing process, why he thought Fitzgerald would get a hand-slap. "After all, it's not a capital crime," Gamble said. "Good lord. Flipper could have gone to Oakland for the tequila and been back sooner than this."

"You're right. Where is he?" Marybeth asked, realizing she missed him. O'Brien had insisted on accompanying her on her shop rounds, constantly at her side, his banter making her meetings with her managers much more fun. She couldn't recall ever hearing so many compliments about a man she dated, and had found herself wondering whether her father would approve.

"Would you like to hear something beyond belief?" Gamble asked, lowering his voice as though he might be overheard. "Truly? This is unbelievable. The police investigated Flipper as a suspect in the Malcolm Knox murder."

"What? You mean his terrible client? He's dead?" Marybeth shuddered, recalling her two encounters with the man. He couldn't be dead.

"You didn't see it in the papers? Of course, with all the murders we have, that one barely made the *Chron's* back page. But how odd that Flip didn't tell you—he never stops talking."

"Oh." Marybeth was stunned. She was aware of her tendency to half-listen—perpetually distracted by her own planning while in conversation—but she couldn't have missed this. Why hadn't he told her? "He probably did, yes, he must have. It must have slipped my mind."

"Anyway," Gamble continued, "some thug tried to rob Knox in front of his house in Sausalito, there was a struggle with a gun—they found a slug in the garage—and Knox caught a punch that crushed his windpipe, killed him."

"One punch can kill a man?" Marybeth asked.

"Yes, but it's so uncommon that even if the thug were caught, a murder charge would never stick." Gamble declared, a professor warming to his subject. "A single punch means it was a terrible accident. No premeditation. A murder charge—even murder two—would be out of the question. The very best our chaps could hope for would be involuntary manslaughter. Even then it would be the devil of a time beating the self-defense claim. Unless of course the killing occurred, like this one, in the course of a robbery. Then the prosecutor's best friend—the felony murder rule—would kick in." He stopped to sip his margarita, realized he'd lost his audience, and chuckled. "Ah, well, they found Knox's poor little dog all alone, scared out of its wits. If only that dog could talk."

"Even if it can't, it's still smarter than half your police," said Eloy.

"Eloy," Marybeth intoned, stern. "Sorry, Blake. Eloy means well, bless his heart."

"Don't call them my police," Gamble said. "I know Flipper didn't do it. He couldn't have done it; he was in Boston the night of the murder. But he would have liked to."

"Of course, he couldn't do it," Eloy said. "He's a pretty boy, he doesn't have the cojones to beat a man to death."

"You're quite correct about that," Gamble said. "Especially someone half again his size. He's no fool. At least not that sort. And when the police determined he was in Boston, the great Flipper investigation ended with a whimper."

"What do you mean, 'he would have liked to'?" Marybeth asked. She'd turned quiet. Flipper couldn't have done it, he hated guns. He'd told her his woodpecker story when she'd offhand suggested hunting with her father as a way to ingratiate himself. Besides, he had been in Boston.

"Well, I'm not telling tales out of school since you already know this. They hated one another. Flipper was positive that Knox was behind his hit-and-run. And the farcical snake-in-his-mailbox thing. Flip was lucky—he always is—some thug wanted Knox's Rolex. My theory is that some lowlife watched him get drunk at the Trident—he was blowing 2.0 that night—saw the gold watch, followed him home and jumped him. Knox put up a struggle and that was that."

"The snake-in-the-mailbox thing?" Marybeth asked.

"Someone put a rattlesnake in Flipper's mailbox a couple weeks ago. I do think it was likely Knox—can't explain why. But no harm came of it. More likely a ham-handed warning than anything else."

Marybeth was distracted. Something was very wrong. Flipper would have crowed Knox's death from a bell tower. She'd have hung on his every word. How could he fail to mention it? "Where was he staying in Boston?"

"At his mother's, enjoying the home cooking," Gamble said.

"At his mother's," Marybeth repeated, wondering. How far would a mother go to protect her son? The dog. She'd seen a small white dog in the car that struck her, and Gamble just said Knox had a little dog. She tasted the salt on the rim of her glass, recalling her hospital conversation with Eloy after his call to O'Brien. Eloy had been contrite, swearing he'd explained her accident in detail. What if…? But no. "Guys, let's not discuss this Knox killing when Flipper returns. Let's not spoil our evening together."

"I'll drink to that," Gamble said. "I hear enough about murders every day."

"Did anyone say tequila?" O'Brien sang out ten minutes later as he flung open the front door, swinging a small shopping bag. "Jesus H. Talk about epics. I had to go to three different liquor stores to get this wormy tequila for you, Eloy. These drinks better be—whoa, nice blouse, Beth, you got to like that. Give me a kiss. Shooters for everyone, women and children first. Anybody miss me?"

Gamble was tempted to reopen his self-defense against Eloy's Oscar Wilde slander, calling upon his friend as a character reference, but he sensed the odious Mexican would smear them both and decided against it. Instead, he invited everyone to attend his manly rugby match the next day in Golden Gate Park.

"Michael," said Marybeth, "would you help me in the kitchen with the appetizers?"

"Sure, Mare, happy to."

"No, don't grab me." She swatted away his hand. "Scoop the guacamole into that ceramic bowl—Eloy ate the first bowl all by himself. Gland problem, my behind. When he called you about my accident, he exaggerated everything, didn't he? Must have said I was near death, right?" she asked, waiting for his nod, tucking her loose hair behind her ear. "Did he say it was a car that hit me or did he exaggerate that into a tank?"

"No, just a car. Maybe he said it backed up and ran over you twice though." He laughed. "Let me fill your glass. Have I shown you how we do shots?"

"And the dog? Did he say it was a German shepherd?"

"Nah, just some little white dog. Let's do a couple shots."

She deftly chopped an onion to add to her lackluster guacamole, thinking it through, chopping hard into the cutting block. Flipper knew about the hit-and-run, he knew about the dog, he must have known it was Knox. Had he rushed home to confront his ex-client? Had his one punch accidentally killed Knox when the older man tried to shoot him? She stifled a grin, thinking she hardly needed him drunk to learn the truth. A few days earlier, she'd asked him about his cousin and received a blank stare; the lesbian cousin, she'd added, and he'd missed another two beats before recovering and waxing about Roxanne and her girlfriend. Annoyed, she'd said nothing and focused on the positive: that he was a pathetic liar was money in the bank.

O'Brien poured two generous shots into Eloy's juice glasses, sliced lime wedges, limed his thumb web, salted it, tossed back a shot and sucked his hand. "There. Nothing to it. Your turn."

"Show me again please. Besides, I really have to get back out there before those two start up again. You missed the fireworks. Eloy can be so antagonizing—bless his heart, but I'm not certain he does always mean well—and Blake's sense of humor doesn't include jokes at his expense."

"Come on, please, take the shot. I'll set it up on my hand so you won't have a mess. That way you can kiss my hand."

"You do the shot and I'll kiss your hand, anyway. That's it." As his eyes swam, she kissed his hand and said, "You were so desperately in love with me you couldn't visit me on my deathbed? That's true love?"

"No, that's not how it was, it wasn't like that, I was really—I couldn't come." He took her in his arms, kissing her. "I really do love you, Beth."

"You did it," she said quietly.

"Did what?" O'Brien asked.

"I know you did."

"Did what? Kiss me and I'll confess to anything."

She kissed him back with an open-mouthed ferocity, pressing against him, locking her fingers in his black curls. Her father would swim the Dardanelles to protect his family; she knew what a man should do when his woman had been attacked. And never say a word about it. Flipper's crushed cheek told her how close he'd come to losing his life while defending hers. She had no doubt the killing was accidental; Flipper was as capable of murder as a Carmelite nun. But he'd gone into mortal combat with a man twice his size. Certain he'd done it on her behalf, she kissed him passionately, sliding her hands down his long back, pressing into him.

"Whoa, there's a switch." He laughed. "Turn her on by getting *myself* drunk. Jesus H. I've had it backwards all these years." He giggled, kissing her again, marveling at his great good fortune in holding such a beauty.

"We better get back out there before Oscar Wilde returns," she said, pulling back, her eyes shining.

Puzzled, O'Brien ignored the reference in favor of more urgent matters. Glancing down at his jeans, he asked, "But what am I going to do with this?"

"Save it for later."

CHAPTER 43

A COOKIE BY ANY OTHER NAME

"That was," Marybeth said, swallowing a laugh, searching for compassion, "quite a surprise." She rubbed her sticky fingers, giggling, wondering about the proper protocol. Wiping them on Flipper's stomach seemed callous, on herself tawdry, like some adult film. She reached over Flipper for the Kleenex on her night stand, arching her lovely body. She smiled at his shiver as her breasts grazed his shoulder.

Their dinner party had ended early. Gamble had abruptly cited his rugby game as a need for sleep. He'd been off all evening—never quite recovering from Eloy's pointed cross-examination—and his announcement surprised no one. Desperate to get Marybeth in bed, O'Brien had raced the dishes into the kitchen and washed them as if setting a speed record, grunting from time to time at Eloy's seamless monologue. Eloy had wanted them to stay; he slept poorly and delighted in company at all hours. Marybeth promised to have breakfast with her uncle instead, asking Flipper to hold her hand as she peg-legged down the serpentine stairs.

"That just proves how faithful I've been to you, Beth."

"Oh, you, you're *terrible*. The way you try to turn everything to your advantage."

"Wait, wait a second, don't go away, I mean it, don't get dressed, please, don't put on your PJs, I'll be right back." O'Brien dashed into the bathroom.

"I'm waiting," she said, lying back on the pillow, plotting her next move. As certain as she was, she wasn't altogether certain. She had to confirm Flipper's heroism. She told herself she was appalled by the killing. A large part of her may have been, but she knew he'd done it for her.

"Don't worry," he said, returning, his body silvery in the moonlight. "It's like a rubber band, snaps back in no time. Five minutes, tops. Then, boom, out of the park. Look." He flicked at it, trying to show her its spring. He gave it a couple shakes. Resilience was not readily apparent.

She giggled, shaking her head. "Maybe you *should* be in advertising, you're always claiming credit where there isn't any, where others would only blush. Lie down, that's it, just relax." Marybeth laid her head on his chest. She traced down his arm, across his shoulders, exploring his lean, muscled body with a proprietary touch. With no idea how long his intermission would last, she felt restive, almost irritated. She patted the welt on his cheek. Would it fade soon? She felt his strong heartbeat, ticking in sync with her bedside clock. "Blake told us about Knox being killed while you were out." She waited for a reply. He stroked her thigh. "You heard about it?"

"Sure, I heard about it. I heard all about it," O'Brien said, tensing involuntarily.

"And?"

"The detectives interviewed me to see what I knew."

"Were you a suspect?"

"Me a suspect? Nah, no way. They just wanted to find out who I thought might whack the bastard. Hang on a sec. I'm getting a cramp in my leg." Alarmed by his racing heart—knowing the conversation might plunge through the ice at any moment—O'Brien stalled for time. Slipping her embrace, he bolted upright. "Maybe if I stand, stretch out this quad." He rose, made a show of gently punching and massaging his thigh and then recalled his guiding principle: throw the first punch. Inspired, he dropped beside the bed, knelt like a schoolboy saying his nightly prayers, and pleaded, "Marybeth Elliot, will you marry me? I really really really love you—you've got to marry me."

"You're jok—no, you're not. I, I don't know, I might love you, too," she said, startling herself with her own words. She'd had several margaritas, but she shook herself, striving for control. "But you don't have a job. What are you going to do? I disengaged one fiancée who wanted to retire and play golf."

"There goes my career on the pro tour." O'Brien laughed. He'd never touched a golf club in his life.

"Come back to bed. I'm not saying no. But let's talk about that later." She again lay her ear against his chest. "What happens to a man's things when he's killed, you know, like Knox's dog?"

"Depends whether he made a will. If he didn't, everything would go to his sons. I don't know about the dog."

Hearing his heartbeat break into a trot, she sucked in her breath, pleased. She toyed with his slight chest hair, her hand poised to stop him from rolling away again. "Michael, why didn't you tell me Knox had been killed? You hated him so much, why for heaven's sake wouldn't you tell me?" Silence. His heart raced.

"Why didn't I tell you? Why—"

"No, don't get up again, I want to snuggle with you. Just stay right there." She draped her arm over his shoulder, nestling into him, pinning him down.

"I didn't want to upset you—you know, murder and all that—well, maybe not murder. It could have been an accidental killing in connection with a robbery, but I guess that's still murder. I just wanted to forget about that bastard, and with your leg and the good news about your business, I didn't want to bring you down."

"How thoughtful, you did it for my sake—you really do need to be in advertising," she snickered, holding him tight, pressing her ear against his heaving chest. "And this scar on your cheek—how'd you get it? Shaving?"

"OK, officer, you got me. I confess. As I was duking it out with Knox, he caught me with a left hook. Happy?"

"Oh, no you don't. I know that trick. The tell-the-truth-with-heavy-sarcasm-to-make-it-sound-like-a-lie stuff. Tell me: what happened?"

"Please, Beth, please. I don't want to talk about Knox anymore. Let's talk about us."

"You heard what he did to me and you came back for him. I know you did, Michael. I know you did it. It's all right, hush now." She placed a finger over his lips. "Hush, I know it was an accident." His telltale heart was all the confession she'd ever get. But she needed nothing more; she knew he'd been her champion. She'd never listen to another word against him…unless she spoke it.

She kissed him deeply, drew back, stared into his eyes. "I love you, too, Michael. I'll never ask about it again." Then she brought his mouth to hers. They began anew. Yes, yes, yes, she felt his heat burn into her, felt their joined sweat. She was dizzy from the tequila, dizzier from knowing he'd gambled his life for her. She felt his hardness, his muscles stretched across a long sinewy body. Yes, don't stop, she murmured to herself, don't stop.

***

"NOW, WILL YOU MARRY ME?" O'Brien pleaded. He caressed her.

"Oh, no, please don't, no more. I'm too sensitive now. Like a million nerve endings just opened up. Did you do that with all your girlfriends?"

"Mare, no more questions. OK? Just say you'll marry me and I'll give those nerves happy endings forever. I'll do whatever it takes."

"Will you get a job?"

"Sure, anything that doesn't have E-S-Q in it. I've been E-S-Q'd enough. God, you look so beautiful lying here with me. I can't believe we're finally together. Will you? Please."

"I have an idea," Marybeth said, as though it were just occurring to her. "Why don't you come work with me?"

"What?"

"I know you think business is beneath your station in life. But you're a natural at it. You must have noticed. You're the one who told me how to fix the cookies, about putting up sidewalk signs, about the advertising, about all kinds of stuff. You could help with the new stores, handle the leases—"

"All I have are ideas. Ideas are penny a pound. How many thousands of hamburger joints are out there with the idea of making a good burger cheap? And how many *McDonald's* are there? Just one. Business is 95 percent hard work and execution. The rest is luck. You're brilliant at it."

"You can be so sweet."

"Besides, what about the Dutch guy and all his money?" O'Brien asked, sitting up, taking her seriously. "I thought you wanted to sell the company to him."

"I do, but I can't seem anxious, can I? If we, if *we* let him wait, let his offer ripen while we open another five or six stores—I have three new locations picked out—Mr. Woudstra's bound to offer a lot more. He's such a nice man. You can be Vice President."

"I don't know." He sighed, staring at the ceiling. He'd heard of men who lived in the twilight of their successful wives, who buried their resentments and own failures by drinking and skirt-chasing at their country clubs. He'd long since decided the hardest way to make money was to marry it. He ran his tongue over his teeth. "Here comes 'Mr. Elliot', the useless boyfriend."

"Oh, that reminds me," Marybeth said. "I've thought of a new name—Mr. Woudstra's right, all the stores should have the same name."

"Makes sense."

"Aren't you going to ask me what it is?" She held her breath.

"Let me guess—Fantabulous Cookies."

"No, silly." Marybeth propped herself up on her elbows, and smiled into his eyes. "Mrs. O'Brien's."

The End

ACKNOWLEDGEMENTS

For their kindness and encouragement, I would like to thank Kara Cox, Lane Goldszer, Michael Harmon, Randy Mondello, Emma Olson, Kay Orloff, Coleen Ramsdale and Mary Taylor. I need to express my gratefulness to the two John Clearys—father and son—for helping me understand a bit about how detectives work in San Francisco. My special thanks to Micki Erickson for her kind support, to Deirdre Kidder for her help and thoughtful recommendations, and to George Eckrich for his enthusiastic, Texas-sized boosting of the novel from the beginning. My gratitude to John J. Geoghegan for his counsel and great advice (the title, among many others). Kudos to Robert Hunt for his beautiful cover art. To my publishing team at 82 Stories, Julie Trelstad, Alexandra Battey, Nora Long, and Hannah Wood. And, finally, my two wonderful editors—Hamilton Cain and Christine Delsol. I cannot thank you both enough. Thanks so much for sticking with me, Chris and Hamilton.

CPSIA information can be obtained
at www.ICGtesting.com
Printed in the USA
LVHW041047150323
741599LV00002BA/294